A RIP
THROUGH
TIME

Also by Kelley Armstrong

Rockton
The Deepest of Secrets
A Stranger in Town
Alone in the Wild
Watcher in the Woods
This Fallen Prey
A Darkness Absolute
City of the Lost

Cainsville
Rituals *Betrayals*
Deceptions *Visions*
Omens

Age of Legends
Forest of Ruin
Empire of Night
Sea of Shadows

The Blackwell Pages (co-written with Melissa Marr)
Thor's Serpents
Odin's Ravens
Loki's Wolves

Otherworld

Thirteen *Living with the Dead* *Industrial Magic*
Spell Bound *Personal Demon* *Dime Store Magic*
Waking the Witch *No Humans Involved* *Stolen*
Frostbitten *Broken* *Bitten*
Haunted

Darkest Powers & Darkness Rising
The Rising *The Reckoning*
The Calling *The Awakening*
The Gathering *The Summoning*

Nadia Stafford
Wild Justice
Made to be Broken
Exit Strategy

Standalone novels
Wherever She Goes *The Masked Truth*
Aftermath *Missing*

A RIP THROUGH TIME

KELLEY ARMSTRONG

MINOTAUR BOOKS
NEW YORK

First published in the United States by Minotaur Books,
an imprint of St. Martin's Publishing Group

A RIP THROUGH TIME. Copyright © 2022 by KLA Fricke Inc. All rights reserved.
Printed in the United States of America. For information, address
St. Martin's Publishing Group, 120 Broadway, New York, NY 10271.

www.minotaurbooks.com

Library of Congress Cataloging-in-Publication Data

Names: Armstrong, Kelley, author.
Title: A rip through time / Kelley Armstrong.
Description: First Minotaur Books Edition. | New York: Minotaur Books,
    2022.
Identifiers: LCCN 2022001169 | ISBN 9781250820006 (hardcover) |
    ISBN 9781250864895 (Canadian) | ISBN 9781250820013 (ebook)
Subjects: LCGFT: Novellas.
Classification: LCC PR9199.4.A8777 R57 2022 | DDC 813/.6—dc23
LC record available at https://lccn.loc.gov/2022001169

Our books may be purchased in bulk for promotional, educational, or business use.
Please contact your local bookseller or the Macmillan Corporate and Premium Sales
Department at 1-800-221-7945, extension 5442, or by email at
MacmillanSpecialMarkets@macmillan.com.

First Minotaur Books Edition: 2022
First International Edition: 2022

10 9 8 7 6 5 4 3 2 1

A RIP
THROUGH
TIME

AUTHOR'S NOTE

Welcome to 1869 Scotland, as written by a 2021 Canadian. Yep, I am not exactly the obvious writer for such a story, which is why my narrator, Mallory, is also a twenty-first-century Canadian. That said, I did want to present the time period as accurately as I could, within the limitations of available data, contemporary interpretations of that data, and my admittedly modern perspective.

If you share my interest in this time period, you'll find both a selected and more complete bibliography on my website. The selected version is primarily books written for a general audience, while the complete includes scholarly articles and primary sources.

In cases where the primary sources differed from the secondary sources, I initially chose to follow the primary sources. However, if my early readers flagged any of those choices as seeming incorrect, I opted for the better-known variation found in secondary sources. This is a novel of historical fiction, after all.

On the subject of fictional license, readers familiar with Edinburgh will note that there is no "Robert Street," where I've placed Gray's town house. This is intentional. Also, in 1869, the Edinburgh police surgeon was Henry Littlejohn, who held that post during a long and storied career, where he did memorable work in forensic science. Let's just say that Gray and McCreadie would have much preferred Littlejohn to my fictional police surgeon, but that would have made for a very different story.

Again, this is a work of fiction, written by an enthusiastic amateur history buff who must accept that she will make mistakes and hopes they'll be forgiven. If readers wish to point out errors, well-intended constructive corrections—with academic source links—are always appreciated.

ONE

My grandmother is dying, and I am getting coffee. I can tell myself that I'm treating the hospice nurses. I can tell myself that Nan is sleeping, and I can't do anything right now. I can tell myself that even if she woke, she would never begrudge me a fifteen-minute break. It doesn't matter. I crossed an ocean to be at her side for her final days . . . and instead I'm standing in an Edinburgh coffee shop, ordering lattes and chais as if it's just another midafternoon caffeine break, as if the doctor hadn't told me, thirty minutes ago, that the person I love most in the world will be dead before the weekend.

The shop is overcrowded and understaffed, tempers fraying, people shifting and sniping, and I want to scream at them all to shut up and be glad for a day where a five-minute wait is the worst thing that will happen. Instead, I'm on the phone to my mom, hunched over for some modicum of privacy. In the midst of this excruciatingly banal chaos, I am telling my mother that unless she can get here in the next three days, she will never see her own mother again.

I want to step outside, but I've already placed my order. I want to say "to hell with it" and reorder elsewhere, but I left my wallet in the hospice and the ten-pound note I brought is now reduced to spare change. I want to tell Mom I'll call her back, but she's on a brief recess from court.

I want, I want, I want. I want so many goddamn things right now.

If wishes were horses . . .

I hear Nan saying that, and with a blink, the coffee shop glistens behind a gauze of tears.

Focus, Mallory. Do not lose it. Not here. Not now.

"I will do everything I can to get there," Mom says. "If I can't, your dad will."

"Dad won't want you to be alone at home if . . . when . . ." I can't finish that line. Cannot.

Her voice drops to a whisper, as if I'm not the only one having this very private conversation in a public place. "We don't want you to be alone there either, Mal."

"I'm not. I'm with Nan."

She inhales. "And I am so, so glad of that. I'm—"

"Two turmeric lattes, one masala chai, one dark roast!" a barista calls, with the exasperation that says this isn't the first time she's announced my order. I can barely hear her over the low roar of discontent around me. Her accent doesn't help. I may have spent every childhood summer in Scotland, but as a thirty-year-old cop chasing career goals, I haven't visited for more than a week in years.

I step forward, phone pressed to my ear. Mom's still talking, and I'm half listening, focused on collecting those drinks and getting the hell out of here.

I make it halfway when my phone vibrates. A glance at my watch shows a number that has me cursing under my breath.

It's an informant who ghosted me a month ago. One I've been desperately trying to contact, for fear her silence isn't voluntary.

I really need to answer this, but there is no way in hell I'm cutting Mom off, not when her voice cracks with grief and fear. I'm the lifeline to her dying mother, and I won't sever that to take a work call, however urgent.

"Two turmeric—!" the barista shouts.

"Mine," I say, waving my free hand as I reach the counter.

"I should let you go," Mom says.

"Sorry, I'm just grabbing coffee for the nurses." My phone continues vibrating as I shove cups into a cardboard tray. "Can I call you back in sixty seconds?"

"Tonight is fine, hon."

"Really, I can—"

"Tonight, Mal. I need to get back in court anyway."

She signs off. I hit the Answer button to connect my informant as I slam the last cup in the tray. I'm opening my mouth as I turn to go . . . and I crash into a man standing right behind me.

The coffee tray hits his chest. I stagger backward just in time to avoid dumping four cups of hot liquid on him. Droplets still splatter his white shirt.

"Oh my God," I say, twisting to set the tray down. "I am so sorry."

"It's quite all right," he says.

In Canada, there is a warmth to such reassurances. Here, it seems as if they're mandatory, spoken with a cool efficiency that always throws me off balance.

"No, it's not okay," I say, handing him a wad of napkins. "Let me—"

He jerks back, as if I were about to touch him.

"I'm fine," he says, and again, the words are cool. No annoyance. No anger. Just the sense that he is terribly busy and wishes I would stop talking. Please.

He moves up to the counter, placing his order as he plucks napkins and dabs his shirt. I hesitate, but an older woman beside me whispers, "He's all right, dear. You go on now. Enjoy your drink before it gets cold."

I nod and murmur my thanks. That's when I realize I'm still holding my cell phone. I glance down to see my informant has hung up.

It's night now. My grandmother is asleep. The nurse warned she might never wake up, and I am not certain that is a bad thing. I want more time, so much more time, but she's so confused and in so much pain that a tiny part of me hopes she will not wake, and a tinier part wonders whether that is for her sake or mine.

I told the hospice nurse I was going for a jog, but really, I'm running away as fast I can, and every footfall on the pavement drives a dagger of guilt through my heart. I should be at Nan's side, and instead, I'm fleeing her death as if the Reaper dogged my own heels.

I'm in the Grassmarket. I remember Mom telling me how she volunteered at a homeless shelter here during uni. It's long gone, and pubs line the street now. It's much too busy for jogging, even at this hour. After fielding catcalls and dodging tourists, I find a quieter street lined with funky little shops, all long closed for the night.

I pass a tourist trap with a hangman's noose painted on the window, which reminds me that the Grassmarket had been the site of executions. Nan took me to the "shadow of the gibbet" when it was first unveiled, maybe ten years ago. There's an old memorial plaque to commemorate some of the executed and, during a renovation, the city had installed dark cobblestones nearby in the shape of a gibbet. Neither Nan nor I has ever been a keen student of history, but when it comes to the macabre, we're there.

As I wonder where exactly that spot is, I catch a flicker of movement. I spin so sharply that my sneaker squeaks. An empty street stretches before me.

At another flicker, I lift my gaze to a cigar-shop flag fluttering half-heartedly in the night breeze.

I roll my shoulders and stretch in place with one foot braced against the storefront. I drink in the smell of a recent rain and the faint odor of cigars. When I listen, there is only the wind, tripping along the narrow street.

I am alone with my grief and my regret and my rage and my guilt, the last one slipping away as I acknowledge how much I needed this break. A chance to run myself to exhaustion, letting tears dry on my face. A chance to lower my guard and gather my thoughts, and then return to face the horror of my grandmother's death.

I finish my stretches and gaze out on the street as a long exhale hisses between my teeth. It is lovely here. Peaceful and quiet and beautiful in a haunting way. I want to linger, but I have what I came for—a sliver of solitude—and it's time to head back.

I'm lunging into a run when a woman yelps. My first reaction is no reaction at all. It may be quiet, but there are people around. That playful yelp only makes me long for a moment that is, for now, beyond my grasp. I can't even recall the last time I went to a bar with friends.

No one on their deathbed ever wished they spent more time in the office.

Nan's admonition from last Christmas creeps up my spine. She was right, of course. If something happened to me tonight—a slip-and-fall or drunk driver—would I regret not making the major-crimes section? Or regret the fact it's been six damn months since I had dinner with friends? A year since I went on a date, and even that was more hookup than romantic evening.

I could swear that first cry sounded playful, like a woman being surprised by a friend, but when it comes again, it's a stifled shriek. A shriek of delight? A woman out for the evening, a little tipsy, goofing around with friends.

Maybe, but I still strain to hear more, just in case.

Muffled whispers. The scuff of shoes on cobblestones. Then silence.

I pivot toward the sounds as my hand drops toward the holster I am obviously not wearing. Blame five years of patrol duty, with a preference for long nights and rough neighborhoods.

The sounds came from down a narrow lane ahead. I roll my steps as I ease that way, and my fingers itch for the knife I carry when I jog at home.

My fingers close around my phone instead. I pull it out, ready to call 911.

911? Wrong country. What is the emergency number here? Damn it, I should know that. I'm sure Mom and Nan and even Dad all hammered it into my head when I was young. 511? No, that's traffic information at home. 411? Directory assistance.

My thumb grazes the screen, but my eyes stay fixed ahead. Get a better idea of what I'm facing, and then I'll pause to search for the local number.

As I approach the end of the lane, I clutch my phone in one hand. In the event of urgent trouble, I'll dial 911 and pray it forwards to an emergency service. I don't expect to need that, though. The closer I draw to the lane, the more I'm convinced that I'm about to interrupt an intimate moment. The woman's date had surprised her and made her shriek. They'd goofed around and then whispered together and then it fell to silence as they settled into a private spot.

That doesn't mean I turn around. I've rousted couples in dark alleys because what I heard didn't quite sound consensual. Half the time, I've been right.

I ease into a shop alcove. At the first indication of shared passion, I'll scoot. I hear nothing, though. Maybe they've moved on, seeking true privacy—

A whimper.

I press my hand to the wall and lean as far as I dare, my eyes half shut as I strain to listen.

A muffled sound, one I can't make out.

Damn it, give me a little more.

I lift my phone and open the browser. I'm halfway through typing "Scotland emergency phone number" when a cry comes, a stifled word that is unmistakable.

Help.

Then another cry, this one of pain and surprise, and I bolt from my spot before I realize what I'm doing. I swing into the lane to see . . .

Nothing.

It's more alley than lane, stacked with boxes and bins for trash pickup. The cobblestones stretch into darkness, and I race along them, following the whimpers and muffled cries of a woman, until I reach the back corner and look around it to see . . .

An empty lane.

It's a narrow alleyway between the rows of shops, and there is nothing in sight.

I squint into darkness lit only by a single flickering lamp over a door. Even without better lighting, I am absolutely certain there's no one here.

They must have moved on. I misunderstood, and the couple moved on.

I'm turning away when a gasp sounds behind me. I spin, fists rising, to see that empty expanse of alley again.

Then there's a flicker. The shifting of light. A flash of cornflower blue, hovering like a haze. The haze becomes a dress. A long dress, half-translucent. A glimpse of light hair. Then another gasp, as the wisp of a figure falls back against the wall, only to disappear as she strikes it.

What the hell?

I blink hard. A projection? It must be. Some kind of video projection from a tour, a young woman in an old-fashioned dress struck down by an unseen assailant. I peer up at the opposite wall, looking for the malfunctioning projector.

Something moves behind me. Do I catch the whisper of a foot on stone? The smell of another body? Or just a shift in air pressure. Nan would call it a sixth sense, but all I know is that my gut says "Turn around now!" and I obey.

I wheel just as something swings toward my head. I spin out of the way and catch a glimpse of rough rope gripped in a man's hand.

Synapses fire, a connection made. An article glimpsed in passing. Edinburgh. Two bodies found in the past month. Strangled. Old rope around their necks.

A spark of realization, smothered by the far more important fact that I am being attacked. *This* is not a malfunctioning ghost-tour video.

My arm smacks up into his, and he staggers back grunting in shock. His face rises, hidden in the shadow of a dark hoodie. Then the hood falls half back and—

It's the man from the coffee shop. The man I spilled coffee on.

If asked what he looked like, I'd have said I had no idea. I only saw his shirtfront, dappled with coffee droplets. But I never ask witnesses whether they would recognize someone if they saw them again, because half the time they'll say no, but if I put a lineup before them, the memory will slam back.

That's what happens now. I thought I didn't see his face earlier, but then this man looks at me—white guy, midthirties, average face, light hair, dark eyes—and I know him. I know him beyond any doubt.

I spilled a few drops of coffee on some suit in a crowded shop, and now he's in this alley, dressed in a black hoodie, with a length of fraying rope in his hand.

It makes no sense, and that is where I fail. My foot was flying up to kick him, and then I recognized him and I falter. He feints out of my way. I stumble and twist to right myself and in a blink, the rope is around my neck.

I claw to get my fingers under it as twenty thoughts explode at once. Twenty instructions, and above all of them, the scream that I should do better. I've taught women how to fight off an attacker in every situation, and here I am, uselessly clawing at a rope already around my neck.

It happened so fast.

It happened so goddamn fast, and part of me screams a curse for every time I calmly told some woman how to fight this. Get your fingers under whatever is choking you. Free some air. Claw. Kick. Punch. Scream.

Scream? I can't breathe. How the hell can I scream?

I do claw, but the rope is already digging in, my nails shredding against it. I kick backward. Rear kick. Side kick. Roundhouse kick. I know them all, but my foot never makes contact. Even when I manage to get my hand behind my neck, all I feel is that length of rope.

He hasn't said a word. Hasn't made a sound.

My sneakers scuff against the stone, and I'm gasping, the world tinging red at the edges.

I am suffocating. I am going to die, and there isn't a goddamn thing I can do about it.

Fight. That's what I can do. Fight in any way possible.

My kicking foot finally makes contact. Hard contact. The man grunts and staggers, and I get my balance again. I throw myself forward, but he's already recovered, wrenching me off balance.

The man yanks again, as if growing impatient. I am taking so long to die. I twist, and down the alley, two figures shimmer. A young woman with honey-blond hair, in a cornflower-blue dress, as a shadowy figure has his hands wrapped around her throat.

The figures vanish, and I fight anew, but I'm off balance and can't do more than flail.

I'm sorry, Nan. I'm sorry I won't be with you. I know I promised—

The world goes dark.

TWO

I wake on a bed. It's not exactly soft, but considering what just happened to me, I'd be happy with a stone pallet. Better than a wooden casket.

There's a rough pillow under my head and a stiff coverlet over me. A hospital? When I crack open my eyes, pain trumpets through my skull, and I shut them again.

My ribs feel tight, as if they've been bound. Nothing else hurts, though. I'm wearing what feels like a hospital gown, tugging at me when I move.

The room is chilly and damp. When I breathe in, there's the smell of . . . camphor? That's the word that comes to mind, though I'm not even sure what camphor is. Something medicinal. Definitely a hospital, then.

Definitely? It seems very quiet for a hospital. No footsteps on linoleum floors. No creaking of gurney or supply-cart wheels. No blipping of machines or whisper of voices.

I try peeking again, but the pain forces me into retreat.

I survived. That's all that matters. A man lured me in with that video, and I fell for it. Someone must have heard the noise and rescued me.

In the alley, I'd remembered an article sent by a colleague. A fellow detective who also had his eye on advancement. According to the article, two bodies had been found in Edinburgh, possibly the baby steps of a nascent serial killer.

My colleague joked that maybe I could investigate it and become a homicide detective with Scotland Yard. I hadn't had the heart to tell him that Scotland Yard isn't in Scotland. Let's just say one of us has a better chance of climbing the law-enforcement ladder than the other.

I'd only skimmed the article, and mostly just to reassure myself that I wouldn't risk becoming victim number three. The victims had been a middle-aged man killed midday in his car and an elderly woman murdered in her garden. While the murder weapon—old hemp rope—suggested a connection, the police suspected the victims themselves would end up being connected. Targeted killings rather than the thrill-motivated actions of a serial killer.

A visitor out for a jog was in no danger at all . . . unless she spilled coffee on the killer.

I'm still trying to wrap my head around that. I was targeted for murder, not because I had a life-insurance policy or a long-standing feud with a neighbor. I was targeted for an everyday offense. An accident, for which I sincerely apologized and tried to make amends. Part of me is laughably offended.

Plenty of time to dwell on that later. For now, my colleague's joke might actually come true. At least the part about me helping in a homicide investigation.

I have critical information on a serial killer. A face, emblazoned in my memory. A motive, as mind-boggling as it might be. A potential location, as the man's jacketless dress shirt had suggested he worked in a nearby office. I know what he looks like and how he chooses his victims and where police can start canvassing for an ID. It'd be much more impressive if I learned that as a cop, rather than a victim. No matter. At least I hadn't actually died.

Died.

Nan.

I lever up in bed, my head and stomach lurching together as I swallow bile. I gag and then force myself to slow down. If I vomit, they'll keep me in the hospital. I need to get to Nan. Everything else can wait.

The room is dark. I blink, in case my eyes are still closed. They aren't. My head booms, and thoughts flit like fireflies, sparks of light that disappear before I can catch them.

Something's wrong.

Hospital rooms aren't this dark. How many times has Nan grumbled about that? Even in the middle of the night, there's so much light.

I'm not in a hospital.

I scramble from the bed, the damned gown binding my legs and nearly toppling me face-first to the floor. While my outfit might feel like restraints, I'm not actually bound. Also, as my eyes adjust, I can make out a sliver of harsh light under a door.

I'm standing on a lumpy carpet, but in one step I'm on ice-cold wood. I catch smells I don't recognize. There's that one that keeps whispering "camphor." The word strikes me as old-fashioned. Maybe something from Nan's house?

Nan.

I squeeze my eyes shut. Great. My thoughts have metamorphosed from lazily fluttering fireflies to a hive of bees, buzzing about, stingers at the ready.

Slow down.

Step one: open the door.

I make it two more paces before the damn gown tangles up my legs, and I stumble.

Why the hell does this hospital gown reach my ankles? It takes longer than it should for that question to form, proof that my brain is still muddled. I tug at the garment. It's more like a nightgown, and there's something under it, something that stops me from breathing deeply. I run my hands up my sides.

Am I wearing a corset?

Holy shit, I'm wearing a corset and a nightgown. Also some kind of wig—I can feel hair against my back where it normally falls on my shoulders.

I'm not safely in a hospital. My attacker has taken me hostage. Strangled me until I lost consciousness and brought me to some . . . I'd say "lair" if that didn't sound so comic-book villain. I've been taken captive and dressed in a gown and a corset and a wig. I am suddenly terrified of the answer to the question "Where the hell am I?"

There might be a serial killer in Edinburgh, but that's not who jumped me. This is a whole other kind of attack. The kind that turns the stomach of even seasoned detectives.

Breathe, Mallory. Just breathe.

I do. I rein in the galloping terror and take deep breaths. Go back to step one. Try to open the door.

I take two steps toward the sliver of light, only to tangle in the skirt again, and I stagger forward, hands slamming down on something hard that twists my wrist and has me uttering a string of curses.

A distant gasp. Then running footsteps.

I back up, fists rising. The door swings open, and that harsh light floods in, making my head shriek, my eyes half shutting, giving me only the barest glimpse of the newcomer. It's a girl, no more than twelve, backlit by that white light, her edges blurred by my throbbing head. She's holding something like a toy sand bucket.

My brain refuses to process. I see a young girl and—considering what I fear has happened to me—I can only think she must be another victim. But she's out and about, running around the house with a toy.

I swallow and force myself to remain calm.

"Hey, kid," I say, my voice coming out weirdly pitched. "I don't know where I am, but could you help—"

She screams. Drops the bucket and races back down the hall. I stand there, staring after her.

It's only as she flees that my mind finishes processing her image. Twelve-year-old girl with brown hair and eyes, a smattering of freckles, and a thin frame. Her hair was swept up under a strange little cap, one that matched a dress that looked like something out of a historical drama, simple and blue with a matching white apron.

I stare down at the bucket. It's made of wooden slats with iron rings, and its contents puddle on the floor, steaming water that carries one of the smells from my room—a medicinal, tar-like scent.

I lift my gaze to the hall. It's a corridor of gold damask wallpaper, the sort I remember from my great-grandmother's house. There's a light right outside my room. A brass fixture on the wall, spitting white flame.

I take another step back, smacking into whatever I hit earlier. It's a cabinet, the top holding a ceramic bowl and jug and a small pedestal mirror. The cabinet is a dark red wood, the two doors held closed by a brass medallion engraved with a Chinese dragon.

My gut squeezes, nausea rising. I've been kidnapped and thrown into someone's sick fantasy version of a Victorian home, complete with a poor kid forced to play the role of maid.

The nausea solidifies into anger as I inhale again. Okay, whatever this is, I can handle it, and I can help that girl. I just need to figure out what's going on and play along. Help the child; catch this bastard; save myself.

As I straighten, my gaze lifts to the mirror, to my reflection in it, and . . .

The blond girl from the alley stares back.

THREE

I stand in front of the cabinet, staring at the reflection of the blond girl from the alley. The obvious answer is that I'm looking at another projection. I don't even get a chance to consider that, because my first reaction is to jerk back, startled . . . and the girl in the mirror moves with me.

Bruises dapple her neck, and there's a dressing on her temple, as if she'd been struck there, and my mind goes instantly to the alley, hearing her gasp and fall back, seeing hands around her throat.

The girl—young woman, I should say—is no more than twenty. Honey-blond hair that curls to midback. Bright blue eyes. Average height with curves not quite contained by the corset over my chest.

Not me.

None of it is me.

I take a deep breath. Or I try to, but the corset restricts the movement. I look down to see I'm wearing a dress. A long-sleeved cotton dress, not unlike the one on the little girl who fled. When I run my hands over the bodice, I feel stiff stays beneath.

Who puts an injured young woman to bed while wearing a dress and corset?

I almost laugh at my outrage, as if this "young woman" is a stranger and I'm incensed on her behalf.

This stranger is me.

Footsteps thump up the stairs. Heavy floor-creaking steps, with lighter ones pattering along. My head jerks up, and I lunge, only to inhale sharply as the corset tightens. I gather my skirts—a phrase I've never had cause to use before—and race to the door, easing it shut before the people reach the top of the stairs.

A few moments later, someone turns the knob, and I brace my back against the door.

"Catriona?" a woman says. "Open this door."

I close my eyes and lean against it, and I have no idea what I'm doing, only that I do not want to face anyone until I've figured out what the hell is going on.

"Are ye certain she's awake, Alice?" the woman asks.

A girl's voice says, "Aye, ma'am. She were on her feet 'n' talking, though what she said . . . Her mind must be addled fae th' blow."

The older woman grumbles. "We dinnae need this."

I struggle to follow the accents, which seem thicker than I'm used to in Edinburgh. My brain smooths their speech into something I can follow.

"Catriona?" the older woman says.

I clear my throat and channel historical-novel dialogue while sending up a thanks to my dad, the English prof.

"I-I fear I am unwell, ma'am," I say. "Might I lie abed awhile longer?"

I wince. I sound like a community-theater player in a period drama. Even my voice isn't my own. It's the higher pitch I heard earlier, with a thick Scottish brogue.

As silence falls, I wonder whether I've laid on the "historical-novel-speak" a bit thick.

More footsteps. These ones firm, soles smacking along the hall floor.

"Sir," the older woman says.

"What the devil is going on?" A man's voice, clipped with annoyance, his brogue softer.

"It's Catriona, sir," the girl says. "She's awake."

"Awake?" Genuine shock sparks in the man's voice.

The knob jangles. The door opens an inch before I thump against it, forcing it shut.

"She's barred the door, sir," the girl—Alice—says again. "She's not herself."

The man mutters something I don't catch, and the older woman snorts.

"Catriona," he says, firm and abrupt, as if speaking to a dog. "Open this door, or I will open it for you."

"I am unwell, sir, and—"

The door flies open, knocking me forward as a man strides into the room. About thirty, he's big and rough-hewn, with a lantern jaw and broad shoulders. He must work in the stables, judging by the dirt on his rumpled clothing. Tousled black hair. Dark beard shadow. Brown skin. A thunderous look on his face that has me locking my knees to keep from shrinking back.

He stalks across the room and yanks open heavy drapes, the gray light of a heavily clouded day filtering through. Then he turns on me.

"What the devil are you doing out of bed?" he says. "Get back in there now."

"Like hell." The words come before I can stop them, and his dark eyes widen.

I hesitate. I want to fight, to demand answers. *Where am I? What's going on?* I know it isn't what I thought at first. This is not the guy who attacked me, and this is not some sicko killer's historical-fantasy game.

So what is it? I don't know, but my gut says to play along. Roll with it. Get answers without making trouble.

"Apologies," I say, in a tone that doesn't sound very apologetic. "I appear to have been struck in the head, and I am not quite myself." Understatement of the *century*. "Pray tell, who might you be?"

"I *might* be your employer, Catriona."

"Name?"

A tiny gasp, and I look over to see the little girl—Alice—staring at me goggle-eyed.

"Your name, please, sir?" I say.

"Duncan Gray."

"*Dr.* Gray to you," the older woman says with a sniff. I glance at her. Her face says she isn't over forty, but she's steel-haired, with a glare to match.

"That is Mrs. Wallace," Gray continues. "My housekeeper."

"And I am?"

His thick brows knit. "You truly don't remember?"

"I fear I do not, sir, due to the bump on my head. If you would please kindly assist me by answering my questions, I would very much appreciate it."

"You'll ask your questions of me," Mrs. Wallace snaps. "The master has no time for your nonsense."

Gray waves her off, his gaze still on me, peering, assessing. A medical doctor, then? I take a closer look at his shirt, and see that what I'd mistaken for dirt is ink stains. Also, possibly a smear of soot. Wait, is that *blood*?

Gray eases back. "You are Catriona Mitchell. Nineteen years of age. Housemaid to myself and my widowed sister, who is currently abroad."

"And this place? It is your house, I presume. But the city? Edinburgh, is it?"

Mrs. Wallace continues to glare, as Alice watches me with that mixture of horror and admiration. As interrogations go, mine is downright civil. Probably still not quite appropriate for a Victorian housemaid.

If Gray takes offense, though, he doesn't show it. "Yes, it is my home. Yes, it is in Edinburgh." The faintest twitch of the lips. "Scotland."

"And the date, sir?"

"May 22."

Before I can open my mouth, he adds, "Eighteen sixty-nine. Today is May 22, 1869."

FOUR

On May 20, 1869, Catriona Mitchell had been enjoying a half day off, only to be discovered that night in a lane, where she'd been strangled and left for dead . . . exactly one hundred and fifty years before I was strangled in the exact same spot.

I woke mid-morning, and the rest of the day passes in a fog of denial pierced by bouts of investigation. I am, after all, a detective. Faced with a question, I investigate. I'm also the daughter of a defense attorney. I play both roles here—as a detective, I build my case, and as my mother's daughter, I try to tear it down again.

What are the possibilities here? I could be dreaming or being tricked, possibly drugged into hallucination. While it doesn't feel like those are the answers, I can't just trust my gut. The first step is to find something that doesn't fit the time period. For that, I automatically reach for my phone to start checking my surroundings against factual history. But without a cell phone—or any internet—I must rely on a layperson's understanding of the Victorian era, and I'm sure I could be fooled. Also, if it is a dream, it would match my expectations anyway.

Still, I try to poke holes in the fabric of this reality. I check the mirror, in case it's a trick one. It isn't, and I'm not sure how that would work anyway when I can look down and see a body that's not my own. That takes me back to the "drugged and hallucinating theory."

I check my hair. Not a wig or a weave. Nothing about me is familiar, and there is no chance I'm wearing some elaborate disguise.

I check my undergarments next—which is an adventure in itself—in case I find modern underwear in the layers, suggesting a logical gap in the hallucination or dream. Nope, my underwear is definitely not modern. It's a pair of drawers—

Wait. Where's the crotch? I have two leg pieces attached and open at the crotch. Did I rip it? No, that seems to be the design, and I think I have indeed found a logical hole . . . until I need to use the chamber pot with layers of skirts and I realize *why* my underwear would be crotchless. Okay, *that* I did not expect.

I also test my mental faculties. I recite the alphabet backward. I walk in a straight line. I pull up the words to my favorite poems. I'm not drugged or inebriated in any way.

When I woke, I presumed my attacker lured me into the alley with a video of a young woman being attacked. Forget the fact that I'm now in the body of that young woman. Does my theory even make sense? He's the guy from the coffee shop. He stalked me. What's the chance that he planted the video along my run in hopes I'd hear it and respond?

No, what I heard was Catriona. What I saw was Catriona. My attacker only took advantage of it. I'd helpfully run into a dark alley, and that was exactly the opportunity he could not ignore.

Later that morning, Alice brings me a late breakfast, which I can't bring myself to eat, not until I've figured out what's going on. I manage to ask a few questions before she scampers off. Gray checks my head wound briefly, and come afternoon, Mrs. Wallace herself delivers lunch with a lecture, neither of which I'm in the mood for, but I pick at the food and pick through the lecture—mostly about how lucky I am to work for a family like this—for useful information. Then, Mrs. Wallace declaring me well enough, I'm moved upstairs to Catriona's proper quarters.

When night falls, I slip from my room and head downstairs. There are a lot of stairs, with a lot of levels, which does make it seem like a dream until I glance out a front window and realize we're in a town house. In Canada, that would mean a relatively small home adjoined to others. This is as big as any suburban mini-mansion, at least four thousand square feet.

Three stories plus a finished attic, where the maids sleep, and a finished basement, with the kitchen and Mrs. Wallace's quarters.

When I first woke, I'd been in a third-floor guest room. Gray and his sister also have their bedrooms on that level. The second floor is home to the dining room, drawing room, and library. I'm not sure what's on the main level—the doors are locked and I can't easily find anything to pick them.

I conduct an otherwise thorough survey of the house, and I find nothing to suggest I'm not actually in the nineteenth century. Moreover, while I see many things I'd expect, I also see things that I *don't* expect, but on reflection, they fit. Like gas lighting and coal stoves. Ask me to imagine this period, and I'd conjure up candles and wood fireplaces. I'm not sure I've ever given much thought to what came between candles and electricity or wood and oil furnaces, but gas and coal make sense.

Also, the decorating is . . . I don't want to say "ghastly." That oversells it. Slightly. There's too much of everything—from paintings to bric-a-brac to furniture—and Victorians obviously never met a bright color they didn't want for their sitting room. I'm saved from eye trauma by the gas lighting, which combines with the heavy drapes to keep the garish colors muted. I imagine the day when Victorians will get electric light, suddenly see their rooms in their full glory, and run screaming, retinas scarred. Again, it's not what I expected, but when I see it, my gut says, "Yes, this is Victorian."

I poke about the house, and I track down Alice to subtly ask about the residents. Gray and his widowed sister live alone. The staff consists of Mrs. Wallace, Catriona, and Alice, plus a part-time gardener named Mr. Tull and a stable hand named Simon.

Between the staff and the elegant home, the family seems to be what I'd consider upper middle class. Oh, and Gray's not actually a doctor. Well, yes, technically he is—I found diplomas for a bachelor's degree in medicine plus a master of surgery from the Royal College. But rather than keeping people alive, he takes care of them after they're dead. He's an undertaker, which seems to be an inherited family business.

I spend that night investigating, while my internal defense lawyer challenges everything. Finally, it isn't my profession or my mother's that allows me to accept what has happened to me. It's Nan's. She's an amateur folklorist who grew up in a family where they'd put out cream for the fairies. If asked whether she believed in such things herself, she'd say, "I don't *not* believe." She'd heard too many stories to slam that door shut. Real fairies? Maybe not. But she did allow for the possibility of concepts beyond the conventional realm of science, like ghosts and telekinesis . . . and time travel.

In the end, I cannot dismiss the words of that fictional saint of detectives.

When you have eliminated the impossible, whatever remains, however improbable, must be the truth.

Something happened in that lane. Two women were strangled a hundred and fifty years apart. On the same night. In the same spot. I don't think I heard and saw an echo of the attack on Catriona. I think I saw the attack itself—through a rip in time. I heard her cries. I came running. And when I was attacked in the same manner, time tangled, and I fell into her.

Is Catriona in my body, lying in a twenty-first-century hospital bed? If I get back to where we switched places, can I reverse this?

I *will* get back there. Right now, though, there's no escaping. During the day I played "confused and befuddled head-injury victim." Which also gave me an excuse for staying in my bed, recuperating as I worked out my situation. Otherwise, I suspect, Mrs. Wallace would have put me to work as soon as I woke.

Once I've accepted time travel as the answer, I head straight to the front door before realizing I have no idea where I am and how to get back to that lane. My brain insists that isn't a problem. Just pull out my phone and let the GPS guide me back to the Grassmarket. Yeah . . .

While the front door is locked, it doesn't require a key to open from the inside, so it's not as if I'm trapped. I'll acquire more data before venturing out.

Mrs. Wallace has already declared I'll resume my duties tomorrow. That's fine. It's the only way I'll get the information I need to return to the lane where I passed through time. Playing housemaid is a necessary evil if I want to avoid being tossed into a lunatic asylum for my odd behavior.

Here, I have food and shelter and a job that can't be all that difficult. Everyone expects me to be "a little off" after my injury. I'll be as sweet and demure as any Victorian maiden, as quiet as they'll expect from a servant girl, while I figure things out.

I have a mission, one with three simple steps:

> Find my way back.
> Get to Nan's side before it's too late.
> Give the police everything I know to stop a killer.

It feels like the middle of the night when Mrs. Wallace bangs her fist on my door. I reach for my phone to check the time and my hand smacks down on an empty nightstand.

"It's almost five," she says as she sticks her head in. "Are you going to lay about until dawn?"

"Sorry," I say, my voice thankfully muffled as I rephrase that. "Apologies, ma'am. I seem to have misplaced my alarm clock."

Her broad face scrunches up. "Your what?"

"My . . ." I cough. "My, um . . ." *How do Victorians wake up, if they haven't invented alarm clocks?* "Apologies, ma'am," I repeat. "'Twill not happen again."

Her eyes narrow, as if I'm being sarcastic. She shakes it off and says, "Get your lazy bones out of that bed. I'll expect you dressed and downstairs in a quarter hour, or you'll not be getting any tea."

She smacks the door closed. I groan. It's been clear from our brief interactions that Mrs. Wallace is not a Catriona fan. I don't know whether it's a personality clash or simply a product of the times, where women have so little power that they wield it against one another with unnecessary vigor.

Unnecessary vigor? I smile to myself. Even my internal dialogue is starting to sound positively Victorian. That's the trick, really. Stilted speech. Five-dollar words—thanks to Dad, I know plenty of those. And for God's sake, do not mention things before they were invented. Of course, the problem is that I don't *know* when they were invented. For the thousandth time in two days, I find myself reaching for my phone to look it up. I've been able to do that since I was a kid, and now I feel lost without that easy access to a virtual universe of data.

You're a detective, figure it out.

Yep, think before I speak. Err on the side of caution. I'm a maid. No one will expect me to say much. At least I've retained Catriona's voice and accent. That will help. Otherwise each word should be uttered with care and forethought until I'm certain I'm not referring to an object twenty years before its time.

I do know one thing that hasn't been invented. Central heating. As I discovered last night, while the house is mostly heated by coal, there are still a couple of wood-burning fireplaces. In my room, there's a small coal one—a brazier—which I'm sure will do a lovely job once I figure out how to use it.

So my room is freezing, despite me closing the window. There's no shortage of blankets, thank God, but once I throw back the covers, it's like stepping into a walk-in freezer. I reach for my bedside lamp . . . only to remember it's oil. My shaking fingers struggle to light it.

My room has gas lighting, but Mrs. Wallace caught me using it yesterday and gave me hell. Apparently, having gas lighting and being allowed to use it are two different things, at least if you're a mere housemaid.

My quarters are the size of a college dorm room, with a narrow bed and tiny window. A dorm or a prison cell. It's a private room, though, with a locking door, and from what I've seen of servants' rooms in movies, I struck gold here.

I pull on my uniform easily enough. I practiced yesterday, so I wouldn't take an hour getting ready this morning. The damned corset isn't even the worst of it. There's layer upon layer of clothing.

I might have been cursing those layers yesterday, but this morning I happily tug them on. At least they'll keep me warm. Maybe that's the point.

Next come my morning "ablutions." I think that's the word, anyway. It sounds properly old-fashioned.

I have an old college friend who adores historical-romance novels, and I take every opportunity to remind her that those dashing dukes would have had yellow teeth and stunk of BO. Judging by Gray and his staff, that's not true, and I don't know whether Victorian hygiene levels are higher than I expected or they're just higher in a doctor's home.

Dental hygiene is not as dire as I feared. Catriona has a bristled brush in her toiletries and a powder that I use to brush with while hoping I haven't mistaken its purpose and will drop dead of arsenic poisoning. Of course, having no idea what's even in Victorian tooth powder, I might still drop dead of it, but at least my teeth will be clean.

I finish getting ready with a bristle hairbrush, soap, and clean water. It'd be even better if that water weren't ice cold but at least it wakes me up.

I'm still washing my face when the downstairs clock strikes the quarter hour.

Shit!

I mean, drat. Er, no, pretty sure that isn't historically accurate either. In fact, I have the very strong impression that demure young housemaids do not use profanity, at least not out loud.

I race into the hall, only to hear a squeak of surprise and turn to see Alice blinking at me. Okay, apparently demure young housemaids do not tear down halls either. I bend a quick curtsy in apology, and her eyes widen in shock.

Right, housemaids wouldn't curtsy to other maids. That's for the master and mistress of the house. Or is curtsying even a thing in 1869?

I wave to Alice, who lifts her fingers hesitantly.

Do people not wave in Victorian Scotland? Goddamn it, this isn't going to be half as easy as I thought. It isn't just modern speech and modern references I need to avoid. It's modern gestures, modern customs, modern everything.

And the longer I fret about that, the later I'll be for starting work. I suspect Mrs. Wallace wasn't joking about missing breakfast. I only need to suffer through a day to two "in service" before I'll have what I need to get home.

I take the stairs down four flights to the basement kitchen. It's a small room, blazing hot and as clean as a surgery, with a horror movie's worth of hanging knives. The smell—fresh bread, hot tea, roast ham—gets my stomach rumbling, and I hurry for the door into the "servants' hall," where we eat.

"Do you expect to be served your tea, Miss Catriona?"

That's when I see the tray on the counter. A steaming teapot. Slices of fresh-baked bread, tiny silver and glass bowls of butter and pickled something. There's also an empty plate for the ham and poached eggs cooking on the stove.

I head for the tray as my stomach growls in appreciation. I'll say this much for nineteenth-century Scotland, the food has been better than I expected.

I'm reaching for the breakfast tray when Mrs. Wallace says, "I'm not done with that yet. Drink your tea and give me time to finish his eggs."

His eggs.

This is Gray's breakfast.

"Apologies, ma'am," I say, and resist the urge to curtsy. "And where might my morning meal be?"

I follow her gaze to a cup of tea and a chunk of unbuttered fresh bread. I glance from her to the meager meal, hoping I'm misunderstanding.

Nope. Well, at least it's not stale bread and water.

I devour the food, trying very hard not to wolf it down like a starving beast. Crossing a hundred and fifty years takes a lot out of a person, and that chunk of bread only whets my appetite.

Once it's gone, I turn to Mrs. Wallace, feeling like Oliver Twist, holding out my plate.

"Please, ma'am, might I have another slice?"

"And let Dr. Gray's breakfast go cold? You'll get your meal after the master has had his." I must look relieved, because she waves at my empty bread plate. "Did you think I'd stopped feeding you? I run a proper household. You'll need a full belly if you're going to get through your chores. The mistress comes home in two days, and you've been slacking, Miss Catriona."

"I was *unconscious*."

"Not since yesterday." She scoops the poached eggs into tiny silver cups. "Now get your lazy self off and start working."

I head toward what I hope is a room in need of cleaning.

She clears her throat. "Are you forgetting something?"

When I glance over, her gaze goes to the meal tray. I glance from it to her. "You want me to take this to Dr. Gray."

"No, I'd like it to fly up to him on pixie wings, but as you're the only one here, I suppose you'll have to do."

I fix on my most contrite look, lashes lowered. "Apologies, ma'am. I know I'm being a trial. My mind is still a wee bit fuzzy after my accident."

"Oh, is that how you're going to play this?" She raises her voice to a falsetto. "*I'm a wee bit fuzzy, ma'am. If I could just have an extra day or two to rest . . .*"

She shoves the tray into my hands. "Be glad you still have a position at all, after getting yourself into that mess."

"Getting myself strangled?"

"You were skulking about the Old Town. What did you expect?"

The Old Town. If I remember correctly, in this era, that was the slums. So what was a housemaid from a prosperous household doing *there*?

Mrs. Wallace continues, "Now take that tray to the master before it's cold, and as soon as he's done with you, get yourself back here, and I *might* have breakfast for you."

FIVE

As I take the tray up the stairs, one smell rises above the others. Is that . . . ? I inhale. Wafting from the teapot is the distinct smell of coffee. Drool tickles the corners of my mouth.

They have coffee in 1869? I don't mind tea, but right now, that coffee smells more tantalizing than the entire breakfast combined. I twist the tray so I can inhale the fumes directly as I wonder whether Gray would miss a few sips.

I imagine Mrs. Wallace coming around the corner to see me drinking straight out of the master's coffeepot. Maybe if I'm the one to collect it, there will be some left.

Yep, my first day as a housemaid, and I'm already reduced to stealing the dregs of my master's coffee.

Also, "master"? Is that really what he's called? I suppose it's the alternative when we can't refer to him as "His Lordship" or whatever. Still, I hope to hell I'm not expected to call him "master."

Gray's bedroom is on the third floor. That's three flights of stairs up. I continue climbing as I remind myself I'm in need of a good workout. Maybe I can go out for a run on my break. As I think that, my long skirts catch my knees, and I look down. Nope, no jogging in this outfit.

I crest the stairs and . . .

Shit. Which door is his?

A chair scrapes against the floor, and I exhale.

I can do this. Detective, remember? Follow the clues.

As I prepare to enter the room, I try to remember whether I've seen or read this scene: a housemaid bringing breakfast to her employer. It's familiar, but the details are lost to memory. Information I never expected to use, oddly enough.

I think I'm supposed to knock first. Either way, that seems safe. I pause to pull on my best speaking-to-the-lord face. Demure. That's the key. I'm a Victorian housemaid. Keep my gaze down and my expression meek. Be seen but not heard. Or is that for children? Close enough.

I rap on the door. After a moment, there's a grunt that I think means "Come in." I ease the door partway open, and a low table appears just to my left. I set the tray on it and murmur "Your breakfast, sir" and then begin my retreat.

"Where the devil are you going?"

I open the door to see Gray at a desk. He isn't fully dressed. He's decent, at least by twenty-first-century standards. Button-down shirt, mostly fastened. The Victorian equivalent of boxers—undergarments that reach to his knees. If they're crotchless drawers, like mine, that particular part is well hidden by his shirt. Long socks cover most of the remaining skin. Well, one sock. The other is on the floor.

If he wasn't at his desk, pen in hand, I'd think I'd interrupted him in the midst of dressing. From the looks of things, it's an idea that interrupted him, and he stopped halfway through to scribble it down.

"Well," he says, the word spoken with an impatient snap. "I'm obviously in need of your services, Catriona."

I freeze. Now, *this* is a scene I have definitely read in books. The pretty young maid, forced to "tend" to the lord of the manor.

Oh, hell no. *You even hint at that, Dr. Gray, and I'll take my chances on the street.*

He looks from me to the darkened fireplace and then back at me. "Well?"

"Oh! You want me to light the fire."

"No, Miss Catriona. I want you to warm the room with your sunny disposition. Yes, I want you to start the fire. Preferably before I freeze to death."

Well, if you're cold, maybe you could finish getting dressed. Or light your own damn fire.

That's exactly what I'd say if a superior officer expected me to light a fire while he lounged half naked. Well, no, I'd tell him to get his pants on before I reported his ass. But Gray employs me to do exactly this. I need to treat it as good practice for going undercover. Bite my tongue, swallow my attitude, and act a part.

"I realize this is your first day back to work," he says. "I am making allowances for that. But I will expect my fire lit before I rise tomorrow."

"What time is that, sir?"

His dark eyes narrow. "The same as always. Five thirty."

Oh joy. Apparently, I need to get up *before* five now. Right after I figure out how the hell to do that without an alarm clock.

I murmur something suitably agreeable and then move to the fire.

It's a wood-burning fireplace, not coal. The master of the house values ambience over convenience, apparently. Helps when you have staff to light it for you.

I can do this. I was a Girl Guide, and I go camping every year with friends. Well, I did, until I got too busy with work and had to recuse myself from the annual getaway. One year off fire making shouldn't matter. Or is it two years? Possibly three . . . ?

Damn it. I've let things slide. Let life slide. I'm going to fix that when I get back. Repair the damage before I stop getting invitations and suddenly I'm forty and wondering why no one calls me anymore.

For now, though, I've got this. Just start a fire.

I stare at the mess in the fireplace, all ashes and scorched wood. Then I spend the next twenty minutes cleaning the fireplace. Gray has resumed his mad scribbling, so absorbed that the only time he even glances over is when I drop the metal poker on the stone hearth.

"Less clatter would be appreciated, Catriona."

I murmur an apology. There's silence, and I think he's gone back to work, but then he says, dryly, "I don't believe you're supposed to clean the hearth with your skirt."

I look down. I'm wearing a uniform—a white apron over a dark blue dress. That apron is no longer white. Neither is the surrounding fabric. I could argue that he's not one to judge—I already see ink spatter on his collar—but I suspect rejoinders are not permitted in this relationship.

I lean back on my heels. "I'm not quite myself, sir."

"I've noticed."

I take a deep breath and make a decision. A risky one.

"My memory seems to have been adversely affected by my illness, and I find myself struggling to recall mundane and ordinary tasks."

He stares at me like I'm speaking Greek. I replay my words, but they seem fine. Suitably stilted and old-fashioned. Maybe it's my accent? It's thicker than his.

"I realize this is unseemly of me," I say, "being a maid, but I must humbly request your forbearance."

More brow wrinkling, now accompanied by what looks like suspicion.

I hurry on. "I'm not trying to weasel—I'm not asking to be excused from my tasks, sir. I understand my convalescence has been an inconvenience, upsetting the smooth operation of your household. I am simply admitting that I may require reminders, now and then, of my tasks, which I will complete forthwith."

"Forthwith . . ." he repeats slowly.

Isn't that the right word? It sounds right.

I continue, "Promptly and efficiently, with the diligence you expect of your staff."

"I see. . . ." His look is bemusement bordering on bafflement. I've done something wrong. I just can't tell what it is.

"Also," I hurry on, "I beg your forbearance with any idiosyncrasies of character I might display. As I said, I do not feel myself. Which is no excuse for lackadaisical workmanship, of course."

His look skewers me, as if I'm a body on the table, ready for dissection. Whatever his rough appearance, Dr. Gray is not a stupid man. Under that gaze, I swear I see his brain spinning faster than mine on my best days.

Here's where I'm going wrong. Well, one of many ways I'm going wrong. I feel superior to these people. I'm from the twenty-first century. So much more enlightened than them. That's bullshit, of course.

I have the advantages of the modern world. Thinking it makes me smarter is the polar opposite of "enlightened." Like looking down on someone who doesn't have a college degree because they couldn't afford to go to college. Gray is a medical doctor with *multiple* degrees. He's as educated as one can be in this world.

Tread carefully. Do not treat these people like primitive cave dwellers. Do not think you can easily fool them because you're from the future.

Under that piercing gaze, all I can do is get myself back to work. Hide in my chores. Speak less. Work more.

I build the fire. It may not be the way he's accustomed to, but it does the job. Heat blazes from it, and I tidy up the hearth and then start backing out of the room. He's eating one-handedly from his tray as he scribbles.

I've almost made my escape when he says, "Catriona?"

I pause.

"It may be Sunday, but I still have to work today," he says.

My gaze sweeps over the avalanche of papers and books carpeting his desk and spilling onto the floor.

"Oh," I say. "Would you like me to tidy your workspace, sir?"

When his brow furrows, I'm about to replace "workspace" with something more period-appropriate, but the word he repeats is "Tidy?"

"Clean up," I try. "Organize your papers and books so—"

"You do *not* touch my papers or books—" He stops himself and, with great effort it seems, arranges his features into something milder. "Yes, obviously, you are suffering from a mental fog, and I will allow the confusion. What I will not allow is any interference with my belongings, particularly my 'workspace' as you call it. It is already organized, thank you."

"If you say so, sir," I murmur.

His gaze shoots to me, suggesting my tone might have been a bit impudent.

I almost chuckle. "Impudent" is a word no one has ever applied to me. I suspect it's used a lot here, though, particularly when dealing with uppity women.

I bite my cheek not to laugh. I could become an uppity woman. It's tempting, in a life goal sort of way. It'd probably land my pretty ass on the sidewalk, though.

I expect that look in Gray's eyes to darken. Instead, he actually relaxes and even lifts a shoulder in what might be a half shrug. "My research is important, Catriona, and it is organized to my satisfaction."

That sounded vaguely civil.

Wait, did he say research? What sort of research does an undertaker, well, undertake? I glance toward the papers, tempted to inch closer. Then I remember my breakfast awaits, and I resume my retreat.

He clears his throat. "Catriona? I have an appointment today. With people who expect me to look presentable."

"Ah." I look around, crouch and pick up his missing sock from the floor. "You'll need this, I take it."

Do his lips twitch? It must be a flicker of the gas lighting. "I believe I'll need more than that."

Please don't ask me to dress you. Please, please.

When I hesitate, he taps his cheek, rough with stubble. Then he motions to the washstand. A straight razor sits beside it.

I babble excuses. I'm not even sure what they are—I just babble.

His eyes chill. "I believe you were the one who convinced my sister that we no longer needed the barber's visit. You are paid extra for this, and if you are using your mental impediment to shirk a duty—"

"I said I wasn't, sir," I say, and I sound like myself, Detective Mallory Atkinson, telling her sergeant that he is mistaken. As Gray's eyes narrow, I reverse course. "It's my hands. They're unsteady after the accident, so unless you'd like your throat slit . . ."

That is *not* reversing course.

He only looks at me, though. Looks very closely, as sweat beads at my hairline.

"Might that additional pay be deducted from my wages, sir?" I say. "If you insist, I'll attempt the shave, but I really am concerned I might hurt you—"

He pulls back, already turning to his work. "Go. Take the tray. I'll manage it myself."

He mutters under his breath. I take the breakfast tray and eye the straight razor. I'm going to need to figure that one out. How hard can it be? Worst I can do is leave him lying in a pool of his own blood, and after a day or two, that might not seem like such a bad idea.

I think I stifle my snorted laugh, but Gray turns, that narrow-eyed look as sharp as the razor.

I murmur something vaguely apologetic, curtsy, and back out of the room.

Apparently, it's Sunday. I'd known that from Gray, but what I'd overlooked was the significance of it in nineteenth-century Scotland. Sunday means church. While that would give me time away from my chores, I can't risk attending a Victorian church service. I'm guaranteed to do something wrong. When I beg off with my "sore head," Mrs. Wallace's grumbles suggest Catriona isn't exactly a regular churchgoer. Skipping out would mean a couple of hours alone in the house, and I can't begrudge her that short break.

Except she wouldn't be alone. Gray doesn't attend either. In his case, I get the feeling that's normal—no one seems to expect him to do otherwise. Either way, it's not as if I could have taken advantage of the time off. I need every minute that day just to finish my chores.

As a teenager, I spent a summer cleaning houses, when my inexperience meant it was that or telemarketing. As I'd scrub a stranger's toilet, I'd reassure myself that someday I'd hire people to do this for *me*. By my late twenties, I could afford a weekly cleaner—the benefit of a decent job and no dependents. Yet when I slapped on a pair of rubber gloves and picked up a scrub brush, I fell back into a world where I could shut off my brain and rely on pure muscle and muscle memory.

I find comfort in cleaning. I start a task, and as long as I keep at it, I see the results. Organized shelves. Sparkling floors. Glistening walls.

That's how I start my day of cleaning. Oh, it's tougher than at home, where I can hit the button on my robotic vacuum cleaner. Harder even than when I was a kid and homeowners would hide away their "good" vacuum and give me the crappy old one. No vacuums here. No spray-bottled cleaners. Not even rubber gloves. I'm on my hands and knees with a scrub brush and water filled with some cleaner that I'm ninety percent sure will later be proven to cause cancer.

I also spend far too much time reaching for my phone to start a podcast, resume an audiobook, even listen to music. That's what I do when I'm cleaning, same as when I'm working out or driving or any time my hands are busy but my brain is not. Here, there's nothing to do except keep uselessly checking my nonexistent watch for the time, which passes with excruciating slowness.

Still, hard work never killed anyone, right?

By midday, I decide that whoever coined that phrase never toiled as a nineteenth-century housemaid. I don't mind the cleaning. Don't mind the hard work. But it never ends. Scrub this. Polish that. Haul hot water.

Empty dirty water. Make the beds. Sweep. Dust. Clean. Oh, and don't even get me started on the chamber pots.

I suppose I should be thankful that I've at least managed to jump into a time period with actual bathrooms. I have not, however, jumped into the era of flush toilets. What looks like a toilet has a basin under it, and Alice and I alternate the duty of emptying that basin and then scrubbing it. We're allowed to use the facilities ourselves, as I discover when Mrs. Wallace reminds Catriona what a privilege it is for staff to be permitted to use the family "water closet." I don't even want to know what the alternative would be.

When I do complain—a bit—about the water hauling, I get a lecture on how lucky I am to be in a house that has the luxury of both hot and cold running water. At least I don't need to heat the water on a fire and haul it the way Mrs. Wallace did back in her day, which was, I'm guessing from her age, only about five years ago. Yep, gas lighting, running water, it's all fairly new, but when it comes to science the Grays have the best. Mrs. Wallace proudly tells me they've even been pricing out the possibility of central heating, coal-fired of course.

I work from sunup until sundown. No rest breaks. No lunch hour. Oh, I get enough food. Breakfast, a cold lunch after Mrs. Wallace returns from church, dinner, even afternoon tea with a piece of cake. No other downtime, though, and my meals are expected to be expeditiously eaten. Tomorrow, though, is my "half day." According to Mrs. Wallace, we get three half days off each fortnight, which is apparently far better than the norm. To me, it just means that I can get back to that alley tomorrow and return to my own time.

By 8:00 P.M., I finally finish the list of tasks that Alice relayed to me. I didn't dare admit my "memory lapses" to Mrs. Wallace. I rely on Alice, who seems surprised every time I speak to her, but happy enough to conspire. In return for her help, I offered to clean the water-closet chamber pot for the rest of the day. She'd looked startled—and suspicious. Maybe it's a matter of pride, not wanting to be accused of shirking one's duties.

I don't know what to make of Alice. She's a twelve-year-old kid, done with school—if she ever attended—and already in a life of service.

I know this isn't uncommon for the time period. If there are child labor laws, they don't apply to children like Alice, in relatively safe occupations. Yet is she really better off than working in a factory? At least there she could go home to her family at night. All she has here is a cranky housekeeper and a befuddled housemaid.

I get the feeling Catriona had been Alice's friend. I catch her looking at me with alternating concern and wariness. Her "big sister in service" is acting odd, and she's worried. If she's lost her only friend, then I should be that friend, which would be so much easier if I had experience interacting with preteen girls. I will be kind. I can do that. The rest . . . Well, hopefully she'll get *her* Catriona back tomorrow.

Tasks done, I detour to the kitchen in hopes of bedtime tea. Mrs. Wallace is madly preparing food for Tuesday, when the "mistress" returns. Something tells me the mistress is a harsher taskmaster than her brother. Gray hasn't rung the service bell all day. He expects the household to run efficiently around him, leaving him to his work. From the way Mrs. Wallace and Alice are freaking out, the lady of the house is another matter.

"Do you mind if I boil water for tea before I retire for the evening, ma'am?"

She turns to me. "Retire?"

"Y-yes. I've finished . . ." I list my tasks. It takes long enough that I could have boiled that water and probably steeped my tea.

"And the parlor?" she says.

I nod. "Dusted it, swept it, and cleaned the silver."

"I mean the funerary parlor."

"The what? Oh. Dr. Gray's place of business. Am I supposed to drop something off there?"

She looks at me like I've lost my mind. "You're supposed to drop yourself off there. It hasn't been cleaned in days, that being your job. Dr. Gray has two appointments in the morning."

"You want me to clean it now?"

"No, I want you to clean it tomorrow night, after his appointments. Let the grieving families discuss their dearly departed amidst the dust and cobwebs."

"Right. Okay." At her look, I correct my speech to, "Yes, ma'am, you are correct, and I apologize for my confusion. I'll grab—fetch—my coat and—"

"What do you need your coat for? If you're cold, you'll warm up as soon as you get working." She waves a hand. "Now off with you."

SIX

When Mrs. Wallace said I didn't need a jacket, she meant I wouldn't need to go outside. The funeral parlor is behind that locked door on the main floor. Entering through the front door, you can arrive in a foyer with two doors. One leads into a hall with a door to the courtyard, steps to the living quarters or a small "staff" door into the back of the funeral parlor. The second unmarked foyer door is on your right and leads into the funeral parlor.

I'm guessing that when Gray is expecting clients, they close the door into the main hall and open the one into the business. The lack of signage seems confusing, but we *are* in a residential neighborhood. Something tells me there's also no sign out front either. Having a neighbor sell fresh-baked pies is one thing; having them store dead bodies is another.

When I step through that door, the first thing I notice is the endless black. Swaths of what I think is called crepe—a lightweight, crinkly fabric—wind around pillars and loop over doorways and cover almost every wrapable surface.

To my left, I find what must be a showroom, with small caskets that I first think, with horror, are for babies. Hey, infant mortality rates in this period are mind-boggling. Then I realize they're samples. Miniature caskets. Or coffins. Or whatever they're called. There are sample headstones, too, also in miniature. When I see a book of photographs, I expect mortuary photos—those creepy Victorian pictures of people posing with dead relatives. Instead, it's sample photos of living persons with memorial dates.

Looking around, I don't see any of the ghoulish stuff I associate with Victorians and death. No photos of deceased loved ones. No dolls made in the likeness of a dead child. Nothing more morbid than hair jewelry.

Up front is a sitting room. It looks like a formal parlor, though the colors are much more muted than the riotous ones upstairs. Other than the somber decorating, there's no sign that this is anything except a sitting area, with a sofa and chairs and tables. I suspect that's intentional, so curious passersby see only a tidy front parlor. Heavy curtains frame a window that looks out onto the street. There's no lawn. It reminds me of New York brownstones, fronting directly onto the road.

I dust and sweep the reception area and showroom. Those take up more than half the floor space. There's no area big enough for loved ones to host the visitations and services. I check, in case there's a small chapel or viewing room. There isn't. Odd. Services must be held elsewhere.

That leaves one other essential part of a funeral parlor: the preparation room. I find a locked door at the rear, which I presume is an office. But then another closed door opens to reveal an office, which is remarkably tidy. Not as tidy as *I'd* like, but more than I'd expect from Gray, with only one stack of books on the floor and a few scattered pages on the desk. Also a book that seems to have fallen from the overstuffed shelf. It's lying open on the floor, pages folded. My fingers itch to pick it up, but I can hear him snapping that he put that book there, exactly like that, and I'd bloody well better not touch it.

I close the office door and make a mental note to find out whether there's anything I should be doing in the office, dusting or such. Then I retreat to finish cleaning the showroom and reception area.

When I'm done, I know I should head off to bed. An hour ago, I'd been ready to cuddle down in a casket to get a bit of rest. Now my work's finally done, and my brain is whizzing so fast I don't think I could sleep if I tried.

That locked door must be the preparation room. It must also be where they keep the bodies awaiting burial.

As a police officer, I've sat—or stood—in on autopsies. My colleagues always tease that I'm such a keener I jump at the chance to prove myself in anything, even autopsy duty. The truth is that I'm genuinely interested.

I've even seen an embalming. I'd been interviewing a mortician on a case, and he'd been up to his eyeballs in bodies, so I'd talked to him while he worked. I suspect that violates some professional code of privacy, but when I'd expressed an interest in seeing the process, he'd happily demonstrated. He also called the next day to ask me out. I said no, but not without a stab of guilt. I suspect putting "mortician" on your dating profile doesn't win you a lot of right swipes.

As for the preparations, I'd found them fascinating. All that work to give people one last look at their loved one, and they'll still complain that Aunt Agnes never wore her hair that way. This reminds me of Nan, but in a strange way, thinking about the dead helps quiet the gibbering voice that whispers my grandmother is probably already dead, probably lying in a place like this.

What if she is? Would that be any different than coming back from my jog that night to find she'd passed while I was gone? I would have felt horrible not being there, but I also must admit that we'd said what needed to be said. I just selfishly wanted more time. If she is gone, then her body may be in a place like this, but her spirit is not and the memory of her is not.

I double-check the door. Yep, still locked. I scan the room for something I can use to pick the lock with. Amazing how many of those "junior police officer" kits come with tools and instructions for opening locks, as if breaking and entering is just part of the job.

I return to Gray's office and ease open a drawer, looking for—

A hard rap sounds at a distant door, seemingly from the front of the house. I slam the drawer shut, wincing as everything inside jostles. I hurry out of the funeral parlor into the main hall. A staccato rap sounds again, and I realize it comes not at the front door but at the rear.

Is a housemaid allowed—or even expected—to answer the back door? I could catch shit either way. The choice, then, is mine. Which means there's no choice at all. It's a late-night knock at the back door to a funeral parlor. Of course I want to know who it is.

I must still play the simpering maid, though, so I set my foot behind the door and crack it open a scant inch, while gripping a letter opener in my hidden hand.

I peer through the crack to see a man far more befitting my mental image of a Victorian gentleman . . . and possibly befitting my romance-loving friends', too. He wears what I want to call a frock coat, with a vest underneath and a starched white shirt. A wide tie with a jeweled stickpin completes the look. He's around Gray's age and has sandy brown hair, sideburns, and a neat mustache. Despite the facial hair not being to my taste, he's handsome in that ordinary way that I consider the best kind of good-looking. Nothing flashy, just really easy on the eyes.

It takes me a moment to notice the man isn't alone. Behind him stands a guy probably not much older than Catriona, wearing what is unmistakably a police uniform.

"Miss Catriona." The older man smiles, and there's a gap between his front teeth, a charming one that I'm glad no modern orthodontist closed. "So good to see you up and about. I saw the light and thought it must be Duncan working late."

"No, sir," I say, my gaze demurely lowered. "It is only myself, finishing my chores. Would you like me to fetch Dr. Gray?"

"Please."

I slide the letter opener into my sleeve as I pull the door wide and invite them in. It's only as the two men move inside that I see the wagon in the courtyard. And a foot hanging out of it.

Oh, my. This *is* interesting.

"I will tell the doctor you're here," I say. Then I pause. "Apologies, sir, but . . ." I rub the bump on my temple. "This has left me a wee bit confused. I know you are an associate of Dr. Gray's, and that we have met before, and that you work for the police. Yet your name escapes me."

He only smiles. "Tell Dr. Gray that Hugh McCreadie is here to see him." He motions at the young man. "And this is Police Constable Findlay, whom I believe you know."

McCreadie's eyes twinkle, and I glance over at Findlay, who nods stiffly.

"Perhaps you two can take a moment to speak later," McCreadie says.

"That won't be necessary," Findlay says, his voice as stiff as that nod.

McCreadie looks between us and sighs. "That's why you've been off today, is it? A bit of trouble between you and the lass?"

"Nothing of concern, sir."

So Catriona had some romantic entanglement with the young constable? That's awkward, and I kinda do hope they *have* had a falling-out, for my sake. Catriona can fix that once she's back.

I turn to the older man. "Inspector McCreadie, is it?" I say, remembering the proper title for police detectives in Scotland.

He chuckles. "I'm not English, lass. I'm a Scottish criminal officer."

When I hesitate, he says, "Detective McCreadie."

Detective. The same title I use in Canada. That'll make it easy to remember.

"Thank you," I say. "I shall tell—"

"No need, Catriona." Gray's voice cuts through mine, and I glance up to see him descending the stairs. "Hello, Hugh. I thought I heard your voice."

"No," McCreadie says. "You sensed that rustle in the air that tells you something is afoot, something interesting. I have brought a fresh intellectual adventure for that brain of yours, so if we may step inside . . ."

Gray turns to me. "I've no further need of you this evening, Catriona."

I bob a quarter curtsy. "Thank you, sir. I left my dusting rag inside. I shall fetch it and depart out the other door."

With a wave from Gray, I'm dismissed. I disappear into the funeral parlor, walk to the rear—staff—entrance, open the door and shut it again loud enough for them to hear. I doubt they noticed—they're already outside bringing in the body. While they do that, I find myself a shadowy hiding spot.

A midnight corpse at a funeral parlor. Delivered by a police detective and his young constable. That hardly seems proper procedure, and I have a very good idea what they're up to.

Body snatching.

Years ago, Nan had taken me to a special exhibit at the museum. I remember a wonderfully lurid diorama of two disreputable men robbing a grave, one digging while the other held a lantern. A raven had been perched on the headstone and a starving dog waited, as if both hoped for any pieces that might fall off the rotting corpse.

Edinburgh was known for its medical schools, and those schools needed bodies, which were hard to come by back in a time when you couldn't—and wouldn't—donate yours to science. An entire trade grew up around providing those specimens. If I recall correctly, there'd been a notorious case of two local guys who realized how much money they could make selling cadavers and decided to skip the whole "waiting for people to die" part.

While grave robbing is one way to get bodies, this would be another one: use the corpses of those who won't be missed. Gray's police friend finds a drunkard dead in an alleyway and brings him to his funeral parlor, as if delivering a body for a pauper's grave. Gray pays a few shillings and passes the cadaver along to his medical-school friends.

I won't question the ethics of what he's doing. I'd never condone it in the modern world. We already treat the indigent as disposable. Here, though, if advancing medical science requires corpses, I'll cut them some slack until we reach the day where people can choose to donate their bodies to science.

I'm not hiding to judge Gray by confirming my suspicions. I'm hiding because he isn't the only one who likes a puzzle. I think I've solved this one. Now I'm flipping to the back of the book to double-check my answer.

Gray helps lift the body. Just rolls up his sleeves and does the work, which would have surprised me for another man of his station, but doesn't surprise me for this one.

They carry in a man's body through the courtyard door, then the staff door and finally through that locked door. I would think one would want a direct door from the funeral parlor to the courtyard, but I suppose that hadn't been possible, when they were retooling a family home to accommodate the dead.

After Constable Findlay helps, McCreadie claps him on the back and tells him to take the rest of the night off, joking that there's time to get a pint before the public houses close. He might also palm him a shilling—or whatever a beer costs. I only know that the young man thanks McCreadie and leaves without hesitation.

McCreadie waits until Findlay's gone. Then he says, "I think the body put him off, poor lad. I do hope not. He has promise, that one, but this isn't a job for the squeamish."

Gray only grunts in response, and then there's a click, as if he's locking the door.

McCreadie's heavy footsteps cross the floor. I wait for the click of him closing the preparation room door, but it doesn't come, and when I poke my head out, I see the door half open, the light from inside flooding out.

Thank you, Detective.

I wait for McCreadie to speak, to be sure he's in that room. When he murmurs something, I creep out and take up position behind the door, where I can peer through the crack. It isn't a perfect sight line. I see the legs of the body, which are oddly drawn up, as if the corpse stiffened in a seated position. The two men block the corpse's upper half.

"In my expert opinion," Gray says, "the cause of death is murder."

McCreadie gives a sharp laugh. "You always were the clever one."

Murder? That surprises me. Yet McCreadie *had* mentioned an intellectual puzzle. Is this more than a body snatching?

"Have you notified Addington?" Gray asks.

McCreadie grumbles something unintelligible and definitely uncomplimentary about this Addington fellow. Then he says, "I'll need to fetch him within the hour, so you need to work quickly."

Gray only grunts. A tap of metal. I peer through to see him leaning over the body, prodding at it.

"My preliminary assessment is that this part seems to have been inflicted postmortem."

"You're certain of that?"

A low growl from Gray. "No, Hugh, I'm not certain at all. That's why I called it a preliminary assessment. You will get a proper ruling from Addington."

"If I expected a proper anything from him, you wouldn't be here."

"I would certainly be here. It is my laboratory."

"Laboratory"? That must be the Victorian word for an undertaker's preparation room. It still makes no sense. McCreadie brought a murder victim to an undertaker, and then he's bringing the coroner *here* for the autopsy?

"I would agree all this seems postmortem," McCreadie says. "What I want is your professional opinion."

"You lack faith in your own judgment," Gray says. "It is a poor quality in a criminal officer."

"I lack faith in my medical expertise, because I am not a *medical* officer, Duncan."

"It doesn't take a doctor to realize how much simpler it would be to do all this if your theatrical property is already dead."

"Theatrical property?"

"A 'prop' as they call it these days. Yes, that is disrespectful to the young man, but there is not anyone here to judge me for my callow phrasing."

"I meant, why do you call him a prop?"

"Because all this is clearly staging. One does not do this to a body unless one has a message to convey."

"Or unless one is a madman."

"Madmen still have messages, perhaps more than those in possession of their faculties. I have no opinions on the mental state of this killer. My interest is the body, which isn't all that interesting."

McCreadie sputters. "How can you call this 'not interesting'? It is the most bizarre murder I have ever seen."

That has me twisting and craning to see more.

"The staging is interesting. My concern is the murder, which is terribly pedestrian. Simple strangulation." Gray lifts something out with what looks like tweezers. "You're looking for woven rough cord. Hemp, I believe. Likely rope."

McCreadie lifts something. "Like this?"

Dangling from his hand is a length of old rope. Exactly like the one used to strangle me.

SEVEN

I stare at that rope. I don't hear what they say about it. I just stare until a word snaps me out of it.

Beak? Did they say something about a beak?

I've obviously misheard, but that incongruous word is enough to bring me back to myself, and with that, I almost laugh. The victim was killed with an antique-looking piece of rope. Uh, because we're in 1869? It's just regular rope here. Old, yes, but otherwise, not nearly as incongruous as it'd been in my time.

Gray is saying something about wanting to remove another rope from the victim's legs to determine whether they're seized in that position. That has me craning forward again, still unsuccessfully. I can see the knees, which are drawn up. I squint until I can make out a length of rope wrapped around the victim's ankles. So he didn't go into rigor while sitting. That would be difficult—he'd need to die seated and somehow not fall out of the chair. Rigor mortis is a temporary condition, starting about six hours after death and dissipating around forty-eight hours.

Yep, I may not have been on a date in over a year, but I am intimately acquainted with the principles of forensic science, having spent far too many nights snuggling with textbooks, hoping it'd help get me into the homicide unit someday.

As Gray cuts the rope, he holds it steady, and I rock forward, wanting to warn that he's getting his fingerprints on it. Or is fingerprint analysis not a thing yet? One area I haven't studied is the history of forensic science, seeing no practical use for it.

Well, that'll teach me.

Gray cuts the rope, and the victim's legs stay in the same position, indicating rigor. He massages one and then the other.

"Death at least eight hours ago and less than thirty-six. I'll let Addington take the core temperature—he can handle that much."

McCreadie mutters something uncomplimentary, presumably about the coroner again. Would it be a coroner? Medical examiner? Or just a doctor with a basic knowledge of pathology?

"Tell Addington you had to cut the rope to move him," Gray says. "I'll leave the hands where they are."

I squint to see the victim's hands, but McCreadie stands between my sight line and the upper body.

"The feathers were intact?" Gray asks.

Feathers?

"There were a few more of them," McCreadie says. "Dislodged when we transported him."

"Hmm. I don't suppose it matters. I have no idea what they signify, but that would be your job. Lack of bleeding suggests they were also inserted postmortem."

Inserted? Feathers? I'm barely able to stand still now, and I keep reminding myself that this has nothing to do with me. I'm a housemaid in this world, which I hope to exit tomorrow.

Forget feathers and beaks and bizarrely posed corpses. This does not concern me, and like Gray, I will deem it quite ordinary. Mundane. Not worthy of my attention.

So why am I still bouncing on my toes trying to see the body?

"That is enough for now," Gray says. "Addington will be here soon, and we must play the game of pretending no one has examined the body. I shall perform a more thorough analysis in the morning."

"Would you like to know who he is?"

"Who *who* is?"

"The poor lad on your laboratory table."

"You know him?"

"Archie Evans. Came up from London a few years back. Fancied himself a proper journalist. Reported on crime for the *Evening Courant*."

"Why the devil didn't you say so? That could be significant."

"I already considered that, Duncan. Evans may have covered the wrong story. Dug too deep where he ought not to. That has nothing to do with the manner of death, though."

"The feathers belong to a pigeon. A pigeon carries messages. A scribbler spreads the message of the news."

"There was also a single raven feather." McCreadie takes a watch from his pocket. "Oh, would you look at the time? I must trot off to meet Dr. Addington."

"Do not *dare* walk out now, Hugh. Where was this raven feather?"

"Oh, do not concern yourself with such an uninteresting murder, Duncan. I'm certain you have better puzzles to captivate that brain of yours. Off I go."

McCreadie walks from the room as I scamper back into my hiding spot. I listen as his boots clomp across the floor, and Gray strides after him, audibly seething.

"Be sure to leave the door open for our return," McCreadie says cheerfully. "No need to stay up. I'll see you on the morrow."

McCreadie leaves. Gray follows him, still asking about the raven feather. I should make my escape now. Get out while I can. But even as I fix my gaze on the back door, my feet take me to that "laboratory" door.

I sneak toward the door the men exited. It's firmly closed. I slip into the lab and sidle up to the table for a look at the body.

I've seen mangled corpses and drowning victims, and other sights that made me wish I hadn't eaten breakfast. This is horrifying in an entirely different way. There's no blood. No gore. Not even stab wounds.

Gray called it a prop. That's what it looks like. The prop from some avant-garde performance art meant to convey God knows what message. Except in art, it wouldn't be an actual body. That's where the horror comes from.

The young man has been staged to look like a bird. Legs bound up and feet broken into a perch pose. Elbows wide. Hands affixed to the torso so the arms form wings.

It all looks postmortem. That hardly matters. It's still grotesque.

Rows of feathers protrude from the young man's shoulders. They've been poked through the shirt and inserted into his shoulders.

Then there is the beak. It looks like a mask from an old play. By old, I mean old-fashioned, in the sense that it's carved from wood rather than plastic formed in a 3D printer. There's a string for fastening it, but when I nudge the beak with my knuckle, it stays fixed. Glued on? That makes me shiver, but then, morbid ghoul that I am, I can think of far worse ways to fasten a beak onto a person's face.

This is what my detective brain seizes on. It's what has my hands moving instinctively to my nonexistent pockets for my nonexistent phone, itching to snap a photo for later study. I see past the grotesquerie of the staging and must grudgingly marvel at the ingenuity and lack of mutilation. I grew up in the era of movies like *Saw,* which I walked out of. I love horror; I hate the torture-porn of body horror. The killer here has managed to capture the essence of that while refraining from true butchery.

That doesn't mean I admire the killer in any possible way. They murdered a young man. The kid barely looks twenty and, yes, the death of anyone is tragic, but I will always feel an extra pang of grief for lives cut so short.

What did McCreadie say? Evans had been a reporter on the crime beat? This boy had accomplished something, and now he's lying in a funeral parlor. What was done to him only makes it that much worse. It's mockery. Using his body as a canvas, using his death as a message, as if his life was worth no more than that.

Staged to look like a bird. A pigeon, Gray said. I eye the feathers and consider taking one for study. McCreadie did say a few had fallen out, so another wouldn't be missed.

I stifle the impulse. Not my circus. Not my monkey. Not even my century. I plan to be gone tomorrow, and I'm sure as hell not disturbing a murder victim's body to satisfy idle curiosity. Because that's all it can be. Idle curiosity.

Presuming they are pigeon feathers, the symbolism is simple. As Gray said, pigeons carry messages. A reporter spreads the news. As for the raven feather near the body, well, ravens prey on pigeons. Corvids have a reputation for being the smartest birds. That's how our killer sees themself. They're the smartest person in the room.

All the creative thought that went into the staging is ruined by the simplicity of the message. That's typical. In movies, detectives drive themselves mad trying to figure out what a killer is trying to say. A single raven feather left by the corpse. What ever can it mean? Surely if we answer that we'll find the killer. In real life, that damned feather is just a feather, either naturally occurring or put there by a killer who presumes detectives will be so engrossed investigating its meaning that they won't pay attention to any actual clues. Yeah, the average detective just pops that feather into an evidence bag and adds it to the list, acknowledging its existence while recognizing that it probably means nothing.

These feathers do mean something, but it's a ham-fisted message, one I hope McCreadie doesn't spend too much time deciphering.

Despite all the staging, the method of murder seems simple enough. There are rope burns around the neck. I pry open an eyelid. Petechial hemorrhaging. Evans was strangled.

Just like me.

Just like Catriona.

My fingers move to the healing bruises around my neck as I look down at the rope. Then I shake my head sharply. There's no connection to either attempted murder. Mine happened a hundred and fifty years from now. Catriona had been manually strangled. The fact that the rope looks similar to the one used on me is pure coincidence, and I need to stop seeing connections where none exist. This—

The front door slaps shut. I spin. I had intended to just take a quick glance in here because Gray seems to have only stepped out, leaving on the lights, as if intending to return.

There's no time to leave. The steps are crossing the room, heading straight for this one. I glance around. One table. One body. Shelves of tools and bottles. No place to hide.

A cloth covers the table, but when I move it aside, it's solid wood beneath, a cabinet with more drawers. I dart to the other side and press myself against the cloth. It's a poor spot, and he'll only need to lean over to see me.

Gray walks in. His shoes squeak as he stops beside Evans's body. A grunt. The clink of forceps. Another grunt.

"You are not interesting," he says. "Bizarre, but otherwise mundane. Death by strangulation. As boring as they come. Not even worth the effort of matching fibers in your flesh to those on the rope, as your killer left it around your neck. Utterly unworthy of my attention."

Another shoe squeak. Another grunt. Another clink. Then a clatter, as if he's tossing down the forceps.

"Completely outside my purview. You would add nothing to my studies. Nothing. Let Dr. Addington deal with you. I have an early start to my day."

With that, he stalks from the room, shutting the door behind him. I wait until he's gone. Then I wait a few more minutes. I'm in the next room when voices sound outside the door. McCreadie and Dr. Addington. I hesitate, feeling the urge to hide again and eavesdrop.

Completely outside my purview.

I give a rueful smile. *You and me both, Dr. Gray. And I have an even earlier morning than you.* Neither of us has time to pursue idle curiosity.

I tiptoe to the back door and creep out just as the front one opens, and McCreadie leads the doctor in.

The first thing I will do when I'm home is run to Nan's bedside. The second? Sleep. So much sleep. As a cop, I've pulled double shifts, and none left me as exhausted as a single day being a housemaid. When Alice wakes me the next morning, I swear I only just drifted off.

Getting out of bed, I also know how Mom and Dad feel. Lately, they've started joking about their age and how it takes a few minutes to get going in the morning, like starting a car with a cold engine. My knees threaten to give way. My shoulders scream. I reach for the bottle of Tylenol I keep in my nightstand drawer. Yep, no nightstand, and no Tylenol.

I stump, stiff-legged, to the washbasin, only to discover it's the dirty water from yesterday. Because I don't have a maid to empty it for me.

I use the water anyway. Sure, since I hope to be gone today, I could say screw it, get clean water, and be late for my shift. Yet I'm well aware of Catriona, the girl who doesn't have an escape hatch to another time. It's like the old concept of a whipping boy. If I do anything wrong, she'll suffer the punishment. Scummy, cold water it is, then.

I dress as quickly as I can, buttoning with numb fingers, shivering the whole time. Then I stagger downstairs, only to still get a lecture on tardiness. It's been ten minutes since Alice came up. How fast am I supposed to dress with five layers of clothing and no zippers?

I suck it up, like I used to when I spent weekends with my paternal grandparents. They lived on a farm and were determined to teach me the value of hard work. What I learned instead was how to push through. Do what I'm told and remind myself that my dad had to do this every day of his life, and at least my term of servitude ended Sunday evening when he came to pick me up.

This term of servitude ends at two. Precisely two, as Mrs. Wallace tells me *twice* that morning.

"Not one minute before. I know your tricks, and I'll be having none of them today."

So Catriona had tricks? Maybe she wasn't quite the meek and guileless creature I imagine. I can't blame her. I consider myself a hard worker, and I'd still be trying to sneak out of this job a few minutes early.

Catriona may leave early herself, but I will not do it on her behalf. Anyone doomed to this wretched life doesn't deserve additional punishment. Yes, yes, I'm well aware that there are people in Victorian-era Scotland who'd have given their eyeteeth for her job, with plentiful food and a private bedroom. But there's always someone worse off, and my very middle-class life back home makes me a grand duchess compared to poor Catriona.

I wait for the clock to strike two before I pack away my broom. By the time I arrive in the kitchen, it's ten past, and when Mrs. Wallace glowers at me, I half expect her to give me crap for leaving *late*.

"Did you scrub Dr. Gray's hearth?" she asks.

I launch into a recital of everything I got done, and with each word, her eyes narrow. There's no sarcasm in my tone, yet she acts as if I'm being a smart-ass.

"I *will* check it, you know," she says.

"Feel free—" I swallow hard. "I mean, I understand, ma'am, and you are more than welcome to do so."

"You're up to something," she says, setting down her wooden spoon. "Don't think I cannot see that. Talking so prettily. Doing all your work." She looks at the clock and sniffs. "I've never known you to linger when it's your half day."

"I know I have not been myself, ma'am," I say. "It is the knock upon my head. I shall be right as rain soon enough."

"You'd better be. I will not stand for these tricks once the mistress returns tomorrow."

"I have no idea what you mean, ma'am." *I really don't.* "But I do hope to be back to myself tomorrow."

She grumbles, turns, and hands me a tray with a pot of tea and a plate of coconut cake. "For the master in the funerary parlor."

I make no move to take it. "My half day started at two."

"Yes, and this was ready before two. The tea will be getting cold now. You'll drop off the tray on your way out. The master had a busy morning—one funeral done and a second to arrange. He barely picked at his lunch. He's overly fond of pastries and this might tempt him. Now off with you."

EIGHT

As I head for the door, I realize I'm wearing indoor boots and no jacket, and a glance out the window shows it's hardly the warm May day I'd expect in Vancouver. I'll stop at the front closet . . . Oh wait, it's the Victorian era, when apparently closets haven't been invented. Where do they keep outerwear? In their bedrooms? Were there warmer clothes in Catriona's trunk?

I glance down at the rapidly cooling tea. I'll take the tray to Gray and then go upstairs and figure out the rest.

The funeral parlor is quiet, the only light coming through open front curtains and precious little of that on this overcast day. I'm about to call for Gray when I realize that's probably not maid-appropriate.

As I walk in, I catch a muffled curse from the laboratory. The door is closed. I rap once and push it open. Gray is standing beside the body of Archie Evans. He seems to be trying to do something with the young man's hand, and rigor hasn't relaxed yet, so the limb is not cooperating.

"Your tea, sir? Mrs. Wallace asked me to deliver it before I left."

He stares at me. Looks at the body, and then back at me.

I just walked in on him wrestling with an autopsied corpse, the poor guy's chest cracked open and roughly sewn. I should have dropped the tray and run screaming.

Little late for that.

"Is that the poor bloke they brought in yesterday?"

His brow furrows at the word "bloke." That's English, isn't it? I am not getting any better at this.

"I shall leave your tea on the table over here. Unless you would prefer it at your desk."

"I think my desk might be cleaner."

"Right." I turn to leave.

"Catriona?" he says. "If you have a moment, there is something I'd like far more than tea."

I bite my lips against a snort, thinking again of my friend's historical-romance novels. I've gotten none of those vibes from Gray, thankfully, and so I just say, "I do need to be off, sir. It is my half day. But I can spare a moment. You seem to be having trouble with that poor chap, er, lad's arm. Shall I hold it for you?"

He looks at the corpse's hand and back at me with a blink of surprise.

"I spent time on a farm," I say, which is true enough. "I'm not squeamish."

"I appreciate that. I *could* use your assistance. I lost my apprentice last month. He decided undertaking was not the profession for him. I have no idea why."

Gray doesn't smile, but his eyes do sparkle with enough self-awareness to tell me this is a joke.

Huh, didn't think you had it in you, Gray.

That's not entirely fair. Duncan Gray doesn't match the stereotype of the dour, washed-out undertaker, a ghoul haunting his own funeral parlor and preying on the grieving. I have yet to meet a funeral director who *does* match the stereotype. But while I wouldn't call Gray dour, he's certainly not trying out for stand-up comedy any time soon. If I had to cast him in a period drama, it'd be somewhere between "mad scientist" and "brooding lord with his wife locked in the attic."

"Not everyone is cut out for such a job, sir."

"I cannot imagine anyone *is*," he murmurs.

He speaks low enough that I'm not supposed to hear, but I can't let that door shut without trying to pry it open. Curiosity is an occupational hazard.

"You inherited the business, yes?" I say. "I presume it was not your dream job either?"

"Dream job." He mulls the words over, and I know I've been too modern again, but he nods, as if presuming this is only a unique phrasing.

In answer to the question, he shrugs. "Fate deals unexpected hands, and we learn to play the cards we are given."

"I know a little of that," I murmur. "Was your family always in the business then? Of undertaking?"

"No, but it is how we made our fortune, and so it behooves me to continue the tradition."

"Was it cabinetmaking?" I say. "I know that is how many undertakers begin."

The faintest hint of a smile. "It is, but no. I cannot imagine my father as a cabinetmaker. He invested in private cemeteries and friendly societies, and he proved a successful speculator, and so he decided to commit himself more thoroughly to the business of the dead." He looks down at Evans. "As you are not squeamish, perhaps you could help me for an hour or so?"

I make a show of biting my lip, and then meekly murmur, "It's my half day off, sir."

"Yes, yes, I know. I promise I shan't take up more than an hour of your time, and I'll send you along with two shillings for your troubles."

His tone somehow manages to be both imperious and considerate. He's dismissive of Catriona's day off—she is a servant, after all. Yet he understands he's asking for extra work and offers compensation. Does that make him a good employer for his time? I could better answer that if I had any idea how much a shilling was worth.

I suppose I should be grateful he doesn't order me to stay all afternoon for no extra compensation. I suspect the Scottish equivalent of Work-SafeBC is still a hundred years from being available to hear employment-standards complaints.

When I don't jump at the offer, he sighs. "It truly will only be an hour, Catriona. I have someplace to be after that. Detective McCreadie wants me . . ." He waves off the rest of the explanation. Being a mere maid, I don't need it. "One hour. Two shillings."

"I'd rather take the time in lieu."

"In lieu?"

"Instead of. It's a local phrase. From where I was born."

His brow furrows. "My sister said you are from Edinburgh."

"May I bank the extra hour, sir?"

"Bank . . ." he murmurs. "That is a clever use of the word, Catriona. To put the extra hour into the bank of your time off, yes? You appear to have picked up many odd phrasings and pronunciations." He's barely paying attention now, having walked across the room to fetch a notebook. "It must be the injury to your head. I've heard of such a thing. A form of aphasia."

"Mmm, yes, that's it. Aphasia. Whatever that means."

Is that another ghost of a smile? "I will not bore you with the explanation, but combined with personality shifts, it is very intriguing. I might ask you to speak to a fellow of mine from the Royal College. He studies the brain. Not really my thing. It is intriguing, though."

He's still only half paying attention. Lucky for Catriona, her boss isn't all that interested in her "personality shifts" and "odd phrasings and pronunciations." He's dismissed them as a sign of mental trauma and moved on to things that do interest him. Including, apparently, this corpse.

"All right," he says as he opens the notebook. "You may bank two hours for giving me one. Now, this will be tricky, but I'm going to ask you to move the cadaver and assist me in observations while I write them down. Begin by holding out the hand with the fingers splayed."

I do as he says, which isn't right, and then I try again, and it's still not right. After the third round of vague instructions and random gestures followed by a snap of frustration, I say, "Fine, here. You do this, and I'll take notes."

He stops. Looks at me. Then he turns his notebook around. "Read the top line."

"The deceased displays pete—pete—I don't know what the rest of that says," I lie. "But if you spell the words I don't know, I can write them."

He's staring at me as if I'm the one lying on the examination table. "My sister told me you were illiterate."

I mentally smack my forehead. Gray wasn't suggesting I lacked the education to spell "petechial." He was questioning my ability to read and write. I am a nineteenth-century housemaid, after all.

I send up a silent apology to Catriona and straighten. "I may have misrepresented my abilities to obtain the position, sir. I didn't want Mrs.

Wallace thinking I was putting on airs. I had some lessons in my youth, and I can read and write adequately."

Of all the excuses I've made, this one seems one of the most reasonable, yet this is the one that has him scrutinizing me as if I'm a five-year-old who has told the most outrageous fib.

"It was my sister who hired you."

Really? That's where he's drawing the line? Forget the fact that his nineteen-year-old housemaid didn't blink at a grotesquely staged corpse or at handling said corpse, he's suspicious because she misremembered who hired her?

"Yes," I say. "All the more reason for me not to want to look as if I'm getting above my station. The lady of the house might not wish to hire an educated girl."

Now he's truly staring at me, as if I've sprouted a second head. Then he thrusts out the pen.

"Take notes, then. I will spell what I need."

I hold the pen over the page . . . and a blob of ink falls onto it.

"I believe your pen is broken, sir."

He sees the blob and sighs. "Have you not used a fountain pen, Catriona?"

Er, right. No ballpoints in the nineteenth century.

He continues, "There is a dip pen at my desk if you prefer, but fountain pens are the writing instrument of the future, and it would be wise to learn how to use one."

Dip pen? I'm guessing that would be a pen you dip into the ink each time, unlike a fountain pen, which has a capsule of ink. I take a closer look at this one. Instead of the cartridge I'd see in a modern fountain pen, it has a small reservoir that I'm presuming needs to be filled.

I test the nib on a corner of the page and nod. I'll need to be careful, but I think I can manage it.

Gray holds Evans's hand in the way he wanted and makes observations, which I jot down. He moves to the victim's head and lifts the rope coiled beside it.

"This was used to strangle him and was also left in situ." He pauses and spells "in situ" and explains it's Latin for "on site" or "in position." Then he continues, "Because we know this rope was used, I can examine the marks it left and the fibers that remained and those observations can be of use in crimes where the rope was removed."

"To find the murder weapon."

"Murder weapon." He samples the phrase. "Yes, that is it precisely. Make a note of that terminology, please."

He returns to his observations, and I look from him to the body. As he talks, there's a note in his voice I haven't heard before. Passion. The passion of an enthusiastic teacher expounding on his favorite subject.

I'd been confused yesterday by Gray, an undertaker, examining a murder victim. Now I remind myself he isn't just an undertaker. He's also a doctor. And he's using that professional combination to study forensics.

To modern police, matching weapons to wounds is as obvious as dusting for fingerprints or gathering DNA. None of that exists in the Victorian world. Oh, I'm sure police have started matching weapons and wounds, but still, it is the early days of it, which makes Gray a pioneer in my favorite science.

This is why McCreadie snuck Evans's body in. So Gray could get a look before the coroner started carving it up, and presumably so Gray could give his friend insights that McCreadie might use in his investigation.

With that, Duncan Gray becomes a thousand times more interesting.

"What do they call what you're doing?" I ask. "Criminal science?"

"There's a word used in medicine," he says. "Forensics. It is used for scientific studies that play a role in the judicial system." He pauses. "The judicial system meaning court, such as in a criminal trial."

"This is forensic science, then?"

"You could call it that, though it's hardly a recognized discipline."

"It's new then? The idea of what you're doing? Matching weapons to wounds and such."

He laughs, and the sound startles me. When I glance over, he looks very different from the man I've been serving for the last two days. He's relaxed and comfortable, absorbed by his work and forgetting that his student is a mere servant. A female servant, no less. Or maybe that's unfair, and it's not so much forgetting as not caring. I'm interested, and that is all that seems to matter.

"No," he says. "It isn't new at all. I have a book on such scientific inquiry from thirteenth-century China, and it's not even the first of its kind—only the first that survives."

"Seriously?"

That very modern exclamation has him looking up in surprise, but his eyes only twinkle with amusement. "What shocks you more, Catriona? That the science is so old? Or that it is not the invention of the grand British Empire?"

"That it's so old," I say, honestly.

When I say that, his nod grants me a point for not falling into the trap of colonialist thinking. That's when I notice his skin tone. Oh, I'd noticed obviously. When we first met, I'd noted it was brown, which had been no different from observing his height or eye color. Yet I hadn't paused to realize that people of color might be less common here. I'm sure they're not nearly as *uncommon* as Hollywood historical dramas would suggest, but we aren't yet in the age of easy travel and immigration.

What would it be like to be a person of color in Victorian Scotland? Worse than being one in modern Vancouver, I presume, and even that's not always easy, as I know from friends. How does the outside world treat him? How did Catriona treat him? I need to bear that in mind. If he seems cool or distant, there may be a reason. Right now, though, he's relaxed, drawn into a topic that clearly interests him.

I continue, "If the science is that old, why don't we already know all this? We've had five hundred years to figure it out."

That smile quirks again. "Perhaps we do know it, just not in this corner of the globe. Or perhaps the need for it in this corner is relatively recent, as our judicial—court—system develops."

"Or as the lawyers get better at their jobs, and police need to work harder to make their case."

His laugh is sudden and sharp. "True enough."

I flip through the notebook. "So this is for police work. Observations on weapon marks."

"Among other things. Now, if you could please make note of the damage under his fingernails."

I lean forward to peer at dark bruises where the nails have separated from the beds. I wince. "He was tortured."

"Tortured?"

At his tone, I pull back. "I mean, it is possible someone did that to him, perhaps as a method of extracting information, by putting something under his nails. It would be very painful. I believe I have heard something like that. Somewhere."

"I am aware of your background, Catriona. My sister told me the full story. I understand that you may, in your felonious circles, have encountered such a thing, so there is no need to dissemble."

Felonious circles? Well, well, you do have an interesting past, Catriona.

I nod, gaze lowered. "Yes, sir. Well, then, may I speculate that this poor lad was tortured?"

"You may, particularly as that would explain this." He pries open the victim's mouth to show a missing tooth, the gum still raw. "The doctor performing the autopsy speculated that it had been knocked out in a blow, but I see no evidence of a head injury. Extraction seems most likely. I have heard of that being used in torture, during times of war, but did not make the connection. Thank you, Catriona. Now if the tooth was extracted, some tool must have been used. Let us take a closer look at the gums for signs of that."

And so he continues, quite merrily examining the victim and theorizing on how the tooth may have been removed. I take notes, make appropriate noises, and send up yet more apologies to poor Catriona, who is about to return and discover that not only is she expected to be able to read and write, but to listen to her employer speculate on methods of torture without batting an eye.

"You shall need to convey all this to Detective McCreadie," I say when he finishes examining the mouth and hands. "It is vital information in solving the crime."

"Is it? I'm not certain about that, Catriona. We do not know what was used to torture the poor lad, and so this cannot help Detective McCreadie."

"It helps because it proves this isn't a random victim," I say. "His killer wanted information from him."

Gray frowns at me. "What's that?"

I hesitate. Then I plow forward. In for a penny, in for a pound. "There are two reasons to torture a person. One is sadism—the torturer enjoys inflicting pain. Two is the, well, practical purpose. Extracting information. This particular type of torture suggests the latter. The killer only damaged three fingernails and took one tooth. I probably shouldn't say 'only'—they are still terrible things to do—but the point is that he did not do more, which would argue against sadism as the motive."

And now Gray is openly gaping at me.

"It makes sense, doesn't it?"

"It . . . does. What was that term you used? Sad . . . ism? Related to the Marquis de Sade, I presume?"

I shrug. "Never heard of him. The point is simply that this is torture for the purpose of extracting information rather than extracting pleasure, either for the torturer or—" I cough. "The point is that this is not a random murder."

"In which case, the staging could be more significant than I presumed. I thought it was simply for shock. To garner attention."

"Could be," I say. "Probably is. What Detective McCreadie needs to know is that the victim had something his killer wanted. That's significant."

"It is. Excellent work, Catriona. Now—" A clock rings the hour, and he curses under his breath.

"If you need a little more of my time, sir, I can spare it."

"Unfortunately, no. There is someplace I need to be. The police are addressing the media regarding this."

"A press conference?"

He doesn't miss a beat at the modern phrase, just waves his hand dismissively. "Some newfangled idea from the commissioner. Personally, I fear it does more harm than good, but sadly, the police are not subject to the Hippocratic oath."

I snort a laugh at that, which has him turning, brows knitting, only for him to remember what he's doing, putting away his tools.

"On second thought," he says, "you should come along, Catriona, if you are heading that way. Tell Detective McCreadie your theory."

"I think it'll hold more weight coming from you."

He frowns at me. "But it is *your* theory."

Having worked in several environments where men were quick to take credit for my theories—or restate them right after I did and win the credit—I find Gray's genuine confusion refreshing, especially given the time period.

If he doesn't understand why a doctor's words would carry more weight than a housemaid's, I won't tell him. While I suspect it's less a sign of enlightened thought than the obliviousness of privilege, I still grant him a point for it. And, as eager as I am to get back to my world, I am curious about a Victorian-crime press conference.

"I shall join you, sir, if that is all right, but I believe the theory should come from you. You are the professional."

"I suppose. I will tell him without taking credit. If the lead helps his investigation, then I will let him know that it was your idea."

NINE

Once Gray is finished putting away his tools, he grabs his jacket—a double-breasted frock coat that falls just past his hips. When he dons a hat, it's an honest-to-goodness silk top hat. It looks remarkably good on him, and not at all as if he's going to whip it off and pull out a rabbit.

As he strides toward the door, I say, "Are we not going to wash our hands, sir?"

He looks at me and then examines his hands. "They seem clean enough."

"You were just handling a decomposing corpse." I peer at him with a dawning suspicion. "If I say 'germ theory,' what do you hear?"

He frowns. "A new theory from Germany?"

At my expression, his eyes glitter. "I am teasing, Catriona. I am well versed in contagion theory as well as the arguments of those who prefer miasmic theory. I lean heavily toward the former. I am quite fascinated by the work of Dr. Pasteur. There is also a new theory from Dr. Lister in Glasgow regarding the use of carbolic acid. I have even read older theories on the possibility of contracting illness through touch, particularly a fascinating account from a doctor in sixth-century India. I tried bringing it to the attention of my medical colleagues, but they called it foreign nonsense."

He strides to the small water closet, which contains a washbasin. "We probably ought to scrub up. The smell can be repellent, and I do try to remember to wash my hands after handling bodies, in case there *is* any possibility of contamination."

He motions for me to go first. As I scrub, he says, "When I was a medical student, my classmates would fairly clamor for the privilege of wearing the apron of a retired surgeon. It had never been washed and was quite stiff with blood and other bodily fluids. They thought that proof of his long and storied career, but I always found it . . ."

"Horrific, repulsive, and utterly terrifying?"

"I was going to say 'somewhat unwholesome.'"

My kingdom for a bottle of hand sanitizer.

I dry my hands and turn to him. "While you wash, I shall need to fetch my boots."

He frowns at the ones on my feet. "Are you not wearing them?"

"These are my indoor boots."

When his frown only deepens, I stifle a sigh. "I suppose they will do. However, I do require a coat."

"Ah." He lifts a hand. "That I can remedy."

He finishes scrubbing and drying his hands, strides into a side room, rummages in a wardrobe, and pulls out . . .

Oh my God, it's a Sherlock Holmes coat. Lightweight tweed with a cape around the shoulders and upper arms. It's gorgeously tailored, which I'm beginning to realize just means a normal piece of middle-class clothing in a world where most is still handmade. I'm reaching for it when I pause.

"That didn't come from a client, did it?" I ask.

"Client?"

"Of the nonliving variety?"

A moment's pause. Then a half-snorted laugh. "No, it did not. This belonged to my apprentice, the one who left."

"Will he mind me borrowing it?"

"Oh, I'm quite certain he has no intention of returning. It was rather an abrupt leave-taking."

"May I ask what happened?" I ask as I pull on the coat.

"A most puzzling thing, really. I'd obtained a cadaver from the Royal College. Perfectly legal. All the appropriate paperwork and such. I wanted to test the marks made by various weapons."

"Weapons?"

"Axes in particular."

"I see."

Gray opens the front door for me and ushers me out. "Scotland had two ax murders within a month, which got me thinking it would be advantageous to be able to compare wound patterns. There are many sorts of axes, particularly in the countryside."

"Uh-huh."

"I asked James to hold the body down while I wielded the ax. The first blow was rather messy. It had to be a fresh cadaver, you see. Decomposing tissues would have reacted in an entirely different way. Also, in my zeal, I may have severed the cadaver's arm, which may have shot up and struck James."

"Uh-huh." We've moved onto the street, and Gray continues talking in a conversational tone, causing two well-dressed ladies to quickly gather their skirts and cross the road.

"I'm guessing that's when he quit?" I say.

"Quite abruptly."

"Probably for the best. It seems he lacked a proper appreciation of science."

Gray nods mournfully. "I fear so. It will be devilishly hard to replace him."

"I am certain you'll manage, sir. Though, if I might offer some advice, perhaps the first step in your hiring process should be to hold the interview *while* you are examining a body. Ask for their help. If they flee, you have your answer."

"That is a fine idea, Catriona."

"You're most welcome, sir."

Nan lives outside Edinburgh, which means that while I've spent time in the city, I don't know it as well as I might if she'd actually lived *here*. It's like when I grew up in a suburb of Vancouver. I knew the city well enough, but my experience was limited to the areas we visited regularly. Here, I know that the spot where I came through is in the Grassmarket, which is in the Old Town, and I know that Gray's town house is in the

New Town, but I have no clue how to find my way from one point to the other.

My main point of reference in Edinburgh has always been the castle. Yep, kind of hard to miss a big castle on a hill. It's like the CN Tower in Toronto. No matter where I am, I can orient myself according to that. As we walk, I spot the top of another landmark—the monument to Sir Walter Scott. I've climbed the two-hundred-odd steps inside, and while it's not quite the CN Tower, I should be able to see it from many parts of the city.

Gray lives in the New Town. That's the new part of Edinburgh . . . or it's new in this time period. Edinburgh, being a royal city, was also a walled city, and while that's great for protection, it's horrible for expansion. Behind its walls, the city grew crowded and it grew upward. Sometime in the Victorian period—before now obviously—those with money abandoned the Old Town and built the New Town across the mound. As we walk, I can see the Old Town rising on a slope, blanketed by the smog of coal smoke that earned Edinburgh the nickname of Auld Reekie.

As we round the corner I make note of the street name. When I'm back in my time, I want to see whether Gray's house still exists. Robert Street. It's a short road, with only maybe a dozen or so town houses. There's a park to our right. Queen Street Gardens?

After a quick walk, we reach a road I definitely recognize. Princes Street. In the modern world, it's a massive thoroughfare. It's the same here, wide enough for five coaches to pass. Busy, too, and lined with shops and hotels.

I try not to gape as I look around, taking it all in. I also need to watch where I'm walking, preferably at the side of the road, away from the mud that I'm sure is fifty percent horse dung. I do look as much as I can, though, taking brief note of the fashions. There are other men in top hats and frock coats, like Gray. The genteel women wear skirts more bell-shaped than my own and . . . is that a bustle? Are they coming into fashion or leaving it? Leaving it, I hope, with a shudder.

We make our way to Princes Street Gardens and cross to the Old Town. It is only as we walk that I realize another advantage to going with Gray. It's my first look at the city in this time period, and it gives me time to orient myself, not just to the landscape but to the customs of the time. I can't afford to call attention to myself before I escape back to my own world.

It's a brisk and overcast day, yet still a fine walk, one I will commit to memory for the sheer novelty of it. Like strolling through the most elaborate period theme park ever.

We've left the town houses and wide streets of the New Town and entered the densely packed tenements and narrow cobbled roads of the Old Town. Now walking gets tougher, as we head uphill. At one point, when I stop to adjust my boot, Gray asks whether I'm all right with the walk. I say I am. He has a groom and presumably horses and a carriage, but he seems to prefer walking. Normally, I would appreciate that, but . . .

Oh, let's not mince words. I don't mind the uphill walk, but streets are filthy. At least in the New Town, the mud and the animal by-products had been in the wide streets. Here, the narrow roads mean I'm walking in it, and I'm pretty sure not all those by-products are animal. While the cobblestones help, there are still unavoidable patches of muck and some very questionable puddles.

I stare down at my shit-spattered boots and try not to whimper. My indoor boots. My lovely, formerly clean indoor boots.

I glance down at Gray's, which might be even dirtier, as he isn't darting about to avoid the worst of the muck. Of course not. He has a maid to *clean* his boots.

As we walk, I'm aware that I seem to be drawing some attention. Or, I should say, Catriona is. Understandably. She's young and fair-haired and "winsome," as they might say in this time. Yet I realize those looks linger less on her pretty face than her stylish jacket. Stylish *men's* jacket. I pull it tighter. It is a lovely coat. I find myself wishing I could sneak it back to the twenty-first century.

I'm not the only one attracting attention. Gray gets his share, complete with uneasy glances and careful sidesteps. He is a forbidding figure, taller than most, his workman's build not quite disguised by his gentleman's clothing. Yet again, I think it's more than that, as I take a closer look at him and suppress a chuckle.

"Sir?" I whisper.

He glances over and I motion to his collar, which is half tucked in. He fixes that with a grunt of annoyance. Next I gesture to his misbuttoned coat. As he does it up, I whisper, "Might want to go one higher," and point at the blood speckling his shirtfront. A put-upon sigh, as if I'm unreasonably insisting he use the right fork at a picnic.

Even after he looks more presentable, he continues drawing those uneasy glances and careful sidesteps, and I remember my earlier thoughts, about how his experiences here might differ, as a person of color. When I look around, I see an Asian couple selling from a battered street cart. Otherwise, the only people of color I recall were back in the New Town, and not residents but staff—a Black coach driver and an East Asian butler opening a door for a matron. That is the true difference then. There are people of color, but I'd guess most are in service or working menial jobs. They are not doctors or undertakers, and not imposing and confident men wearing a gentleman's attire. *That* is what makes people uneasy. Gray has stepped out from the box in which they'd like to keep him. Not that different from home, really.

We find McCreadie's police station. I presume the city has a main station, and that this is not it. I had the impression that Old Town in this period was tenements and slums. My impression was wrong. The station is in a working-class neighborhood, surrounded by shops and services. I don't recognize it, but without specific landmarks, there's not much of Edinburgh I will recognize here.

Gray escorts me through a side door of the police station, bypassing the front desk. We go up a flight of stairs to what looks like courtroom space. Huh, that's interesting.

Before I can look around, Gray steers me into the first room. I glance at the sparse gathering and whisper, "Are we early?"

He checks his pocket watch and shakes his head. "Scarcely on time. It will begin any moment."

I frown at the half-dozen reporters surrounding us. Only three even have notepads at the ready. Wouldn't a case like this garner more attention? Maybe people in Victorian Scotland weren't all that interested in murder.

As I look around, I get looks back. Looks of confusion, paired with frowns. I realize I'm the only woman there and edge closer to Gray, in explanation.

Why, yes, I am here with this distinguished gentleman. A pretty bauble for his arm. Pay me no heed, good sir.

When Gray murmurs something to me, I glance to see a gray-haired man stride through the door. He's joined by a florid-faced man of perhaps forty, who lifts his chin with a pompous semi-smirk. Both ascend the rough platform.

"Where is Detective McCreadie?" I ask, rising on my toes to scan the front of the crowd.

Gray only makes a noise deep in his throat. A near growl of discontent. Before I can ask what's wrong, the older man begins. He's a lousy public speaker—a senior officer who's been handed this position for his seniority rather than his leadership skill. He stumbles through opening remarks and then introduces the criminal officer in charge of the case— the guy standing beside him.

I rise on my toes, and Gray bends to let me whisper in his ear.

"Has Detective McCreadie been removed from the investigation?"

"No," he murmurs in my ear. "He is only being deprived of the recognition for it."

When I frown, he says, "They have put a more senior officer in charge. Detective McCreadie will answer to him. But Detective McCreadie will do the work."

Huh. Some things don't change, apparently.

The two men on the podium do a bang-up job of making a fascinating case seem dull as dishwater, so I focus my attention on someone a little more interesting: Gray. I watch his reactions as the men speak. His tight face as he listens. His cheek tic of annoyance when the other criminal officer boasts that he'll find the killer. His full-body stiffening when that officer brags about all the information he personally gleaned from the body—all the information Gray and McCreadie provided.

Otherwise, it's a routine press conference. The criminal officer and his superior talk about the case. The reporters ask questions.

We're walking out when someone taps Gray's shoulder, and we both turn to see McCreadie, as nattily dressed as he'd been last night, smiling with an ease only barely betrayed by a tension in his eyes.

"I had hoped to see you up there," Gray says.

McCreadie shrugs. "Someday."

"That man is an incompetent boor. He solved one case twenty years ago, and he's skated on his reputation ever since."

"It wasn't *one* case, Duncan," McCreadie says as he steers his friend to the side.

"Yes, it was. Three consecutive murders but only a single investigation. That makes it one case."

"A serial killing?" I say.

Gray frowns at me. "Serial . . . Yes, I suppose that's what one would call it."

"Catriona?" McCreadie says as if just seeing me there. "What ever are you doing here? And what are you wearing?"

"A fine gentleman's jacket," I say. "Is it not stylish?"

I twirl, and one corner of his mouth rises. "It was . . . about five years ago. But I daresay it looks better on you than it did on young James. It's a bold fashion statement. I approve."

I half curtsy. "Thank you, kind sir."

His look is half amused, half bewildered. Apparently, I'm not acting like the Catriona he knows.

He gives his head a shake and says, "As for the original question, what are you doing here with Duncan?"

"She was helping with my laboratory observations," Gray says. "I daresay she did a sight better than James. Perhaps it's not only his coat she shall take over."

I expect McCreadie to laugh, but something in his face tightens.

Gray continues, "Catriona made a few astute observations of her own."

"Did she? And our young Catriona evidenced a never-before-seen interest in your work, I presume?"

"It *is* very interesting," I say. "I did not realize so until now."

McCreadie's tone chills. "I see."

We head outside. The two men talk for a few minutes, and I'm looking around, ready to take my leave, when McCreadie says, "Catriona?"

I glance up to see it's just the two of us. I peer around for Gray.

"I sent Duncan to fetch us pies from the seller," he says. "I wanted a word with you."

He motions me around a corner, and I'm about to say we should tell Gray where we've gone when I realize that's the point.

"Yes, sir?" I say after I've followed him.

"So you've discovered a sudden interest in Duncan's scientific inquiries?"

"As I said, they *are* interesting."

His face hardens. "Do not take me for a fool, Catriona, and do not forget who took you to Isla. I believed you could be redeemed, and you have done nothing but prove I am a very poor judge of character."

Isla? Is that Mrs. Wallace's first name? No, Gray said his sister hired me. That must be Isla.

Wait, *redeemed*?

Right. Gray did say something about Catriona's felonious past.

McCreadie continues, "I cannot count how many times I have bit my tongue against telling Isla the rest of your story. The parts I misguidedly decided were not your fault. I know better now. There was no Fagin in your life, Catriona. It is all you. The only reason you are still employed is because Isla is too good-hearted—nay, too *stubborn*—to accept defeat. And Duncan is too caught up in his work to see you for what you are. But I see you, and I will not allow this."

"Allow what?"

His eyes narrow. "I warned you not to play me for a fool, Catriona. You owe me the respect of honesty. You did not take a sudden interest in science. You took a sudden interest in the man behind the science."

I stare up at him. Then it hits. "You think I'm trying to seduce Dr. Gray?"

"I think you liked your stay in their guest room. I think it made that scheming mind of yours do what it does best."

"Scheme?"

"Do not mock me, Catriona. You tread on very dangerous ground here. If I told Isla the rest of your story—and if Mrs. Wallace stopped shielding her from the worst of your misdeeds—you would be out on your arse. You have set your cap on Duncan. You are a pretty girl from a decent family, and Duncan is a very busy man with no time to look for a wife. You see an opening."

A doctor marrying his housemaid? I want to say someone else has been reading romance novels, but then I realize it might not be so implausible. Gray isn't a lord or an earl and, from what McCreadie is implying, Catriona didn't grow up in tenement housing. She's a girl from a good family who made poor choices, one who might be looking to climb back up to her old status.

"It will do you no good," McCreadie continues. "That's what I pulled you aside to say. I could warn that I am watching you and you'd best not try anything, but I needn't bother. We both know how he is."

"How he *is*?"

McCreadie eases back, a little of his anger dissipating. "An illustrative example, Catriona, in case you have failed to notice these things on your own. Last month, we were in a public house, and Duncan got into a brawl."

"Dr. Gray?" There's honest incredulity in my voice.

"He did not start it, which I should say makes the man happier than is decent. He does love the excuse for a good bout of fisticuffs. In this case, he had it, having been struck with a knife."

"*What?*"

McCreadie waves off my concern. "He stitched himself up later. Again, not the point, which is that his blood cast a pattern on the wall. He began sketching it and comparing it with the wound and the angle of the blow. When a young lady evidenced great interest in what he was doing, he quite happily explained it to her, never once realizing that she was not interested at all in the blood pattern and was rather more interested in his—" He coughs. "In his ability to pay for her services."

"Ah, she was a sex worker."

"A *what?*"

"Lady of negotiable affections?"

He gives a short laugh. "I suppose so. Though I have the feeling she would have negotiated a very low price for those affections. They always do for Duncan. Yet the point is that he was oblivious. He is always oblivious to attention from the fair sex."

"Because he prefers men?"

McCreadie's eyes round, and he sputters incomprehensibly before saying, "No, he likes women. But the women he likes are not pretty shopgirls or fetching pie sellers or winsome housemaids, and they are certainly not 'ladies of negotiable affections,' as you put it. He will never notice your interest because he will not share it, and if you force him to notice it, he will find you alternate employment within the week. You have chosen your target poorly, Catriona."

"Perhaps you mistake my interest, sir."

He snorts. "So you're actually interested in the science of dead bodies?"

"As you say, I come from a good family. While I have thus far concealed it, I do possess an education. And a brain, though you obviously do not think it."

"Oh, I never doubted that, Catriona."

"Yes, I see an opening here. An *employment* opening. Dr. Gray is in need of an assistant, and as I am not squeamish, I see no reason why I should not angle for the position. Yes, that might require exaggerating my interest in the subject. It *is*, however, vastly more interesting than scrubbing water closet pots."

He eyes me, and I can tell I have made a valid argument. I only hope Catriona thinks so when she returns.

"All right," McCreadie says slowly. "I will not interfere with your pursuit of the position. If your pursuit turns *elsewhere*, though . . ."

"It will not," I say with a conviction that seems to settle his mind.

He leads me back around the corner to where Gray is scouring the area. Spotting us, Gray strides over, pies in hand.

"What the devil were you doing back there?" he asks.

He seems genuinely perplexed, failing to presume the natural reason a man might take a pretty maid around a shadowy corner. McCreadie is right, then. Gray does not see Catriona in that light. Which is a relief.

Gray hands me a pie and then explains my torture theory about the fingernails and the missing tooth. As promised, he doesn't credit me, but neither does he take credit himself, crafting his words in a way that allows McCreadie to presume it was Gray's idea but with an opening to correct that later. I can't imagine Catriona will care who takes credit, but Gray is going out of his way to be fair-minded, and I appreciate that.

When McCreadie is called back into the station, Gray turns to me. "Now you may begin your truncated half day off, Catriona, which I will repay doubly."

"Thank you, sir. Before I go, might I ask you an odd question?"

One brow rises with interest. "Of course."

"Where was I found after my attack?"

"Where were you found . . . ?"

"I wish to go there and see whether it jostles my memory. I have no recollection of the evening, and I would like to know what happened to me." I glance toward the police precinct. "I presume there is an active investigation?"

He hesitates, and as he does, dark color creeps into his cheeks. He glances toward the station and then plucks at his necktie, as if it's suddenly too tight. "Er, yes. I mean, no, there is not an investigation. Had you perished in the attack, there certainly would have been, but you did not and . . ."

"I am only a housemaid."

I expect him to deny it, but he says, "Partly that and partly because, in the area of town where you were found, such attacks happen thrice a night. Perhaps not as serious as yours, but assaults are common enough that the police do not involve themselves unless it results in murder."

"Which I'm sure is a great deterrent to the area's thieves, ruffians, and rapists."

He colors more. "Er, yes, as to that, you were not . . ." Another tug at his collar. "As the attending physician, I felt obligated to check for signs of tampering with . . ."

"My virtue?"

"Yes. Had that occurred, I would have insisted on an investigation, but that did not seem to be your assailant's goal. Also, I assure you that I did only the most circumspect of inspections."

"It was a medical exam," I say. "It's fine. Now, regardless of whether there's an investigation, I would like to jar my memory if possible. I fear I was assaulted by someone familiar to me, someone I might trust."

He frowns. "There was no evidence it was anything but a random assault."

Was it? The detective in me can't help analyzing what I heard that night. The first cry had sounded like a playful squeal, as if Catriona had been surprised by someone she knew. Someone she knew well? Or a mere acquaintance?

Again, not my monkey. Not my circus. With any luck, Catriona will return today and be able to name the attacker herself.

"Will you tell me where it happened?" I ask.

"I will take you there."

I shake my head. "You have better things to do, sir."

"I do not at the moment. Also, as I said, it is not the neighborhood for a young woman. I insist on escorting you."

TEN

Gray was not exaggerating. When he shows me where Catriona was assaulted, I can only gape and wonder what the hell a nineteen-year-old housemaid was doing here. As I theorized, it's the same spot where I was attacked in the modern day. Ironically, in that period, this is a picture-perfect tourist street designed to make you feel as if you've stepped into lovely Victorian Edinburgh, when the reality is that it'd been a street no Victorian tourist would set foot on. The narrow, cobbled road—quaint and cozy in the twenty-first century—is so dark and shadowed that it might as well be labeled Battery Boulevard.

As we walk through the neighborhood, I resist the urge to pull in my skirts like a proper little miss, my pretty nose upturned, curls flouncing. While I'd patrolled in modern tenement neighborhoods, this is worse than anything I'd seen in Vancouver. This is true squalor, with the stench to match, the kind of place that reminds me how, only hours ago, I'd acknowledged that some people would happily take Catriona's job. Now I *see* those people, for whom a daughter in service would be "the one who got out"— the pride of the family, sending home whatever shillings she could spare.

Catriona wasn't from this neighborhood. So what was she doing here? The answer, apparently, can be found just a few steps from where her body was discovered.

As we stand in that alley, Gray points to a hand-lettered sign in a nearby grimy window. "You were in there, having a drink."

"It's a pub?"

He clears his throat. "It passes for such, but Hugh—Detective McCreadie—says it is a known den of . . ."

"Iniquity?"

He looks startled. "No, not at all. There's nothing of a salacious nature about it. I was going to say den of thieves, and then realized my phrasing might be offensive."

"Not if I used to be a thief."

"Yes, but you are no longer one. So I presume you were meeting a former compatriot for a drink. A social engagement."

I look at that grimy window and try not to shudder. You'd need to *pay* me to drink anything served in there.

"All right, so I was spotted in that . . . establishment," I say.

"Spotted *leaving* it," he corrects. "The proprietor would not confirm you had been a patron."

"But I presumably was. Then I came out and was pushed into this alley here, where I was hit on the head and strangled. Or I was strangled and struck my head in falling."

I drift into memories again, trying to remember exactly what I'd heard and seen. A shadowed figure throttling Catriona. She'd been conscious, so she must have hit her head when she fell.

Stop that. Solving the attack on her isn't my business. Getting home is my business. My only purpose in being at this spot.

I start to walk down the alley and halt. I don't want to cross through time with Gray standing right there. I owe him better than that. I stop short and wave my hand. "Do you know precisely where I fell?"

He shakes his head. "You were not discovered for several hours. When you were, it was by a passing constable. He recognized you—having seen you once before with young Findlay."

Constable Findlay? Detective McCreadie's assistant?

I open my mouth to ask why I'd been with Findlay, but then I remember yesterday, when McCreadie had seemed to expect that Findlay might wish to speak to me. I'd thought it might be a romantic entanglement. They were of an age, and Findlay would be a good social match for Catriona.

Gray continues. "Recognizing you, this constable sent for me, and I attended you here before bringing you home."

"No one had noticed me missing?"

"It was one of your half days off."

So Catriona had a half day off, and that night, instead of being home in bed, she was here, in this pub, possibly meeting an old colleague, possibly continuing her "felonious" ways.

As a detective, I'd start there. Former—or not-so-former—thief gets attacked leaving a black-market dive bar. While it's possible it was a random attack, it's more likely connected to her criminal endeavors. She pissed someone off. Double-crossed someone. Or even just refused a gig, that classic "one more job."

Of course, none of this matters to me. I'd love to solve the attack on Catriona, as an apology for borrowing her body. But even if the answer miraculously fell from the sky, I doubt her attacker would ever see justice. She's only a maid, and this was only a physical assault in a neighborhood where it might happen to anyone alone at night.

I suppose Catriona figured she could take care of herself. Just like the detective who ran into this alley a hundred and fifty years from now, alone at night, following the cries of a woman in distress.

Seems we both aren't as street-savvy as we thought.

I turn to Gray. "Thank you, sir, for bringing me here. I think I shall linger and see whether any memories return."

"Leave you here?" He looks around in horror. "Absolutely not."

"It's daytime, sir. I will be fine."

"In the very spot where you were brutally attacked and left for dead? No, look around all you wish. I shall wait."

I don't let Gray wait. Oh, I can't convince him to leave. McCreadie grumbled about Gray's sister being stubborn. Apparently, it's a family trait, and when a man of Gray's size decides to park himself somewhere, he stays parked. I won't try to cross through time with him watching, so the only way for me to break the impasse is to pretend to skulk about with dramatic pauses for deep contemplation and deeper sighs before declaring I remember nothing.

"We will head back through the market," he says. "I'll leave you there to do your shopping."

"Shopping?"

"Spending some of your quarterly wages."

"And what would I spend it on?"

He throws up his hands. "Confits? Ribbons? A new bonnet. Whatever you like."

Candies and pretty bows? Is that truly where he imagines a housemaid's salary goes? In his defense, maybe he hopes it does. Catriona's daily needs are covered—food, shelter, uniform, and such—and so he expects wages to be like pocket money.

If I *were* a maid, I know exactly what I'd do with my salary. I'd save it up in hopes that I wouldn't be scrubbing chamber pots into my twilight years.

While I don't actually have any wages to spend, I'll let Gray escort me to the market. Once he leaves me to shop, I'll sneak back to that alley.

This neighborhood is known as the Grassmarket because it used to be the main market for Edinburgh. It's now more of a hodgepodge of shops and tenement housing, all of which have seen better days—hell, better *centuries*—but there's also an open market space with stalls, and there's where we go.

I expect Gray to deposit me at the edge, but he seems quite content to wander at my side. That is, he's content to do so until a cart of antique books catches his eyes.

"Is that Paré's plague treatise?" he murmurs to himself as he wanders off.

"Thank you, sir!" I call after him. "I shall see my own way home this eve!"

Unfortunately, the sound of my voice reminds him of my existence. Gaze still half on that book cart, he takes two long strides my way as he roots in his pocket. When he reaches me, he passes over a coin.

"For your help today, Catriona."

"I thought we agreed to time off instead?"

"You earned both." A faint smile. "Spend it on something that makes you happy."

I don't even have time to thank him before he's heading back to those books, leaving me staring at his back and thinking that, of all the fascinating things in this world, he might be the one I'll most regret not getting to know better.

"I'll look you up when I get home, Duncan Gray," I murmur as he bends over the cart of old books. "I expect you did some amazing things."

I lift my fingers in a wave, even if he can't see it, and then I hurry from the market.

I have been in the right spot for over an hour, pacing and wandering, and at one point—when the lane is clear—even dropping to the ground, as if I can somehow pass through time that way. I realize that is ridiculous. Just like I realize this entire plan is ridiculous.

I'm trying to pass back through time by returning to the place where I crossed over. My brain says that makes logical sense, but I am well aware that it only makes sense because I've seen it in movies and read it in books. To return to your own time, you go back to that spot—that magical bridge between worlds. Or you go there and do something you did the last time and that makes you cross over. Maybe it's a word or a phrase or an action or an emotion. Do that thing, and it will unlock the door through time.

Which is like saying that if I tap my ruby slippers three times I can go home again. I am basing my entire theory on the imagination of fiction writers. Not scientists, because there is no science. People can't travel through time. Therefore, writers don't need to worry about "getting it right." They make up whatever they want.

To return to your own time, child, you must find the spot where you crossed, during the same alignment of the planets, and then eat one hundred and fifty leaves of thyme, one for each year you must travel.

I knew this was a preposterous plan. Yet it was the only one I had, and what was the alternative? To throw up my hands and resign myself to the life of a housemaid when a walk across town might have been the key to returning? If so many writers used that particular trope, maybe there was a kernel of truth to it. It's like meeting a vampire while holding a vial of holy water and *not* throwing it at him.

I don't know what happened to me. I cannot begin to understand it, because the possibility doesn't exist in any reality I know. I suspect modern theoretical scientists would have ideas, but it's not a subject I've ever needed to research. I am hoping, then, that some author or screenwriter did the research for me and this whole "return to the spot where you passed over" idea is sound.

What I suspect, though, is that what I encountered here was a rip in the fabric of reality. I was strangled in the same spot, on the same day, at the same moment as a young woman a hundred and fifty years earlier. That caused some crossing of wires in a cosmic sense, and my consciousness—my soul or whatever you care to call it—somehow swapped with that of Catriona Mitchell.

Can such a thing be undone? I can't even contemplate a negative answer. The despair would swallow me whole, and I might find myself taking the most desperate action to get home again. To put myself in those exact conditions. To die on that spot and hope that took me home because I cannot imagine being trapped here forever.

There are worse fates than being a maid in a decent household. I have a job and food and a roof over my head. There's even the possibility that I could become the assistant to a man doing work I find fascinating—work I could surely help with. But those are only scraps, barely enough to keep me from lying down on this spot and strangling myself.

Yes, there are things in my real life I'd like to change, but I want the chance to do that. I need to see Nan and tell her all about this before she dies. Give her a glimpse into true magic, a goodbye gift, one last secret between us before she's gone.

I want to make other changes, too. Work less. Play more. Renew friendships. Fall in love. Compared to Catriona, though, I had an idyllic life. A challenging job that I love. A cozy condo and a loving family and my freedom. Most of all, I had my freedom. I could go where I wanted, do what I wanted, be who I wanted. This is not my world, and I do not want to stay in it.

So I will sustain my spirits by telling myself there must be a door. That I can get back, and either I'll figure it out or I'll return when the universe repairs its glitch.

Until then, I'll make the best of it. Be Catriona Mitchell. Do whatever I can to make that role mine. To be a version of this girl that I can live with and not go mad. Also, to not act in any way that'll have me *labeled* mad. Keep my secret, blend in, and do my best.

I pace the alley one last time, as if the thousandth will make a difference. When footsteps sound, I stiffen. I'm not alone on this lane. I've had my share of curious looks. I entertained two offers of "companionship" before I learned to busy myself whenever anyone passed. Still, it's been safe enough. However bad the neighborhood, it's still daytime and even the offers had only been for a drink, while naturally hoping it'd lead to more. It's not as if anyone has honestly mistaken me for a sex worker. At those footsteps, though, I still steel myself as I turn.

It's a woman, maybe in her late twenties. Dark-haired, with a scar across her cheek and a narrow-eyed look that dares anyone to ask her how she got it.

"Well, look at the little kitty-cat, slunk back to see what's left in the cream bowl. I thought you'd never show your face here again, not after last week. I heard someone taught you a lesson. Much overdue, it was."

The woman smiles, revealing exactly the sort of teeth I expected from an era before regular dental cleanings. Then I realize what she's saying. She knows me—knows Catriona. And something else.

"You know what happened to me here?" I say. "When I was attacked?"

"Everyone does. They're wagering on who done it. Too many people wanted you dead. I can't say I blame them." She leans forward, foul breath washing over me. "If you want to make a wager yourself, we can put it under my name. Earn ourselves both a bit of money."

I shake my head. "I don't know who attacked me. I don't even remember why I was here." I tap the fading bruise on my temple. "I've lost my memory."

She laughs so hard a rat squeaks and scurries off. "Oh, is that your story? And such pretty manners, too." Her eyes narrow. "What are you up to?"

"Trying to figure out who tried to *kill* me."

More eye narrowing. "Do not forget who you're talking to, Miss Kitty-Cat. I know all about that canny mind of yours. I've been a victim of your schemes as often as I've helped you build them. You might be able to fool the lads, but I see past that pretty face."

Before I can speak, she rocks back on her heels. "Is it the doctor?"

"What?"

"Your master. Dr. Gray. I heard he came to fetch you. Nursed you back to health. Have you decided to take my advice? Is that what the pretty new speech is for? The pretty new manners? You've finally set your sights on the master?"

She bats her lashes and simpers. "Oh, kind sir, I don't remember anything with this lump on my skull. I am but a poor, innocent lassie in need of a strong man's protection. A strong and *rich* man's protection." She cackles. "He may not be a proper toff, but he's got a fine house and a fine income. No proper lady will have him, so you might as well."

"Dr. Gray's occupation would hardly prevent him from finding himself a proper lady."

"His occupation?" She snorts. "You have indeed taken a hard blow to the head if you think that'd be what stops them."

"I *did* take a hard blow, and I have no idea what you're talking about."

"Are you daft? Even if you've forgotten the scandal, surely one look at the man will jolt your memory."

She taps her cheek and arches her brows. Does she mean because he's not white? What would that have to do with a scandal? Ah, I bet I know. His skin tone suggests one of his parents is white and the other isn't. Such a union would probably be shocking in this day.

"Whatever the issue," I say, "I cannot imagine Dr. Gray lacks for female companionship. And no, I have not changed my mind on that count. I'm not sure how traipsing around this neighborhood would help me win him to my bed."

"Traipsing? My, my, you speak like a properly educated lady yourself." She eyes me. "I've heard you come from a good family, however much you denied it. That could be useful. Get little Miss Kitty-Cat into places no alley-cat girls can go."

I shake my head. "I just came to see if I could find out what happened to me. If you have anything to add, I'd appreciate the information. Otherwise—"

She grabs my arm, fingers digging in. "Pretty words and manners are all very fine, but don't you go putting on airs with me. Do not forget I know things that would get you tossed from your fine doctor's home."

"Yes," I murmur under my breath. "I've heard that before. Today in fact."

She twists my arm. "Do not mutter insults at me, Catriona."

"I wasn't," I say, "and I apologize if I was being rude." I pause. "Perhaps we could have a drink, for old times' sake."

If this woman holds something over me, I need to be nice. Also, I'd like to know more about the young woman whose body I inhabit, and this seems an excellent opportunity to do so.

"A drink?" The woman scowls. "Is that a joke?"

Fortunately, my expression must answer for me, because she eases back, still eyeing me sharply. "You really have lost your memory. No, kitty-cat, I do not want a drink. I don't imbibe. Neither do you, and that piece of advice I'll give for free. Lose yourself in a bottle, and soon you'll be lifting your skirts for more. That's not the life for us."

"So what *is* the life for us?" I say. "Forget the drink. May I ask you some questions?" I take out the coin. "I can pay."

"With two bob? That'll buy you two words." She makes what I presume is a rude gesture and then puts out her hand.

I pocket the coin. "How much for more?"

"I'll give you the going rate for a high-class whore. A pound will buy you twenty minutes of my time." She starts to walk away. "You know where to find me, kitty-cat."

"No, actually, I don't."

She laughs and points at the dive bar where Catriona had been spotted the night she was attacked.

"Can I get your name?" I call after her.

She turns and puts out her hand. With a sigh, I drop the coin into it.

"Davina," she says, closes her hand, and walks away.

ELEVEN

By the time I get home, I'm starving, and I've missed dinner. I'm not even sure I'd have been entitled to it on my day off. While I doubt Gray would have begrudged me an extra meal, Mrs. Wallace is an entirely different matter.

I stand in the doorway of the darkened kitchen. It's past eight, and the housekeeper has cleaned up and gone to her quarters. There's food here somewhere. Catriona wouldn't think twice about taking it, and if I want to convince them I'm Catriona, I should do the same. Yet I can't bring myself to step into the kitchen.

I'm not Catriona. I don't want to be her.

At first, hearing of her "felonious past," I'd been intrigued and a little impressed. Not such a meek housemaid after all. A cop shouldn't be impressed by a thief, but I've always had a keen appreciation for circumstances. As a patrol officer, if I got a call for some kid in two-hundred-dollar running shoes swiping a candy bar, you can bet your ass I'd be speaking to her parents and writing it up. Make that a teen runaway swiping condoms so he doesn't knock up his girlfriend, and I'd point him to the nearest Planned Parenthood and persuade the shop owner not to lay charges.

I do not judge lives that have seen the kind of hardship I struggle to comprehend. I was raised in an upper-middle-class family, the only child of a tenured professor and a law-firm partner. My parents made damn sure I understood just how much privilege I had, whether it was weekends on the farm or weeknights in a soup kitchen.

I'd imagined Catriona as a girl who'd grown up fighting for scraps. A victim of circumstance who'd done what she had to and "worked up" to housemaid in a prosperous home owned by a decent man. It might not seem like much to me, but it was a Victorian success story.

Except that's not how it went at all, was it? Catriona didn't grow up in Old Town poverty. That doesn't mean she didn't escape horrors of another kind at home, but I'm getting the sense she's less a scrappy success story than a remorseless criminal.

Maybe there's more to her. Maybe, even if there isn't, I can't completely blame her, given the restrictions she faces in this world. But I know one thing: I don't want to be her.

If I'm temporarily stuck here, then I will become Catriona version 2. Gray mentioned that brain damage can cause personality shifts. I remember the case of Phineas Gage from Psych 101. The guy got a railroad spike through his head, and it completely changed his personality. While I think that kind of shift only occurs with actual damage to the brain, if Gray—as a doctor—doesn't know better, I should take full advantage.

Yep, a blow to the head changed my personality. It made me, apparently, better spoken and better mannered, which would be hilarious to anyone who knows me. I might come from privilege, but I've always been what one might call a little rough around the edges, more of a beer and nachos, jeans and sneakers, rough-and-tumble kind of girl.

Ironically, compared to Catriona, I *am* the sweet-tempered housemaid I expected her to be. I can make adjustments, though, closer to the real me. Catriona clearly had an edge, and therefore so can I. She had a brain, and she had an attitude, and she had a healthy dose of self-confidence. Therefore, I do not need to rein in that side of myself as much.

As Catriona v2, do I want to steal from the larder? No. Or that's a fine excuse. The truth is that as I stand in the kitchen doorway, the despair from earlier rushes back. I think of my apartment, where the only question would be whether there's anything I *want* to eat in the fridge. I never even had to sneak cookies as a child. My parents kept a shelf of kid-friendly snacks, and I was welcome to help myself. Nan had fruit on the counter and the ever-present biscuit tin. Even my dad's parents, as strict as they were, bought little boxes of raisins and animal crackers for my visits long after I passed the age for either.

Access to food. It's a silly thing that looms huge right now. A symbol of what I had and what I face. A life where if I miss dinner, I go hungry until breakfast. A life where there aren't coins in my pocket to slip out and buy something to eat. A life where I'm not *allowed* to just "slip out," and even if I did, I'm not sure where to *find* dinner or if I'd be welcome, as a young woman alone.

This world may not be hell, but it is another sort of nightmare, one where my rights and freedoms have been snatched away, and I am powerless to fight back.

That might be the worst of it. I want to fight, and I cannot because it would land me in the streets or an insane asylum.

Be a good girl. Do as you're told. Don't make waves.

Words so many other women grew up with. Sentiments I was never taught. I don't know how to do this. I'm not sure I *can.*

I want to go home. I just want to go home. I need to get to Nan, if I can. If she's still alive. And if she's not? Were her dying hours spent frantically wondering what happened to me and then passing without ever knowing the truth? And my parents. Oh God, my parents. They'd have been notified I was missing and would have dropped everything to fly to Edinburgh. Instead of spending Nan's final days with her, did they spend them looking for me? Were they facing the possibility of grieving us both?

Am I missing? I realize with a jolt that I might not be missing at all. I might be walking around the modern world . . . with Catriona puppeteering me.

What if Catriona took over my body? A thief and a con artist in my body. With my grandmother. With my parents. She'd only need to be found wandering and confused, and someone would have taken the ID from my pocket and contacted my parents.

What damage could she do? As a police officer? As the only child of doting and well-off parents?

"Catriona?"

At the voice, I spin to see Alice. When I move fast, she shrinks on herself before straightening.

How many times have I seen her do this? How often have I lifted a hand, and she's flinched? Moved toward her, and she's steeled herself? Spun to face her, and she's drawn back?

Such a timid little thing, I'd thought. Scared of her own shadow. That must be what life is like for girls her age, not even a teenager and already in service. Yet now that I reflect on it, I realize I've heard her chattering away to Mrs. Wallace. I've seen her take coffee to Gray, her demeanor relaxed and confident. She doesn't flinch from them. Doesn't draw back from them. Just from me.

No, just from Catriona.

Alice has always been quick to answer my questions. Eager to help. Solicitous of my well-being. I remember hoping, for her sake, that her "friend" would return when I left this body.

Friend? No. Alice isn't quick to be helpful because she likes Catriona. She's quick because she's afraid of her. Because, on top of all her other charming qualities, Catriona is a bully.

I want to ask Alice if I'm right. Yet how would I do that?

Er, have I ever hit you? Pinched you? Slapped you? Just . . . asking.

I don't need to ask. I'm a damned detective. I can follow the clues, and the fact that I misunderstood before now only proves how distracted I've been. More Psych 101. The brain likes stereotypes because they are mental shortcuts. We have so much data to process in everyday life that we rely on these shortcuts far too much.

In this world, the data is overwhelming for me. So I've shut down the part of me that I'd like to think is bias-light, and I shoved everyone into boxes. My undertaker employer will be grim and foreboding. As a man with servants, he'll be an inconsiderate asshole. The body I inhabit is that of a pretty teenage housemaid. She'll be meek and mild and not terribly bright. Oh, wait, she was a thief? Then she did it out of desperation, a girl from the slums driven to steal for a living. The twelve-year-old scullery maid flinches from me? She's a poor and timid creature. Oh, she's also nice to me? Because we're sisters in service, bound by circumstances.

Sisters, yes, in the worst of ways. Two girls forced to live together, one of them taking full advantage of her superior size and position. The kind of sister that made me glad I was an only child.

Catriona bullied Alice. Of all the things my host-body has done, that upsets me the most, and it's a lead weight on my mood, dragging it deeper into the gloom.

"Hello, Alice." I speak as kindly as I can, and she still tenses, as if that kindness is a trick. She's not a timid girl. Not a fearful one. Just one who has learned her own tricks to avoid punishments she doesn't deserve, like abused children in every time period.

I want to say something. I cannot. I can only show her that I have changed.

"I've missed dinner," I say. "And I can't remember whether we are allowed to take food from the larder. Is there something I may have?"

She eyes me, and I see the problem. Catriona doesn't ask—she takes. Maybe this is the trick. I will eat something and blame Alice for saying it was okay.

"Never mind," I say. "I'll ask Mrs. Wallace in the morning. I'm fine tonight."

I've started to step past her when she says, "We're allowed to take any leftover bread or rolls, as Mrs. Wallace will bake more when she rises. But there's none tonight. She has been running herself ragged preparing for Mrs. Ballantyne's return, and I think she may have reheated day-old rolls for the master." Her lips quirk. "He was too distracted to notice. He always is."

"Ah, well, thank you for letting me know." I pause. "I know I'm asking a lot of silly questions."

"Your memory is affected. That's what Dr. Gray says."

"It is, but . . ." I glance around, as if being sure we are alone. "I fear letting him know how badly it is affected. I realize I do not seem myself, and that is because I scarcely remember myself, and I fear if the master finds out, he'll have me sent away."

She frowns. "Dr. Gray would not do that. He might try to study your affliction, but if it becomes overtaxing, Mrs. Ballantyne will stop him."

"Perhaps, but I am still anxious. So I appreciate your answering my questions, and I apologize if I do not seem like the person you knew."

Her gaze goes wary, but she only nods.

When I start to leave again, Alice sighs. "You ought not to go to bed without dinner. There are biscuits in my room. When Dr. Gray does not finish his, I take them, as Mrs. Wallace would only throw them into the rubbish. You can have the ones from today."

"I won't take them all, but I would appreciate one. Thank you."

Alice helps me fix tea and gives me two of the biscuits she took from Dr. Gray's tray this afternoon. I thank her again and ask how her day was. The question seems to throw her. Because each day is the same as the next? Or because Catriona would never ask and therefore it's suspicious? Probably the latter, and there's nothing I can do except vow that we'll get past it.

And what will happen when her tormentor returns? Because Catriona will return. I cannot—will not—acknowledge any other possibility.

Since it seems I'm not leaving any time soon, I'll have time to teach Alice how to deal with the return of the person who owns the body I currently possess, and I'll try not to think about *that* brain twister too much.

When I enter my room, the first thing I see is a book on my dresser. *Records of Washing Away of Injuries,* by Song Ci, translated by W. A. Harland. I crack it open and smile for the first time in hours. It's the thirteenth-century Chinese book of forensic science that Gray had mentioned. Underneath is a folded note. I open it to see calligraphy-worthy penmanship. However messy the man may be in his personal habits, his writing is enviable.

> Catriona,
> This is the book I mentioned, in case you care to read it. Please do not feel obligated to do so. In fact, I would be more annoyed to discover you forced yourself to read it rather than admit you are not interested.

He signs with a flourish that makes me smile again. It is the stereotypically illegible doctor's signature, and yet still as beautifully scripted as the rest.

Do I want to read this book? Hell, yes. I'd never even heard of it, and my heart does a little flip of joy as I take it to the bed with my biscuits. I reach for my cell phone to use the flashlight and . . .

I get the damned oil lamp burning and set it up beside the bed. When I open the book, I need to adjust the flame, and I'm still squinting. I'm reminded of being on a car trip with a friend, and when I tried to read in the passing streetlights his parents had warned that I'd ruin my eyesight reading in the dark. Still not sure whether that's a thing, but I do wear contacts.

No, I *did* wear contacts.

I hadn't even realized I'm no longer wearing them. I peer across the room and then down at the book. I can see it perfectly. Thank God for small mercies—I imagine in this world, unless a maid is half blind, she's not going to get spectacles.

I settle on the bed and open the book to the first page. There's an inscription.

> *To my darling genius son,*
> *I found this in a shop, Duncan, and thought you might enjoy it.*
> *Please don't let your sister get hold of this one. You know she'll insist on reading it, even when it will give her nightmares.*
>
> > *Love always,*
> > *Mama*

The warmth of those words settles over me. When I smile, my eyes glaze with tears. I don't know this woman—I presume she's gone and I'll never get that chance—but in her words, I am reminded of my own mother.

When I graduated from university, I overheard extended family whispering about how disappointed my mother must be that I wasn't going to law school. Did I not have the marks? Such a shame. Such a disappointment. I didn't bristle at those words. I inwardly laughed at how little they knew my mother, who had never once tried to nudge my dream in line with hers. No more than my father tried to nudge me toward English when I wanted to study criminology and sociology.

I might be an only child, but my parents never made me carry the weight of their dreams. They'd found their own and encouraged me to do the same. I feel that same sentiment in these words, and I am happy for Gray in having that.

Does that make me think again of my own parents? Of what they'll go through if I never return? Of what I'll go through if I never see them again? Yes, it does, but this time it's only a pinprick of pain, washed away by the certainty that I *will* see them. The determination to do so, to find a way. My mood has lifted again, and so I am able to set that aside and focus on the moment.

I turn the page, and I tug the coverlet over me, and I pick up a cookie—*biscuit,* I remind myself—and I begin to read.

TWELVE

W hat is *this*?" a voice thunders, and I leap up, all four limbs flailing. One knocks the book off the bed, and before I can blink myself awake, Mrs. Wallace is scooping it up. The housekeeper stares at the book and then opens it and stares some more.

I'm about to ask what emergency brought her here in the middle of the night. Then I see dawn's light seeping through the curtains. That doesn't necessarily mean it isn't the middle of the night, as I've already realized. We're in the north and we predate daylight savings time, meaning "dawn" comes around four A.M. at this time of year.

I rub my eyes and give my head a sharp shake. I'm still dressed from the day before, having fallen asleep reading.

I squint behind Mrs. Wallace.

"No," she snaps. "Alice did not come to wake you, because I had a more important task for her. I realized you were still abed and came to get you myself and found you've been eating pilfered biscuits. That was bad enough. But this?" She waves the book. "You stole from the master's *library*?"

From her tone, you'd think I'd stolen from the family safe. "No, I didn't—"

"It is bad enough you pilfered from the good silver," she says. "Bad enough I caught you with one of the mistress's bracelets. They will not notice that. *This* they will notice."

She waves the book again.

"I didn't—"

"I covered for you, missy. I let you cry and promise you wouldn't do it again. I knew better. I could hear the lie in your voice, see the crocodile in your tears, but for Miss Isla's sake, I allowed you one final chance. This is the last straw. This time I will speak to the master."

"Speak to the master about what?" a voice says from the hallway.

Mrs. Wallace turns in horror. Then she sprints—astonishingly fast given her long skirts—and blocks the doorway, as if shielding me from Gray's view.

"What ever are you doing in this part of the house, sir?" she says.

"This being my house, I believe I am entitled to be in any part of it," he says dryly. "Excepting, of course, the bedchambers, which is why I stopped in the hallway to voice my question. As for why I am in this part of the house at all, I ventured out in search of coffee and heard raised voices."

Mrs. Wallace glares at me. "The master should not *need* to venture out in search of his morning beverage."

"Perhaps," Gray muses. "But the master is quite capable of not only venturing out but even brewing his own."

She shoots him a meaningful glance.

He clears his throat and says, "It was a very small fire."

I catch the barest quirk of Mrs. Wallace's lips, but when she turns to me, her face is stone again. Seeing that softening, I'm reminded that I've never heard the housekeeper do more than mock-sternly admonish Alice. In other words, she's not usually the gorgon I've seen. I get that side of her because Catriona has deserved it. Yet another person I've shoved into a box—the dour and strict housekeeper, overly proud of her position and lording it over her staff.

"The master should not need to venture out in search of his morning beverage," she repeats.

I scramble from the bed. "Yes, ma'am. Apologies, ma'am. I seem to be having difficulty rising without a . . . without Alice. I stayed up too late reading."

"Reading?" She lifts the book. "Is that really how you wish to do this? All right then." She turns on Gray and dips her chin. "I regret to say, sir, that—"

"He lent it to me."

She wheels on me, face suffusing with red. "Do not dare pull Dr. Gray into this. If you expect him to lie for you—"

"I do not, and I apologize for interrupting, ma'am, but I did not get a chance to explain earlier, and I didn't wish Dr. Gray to think I was causing trouble to embarrass you."

I smooth my rumpled dress and turn to Gray. "Mrs. Wallace found your book here, and she mistakenly believed I had stolen it because of my felonious past, as you called it. Also, she has caught me stealing before, and she kindly gave me a second chance. I did not yet have the opportunity to explain that you lent me the book or show her the note that accompanied it."

I find the note and pass it to Mrs. Wallace. "I professed an interest in the book yesterday, when I was helping Dr. Gray, and he kindly lent it to me, and then I stayed up too late reading."

"And the biscuits?" she says, her gaze only skimming the note.

"I did take the biscuits," I say. "And I am sorry."

"Where did you take them from?" Gray asks.

"The, uh, pantry."

"Exactly where?"

When I don't answer, he turns to Mrs. Wallace. "I believe Alice gave Catriona the biscuits. I have noticed her sneaking uneaten food from my tray."

He glances down the hall, as if making certain Alice isn't there, though he still lowers his voice. "I have spoken to Isla about it, and she says I ought not to comment. Alice has known want in the past, and so it eases her mind to store food in her quarters. It is, after all, unwanted food, and no harm is done. I would prefer to give her some to put away, but Isla does not wish to embarrass the girl."

"She has food-security issues," I say with a nod. "Even if she has plentiful meals now, she'll rest easier knowing she cannot go hungry again."

"Precisely." Gray looks from me to Mrs. Wallace. "Have we settled the matter then? Catriona stole nothing. Neither did Alice, who is only caching unwanted food."

"Like a squirrel," I say.

His lips twitch. "Like a squirrel. Now, if this is done, perhaps Catriona can have a few moments to dress before I get my breakfast. There is little rush, though I'll happily take my coffee as soon as I can get it." He points to the book. "Are you still reading that?"

I nod. "I got most of the way through before I fell asleep. I'm up to 'suicides by edged weapons.'"

His brows rise. "You are a quick reader."

"No, I just stayed up very late, which is why I'm still fully dressed." I hitch my skirts. "I don't even want to think what my hair looks like."

"It could use a brushing."

"You're supposed to tell me it looks fine. Lie."

His lips tweak again, at the same time Mrs. Wallace's tighten. I'm being overly familiar with the master. He won't care—the man doesn't stand on ceremony. But even if Mrs. Wallace doesn't accuse me of flirting, she's definitely going to see my easy banter as a sign that I am forgetting my place.

I nod to Mrs. Wallace. "I shall dress as quick as I can, ma'am, and bring Dr. Gray his breakfast posthaste."

She grunts, sets the book on my dresser, withdraws with Gray, and shuts the door.

I take Gray his breakfast. He's working in the funeral parlor, and I deliver it there. I'm hoping he'll invite me to stay, and help, but he barely seems to notice me dropping off the tray. He's leafing through files and gives a distracted wave with, "Just set it over there," and I suspect it'll still be full when I return with his morning coffee. I can see he's drained his first cup of the day, and crumbs suggest Mrs. Wallace included a biscuit or two, which he's eaten.

Back in the house, I start into my chores. I'm passing the kitchen when Mrs. Wallace looks up from where she's making pastries.

"I wish to apologize for my earlier accusations," she says stiffly.

"I deserved them. I know I have not earned your trust, and I intend to do so." I pause and add, with a faint smile, "Though I will understand if it takes a while for you to believe I am sincere, and not attempting to earn your trust with the plans of later betraying it in a spectacular heist. I do have my eye on Dr. Gray's library. Did you know he has a first edition of *Moll Flanders* in there? My father—" I cough softly. "I know people who would kill for that. Well, not literally. All right, possibly literally."

She's quiet long enough that I realize I've misstepped. Too much Mallory, too little Catriona. I'm looking for the way back when she says, "You are behaving very differently these days."

I sigh, perhaps a bit too dramatically, but that strikes me as something Catriona and I probably have in common. "People keep saying that. Dr. Gray believes it is the bump on my head. Everything is a wee bit muddled. I'm mispronouncing words I should know. I'm using words I never used before. I'm making up words, too. Perhaps it will pass. If it does not?" I shrug. "I shall make the best of it."

When I turn to go, she says, "Would you like some tea? I've a batch of these tarts that didn't quite turn out, and I'd rather not throw them in the rubbish. Alice says they're quite good."

"I'd love some," I say. "As for the tea, is there any chance I can push my luck and ask for coffee? Or is that all for Dr. Gray?"

"Since when do you drink coffee?"

I shrug. "It smells good."

"And tastes disgusting. I'll put on the pot, and you'll see what I mean soon enough."

On a ten-point scale from gas-station swill to hand-roasted brew, the coffee rates a three. In other words, yes, it smells better than it tastes, but somehow, I doubt Gray is forcing Mrs. Wallace to buy the cheapest stuff available. While his tastes are far from extravagant, they are solidly good, meaning this must be the best coffee widely available at this time. Or perhaps it's not the beans but the brewing method, which seems to be a drip pot. I wonder whether I could rig up a decent French press? At any rate, having not had coffee in nearly a week, I'll raise the score to a solid five and won't turn down future offerings.

I'm finishing my cup when Alice bursts in.

"Something is happening at the funerary parlor," she says. "There is a cart in the mews, and I heard Detective McCreadie's voice. There is also a coach in the front."

I bolt upright. Another murder? If so, Gray might need my help. Or so I hope, because unlike former clerk James, I'd happily hold a body while Gray hacked into it, especially if the alternative is scrubbing fireplaces.

I take my coffee and follow Alice up the two flights of stairs to the drawing room. As soon as I step into the room, I pause and look down at the cup. Am I allowed to bring it in here? I glance at Alice, but she's already plastered to the window.

I glance out. There is indeed a commotion in the funeral parlor. Voices sound from downstairs, and there's a carriage pulled up in front. It's fancy but shows signs of wear. I'm squinting at it when another door slams, and we both jump. I bump into Alice, and in my fear of dumping my coffee on her, I overcompensate and end up on my knees, cup held aloft like a touchdown football.

Alice claps. "You ought to be an acrobat."

I almost joke that I'm too old for that when I remember that I'm not. Or, at least, my body isn't.

This body may be younger, but it often feels like driving a clunky rental. Catriona's strength isn't the kind I'm accustomed to. Legs that are used to standing all day, yet balk at moving faster than a walk. Arms that can hoist a full water bucket, yet ache after an hour wielding a pen. And don't even get me started on my core. Remove the corset, and I can barely manage a proper sit-up.

I keep thinking I need to incorporate body-strength exercises into my pre-bed routine, which reminds me of the days when I'd plan a five-mile run after work, only to drop from exhaustion the moment I came through the door. The mind is willing. The body says, "Screw that."

I'm rising from the floor when Gray's voice rings out. "Catriona? Catriona? Where the devil is that girl?"

"In here, sir!" Alice calls before I can.

He thunders into the room, gaze sweeping over us, only to land on the cup in my hand.

"I was on break," I say quickly. "I heard a commotion and came to see what it was. I did not mean to bring a hot drink into the drawing room."

"I only wondered why you are cradling that cup as if it is a newborn kitten. Finish it or bring it along. They came for young Evans's body just as I discovered something of interest."

I'm about to ask for more when the front door opens with a flurry of voices and activity, a woman telling someone to set her bags over there.

Gray's eyes widen in alarm, and he curses under his breath. Then he strides off toward the stairs.

"Isla," he calls as he descends. "I thought you returned this evening. Please do not tell me I forgot to pick you up at the station."

A woman's voice answers with a warm lilt. "No, Duncan, you did not forget. You have done so often enough in the past that I learned to arrange my own transportation home. However, if you feel terribly guilty, you may pay the driver for me."

A *slap-slap*, as if Gray's patting his pockets.

The woman sighs dramatically. "Or I shall pay and you, little brother, may owe me. Now let me give you a hug." A moment's pause, as if they are embracing, "And now you may run back to whatever has currently seized your attention. *Lovely to see you, Isla. Did you have a good trip? Yes, yes, we shall chat later, dear sister.*"

I peek down the stairwell. I can see a woman's pale hand patting Gray's arm and then turning him around and giving him a light push toward the stairs.

"I do not mean to run," Gray says. "It is only—"

"Something dreadfully important. I can see that. Off you go."

As Gray steps away, Isla Ballantyne appears. Like her brother, she's tall and sturdily built, but the resemblance ends there. She has an artfully woven crown of copper hair with curls trailing down. Milk-white skin with freckles. Bright blue eyes.

A handsome woman. That never seems like a compliment, but I mean it as one. "Pretty" implies a fleeting attractiveness. Catriona is very pretty, and I have no idea how much of that is true beauty and how much is simply youth. At sixteen, Isla Ballantyne would not have been the most attractive girl on the dance floor, but I have no doubt she will be at sixty.

Isla wears a gorgeous dress, dove-gray wool and dusky blue silk. The fitted bodice dips deeper on the waist than mine and it's trimmed with enough bows to thrill a five-year-old, but they're all discreet decorations that only enhance the dress. Her skirt is much wider than mine and perfectly belled, like the fashionably dressed women I saw in the New Town. Does that need *more* petticoats? I think I'll stick to my less fashionable attire.

Gray murmurs a few words before Isla pats his arm again and shoos him off. Then he nearly swings right past me down the hall before stopping so abruptly his shoes squeak.

"I have need of you," he says. "Accompany me."

"You have need of *Catriona*?" Isla says, pulling off silk gloves after she's paid the driver.

"Yes, she is assisting me in my work. I lost James."

Another dramatic sigh from Isla. "I do hope you don't mean that literally, Duncan."

"Of course not. I mean he quit."

"Dare I ask what you did to him?"

"I asked him to assist. That is what I hired him for, after all. Now he has left, and Catriona is temporarily aiding me instead." He waves for me to hurry, as if I'm a dawdling child. "I will dictate, and you shall take notes."

"Duncan?" Isla calls after us. "I hate to interfere, but I must point out that Catriona cannot write. Not yet, although I have hopes of teaching her."

"She can. She does. Her handwriting is wretched. If you wish to teach her something, please make it penmanship."

"Catriona?" She stares at me, one glove still half off. "You know your letters?"

I bow in what I hope is a proper curtsy. "I do, ma'am. I must apologize for keeping it from you, but I feared you might think I had airs above my station."

"Airs above your . . . ?" She arches a brow at Duncan. "This *is* Catriona, is it not?"

"I fear I am somewhat changed, ma'am," I say. "Due to the concussion I received during my incident."

"Concussion?"

"Er, my head was . . . concussed. I believe that is the word, though I have been doing some odd things with language lately, ma'am. Putting together the wrong words and coming up with new ones altogether."

"All right," Isla says slowly. "This started after you fell and struck your head?"

"I am not certain I fell. It is possible that I was struck in the head with a blunt object before I was strangled. The blow was hard enough to cause prolonged lack of consciousness."

Her gaze shoots to her brother. "Is there something you wish to tell me, Duncan?"

"I sent you a telegram. Or I thought—" He pauses, frowns. Then he nods abruptly. "No, I recall writing it and giving it to Mrs. Wallace."

"I will speak to Mrs. Wallace," Isla says. "I understand she wanted me to have a relaxing holiday, but I do hope she didn't withhold that message."

The look that passes between them says Mrs. Wallace most certainly did withhold it. The lady of the house was on vacation, and the housekeeper wasn't about to disturb her with news that might bring her home. Not when it was about a maid who didn't deserve such consideration.

I clear my throat. "If you did not receive the telegram, ma'am, I am glad of it. I recovered, and your holiday was not disturbed. I only mention it to explain the lingering effects on my vocabulary and, apparently, my personality."

"I see. Well, then, I am glad to hear Duncan has found a—"

"Duncan?" The front door opens, McCreadie popping his head in. He sees Isla, blinks, and hurries inside, striding to greet her with an embrace that I suspect, in this period, suggests a long-standing and close acquaintance.

"Isla, when did you arrive?" he says.

She lifts her still-half-gloved hand. "Just now. I haven't even had time to take these off, and I've already discovered that my poor maid was strangled and has experienced a brain injury."

"Ah, yes. Catriona. She seems fine enough." McCreadie picks up a small suitcase in each hand. "I'll run these upstairs for you."

"Did you not just come to fetch my brother?" she says. "On the urgent matter in the funerary parlor?"

"Er, yes. Of course. Duncan, you need to show me what you found before they remove the body."

"Body?" Isla perks up. "Is it a murder?"

"Yes, but—"

"Come, Catriona," Isla says. "There is a murder victim to tend to. This is terribly exciting. It's been months since we had one. No wonder Duncan is so distracted." She beams at him. "Is it an interesting case? Please tell me it is interesting."

McCreadie steps into her path. "No, Isla. Duncan has Catriona to assist him. You are not seeing this one."

Her brows arch. "I beg your pardon? It sounds as if you said I *am not* to see him, when you meant that I *ought not* to."

I bite my lip to suppress a smile, half at her words and half at the flush that creeps over McCreadie's face.

"Er, yes. 'Ought.' That was the word I meant. You ought not to see the body."

"But I can, and so I will."

She starts to pass him.

Gray clears his throat. "Isla . . . ?"

She keeps walking. Gray sighs, follows, and leans past her to brace one hand on the door.

"Hugh is correct," he says. "It will give you nightmares."

She looks between the two men and straightens. "May I remind you that I am no longer a child needing you two to protect my delicate sensibilities."

"It's your delicate *stomach* that's the problem," Gray says. "And your overactive imagination."

"Overactive?" she huffs.

"This is not a science project, Isla," Gray says. "It is a murder victim."

Her lips tighten. She doesn't like that, particularly as her brother does indeed use murder victims as objects of scientific study. But I presume she doesn't study forensics, and so his point is valid enough to accomplish what he intends—make her reconsider her zeal to see the body.

Finally, she flutters her fingers. "All right. Off with all three of you then, and I shall await the report. There will be a report, yes? And if there are any unknown substances to be analyzed, you will bring them to me?"

"We shall report and, of course, anything requiring chemical analysis shall be delivered to your laboratory."

THIRTEEN

Gray and I wait while McCreadie carries Isla's bags to the third floor. Then we head back down to the main level.

"Why is Evans being moved?" I ask as we start down the stairs.

Both men frown at me.

When Gray replies, it is with all the patience of an excellent teacher. "We need to remove him before his body begins to break down in the process known as decomposition. He will become quite odorous, and it is best to relocate him to a morgue, as his funeral cannot be held until Thursday."

"Is there nothing an undertaker can do to halt the decay process?" I say, seeing the opportunity to answer questions I've had from the start.

"Such as preserving the body in spirits? For medical examination, yes, but I doubt the family is keen to purchase ten gallons of whisky to pickle him."

"*He* might appreciate it."

McCreadie chuckles. "No doubt he would. The lad was fond of his spirits."

"So what *do* you do to the bodies? To prepare them for burial?"

"I do nothing to the bodies, Catriona." Gray's dark eyes grow darker. "If you have heard otherwise—"

"I haven't," I say quickly. "I only wondered about an undertaker's role in regards to the body. Dressing it? Making it look presentable?"

"You have a very odd concept of my occupation. Dressing or beautifying a corpse is entirely the responsibility of the family or whomever they hire. I simply make the arrangements. I free the bereaved from such details."

"Ah, then you are a funeral *director*."

His lips purse as he resumes walking. "Yes, I suppose that is an apt way of phrasing it. I direct all details of the funeral itself—the procession and the service—as well as supplying the necessary commodities, such as the coffin and the cemetery plot."

Interesting. To me, the term "undertaker" always had a hint of the morbid, and I presumed it described the person who dealt with the body itself. Instead, the modern title of "funeral director" seems more apt. Like a wedding planner for death.

"But if you have found something, should you not be permitted to further examine the body?" I ask. "Even after the coroner does his work, the body cannot always be released to the family promptly."

"Coroner?" Gray's brows shoot up. "We are in Scotland, Catriona."

"So Dr. Addington is called . . ."

"The police surgeon."

"Couldn't *you* be licensed as a police surgeon, Dr. Gray? Then you could perform the autopsy."

Gray stiffens at that. Before I can apologize for an apparent misstep, McCreadie says gently, "Dr. Gray possesses a medical degree, but he cannot—er, *does* not—practice medicine. Even if he did, there is only one police surgeon in Edinburgh. It is an elected position. The police surgeon autopsies the victim. I examine the scene and make observations regarding the body."

"So you're trained in the principles of forensic science? I presume it is part of your policing education."

McCreadie frowns at Gray.

"She means the science I am doing," Gray says. "'Forensic science' is her term for it. As for the education a criminal officer receives . . ."

McCreadie snorts. "A high-minded ideal, Catriona, but I believe the breadth of my professional instruction was 'Can you wield a cudgel? Yes? Excellent!'"

"Hugh is joking," Gray says. "But only slightly. As with many new areas of study, being new means your 'forensic science' has not been proven to the satisfaction of those who oppose change. Most officers of the law, not being scientists, mistrust the science. They solve a robbery by questioning witnesses. Not by matching finger marks left on the window frame to the fingers of a suspect."

"Still not convinced of that one myself," McCreadie murmurs.

"Remind me to lend you a treatise on the matter."

"Please don't. The only thing those articles are good for is helping me sleep. Finger marks are intriguing, but there's no possible way they can solve a crime."

"Why not?" I say. "Everyone's prints are different, which makes them a unique identifier."

Both men turn slowly my way.

"Er, that was something I, uh, read," I say. "I think. Possibly?"

Gray is about to comment when a noise from the examination room catches his attention. He strides toward it and flings open the door. I think he's going to give hell to whoever's in there, but it's only Constable Findlay, protecting Evans's body from being taken. The young man stands on the other side of the room, taking great interest in a medical clamp.

"You may leave, Colin," McCreadie says. "Thank you for your assistance. I do hope the sight hasn't put you off your lunch."

The young man straightens and demurs, but when his gaze flicks toward the body, he turns away quickly.

Findlay catches my eye and lifts his chin. A stiff "Miss Catriona," and then he strides past.

"What ever did you do to my constable?" McCreadie murmurs as he leaves.

"I-I honestly do not remember, sir."

"I was teasing, lass. A young woman is entitled to change her mind, as much as a young man may wish otherwise. He will be himself soon enough. Now, to work?"

As we stand beside Evans's body, I realize why poor Findlay looked so uncomfortable. Evans's chest has been unstitched and cracked open again. McCreadie sees that, stops abruptly, and reverses course to stand by the wall. If Gray notices, he ignores it.

"I credit Catriona with this discovery," Gray says. "Or our conversation from yesterday, at least. We discussed Song Ci's book, which I took to her last night, and with that playing upon my mind, I bolted awake in the middle of the night remembering something. Then I went back to sleep and promptly forgot it until I had my coffee this morning."

"All praise the goddess of caffeine," I murmur under my breath. Both men glance over, but clearly decide they have misheard.

Gray continues, "When I examined the body yesterday, I found signs of damage to the lungs. I presumed it was from the strangulation, robbing the body of air, but it must have been bothering me, because last night, thinking of Song Ci's book, my mind turned to the section on how to identify a victim of drowning. I opened him up again and found this in his lungs."

Gray hoists a vial like it's the Holy Grail. Inside is an opaque liquid.

"Mucus?" McCreadie says.

"Water," I say, before I can stop myself.

Gray smiles at me. "Very good, Catriona. It is water. There was a significant quantity of water in his lungs, meaning he inhaled it shortly before his death."

"So he died of drowning?" McCreadie says. "Not strangulation?"

"Well, that is the question. I do not believe there is any foolproof way to tell the difference, though I shall research that further, of course. Yet if I were pressed on the matter, I would say the strangulation caused his ultimate demise. If that is the case, what was the purpose of the drowning? I'll have Isla examine the water, of course, but from my preliminary examination, I believe the lack of soil particles indicates household water."

"There are signs of restraint, are there not?" I say, moving to get a better look at Evans's arms.

"Yes, soft restraints on both the wrists and ankles."

"Then it's waterboarding," I say.

Both men stare at me, their empty expressions telling me I'm using a modern word.

"Er, I, uh, do not know the proper terminology for it," I say. "That is the word I have heard, I think. I mean the method of torture in which one pours water over the victim's mouth and nose, to inflict the sensation of drowning."

More staring, and I realize my explanation sounded far too technical for Catriona. Either that or Gray's rethinking having anyone in his home with such a well-rounded knowledge of torture.

"Inflict the sensation of drowning?" McCreadie smiles. "That hardly sounds like torture, Catriona."

"You don't think so?" I wave at Evans. "Switch spots with him, and I'll grab a pitcher of water."

He only laughs and shakes his head. "I know Duncan speculates that the missing tooth and damage to the nail beds are signs of torture, and it seems you and I have run in opposite directions with that baton. I believe he is mistaken, and you have embraced the theory. No, Catriona, I will accept the possibility of torture, but one cannot achieve such a thing with a little water."

McCreadie glances at Gray, as if expecting his friend to chime in with laughter. Instead, Gray frowns, thoughtful.

"It is an intriguing idea, Catriona," he says.

McCreadie clears his throat. "Er, yes, I did not mean to laugh. We may disagree on debate theories, but we ought not to mock them, and I apologize if that is what I seemed to do. I was amused by the thought, that is all. Please do share such ideas with us, Catriona, with no fear of mockery."

"Yes," Gray says. "While I shall need to think on this more, I welcome all speculation. The water is important, in some way, and must be investigated further. For now, I wished to show Catriona the damage to the lungs, and then I'll get him stitched up and off to the morgue."

Evans's body having been removed, we're in the drawing room having tea. Tea that I served, I might add. I could bristle at that. I just finished taking notes and helping examine a body. They listened to my observations then. But now it's "Catriona, would you bring us our tea, please?"

It does rankle, obviously. I'm a police detective, damn it. Even if they don't know that, haven't I proven I'm more than a housemaid? Yes, I have, and thus they treated me as more, and I must acknowledge that.

It reminds me of all the times someone told me I was lucky to have a detective partner who treated me the same way he would a male partner. Lucky? To have a *partner* who treated me as an equal? If I do the job as well as a man, should treating me like one be commendable? The fact it is only proves how screwed up the system still is.

Here, it's different. Here, I must acknowledge that I cannot expect to be treated as a man because we are light-years from sexual equality even being discussed in all but fringe circles. I may not know much about history, but I know we predate the women's vote. We may even predate the women's suffrage movement.

My gut tells me that I *am* lucky to have landed in a household where I'm considered a suitable assistant to a forensic scientist. Lucky to have these two professionals consider my observations. I'll credit the woman bustling about upstairs unpacking. It's obvious McCreadie is an old family friend. It's also obvious that Isla is a chemist—a scientist in her own right—and that this is accepted as normal within these walls.

Is it normal outside them? Again, I'm kicking myself for not taking a history course or two in university. My knowledge of this period is one big blob of Victoriana. If I recall correctly, Queen Victoria reigned for over sixty years. That's like lumping the twenty-first century with the World War II era and calling it all the same. I know Isla traveled without a chaperone. Is that normal for women? Or only for widows? Or is she defying norms and expectations on her own? I have no idea. All I know is that Gray and McCreadie seem more open to including me than I expected.

Which does not keep them from expecting me to serve tea . . . because it's what I'm being paid for. I'm a maid, not a colleague. I serve the tea, and then I leave, with Gray promising to summon me if he requires my assistance with anything else.

Gray does not summon me. I wait all afternoon and into the evening, like a dog with her ears attuned for the sound of the master's voice, the pound of his boots, the slap of his door. I hear all those, but whatever he's doing, he's managing on his own, and I am left to my scrubbing and washing.

Dinner comes, and Gray and his sister take it in the dining room. Mrs. Wallace insists on serving—not trusting me, apparently—meaning I have no opportunity to speak to him about the case. Afterward, he disappears into his quarters with the door shut. I offer to take him tea, but Mrs. Wallace says he's asked not to be disturbed.

It's past eight at night. I'm lingering in the drawing room. My chores are long done, despite the interruption. I had fewer today now that the mistress-returning heavy cleaning is done. I almost wish I were as bone-tired as I've been the last couple of days. I'm wide awake, my detective brain popping. With this case, a window keeps cracking open, just enough to let in the sweetest whiff of fresh air and a view of possibilities beyond housemaid drudgery.

An opportunity to experience police work in a past century. A chance to work with a pioneer of forensic science. This is how I could bide my time without losing myself in a gibbering endless panic that I'll never get back home, that Catriona could be in my body, wreaking havoc on my life, taking advantage of those I love.

Yet that window opens, and I barely get a chance to peek out before it slams shut, and I need to wait until Gray opens it again. As with waiting for the door between centuries to reopen, I am at the mercy of fate, and I don't do well with that. I make my own choices. I control my destiny as much as I am able to. Hell, I don't even like to let someone else drive. And now the universe has snatched the steering wheel from my hands, and I swear I hear it laughing at my frustration.

"Catriona?"

I spin to see Isla in the doorway. I quickly smooth my dress and straighten. "I apologize if I am not to be in here, ma'am. I thought I saw something outside."

She walks up beside me and peers out the window.

"It is nothing," I say quickly. "A passerby who looked suspicious, that is all."

"Ah, well, you are quite welcome to sit in here when it is empty, Catriona. As it seems everyone else has retired to their quarters, please have a seat. We should talk. I am most distressed to hear of the attack you suffered."

"I am fine, thank you. There are only the lingering effects of this." I point at the bruise on my temple. "I will not disturb you further. I'll retreat to my room—"

"Please sit." Her voice is honey-sweet, but that "please" is a formality slapped onto a direct order.

I lower myself into an ornate armchair. She takes the more comfortable settee beside it.

"Tell me about this injury, Catriona," she says. "My brother says you were unconscious for more than a day."

I nod.

She waits for me to go on. Keeps waiting, as the grandfather clock ticks past the seconds.

"What do you wish to know, ma'am?" I say.

"Whatever you can tell me. While the medical sciences are my brother's domain, I am always interested in them, even if my traitorous stomach disagrees." Her smile is light and self-mocking, but her gaze stays fixed on me, as sharp as her brother's.

"Tell me all about the effects," she says. "What you have experienced. I am dreadfully interested, and I hope you will indulge my curiosity."

Indulge her curiosity, my ass. Over the next thirty minutes, Isla Ballantyne interrogates me like a suspect in the box. An apt description, because she does suspect me of something.

So far, everyone has bought my story. Blow to the head muddling my mind and my memory. Gray, the medical expert, accepted it at face value. Both McCreadie and Mrs. Wallace have their doubts, thinking "Catriona" is up to some trick, but they've stepped back to watch and judge. Isla dives in with a razor-sharp scalpel. Without even a skeptical raised eyebrow from her, I still feel my story falling apart around me, eviscerated by her questions.

"Well, that certainly is interesting," she says when I've finished.

"The mind is a mysterious thing." Even as I say the words, I want to smack myself. They're ridiculously trite, and her lips twitch a little, but she says, with all solemnity, "It is indeed."

"Is there anything else you needed, ma'am?"

"No, Catriona. You are free to enjoy the remainder of your evening."

I rise before she says, "Oh, there is one last thing."

Every muscle in my body tenses, and I have to rearrange my features into some semblance of blankness before I turn to her. She's taking what looks like a small pill from a tiny box. When she pops it into her mouth, I catch the distinct odor of peppermint.

"Yes, ma'am?" I say as she closes the box.

"You didn't notice my locket when you cleaned my bedchambers, did you?"

"Ma'am?"

"My locket. The one I always wear, except when I travel." She catches my blank look. "Ah, yes, your memory."

Do I imagine a sardonic twist on that last word? I don't think I do.

She continues, "It is an oval locket. Silver and rather simple in design, with a distinctive rod of Asclepius on the front."

"Rod of . . . ?"

"A staff entwined with a serpent. It was given to my grandmother by my grandfather."

"A gift between your grandparents," I say, as a sick dread settles in my gut.

"Yes. It is the only locket I own, and therefore if you have seen one, that would be it."

"I did not clean your quarters before your arrival, ma'am. Mrs. Wallace aired them out and told me I was not to enter."

"Well, if you do see the locket, please let me know. There are several pieces of jewelry missing. That plus a ring and a set of earrings from my late husband."

The dread congeals as I repeat, "From your late husband. Yes. I can see how you would be concerned. Those would be of great sentimental value."

"No," she says flatly. "Only the locket is. My grandmother gave it to me on her deathbed, in recognition of the fact that we shared something in common. She had secretly trained to be a doctor and yet was recognized as no more than my grandfather's assistant. I received training in the pharmacological sciences, but have no hope of being recognized as more than a woman who dabbles in herbal remedies."

When I say nothing, she waves her hand, mistaking my silence for disinterest. "I say that only to impress upon you the personal value of the piece, Catriona. I do not care about the other items. Only the locket." Her gaze meets mine. "If it found its way back into my bedchamber, I would not question where it came from. I would only be glad to have it back."

I nod and mumble, "I understand."

"I sincerely hope you do. Now please enjoy the rest of your evening."

FOURTEEN

The rest of my evening is spent tearing through Catriona's room looking for that damned locket. What the hell had the girl been thinking? Mrs. Wallace must have already caught her stealing from Isla's room, which is why I'd been forbidden to air it out for the mistress's return. After being caught and let off with a warning, Catriona steals the very necklace Isla is guaranteed to notice missing.

How could she be that stupid?

It's not stupidity. The more I hear about Catriona, the more I see her reflected in a dozen young criminals I met as a cop. Having a degree in criminology and sociology means I'm very aware of how an early bad start can send a life careening down the wrong path. Or how a little redirection can steer it on a better one.

For every four kids I worked with, there was always one beyond my help. And for every twenty, there was a Catriona, a teenager who professed to desperately want to get out, their eyes shining with tears as they thanked me for putting them in touch with social agencies. They wanted to make better choices. They wanted to overcome their pasts. And the minute they were out of my sight, they were picking another pocket or rolling another drunk, and when they got caught, it was all "Please call Detective Atkinson. She'll understand."

Oh, I understood. I understood that I'd been played by a pro.

That is Catriona. She played McCreadie to get this job. She played

Mrs. Wallace to keep it. Most of all, she's played Isla, who took her in and gave her a chance, and in return, Catriona blatantly stole her most prized piece of jewelry. If Mrs. Wallace turns her over this time, she'll cry and sniffle and tell Isla that she's a bad seed, unredeemable, and should be cast out on the streets, and Isla will embrace her and promise her another chance.

I have been in Isla's place. I know how much it stings to have your kindness repaid with inward sneers and eye rolls as your pocket is picked clean. It is painful and humiliating. Still, all that suffered was my pride. I'd never had anything of value stolen, certainly not a cherished locket.

The locket. A deathbed gift from a woman who'd understood Isla, in a way even the best parents never quite can. A bond forged by shared passions and shared disappointments. This barb could not strike closer to my heart if it'd been aimed there.

Where the hell did you hide it, Catriona?

I tear the room apart as quietly as I can. I find the first hiding place in a false-backed drawer where she's stashed a dainty box of bonbons. It's half full of sugary confections with a tiny card that reads "For the sweet Mrs. Ballantyne, Fondest regards, Mr. Edwin Perry."

I curse under my breath. I'd bet my ticket home that Isla didn't pass on this would-be suitor's gift to Catriona. I picture Catriona in bed, munching away while rolling her eyes at the sucker who'd asked her to deliver the box to her mistress.

I find the second hiding spot behind a drawer. An opened envelope addressed to Gray.

I hesitate. While I hate to look at his mail, I need to know what Catriona was doing with this.

I unfold the letter and the smell of jasmine rushes out. If that didn't suggest a female sender, the looping script does.

My Dearest Duncan,
I know you think we ought not to see one another again, but I must
implore you to reconsider. Perhaps these memories will spur your return
to my doorstep.

I stop after two more lines. Okay, so by sharing "these memories" what she really meant is "let me send you a very explicit description of the last time we had sex." Well, gotta give Gray credit for that—he definitely left her wanting more. And left me deciding I don't want to *read* more.

I skim down to the closing lines and see that the woman has not only a name but a title. Well, two titles, if you include the word "widow," which seems intended as a reminder to Gray that Lady Inglis is neither maiden nor adulteress.

McCreadie made some comment about Gray not noticing pretty shop-girls and fetching sex workers. Nope, because his tastes run to women his own age who don't expect cash or commitment. Although they apparently may expect more return visits than he cares to pay.

Catriona has been intercepting the post. Taking anything that looks interesting, like a box of candies. Or anything that looks useful, like a letter for Gray in a woman's handwriting. I am furious on their behalf. For someone like Catriona, decent people are nothing but suckers who deserve whatever she dishes out.

So what might she be doing if she's in my body? With my family? Yes, I'm still obsessing about that, but I need to remind myself that my parents aren't fools. If I start abusing their trust—or asking for large sums of cash—they'll know something is wrong, and they're not going to let Catriona empty their bank accounts. Whatever she does in my body, I can fix it.

I keep searching until I find hiding spot number three, and when I do, I let out a truly spectacular string of curses. I've spent nearly an hour searching the floorboards, and the whole time, I'd been rolling my eyes muttering that I'm being melodramatic, no one actually hides things under floorboards. Then I find the loose nails. I pry them up to uncover Catriona's most secret of hiding spots, containing a switchblade and a black pouch.

I take the pouch out, and dump the contents onto my bed. It will be the necklace. I am sure of that. The pouch jangled and had the weight of jewels, and here will be all her prizes.

It is not her prizes. It is the proceeds from her prizes. Money. That's what lies scattered across my bed. A fistful of coins that adds up to twelve pounds.

Yesterday, Gray gave me a two-shilling coin. It must not be worth too much, because Davina scoffed at it, but it has to be enough to buy a few treats from the market. If I were to guess, I'd say that it'd be like handing over a twenty-dollar bill in modern times, at least as far as buying power is concerned.

If I stumbled over a twenty in the market, I'd grin and buy myself a treat or two, rather than stash it away as a true windfall. Of course, how I'd treat twenty bucks back home as Mallory Atkinson is a lot different from how I'd treat it here as Catriona Mitchell. I seem to recall that twenty shillings equals a pound, making this stash worth more than a hundred times what Gray handed over as pocket money.

Twelve pounds. A small fortune for a housemaid. And it must be what remains of Isla's locket and whatever else Catriona stole and pawned.

This might be her grand plan. Save up enough money to leave service. To go into business on her own. I'd respect that if she were doing something like selling flowers on her days off. But this is theft from people who do not deserve it, and I am furious.

I am furious and also helpless to do anything to fix it. This is what remains of Isla's most prized piece of jewelry, and no alchemical magic will turn these coins back into a silver locket.

Yesterday, I bounced back from my despair over not getting home. I've been underplaying that despair, telling myself I didn't actually expect "going to the same spot" would work. Also, it's not as if I'm trapped in a Victorian poorhouse.

Nan preached the power of positive thinking. Mom taught me that her mother's words are wonderful advice that will only take you so far before you need to acknowledge that something *is* wrong and deal with it. I will be honest then. The disappointment of not getting home had crushed me, and I'd been pleased with myself for indulging in only a single evening of despair before brushing myself off and moving on. Yet this morning, it is my mother's teachings that prove their truth, as I am forced to realize how much of my "chin up and carry on" was self-delusion fueled by a temporary spurt of willpower.

That willpower and that delusion evaporated when I found the pouch of money and lost my chance to make things right with Isla. She is onto me, and she will not drop this as easily as McCreadie did.

It doesn't matter if this house belongs to Gray. It's Isla's childhood home, and only her sex kept her from inheriting it, and my gut tells me that Gray considers it as much hers at his. She is mistress of this manor, and she can kick my ass to the curb as easily as he can. Easier, I bet. The household is her domain, freeing Gray to run the family business and pursue his studies.

In short, without that locket, I am in deep shit, and as the morning progresses, I feel the weight of it. Every bit of traction I've gained has been ripped away. And here is the proof that I haven't truly recovered from the disappointment of not crossing over: the concession that my despair has little to do with the locket situation and everything to do with feeling powerless in this world. The locket issue only brings that into sharper focus.

The disappointment starts from the moment I take Gray his tray, and he barely acknowledges my presence. I'd hoped he'd have work for me. Real work. I planned to ask, but he's so wrapped up in writing that I can only drop off the tray and retreat.

I don't get coffee that morning. I ask, as sweetly as possible, and Mrs. Wallace snaps that I'm getting above myself. I take tea . . . and the cup slips from my hands, and of course she sees that as me intentionally breaking it because I didn't get coffee.

As for Isla, she leaves right after breakfast, which Alice serves her. I don't get a chance to say hello or even gauge her mood. She could have said good morning to me if she wanted—the town house is hardly a fifty-room mansion—but she did not. That is telling.

I'm supposed to clean Gray's bedroom as soon as he leaves for work. That day, though, it is past ten, and his door remains closed. I slip in to find him at his desk, fingers tapping the top. He's obviously deep in thought, and I should take his tray and leave, but I feel like when I was a kid and my parents' moods were off, and I just *had* to know whether it was because of something I'd done.

"May I bring you fresh coffee, sir? This has gone cold."

He waves me off, and I pick up the untouched tray. I'm about to leave when he says, "Is there any jam?"

"Jam, sir?"

"Jam and bread. Tea with honey. I'm not focusing as well as I like, and that is usually the problem."

"Low blood sugar. That'll do it."

He frowns over, and I realize my words won't make sense to him. What catches his ear, I bet, is the word "blood."

I say, "I mean that I often find that if I do not eat in the morning, I cannot concentrate as well."

He seems to be half listening. I don't take offense, considering that's twice as much as he's listened to me so far today.

"I will bring bread with lots of jam and tea with lots of honey." I pause. "You do seem very busy, sir. If there's anything I could do? Note-taking perhaps?"

He shakes his head. "I will not pull you from your duties today, Catriona."

Pull away. Please.

The words are on the tip of my tongue. At first, I hold them back because the phrasing is too modern, but that pause gives me time to realize the truth of what he's saying. If I don't do my chores, who does? Mrs. Wallace? Alice? To ask for case work means pushing my maid duties onto the shoulders of others.

Damned ethical dilemmas.

Let's try another angle.

"I finished the book you allowed me to read, sir. Thank you very much for that."

"Oh?" That catches his attention. "Already?"

"It was very informative. Did you notice Song Ci mentions looking under fingernails for signs of bamboo splints, indicating torture? I have marked the page if you would like to show it to Detective McCreadie. In the meantime, perhaps there is another book I could read on forensic science?"

"You are welcome to any in the library, Catriona."

Not quite what I was hoping for, but he really *is* distracted by whatever he's doing, and the fact that he hasn't shooed me out should prove that Isla hasn't shared her suspicions.

"Thank you, sir. Again, if there's anything I can do, I will ensure I still complete my chores and do not force anyone else to perform them."

He hesitates, and my breath catches.

He runs his hand over his chin, dark with stubble. "I do not suppose you have remembered how to shave."

As my hopes plummet, my brain spins. Could I manage it? That would make him happy and give us time to talk, give me time to prove I'm genuinely interested in his studies and would make an excellent replacement for James the lost assistant.

Except I have no idea how to use a straight razor and might slit his throat.

Damned ethical dilemmas.

He rubs at his stubble, and I can't help noticing the strong line of his jaw, the curve of his lips, his ink-dappled fingers.

The letter. I have done so well forgetting that damned letter, and I really don't need it creeping back now.

Yes, Gray's a good-looking guy. Yes, he's an interesting guy. But he's my boss and hell, no. Scrub that letter from my brain, please.

"Catriona?"

I wrench my gaze away and manage a shallow curtsy. "Apologies, sir. I was thinking of how much I hate to refuse such a simple request, but I do fear that if I wield a razor, we may end up with an unexpected display of blood splatter to study."

His laugh is so unexpected that I jump a little.

"I understand," he says. "If you do recall how to use a razor, though, I would appreciate it. While I have no interest in expanding the household, that is the one downfall to a lack of male indoor staff."

"I'll try to recall the skill, sir."

"Please do. Oh, and speaking of male staff, Simon is gathering the day's papers for me. Please bring them to me immediately. I am most interested in what the press has to say regarding our killer."

Our killer? That's promising.

"Might I read them after you, sir? I am also interested."

"Of course," he says, and he returns to contemplating the mysteries of the blank wall before I'm even out the door.

FIFTEEN

I'm dusting in the drawing room when boots clomp in the hall. I've come to dread that sound, because it means someone just came in from outdoors, and they're tracking mud across my clean floors. I can't just say, "Screw it, I already washed those." Nope, I need to grab a bucket and re-mop before Mrs. Wallace spots dirt.

All of this could be solved if they'd take off their damned boots or shoes at the door, like a proper Canadian. I remember the first time we visited American friends, and I realized they don't even switch to indoor shoes. What kind of heathens traipse through the house in the same shoes they just wore outside, through mud and dog dirt and God knows what else?

At least I must credit the average non-Canadian with having the sense to remove obviously dirty footwear. Not so in Victorian Scotland, where guys walk in from tromping along a horseshit-laden road and track it all on my clean floors. Why? Because I'm here. I exist to clean it up.

"So they were not telling tales," a male voice says in a thick country brogue. "You really did rise from the dead."

I turn to see a young man. He's in his late teens, with a mop of dark brown hair, sharp features, and a grin that lights up blue-gray eyes.

"Not even going to say hello, Cat?" he asks. "I suppose it takes more than a bump on the head to forget you're angry with me."

That's when I notice the stack of newspapers in his hand.

"Simon," I say, and try not to add a question mark.

"Well, I ought to be glad you didn't forget my name." He walks into the drawing room and slaps the stack of papers on a side table. "These are for Dr. Gray. See he gets them as quick as you can. And . . ." He casts a glance around and then lowers his voice. "I know you are displeased with me, Cat, and I wish it were otherwise. I miss your conversation."

His grin sparks, and I try not to inch back. *Dear lord, Catriona, how many boys were you dangling on your bonnet strings?*

Simon sobers. "Yet as much as I miss you, Cat, I won't be changing my mind. Colin Findlay is a good man, and I'll not have you doing him wrong for a bit o' fun and a few bob."

"Police Constable Findlay?"

His brows rise. "You know another?"

"No, just . . ." I clear my throat. "Remind me why we are at odds over Constable Findlay."

He arches one brow, and I tap my temple. "My memory, remember?"

"We are 'at odds' as you put it because the poor man is besotted, and you bat your eyes at him, so he'll court you with pretty trinkets and baubles that you sell as quick as you can. It isn't right."

"Would it be more right if I gave him something in return for those trinkets and baubles?"

Simon's face turns serious again as he meets my eye. "In truth, it would, Cat. At least then it would be an honest exchange. 'Tis a poor trick to play on a man who does not deserve it, and I'll not change my mind on that. If you want to come visit me in the stables, you cannot be leading him on anymore."

I stop myself before saying I'm no longer leading Findlay on. True, but nor do I want to be "visiting Simon in the stables."

Then I rewind our conversation and pause. "You said I sell whatever gifts he gives me."

"Do not pretend otherwise, Cat. You bragged about it a fortnight ago."

"Yes, but where do I sell them?"

He frowns. "At a pawnshop."

"Do you know which one? Have I ever said?"

"No, why—?" He gives a short laugh. "Ah, having lost some of your memories, you forget where to pawn your pretties. I cannot help you there."

"Cannot? Or will not?"

"Both." He slaps the stack of papers. "Take these up to Dr. Gray and leave poor Findlay be."

I nod, and he shakes his head and tromps out, leaving dirt in his wake.

Okay, so I'm starting to get a picture of Catriona's love life.

She seems to be casually involved with Simon. I suspect their relationship was more chaste than the twenty-first-century version of "friends with benefits." Oh, I'm sure there was plenty of sex happening between unmarried teens. But I'm also sure we predate reliable birth control, and Simon's smiles felt more flirtatious than lascivious.

Meanwhile, she's been flirting with Constable Findlay, who's showering her with gifts when she has no intention of doing more than batting her eyelashes at him. Or does she? Could Catriona have had plans that she didn't share with Simon? Did she intend to win the young officer as a husband? That would be a step up, wouldn't it?

From the way McCreadie dresses, detectives make a decent wage. Not exorbitant. He's unmarried with no obvious dependents, and so he can afford to spend a little extra on his tailoring bill, in the same way I could afford a condo—albeit a tiny one—in Canada's most expensive city.

Catriona accepts Findlay's wooing gifts and accepts his wooing, while playing the shy maiden who won't do more than hold his hand before the wedding day. She certainly isn't going to tell Simon that. They might be casual, but no guy wants to hear that a girl is only with him while she makes a play for someone else.

What happened between Catriona and Findlay? Something for sure, considering the cold shoulder he's giving her. Did she tell him to put a ring on it, and he backed off, not being in the market for a wife? Or did he make a pass that she rebuffed?

None of this should matter. I'm not Catriona, and I have no interest in either young man, both being roughly two-thirds my age. It's like watching a soap-opera romance. Except the friend-with-benefits is a coworker and the suitor-without-benefits is McCreadie's assistant, which means I can't avoid either guy. I'll need to keep both at arm's length, which shouldn't be difficult, considering they're both unhappy with Miss Catriona.

I resist the urge to read the papers before I run them upstairs to Gray. There are several newspapers plus a few single flyers and pamphlets that I mistake for advertising until I see they're about Archie Evans's murder. Huh. I skim one "flyer" as I climb the stairs. It's a large single sheet that details the crime from the report of "an intimate observer." According to the sheet, Evans had been brutally murdered, his limbs "gruesomely fashioned" into a bird's wings and limbs in a "manner this writer dares not describe, so great the horror." Uh, they'd been *tied* in place.

The story has been poorly printed on cheap paper. There's a byline, though, one that proclaims the author "Edinburgh's Foremost Reporter of Criminal Activities." The other sheet is a similarly fictionalized account of the murder. It's as if I said to the writers, "Hey, some guy was murdered and made to look like a bird," and their imaginations filled in the rest. Imaginations that produced a picture far bloodier and more lurid than the actual murder.

I'm reading through the second account when Gray's door opens. I'm standing there, sheet in one hand, the other raised for a knock that I have yet to give.

"I believe those are mine," Gray says.

"Uh, yes. Apologies, sir."

He waves me inside. "Put them on my desk, please, Catriona. You may keep that one and finish reading it, if you like. I presume you *would* like that?"

His lips twitch in a way that rankles a little. It's kind but indulgent, too, as if I'm a child. Then I catch a glimpse of myself in his mirror and see a teenager who looks like a milkmaid, all rosy-pink cheeks and honey-blond curls and cream-fed curves.

In this world, there are two options for a man of thirty with a nineteen-year-old female assistant. Either I'm a delectable morsel, his for the taking, or I'm a clever girl he's encouraging to explore higher educational interests. Gray is thankfully embracing option two. He's treating me like a child, because to him, that's what I am.

I half curtsy. "That is most kind, sir. I'll read it and be out of your way."

He waves a distracted hand at a chair. "There are quite enough papers here to keep us from quarreling over them. I would appreciate your thoughts as you read."

I straighten a little at that. "Thank you, sir."

"I daresay you shall bring a very different lens to the reading. One untainted by expertise in these matters."

I bite my tongue. Bite it so damned hard. Instead, I lower my lashes. "Of course, sir. I am flattered that you think a housemaid could have anything to add."

"Everyone has something to add, Catriona. Do not discount yourself like that. With enough learning, you could be a proper little detective. You seem to have some talent for it."

"So kind of you to say so, sir."

Reading those damn papers is an exercise in restraint. In restraining myself from dissecting the accounts of the crime and giving a commentary that will leave Gray gaping.

I am an observer in this world. I cannot risk raising the suspicions of the one person who does not suspect me of anything untoward. I can make the occasional observation—such as noting that Evans had been tortured—but I can't overdo it.

In truth, as much as I want to show off, I'm not sure I could. There's nothing in these accounts we don't already know. Well, nothing of truth. Even the newspapers are rife with fabrications. One journalist, who claims to have known Evans personally, says he was an "unusually handsome young man, with curly hair and the smooth face of an angel." The guy on Gray's examination table had been bearded, with straight hair.

"They're making it up," I say. "Even the newspapers."

"Of course."

"But why? There was a press conference. I hardly saw anyone there."

Gray shrugs, his eyes still scanning an article. "Why bother attending that when they can invent something more entertaining? They are wordsmiths, crafting a narrative to suit their audience."

"And these?" I lift one of the single pages. "These are pure fiction."

"Yes, and probably written by the newspapermen under a *nom de plume*. They could not get away with *that* level of insinuation and lurid detail in the regular press."

He glances over his newspaper at me. "I know broadsides are going out of fashion, but I am surprised you have never read one."

"Why would *anyone* read them?"

"Presumably for the reason they are written. Entertainment. Crime is a profitable business. My sister has, more than once, threatened to turn my cases into novels to make her fortune. I think she was joking, but I am not actually sure."

I flip through the pile of newspapers, along with the two "broadsides" plus two pamphlets that go into slightly more—equally fictional—detail. "The case is getting a lot of attention."

He tilts his head. "I presume you speak in jest."

"This isn't a lot?"

He gives a low laugh and then rubs away his smile. "I do not mean to mock. You obviously fail to share the public's fascination with murder, and so this might seem like a great deal of attention. It is the opposite, in fact."

"Why? It's a strikingly singular murder."

"Too singular, and in entirely the wrong way."

"Explain." I cough. "I mean, please explain your thinking, sir, if you would."

"It is singular in its staging. As an intellectual exercise, poor Evans's death is fascinating. What person conceives of such a thing? I am no alienist, but even I must wonder at such a mind. It is almost, dare I say, artistic."

"The killer has a vision. Or else he is plagued by inner demons, and this is his way of expressing it. A compulsion."

Gray's eyes light up, and I feel like a student giving a perfect answer. "Quite right. That makes the murder and the killer remarkably interesting to me, and apparently also to you. However, to the average citizen, Evans's murder lacks passion. It is a cerebral killing, and therefore quite dull. Nary a severed limb to be found. They're bloodless crimes, and as such . . ."

I feign a yawn, and that has his face lighting up in a way that makes my heart stutter.

Gray leans forward, warming to his subject. "They are *boring*. That is why we have this." He lifts one of the broadsides. "Writers doing their best to work with what little they have."

"What are people looking for?" I ask. "Blood and gore?"

"That is the question, Catriona, and one you ought to discuss with my sister, who is fascinated by which crimes do—or do not—catch the public's attention. As soon as one thinks one has the answer, there is an exception.

Blood and gore, as you put it, certainly sells papers and broadsides. Yet you will also find such cases knocked clean off the front page by a man falling from a ladder and dying of internal injuries."

"Because there's more *story* to the man on the ladder? He was about to marry or have his first child or such?"

"Pathos, yes, that certainly plays a role. Violent and pathetic deaths. An innocent babe, murdered alongside her sweet mother. A promising young man, his head bashed, bits of brain on the ceiling. An elderly woman, throat slit as she awaits the first visit from her great-grandchild. Yet again, Isla could show examples of the most tragic situations that barely rippled the public's attention. Also, one must account for competing events. I was following one particularly fascinating case myself four years ago, when it disappeared from the press, swallowed by a foreign murder." He waits, as if to see whether I'll figure it out. "The shooting of an American president."

"Lincoln?"

His lips twitch. "You truly do not follow the news, do you? Yes, the assassination of Abraham Lincoln. That month, the most horrific deaths would not have made the front page. Then there is the issue of urbanization—"

He cuts himself short and pulls back with the faintest smile. "I will spare you that particular lecture."

"No, please. Go on." I meet his gaze. "I *am* interested."

"Briefly, or we shall be here all day. While murder is hardly a new invention, it became far more commonplace in the city, where one might hope to escape justice in the way one could not in the country."

"Where everyone knows everyone else's business."

"Yes. In the city, we are more anonymous. Some might also say that population density breeds apathy. Too many people to care about. When you look back at murder fifty years ago, each one was a public sensation. The appetite for details was insatiable. People could eat for months telling the story of how they once dined with the killer in a public house. If the victim died in a barn, that barn could be dismantled and sold for a king's ransom, everyone wanting a piece. But as cities grew and murders multiplied . . ."

"People became jaded. They need stories that strike an emotional chord, whether it be horror or sympathy. The murder of Archie Evans is passionless and bloodless. It is getting some attention, because it is odd, but it will not inspire penny dreadfuls."

He sets down his paper. "There is nothing in these. I feared as much, but I wished to be thorough. My task—*our* task—is to find clues that will help Detective McCreadie and, if I am fortunate, some of those clues will also prove useful for my studies." He checks his pocket watch. "Speaking of Hugh, he is due for lunch to discuss the case, and if you'd be so kind as to serve the meal, you may join us and listen in."

And as a special treat, little Catriona, you may join us after you've waited on us hand and foot.

Yes, once again, my back went up at that, but Gray isn't a senior officer expecting a female detective to serve the coffee and doughnuts at a staff meeting. He's a guy expecting his employee to do her job, while he also encourages her outside interests.

I've been part of only a few sting operations, and I find myself wishing I'd had more undercover experience to slide into this headspace. I *am* Catriona. I *am* a housemaid. I was hired to serve Gray's meals, and I'm damn lucky he's letting me join their lunchtime conversation.

He doesn't make me sit in the corner with my servant's lunch either. I am given a seat at the table and expected to fully share in their more sumptuous meal. I don't miss Alice's shocked face when she pops her head in, and I hate to even *think* what Mrs. Wallace will say.

As for the lunch conversation, while Gray might say his only interest in the case is forensic, that's obviously not true. Nor does McCreadie treat him like a crime-scene tech. Lacking a detective partner, McCreadie bounces ideas and theories off his old friend.

I also get the impression Gray isn't the only one who helps. When McCreadie walks in to lunch, his first question is "Where's Isla?," and when Gray says she is away, McCreadie can't hide his disappointment.

The two men discuss the case. Isla has analyzed the water and believes it is from a tap. It's definitely fresh water rather than salt, and the lack of foreign particles suggests it's not from a body of standing water, like a puddle. They still aren't sure what that means—my waterboarding hypothesis has obviously been dismissed.

Next McCreadie brings Gray up to speed on the day's work. They've canvassed people living near the park where Evans was found. One person reported seeing a masked man in a black cape. Then there's the guy who insists he saw a huge raven land and grow to human form.

"The young men Evans was living with still refuse to speak to me," McCreadie says. "I am, apparently, the enemy." He rolls his eyes. "It's a household of young radicals, all convinced the police only exist to deprive them of their rights."

"Kids these days," I mutter, too low for them to make out the words, but McCreadie glances over at the sound of my voice. "You agree with them, Catriona?"

"I agree that some people have sound reasons to fear the police, not only those who engage in criminal activity, but those who have been unjustly persecuted in the past. There are bullies in any organization, but police do have the ability to ruin a life, and some do."

"Perhaps, but to tarnish me with that brush is unwarranted."

I shrug. "Uncomfortable more than unwarranted. They don't know you, but you don't know their situation and their experiences with the law. If they are radicals, those experiences have likely been negative. Police are the enemy of protesters because *they* are often seen as enemy *by* police."

"It sounds as if you have some experience with this."

"I have never been what you would call a radical. I know some who are, though. Getting them to speak to you is going to take time you can ill afford when you only wish to question them. I would suggest you send in someone they will speak to. Perhaps me."

Gray frowns. "Why would they speak to you?" He pauses. "Ah, yes. You alluded to knowing radicals."

McCreadie gives him a look. "They will speak to her because she's a fetching young lady and they are a household of rowdy young men. That would be obvious to anyone but you, Duncan."

"No," Gray says coolly. "I did not mention it because it might suggest we expect her to employ her feminine charms."

"I'm fine with flirting," I say. "Help me come up with a cover story and tell me what you want to know."

SIXTEEN

That afternoon, I'm taking on my first Victorian undercover mission. I'm shocked by how readily McCreadie agreed. Yet more proof that policing is very different in this world. He didn't need to clear it with a supervisor. He doesn't need me to sign a waiver. He barely even hesitated when I suggested it.

He's putting a lot of trust in a layperson. He can't even mike me to get a recording of the interview for court. Of course, I must remember that Scotland has only had an established police force for about fifty years. This is still the Wild West of policing, and I should be impressed they're as far along as they are, with "criminal officers" and homicide investigations.

Gray doesn't try to stop me either. He only makes sure I'm comfortable with the situation. He lets me know I can back out at any time and that if it goes wrong, no one will hold it against me. He does, however, insist on accompanying us, though I suspect at least part of that is just for the excuse to escape his armchair-investigator role and get into the field.

McCreadie will join us in the Old Town with Constable Findlay. Gray needs to attend to a client first, and by the time he's finished, we're running late, so he decides to take the coach.

As I climb in, I look around the interior. It's all black, down to the painted metal trim.

"Is this a hearse?" I say.

Gray gives me a look as he settles in on the seat opposite. "Do you see a place for a coffin, Catriona?"

"It could convert to one. Lay down a few boards to transport the dearly departed, and then flip up the seats for daily use."

"Somehow I do not think my guests would appreciate traveling in anything used to convey the dead."

I shrug. "Wouldn't bother me."

"The smell might."

I have to laugh at that. True enough if bodies aren't being embalmed yet.

He settles into his seat. "As for the coach, yes, you will have noticed it is rather austere. It's used in funeral processions. The hearse—which I am certain you've seen—has glass sides to display the coffin. This one is used for the chief mourners, but it is expedient to also use it personally, as it is of a much higher quality than I'd otherwise purchase."

I watch out the window as we go, and as much as I enjoy a pleasant walk, I'm glad to be in the coach today. Scotland has a reputation for overcast, drizzly weather, but in Edinburgh you get the wind thrown in for free, and today it's wicked, driving that drizzle in my face and making me feel like I'm back in Vancouver in November. I try not to think of what it's like at home right now—sunny and warm, the beaches starting to fill. Still, while I might not love Edinburgh's weather, the city itself makes up for it, with its gorgeously vibrant gardens and green spaces alongside soot-stained medieval buildings.

When we arrive in the proper neighborhood, McCreadie and Gray decide they're going to hole up in a pub, with a nice hot toddy. And who will escort me closer to the radicals' lair? That would be Constable Findlay, the guy who's been doing his best to pretend I don't exist.

Wonderful.

We leave Gray and McCreadie at their toasty-warm pub, and we continue on foot to Evans's lodgings. Simon has taken the coach home—I can't exactly pull up to the rooming house in a gleaming black coach. We must walk, and walk in silence it seems. I get two blocks before I turn to Findlay. Time to get this over with.

"I know I have done something to upset you," I say. "The blow to my head means that I do not remember what it is. I must ask you to tell me so I might apologize."

"I do not wish to discuss it."

He pulls his cap down over his ears and marches on against the wind. He's in his civvies, and without his uniform, he looks less like a scrubbed-cheek cadet and more like a regular guy—a kid even, no older than Catriona herself.

I should drop this. The last thing I want is this young man trying to rekindle "our" relationship. Yet if I'm going to help Gray with the case, then I need to calm these waters with Findlay.

"Whatever it is, please know that I am sorry for what I have done. I was not a good person, and it took a brush with death for me to realize that. I have hurt people, including you, and I am sorry."

He only grunts.

"I just wish to say—"

"You aren't going to let this drop, are you? Fine. I am not *hurt*, Catriona. I am disappointed, that is all. Detective McCreadie tried to warn me about your past, and I told him he was mistaken."

"And he was not," I say softly.

"There. We have said all we need to say on the matter."

"I *am* sorry. Truly sorry."

"You made a fool of me," he snaps. "I could have lost my position. You know how hard I worked for it."

"You could have lost your position because . . ."

He hunkers down against the drizzles and picks up his pace. "I believed you when you said you were interested in my work. You only wanted information you could pass on to your friends."

Goddamn it, Catriona. Just when I think you couldn't stoop any lower, you need to prove me wrong, contrary wench that you are. So that's why she flirted with Findlay. Not for his trinkets. Not for the hope of a wedding band. For information she could sell.

Wait.

How angry *was* he?

Angry enough to ambush her in an alley?

I say, carefully, "I am sorry to push this. I truly have lost my memories. That attack . . ." I shiver. "It was nearly the end of me."

As I speak, I watch his face for even a flicker of guilt. Nothing passes behind his eyes except a spark of hard anger.

"Yes," he says. "It was. When I heard you had been hurt, I silently vowed that I would bring your attacker to justice myself. I started asking questions, poking about the Grassmarket, and what do I hear? How you were selling my information the very night you were attacked."

So Findlay didn't know about Catriona's betrayal until after the attack. No wonder he's so angry. He strode in, determined to bring her assailant to justice . . . only to discover his sweet maiden had betrayed him. That she had been in the *act* of betraying him when she was assaulted.

Catriona had been attacked while selling police information.

That's a solid clue. I know she was in a black-market pub. Now I know why.

"You have nothing to say to that, do you?" Findlay says.

"I—I am not certain how to respond, beyond apologizing with all sincerity. I have wronged many people including you. I am sorry." I meet his gaze. "Very, truly sorry."

He glances away and says abruptly, "Let's get this over with."

The address leads to a town house sandwiched into a row of them. Several have ROOM TO LET signs. This one has a sign in the window politely declaring it MRS. TROWBRIDGE'S ROOMING HOUSE FOR YOUNG GENTLE-MEN.

When McCreadie said Archie Evans lived in a house with other young men, I pictured the modern arrangement, where a bunch of guys rent a place together. Which is silly in Victorian times. If there isn't a woman in residence, they'll starve to death, dying in a bed that hasn't had its sheets changed in a year. Okay, yes, I'm sure there are self-sufficient Victorian bachelors, but I suspect far too many would be like Gray, setting the kitchen aflame when he tries to make coffee. Someone has always done that for them. The solution, naturally, is a boardinghouse, where the proprietress may bridge that inconvenient gap between leaving Mommy and snagging a wife.

I climb the steps and, before I knock, I open the box in my arms to reveal the meat pies within. Then I rap smartly and wait. When no one answers, I rap again.

There's a male shout, a period-appropriate version of "Someone answer the damned door!" Boots clomp, and the door flies open to reveal a young man a year or two younger than Catriona. He's dressed in rumpled clothing with no necktie, which in this world is like answering the door shirtless. He looks from me to the pies and back again. Then he smirks.

"Did someone order a tart?" he shouts into the house.

"Excuse me?" I say.

He blinks.

"Did you just call me a tart?" I say.

His mouth works, and his gaze flies to the pies. "I meant the pastries."

"Of course you did."

Another young man appears behind the first and slaps him on the shoulder. "Ignore this lout. He's already nipping the brandy. I'm Henry, by the way."

This young man wears a tie and looks moderately less rumpled. There's still a glitter in his eyes that I know well. He's seen an opening, positioning himself as my savior, and I'm supposed to swoon in appreciation.

"I heard the news about Archie," I say. "I wanted to say how sorry I am. May I step in? Presuming Mrs. Trowbridge is at home and would find it appropriate."

"She's here somewhere." Henry winks. "She tends to hide when we're home from classes."

He ushers me through a dreary hallway and waves toward an open doorway. Through it, half a dozen young men lounge about. Two are arm-wrestling while another two egg them on and share a bottle. A fifth is stretched out on the floor with a textbook, and the guy who answered the door has gone back to reading something that is definitely *not* a textbook, given the cover art of a very buxom lady in her underthings.

It's a Victorian frat house.

When I walk in, all six turn to look at me. All six mentally undress me, and the one reading the porn doesn't even bother to hide the cover. In fact, he lifts it to make sure I see it. Yep, definitely a frat house.

"Well, well, what have we here," says one of the drinkers, getting unsteadily to his feet. "Did Thomas say something about tarts? Please tell me your wares are for sale, miss. Cheap, I hope. I am a poor student after all."

Henry raises a hand. "None of that. The young woman is here to pay her respects. She has brought us pies."

I half curtsy. "I am so sorry to hear of Archie's passing. I know you are all in mourning, but I did wish to bring these pies."

I step farther into the room, arranging my features in the appropriate look of sorrow. "I cannot believe he is gone. And in such a grisly fashion."

One of the lounging boys snorts. "He was strangled."

"You do not think it terribly macabre? Staged to look like a bird?"

"Macabre?" A loud laugh from Thomas—the guy who'd answered the door. "Look at the big words coming from that pretty mouth. Where did you learn that one? On the back of a penny dreadful?"

"It *is* macabre," says the one who is actually studying. "She chooses her words well. I fear we are dealing with a madman. I hear one escaped from the asylum."

I presume he's mocking me, but his face is somber, and two of his roommates nod.

"Perhaps," I say. "And yet . . ." I bite my lip. "I ought not to say this, but I am devilishly curious."

Thomas waggles his brows. "Devilishly curious? Are you now?"

I focus on the young man with the textbook. His ogle had been perfunctory, like an obligation he had to fulfill and thus got out of the way as quickly as possible.

"I have heard . . ." I begin.

They all lean in to listen.

My target shuts his textbook. "Heard what, miss?"

"The rumor is that poor Archie was tortured. It was not a random murder. His killer wanted something from him." I pause for effect. "Information."

There's an audible shift in the room, and a palpable one in the air. Thomas rises from his seat and steps toward me.

"Is that what you heard?" he says.

From his tone, I'm supposed to step back, to drop my gaze, to stammer that perhaps I am mistaken. Instead, I laser-focus on him, that shift in the air telling me I've stumbled into more than a Victorian frat house. McCreadie did call them radicals, even if I've seen no sign of that.

"That is the rumor," I say. "Though I can't imagine what anyone would want from poor Archie. I do know he wrote about local crime for *The Edinburgh Evening Courant*. I can only guess some ruffian thought he knew too much and killed him for it."

The young men exchange a look.

"That must be it," Henry says smoothly. "We always told Archie he needed to be more careful in such a dangerous line of work. He had quite the habit of talking when he ought to hold his tongue."

I bet he did.

I gaze around the room, as if I have not only lost track of what he was saying but lost interest, too. Ideas, they are so difficult for my female brain.

As I search the room, I spot something near the settee. A crate filled with folded papers, like the crime pamphlets Simon brought for Gray. There's a hideously ugly embroidered pillow right next to the box, and that's what I pretend to focus on.

I wander over to the pillow and touch it, murmuring that it's such a pretty design. Meanwhile, I sneak a look at the pamphlets in that box. Then I blink, trying to hide my surprise. McCreadie called these boys radicals. He also said they hate the police, and so I presumed that meant left-leaning student activists. But what I see in this box is something all too familiar.

A month before I left for Edinburgh, I'd been working a hate-crime case, and I'd helped conduct a search on one of the suspect's apartments. On his hard drive, I found a massive trove of memes for redistribution. Indescribably ugly hate, the sort that if I showed it to some of my friends, they'd swear it wasn't real, that it belonged in another century because no one thought like that these days. What I see in that box is the Victorian equivalent. Pamphlets screaming about the "foreign menace invading proud Scottish lands."

I jerk my head up before anyone notices where my attention had gone, and I turn toward the young men. My expression is blank. That's a skill I learned on my first case dealing with white supremacists. Don't let them see how disgusted you are, not unless it'll serve your purpose. It won't here.

I adjust my grip on the pie box. "Yes, I fear poor Archie did always talk too much, and it has doubtless been the death of him. I wonder, though—"

A string of curses has me turning to see Thomas peering out the front window. "There's a police constable out there."

"What?" Henry strides over to look. He adds to the curses. "Does he think we will not recognize him without his uniform? It's a wonder we didn't smell the stench from here."

I stroll over until I can see Findlay across the street. Yes, he's not in uniform, but his bearing gives him away, spine ramrod straight, gaze scanning the street as if he's on patrol.

"That lad is a police constable?" I say. "He looks terribly young."

Thomas wheels, advancing on me so fast that I do step back this time. "You brought him here."

"Wh-what?"

"We should have seen it straightaway. Just look at her yellow hair." He grabs a lock before I can get out of reach. "She's German. Maybe Russian." Thomas sneers. "Russian, I wager."

"Do I sound Russian?"

I see the slap coming. His expression telegraphs it, but my brain still doesn't react fast enough. It would in the modern day, but this is Victorian times, and I am a fair maiden on a condolence call. Surely, he will not strike me.

He does exactly that. Or he tries, because while I may inwardly curse my delay, I still manage to duck the slap. He doesn't expect *that,* and his face goes bright red, and when he spins on me, it's not a mere slap he telegraphs. It's a right hook.

With no room to escape, I block instead, my arm flying up to stop his, the pies falling to the floor as someone gasps. I think they're gasping because this guy is attacking me. Or maybe even because I dropped the damn pies. But then I see faces turned my way, the shock on them, and I catch a glimpse of myself reflected in a glass cabinet door, and I see *me.* Mallory. Oh, it's Catriona's body, but the expression is my own, a cold rage that stuns everyone except the guy attacking me.

Thomas sees that look, and he sees me blocking his blow, and he tries to stomach punch me. I almost make the mistake of kicking him away. A mistake because I'm wearing four layers of skirts. My knee rises, and it registers the confining fabric just in time. I grab and twist his arm instead, spinning him around. Then I shove him. He smacks into a dainty side table, toppling it with a crash.

A door flies open, and a white-haired woman appears. While Henry might have made a snide crack about Mrs. Trowbridge "hiding," when she barrels through that door, Thomas scrambles up, brushing off his shirtfront.

I rush toward her, my eyes wide with feigned terror. She puts up a hand to stop me and then sets her hands on her hips.

"What's this all about, lass?"

"I-I-I pushed him into the table, ma'am. I am so terribly sorry. I came to pay my respects for poor Archie. This young man accused me of being a foreigner and tried to slap me, and I dropped the pies, and then he tried to hit me again, so I pushed him."

"Foreigner?" she says, as if this is the most important part of my recitation. She glares at Thomas. "Are you daft? How does this poor lass look like a *foreigner*?"

His mouth works, nothing coming out.

"Even if she were—which she is not—there is no call to slap her. I won't have that nonsense in my house. You will apologize, and you will pay her for the pies."

"Pay her?" he squeaks.

"Apologize and pay her *double* for the pies, or you can pack your bags and go. The lass came to pay her respects, which is more than any of you have done. Poor Archie has been murdered, and you carry on as if nothing happened. When the school term is done, I want the lot of you gone."

There's satisfaction in her voice, as if she's wanted them gone for a while and is happy for an excuse. They haven't seemed too torn up over Evans, and her words prove they aren't. Together with Thomas's comments about Evans not knowing when to keep his mouth shut, I have a reasonable theory about why Evans was tortured. Someone identified him as the weak link in this group, the one most likely to talk.

I'm not getting anything else from Evans's roommates. Mrs. Trowbridge might be another matter. For now, she's a potential asset to stick in my back pocket.

Thomas's apology is half-assed. He does pay, though, and I try to give the coins to Mrs. Trowbridge for the table. That wins me brownie points I can use later, as her gaze softens and she pats my hand and tells me I'm a good girl but no, the young lads will pay for the table.

By the time she escorts me to the door, Findlay has made himself scarce. I thank Mrs. Trowbridge and head out into the street to go find him.

SEVENTEEN

For my efforts, I am rewarded with a piping-hot drink. Not a hot toddy, sadly. Okay, I don't actually know what's in a hot toddy, but it always sounds delightful. Catriona doesn't get that. She doesn't even get a toasty little pub to warm her bones. She gets a formal tearoom, which is supposed to be a treat, but damn it, I want my boozy drink and roaring fire.

Also, may I point out that the person who most enjoys my treat is the one who suggests it? Gray is practically vibrating as he surveys the pastries in the window. Ignoring the tiny sandwiches and currant-studded scones on our tray, he goes straight for his cakes and tarts and then starts eyeing everyone else's.

Findlay hands his over quickly, as if Gray's sidelong look is an order from on high. McCreadie sighs and gives him one of his tarts. I pretend not to notice Gray eyeing the petits fours that McCreadie bought me separately in appreciation of my "fine efforts." Those are mine, damn it, and I'm eating every crumb if I need to choke them down.

As for the investigation, it seems when McCreadie called the young men radicals, it wasn't because he misunderstood the nature of their campaign. To him, a radical is anyone trying to cause trouble, for both worthy and despicable causes. The positive ones fight for things like sanitation. The negative ones fight against things like immigration.

"I fully support immigration," Findlay says, his first words since we sat down. "It broadens and strengthens our country."

"I agree that it does," Gray murmurs. "Though I have no idea why you are looking at me as you say that."

The poor young man's gaze drops. "I—I didn't mean—That is to say, if I implied anything, it was not intended as an insult. You are a man of means, both educated and respected."

"Best quit while you can, lad," McCreadie says. "Dr. Gray is as Scottish as I am. He was born here."

"Whatever these young men believe," I say, "the important thing is whether it is connected to the murder."

"How could it not be?" McCreadie says. "If the young man was tortured—and I'm beginning to believe Duncan was right about that—then it must be connected to the murder. That is the information he had. Something to do with these radicals."

"Does that explain the bird staging, though?" Gray says. "Are we to presume it is what detective novels call a false clue? Something to distract us from the killer's true intent?"

"Stool pigeon," Findlay murmurs.

McCreadie looks up, raised teacup in hand. Gray glances over.

Findlay lowers his gaze again. "I-I could be mistaken, sir, but I thought perhaps the pigeon could signify a stool pigeon. An informer."

McCreadie smiles. "That is brilliant, my boy. *Excellent* insight."

"Thank you, sir."

Gray nods. "Hugh is right. That is an excellent theory. If that were the case . . ."

The discussion continues. I cut one of my petits fours in two and pass half to Gray, who lights up so much I have to smile. Then I settle in to join the conversation, feeling happy and at home for the first time since I arrived.

I spend the rest of the day catching up on my chores, working straight through dinner and into the evening. Alice tries to help me refill the coal. I tell her no. Mrs. Wallace says the silver doesn't need to be polished yet. I insisted on doing it. This is my job, and I will show I can do it *while* helping Dr. Gray, at least until I've proven myself enough for Isla to decide her brother needs me more than Mrs. Wallace does.

What really drives me that evening is Isla herself. Oh, she isn't watching me. Isn't judging me. She's not even home, and that's the problem. She's been gone all day, and I sense trouble. Mrs. Wallace expected her back for dinner, and Isla sent a note that she was dining out, which seemed to surprise Mrs. Wallace. When the door opens after eight, I tense, every muscle held tight as I will Isla to continue on upstairs for the night.

Instead, her footsteps tap into the dining room, where I'm polishing the silver. "Catriona?"

I turn to see her in the doorway.

"I'd like to speak with you in the library, please," she says. "You may put away your polishing cloth. You are done for the evening."

I reluctantly return the cloth to its place and try not to trudge into the library like a prisoner awaiting sentencing.

"Close the door, please, Catriona."

I do, and when I turn, I find her seated behind the desk, the huge wooden barrier between us.

I eye an overstuffed armchair that I've dreamed of curling up in with a book. I look at it now, tear my gaze away, and take a hard-backed chair near the desk.

"Have you had any luck locating my locket, Catriona?"

Inwardly, I wince. Outwardly, I look as mournful as I can. "No, ma'am. I have not, but I have scarce had time to search. I was thinking it may have fallen—"

"Let us abandon the charade where we both pretend to have no idea what happened to my locket. Where we pretend you have been a saint since Detective McCreadie brought you to me. I did not expect sainthood, Catriona. I fancy myself more worldly-wise than the charitable matron who gives a ha'penny to a beggar child and is shocked to find her pockets picked. My birth placed me three rungs up from you on the ladder of life. I am reaching down to give you the boost denied by fate. That is all."

She folds her hands on the desk. "I did not expect you to immediately abandon your old ways. It was half a year before Alice stopped picking the pockets of our guests. I did not scold her. I simply gave her the support she required to finally accept that her life here was secure, that she would not soon need those pennies to survive."

Isla rubs a hand over her face. "Now I sound exactly like those I seek to rise above, the matron so smug about her goodness and charity. I am tired, Catriona, and I am frustrated, and I am trying to explain something that you already ought to know, because you are not a ten-year-old child. I know you have stolen from me. I know Mrs. Wallace has caught you and not told me. Little goes on in this house of which I am not aware. My point is that I know you stole my locket, and I will no longer dance around the accusation. You have it, and I want it back. It is not like the pennies Alice stole, easily replaced. Return it, and we shall speak no more on the matter."

"I . . ." I take a deep breath. "I do not doubt that I stole it, ma'am, and I have upturned my room searching for it. I *do* hope to find it. Only I cannot remember that I took it and where I put it."

"On account of your head."

"Yes, ma'am. My memory is worse than I have been letting on for fear of losing my position, but I do not feel right hiding it from you."

"Your memory is damaged, and yet you clearly remember how to speak, even better than before. Your vocabulary is much expanded, your diction is higher, and you have suddenly remembered your ability to read and write. It is almost as if that blow to the head *improved* your memory rather than damaging it."

"I realize that may seem odd," I say, "but I suspect it's not that I've suddenly remembered manners or vocabulary. Rather I have forgotten that I am supposed to be playing a role. Clearly my life before this was such that I learned to hide my upbringing and education for fear of seeming to act above my station."

"Which you continued with me, lest I think you were putting on airs knowing how to read and write."

"Er . . ." I remember saying something like this to Gray, and his obvious confusion. That makes much more sense now that I've met Isla. Also now that I've realized that when Alice disappears for half the afternoon, she's doing lesson work. I've seen Mrs. Wallace reading, and I suspect Simon reads, too.

"I have long suspected you may have lied about your ability to read and write, Catriona. This is Scotland, after all. Your excuse always seemed exactly that."

Okay, so maybe it's not just this household where a servant would know how to read and write. Was Catriona truly an exception? Or did she lie?

I clear my throat. "I no longer remember why I chose to hide it. I must have thought there was some advantage to pretending. As Dr. Gray has pointed out, my handwriting is atrocious, and if you asked me to pen letters for you, as a lady's maid might do . . ." I trail off, realizing my excuse is getting even more ridiculous by the word.

"I do not know my reasoning," I say finally.

"You only know that you barely remember your old self and feel like an entirely different person, because of the injury to your head."

"Yes. That is it exactly."

She folds her hands on the desk. "Do you know where I have been today, Catriona? Consulting with experts in the field of neurological science. My brother may be the medical doctor, but the brain does not interest him. Well, not unless it is splattered around a dead body. He has doubtless read some journal article on personality changes due to brain trauma, and so he has decided that explains your situation because it is a convenient solution."

She taps an ornate wooden box. "This is what my brother likes to do with inconvenient and inconsequential problems. Box them up and shove them aside so that he may focus on the meaningful ones. His maid seems different? That is odd, but she is still filling his coffee cup and cleaning his house, so it is of no matter. She suddenly knows how to read and write? Also odd, but she can take notes now, and that is quite useful. Once, when we were children, I thought to play a delightful trick on him. Each day, I'd move something in his room at night. I planned to blame ghosts. Except my brother didn't mention the moved objects until I pulled his dresser into the middle of the room, and he banged into it in the night. While he had noticed items had moved, until they inconvenienced him, he presumed some logical cause and carried on. Hugh joked that even if Duncan had discovered it *was* ghosts, he would only have processed the information and carried on, so long as they did not cause him any trouble."

I say nothing. I know where this is going, and I'm not rushing it along. I'm too busy thinking of a way out of it.

"My brother believes brain trauma is the answer, and so he has neatly boxed that up and moved on. He sees no harm in our maid having a new personality, not if it is a far more pleasant one. But I see harm, Catriona, because I see deceit. You are up to something. I wanted to give you the benefit of the doubt, and so I consulted with experts, all of whom assured me that what I described is impossible. You hit your head. You did not suffer actual damage to your brain, not the type seen in personality changes. In short, you are lying."

I say nothing. I need to let that accusation sit, to give it room and weight before I reply. When it's had what it needs, I say, slowly, "Is it possible, ma'am, that if I am deceiving you, my motives are indeed harmless? If my brush with death has made me realize the—"

"—the error of your ways, and now you repent, and have become a changed person? Like Ebenezer Scrooge after facing his three Christmas ghosts?"

"I know you are mocking me, ma'am, but I do want to do better, and perhaps I would *like* to forget who I was. I am simply going about it the wrong way, blaming the injury."

"That's the truth then? That this is the new Catriona Mitchell? Not a guise pulled on to please?"

I frown at her.

She leans back in her chair. "Come now, Catriona. Do you think me that gullible? You were attacked in the Grassmarket, where you ought not to have been. I was on holiday, and you took advantage. You became involved in something that led to a near-fatal attack. When you woke, you feared my brother would send you on your way. If not, surely I would when I returned. Is it possible you had a change of heart? A near-death turning point? Yes, but you are presenting us with an almost unrecognizable Catriona. One who is well mannered yet not fawning. Confident yet not haughty. Intelligent. Hardworking. Respectful to Mrs. Wallace. Kind to Alice. And instead of your usual disgust at working for an undertaker, you are *greatly* interested in his studies, even reading a thirteenth-century translated work on it."

"I *did* read that. I *am* interested."

"This is not you, Catriona. Unless you are claiming to be proof of changelings. A human girl who has cast out her fairy doppelgänger and reclaimed her rightful place."

"I—"

"You have been here long enough to assess what type of young woman we'd most like in our home, and you have called upon your upbringing and education to become her."

"That is not the case, ma'am."

"No? This is the new Catriona, is it? Not a brain injury but a transformation?" She doesn't give me time to answer. Looks me in the eye and says, "Then return my locket by morning or you will pack your bags."

EIGHTEEN

I walked right into that one. Ran into it. Isla had seen through my "brain injury" story. Researched it and found it wanting, and in my haste to fix that, I trapped myself. There is only one way out of this mess.

Get the necklace.

Earlier today, I'd asked Simon for the name of Catriona's usual pawnbroker. He didn't know it, but Davina will. She offered me twenty minutes of her time for a "sovereign," which seems to be a pound. I'm getting the idea that's a lot of money, but Catriona has it. I can use it to buy information on Catriona's past and get the name of her pawnbroker. Then I'll pray the shop still has the locket and use more of Catriona's ill-gotten gains to buy it back.

I'm taking Isla at her word on this. Like her brother, she strikes me as a fair dealer. She says she'll drop the matter if I return her necklace, and I believe she will. That doesn't mean she'll accept that I've turned over a new leaf, but she will allow me the space I need to prove that.

When I first arrived, I'd been so sure of what I'd fallen into. I'd assessed at a glance, based on every Victorian-era movie I've ever seen, every book I've ever read. One sweep of my surroundings, and I formed a narrative. Bachelor doctor and his grief-stricken widowed sister, living together with a few servants. Nothing terribly interesting, and nothing I hadn't seen before, complete with shy preteen parlormaid and a gorgon of a housekeeper.

Except that the doctor is also an undertaker and a pioneer in foren-sic science, and the sister is also a scientist and—if I'm interpreting correctly—not all that grief-stricken. Oh, and the servants? Appar-ently, I'm not the only one with a criminal past. Again, if I'm interpret-ing right, that's Isla's thing. Not the do-gooder intent on "reforming" criminals. Not Lady Bountiful opening her doors to the destitute. She's providing a leg up the ladder, as she said, but also safety and sanctuary and the chance to start over, if that's what her employees want. My challenge is to prove that, after my near-death experience, Catriona is finally ready to embrace that second chance. And she'll start by return-ing the locket.

I change into a pale lilac dress and find my coat and walking boots. Catriona's switchblade goes into my pocket. Then I slip out the rear door into the darkness. The clouds have passed, and it's a clear night with stars overhead.

There's a garden here, one that I'd first dismissed as "just a garden" and later, realizing it didn't have any flowers or vegetables, decided was an herbal one. Now, knowing Isla is a chemist, I pause at the garden for a closer look. That's when I notice the skull and crossbones engraved oh-so-discreetly on the locked gate. Okay, well, *that* just got a whole lot more interesting.

No time to investigate. Behind the garden is what I've heard Mrs. Wal-lace refer to as "the mews." Now that I get my first up-close look, it's kind of fascinating. Gray and Isla live in a town house. So where do they keep their horses and coach? In the mews—a row of stables along the back, on their own lane, with other stables across the lane for homes on the road behind theirs. I wonder what this looks like in the modern world. Have the mews been turned into garages? Or is the "mews lane" now a distinct street, the stables reborn as houses?

I'm passing the stables when I bash into a dark-hooded figure. I scramble back, fists rising. A hiss, and then a spark of flame illuminates Simon. He sees my fists and laughs. "Expecting to be waylaid in your own yard, Cat?"

"What the blazes are you doing, skulking about in the dark?"

"Skulking?" His brows arch as his lips twitch. "I was feeding the horses." A wave at the stable.

I can see now that the "hood" is just a dark cap atop his dark hair. He's wearing a long black coat that looks a little too nice for feeding horses. Also, wouldn't that be done earlier in the day?

I remember what Isla said about Alice. Does Simon have a criminal past of his own? If so, does that mean Catriona isn't the only one who hasn't fully retired?

"I might ask the same of you, Cat," Simon continues. "Where are you off to at this hour?"

"I'm done my chores. My time is my own."

"That it is. I'm just hoping you aren't 'skulking' off to cause trouble."

"I'm not."

"Then you won't mind me coming along."

I start to snap my refusal and then swallow it back. Simon is suspicious of my plans, which I've earned—or Catriona has. His half smile is nothing but mingled amusement and exasperation, as if for a younger sibling caught sneaking out.

"Another time perhaps?" I say, looking up to meet his eyes. "I'm not getting into trouble, Simon. I'm trying to get out of it."

Concern touches his dark eyes. "All the more reason to permit me to join you, perhaps?"

I shake my head. "Not tonight. Please. I'll be fine."

While he's obviously reluctant to let me go, he doesn't argue, just warns me to stay away from the Grassmarket. That's exactly where I'm going, but I murmur something like agreement. Then he follows me to the lane and watches me go.

When I turn back to check, he seems to be gone, but I swear I see the hem of that long black coat catch the wind, flapping like the wing of a bird. I round the corner at the end of the mews and take the road up, looping me back to Robert Street.

I'm squinting over my shoulder when a double boot clomp has me stopping short. I backpedal behind the shadow of the town-house row. Someone's coming in the other direction, walking along this side of Robert Street.

It's barely nine. Not exactly the witching hour. It feels like it, though, being already dark, twilight falling earlier in the pre–daylight savings era. It reminds me of the suburbs, when the sun dropped and the streets emptied, people retreating to their backyards. An eerie silence has fallen over the row of town houses. During the day, it's much quieter than

Princes Street or Queen Street but there are coaches, a few delivery carts, the occasional duo or trio of residents out for a stroll, perhaps a maid or a groom zipping along. Flickering gaslight ripples behind dark windows. Otherwise, it's silent and still. Except for that man, who has now stopped at 12 Robert Street. Gray's house.

I pause to size him up. People are shorter in the Victorian era. I think I'd heard that somewhere, but at first, I'd thought it wasn't true. I'd pegged Gray at about six foot three, he towers over me, and he's a good four inches taller than McCreadie and his constable. Then I was in the drawing room today when Mrs. Wallace was measuring Alice for a new dress. I would have guessed Alice is about five foot two. She's four foot eleven. I'm maybe two inches taller. That makes Gray around six feet tall.

The guy stopped near the town house stairs is about five foot eight. He's well built. Dressed in a long dark coat, not unlike Simon's. Wearing a hat and gloves and boots. He looks as if he belongs, his clothing befitting the well-to-do neighborhood. Just a resident out for a stroll?

The man turns around, patting his pockets as if he's forgotten something. Or as if he's spotted me and turned his back.

I'm being paranoid. I'm unsettled tonight. First Simon and now some innocent homeowner making me jump as if I'm in the Grassmarket already.

I step out and glance at the man again. He's still looking the other way, but viewed from the back, he looks familiar. From the front, my gaze had naturally gone to his face, which I couldn't see in the dusk. From the rear, his jacket and his figure and even his stance shout an ID, as if I'm at trivia night and the answer just hit me.

Detective McCreadie.

I frown and squint. The man is the right body shape. Dressed the way I'd expect. The right color of hair. A hint of sideburns from this angle.

It's him. I'm sure it is. So why am I standing here, telling myself I must be mistaken? There's no reason it *couldn't* be McCreadie. He's working with Gray. It's not yet too late to call, especially when there's a light on in the funeral parlor.

As if hearing my thoughts, McCreadie steps up to the door. He's come to talk to Gray. Nothing odd about that. Nothing alarming . . . except for the fact that Gray is about to answer the door, look out, and spot me. I hurry the other way, my soft boots tap-tapping along. Soon I'm at the corner, where I take a moment to orient myself and mentally map out the mile-long walk to the Grassmarket. Then I'm off.

In the daytime, this area of the Grassmarket is the sort that makes people quicken their steps and guard their purses, while guiltily realizing they're making terrible assumptions about a poor neighborhood. By night those assumptions are valid, as are any attempts to hide your valuables and watch your step. There are probably better parts of the neighborhood, but this particular corner of it screams trouble.

I'm not as concerned as I might be. I've worked the modern equivalent of these neighborhoods, and I know that their bark is much worse than their bite. Follow basic rules of caution. Don't wander the street in a drunken stupor. Don't flash your valuables. Don't cause trouble. Act as if you belong. Catriona belongs, and so I walk with my chin up, and while I attract more than my share of catcalls and propositions, they seem more perfunctory than serious.

I head straight for the dive bar Gray pointed out the other day. I walk up to the door and knock. Inside people laugh and talk, but no one answers. I try the knob. Locked. A private club, then. Please don't tell me there's a secret knock.

I rap again, louder. A shadow passes behind one of the grimy windows. Then the wooden door creaks open an inch before a boot stops it and a man's voice says, "No."

"I'm—"

"I know who you are, and the answer is no. You aren't welcome here. Get on with you."

"I need to speak to Davina."

"And I need to speak to Queen Vic. Neither is happening tonight."

"She said I could talk to her if I paid. I'm ready to pay."

A grunt. Then, "I'll pass along the message."

"May I come—"

"You'll wait at least ten steps from my door. Now go."

NINETEEN

O nce I realize Davina isn't hurrying out, I slip over to where Catri- ona had been attacked. The scene of the crime. I search, but any evidence is long gone. I focus instead on trying to recall what I heard and saw that night. Being in the spot could nudge additional details from my memory. It doesn't.

When Catriona first cried out, it sounded like a yelp followed by a play- ful shriek. I'd thought that meant she knew her attacker, but it could also have been a defense mechanism. A stranger steps out from the shadows, and she tries to pretend she's only startled, not frightened.

There'd been the muffled whispers of conversation next. Angry? An- noyed? Calm? Hell if I know—I can't even be sure it'd been a two-way conversation.

I'd seen her being throttled, but the figure doing the throttling re- mained in shadow. And that's it. That's all I've got, which is no more than I already had.

I return to my spot outside the dive bar. Soon a distant bell tower chimes ten thirty, and I'm still waiting to speak to Davina. By now, I've realized that whoever answered the door never actually said she was inside. I've also realized that even if I do get a pawnshop name, it'll be closed by the time I arrive, if it's not already.

Forget Davina. I'm sure the pawnshop is in this neighborhood. I can return tomorrow and check them all. Yes, Isla gave me a deadline, and yes, I'll need to cut out on work, but I don't know what else to do.

I need to figure *out* what else to do if it goes to hell. I have Catriona's money. I trust Isla will pay my back wages when I leave. I also have Catriona's face, which should get me a position somewhere.

I will survive. I repeat that mantra so much I start humming the disco tune. It's all I can do. That and keep from attracting attention. At first, I pace the street, only to be reminded there's a reason sex workers are also known as streetwalkers. I move on a little farther and attempt to install myself at the mouth of an alley, but every time I look away from it, the hairs on my neck prickle, as if a would-be attacker is creeping up behind me. There's no one there, and yet I cannot shake the feeling, so I move out into the light again.

I have now reached for my phone at least a dozen times. I want to look busy, and that's always the answer. Pull out my phone and play a few rounds of solitaire or surf the news. Without that, I'm not sure how to seem busy. Then I find one of those pamphlets tucked into the pocket of Catriona's coat. It's an old one, telling the story of a horrific murder from four years ago, when a serving girl was attacked in her workplace, her throat slit and her body trampled by her killer.

My detective brain pounces on this. If Catriona kept the pamphlet, there must be a link between her and the crime. Clearly, she's related to the poor woman in the tale, and she's vowed revenge on the killer and keeps this in her pocket to remind her of her eternal quest.

Yeah, that would make a whole lot more sense if the pamphlet doesn't say that the guy had been caught right away and later executed. While there's a chance it's significant, I have a feeling Catriona used it for exactly the same purpose I do: distraction.

I stand in the moonlight and pretend to read the paper, over and over, until I've memorized the damn thing.

If I get any insight from that pamphlet, it's into the sort of story Victorians are willing to shell out a penny to read. The horrific broad-daylight murder of a young woman, killed because she dared criticize a man. According to the pamphlet, on hearing the news of the girl's death, her mother went mad and had to be committed to an asylum.

"You'd best not have pulled me from my tea for nothing, kitty-cat."

I glance up to see Davina bearing down on me.

"I had the best seat in the house, and I'll have lost it now." She puts out a hand. "Make it worth my while, or I'm nipping back inside."

I hold up a sovereign, and her eyes gleam.

"Well, well, found your purse, did you?"

"I found this. It's all I've got, and it will buy me twenty minutes of your time, right?"

"Depends on what you're looking for. I don't come cheap."

"All I need is answers." I glance up and down the dim, narrow road. "May we go somewhere else to talk?"

Her laugh rings out, echoing off the stonework. "Do you think me daft, kitty-cat? No, we'll talk right here, and every minute you delay is a minute off your time."

I hand over the coin.

She pulls out a tarnished pocket watch. "You have fifteen minutes left."

"What? I paid for—"

"Every second you annoy me costs you a minute. You're down to fourteen."

"I need to know where I pawn my wares. I sold something I ought not to have taken, and my mistress demands its return."

She lets out a cackle. "The kitty got caught stealing the cream, did she?" She holds up the gold coin, flipping it between her fingers. "Perhaps I did sell myself too cheap."

I should have known better than to admit vulnerability. No honor among thieves. How often had I relied on that to turn one suspect against another?

"It's not as dire as all that," I say. "I am already making plans to move on to a new position. To do it now would be mere inconvenience. But, yes, I'd like to return what I took if I can."

"Uncle Dover's," she says. "The old man gives you extra because he likes the looks of you."

I glance around. "Where would I find his shop?"

She sighs, points, and machine-guns directions.

"Thank you," I say. "Now, I know I've used some of my credit, but I'm hoping you can tell me more about what I was doing the night I was attacked."

She puts out a hand.

I nod at her watch. "I have eight minutes remaining."

"Some information costs more than others. That bit was valuable to you, wasn't it?"

Her eyes glitter as she smirks at me.

I want information on Catriona. I might need it, if solving her murder would get me home again. But the only money I have on me is for the locket. I calculate quickly. I have two pounds left. Nine more in my room—I wasn't foolish enough to bring it all to this neighborhood. The pawnshop is almost certainly closed. I could pay Davina for more information and then return in the morning to buy the locket.

What if Isla kicks me out before that? What if I can't get the locket back and she kicks me out *after* that? Either way, I'll need every penny I can get.

I'm gambling. Betting on getting the locket and winning Isla's forbearance versus betting that Davina's information will lead to Catriona's attacker, which might—based on nothing but a faint hope—get me back home. One path is straightforward; the other winds and bends and may lead off a sheer cliff.

Davina waggles her fingers and her brows. "I'm catching a chill out here, kitty-cat."

"I'll need to come back with the money."

"You do that, then. You know where to find me."

Damn it, I'm on edge tonight. I keep telling myself I'm fine. I have Catriona's switchblade. I'm staying out of alleys and dark corners. Yet I cannot shake the paranoia that first blossomed outside Gray's town house. The sense that danger creeps along behind me, close as a shadow. Yep, if I do make amends with Isla, maybe we can write penny dreadfuls together.

I know I'm being silly. I also know, as a cop and a woman, that "feeling silly" is no excuse for carelessness. If I have the choice of two streets, I take the better-lit one, even if the darker choice might shave a few meters off my journey.

Earlier, I'd speculated that there were probably better areas in the Grassmarket. The pawnshop is in one of them. It's not exactly the New Town but at least here I can stop clutching that blade. It's busier, too, with people spilling from pubs and shops. I quicken my pace and pray the pawnbroker is still open. I see the sign UNCLE DOVER's down an alley just as the distant bells strike eleven and a dim light inside the shop turns out.

I hurry down and rap on the window. When I shade my eyes to peer through, I catch movement, but the lantern stays off. I rap louder.

"Looking to sell your pearl, lassie?" a voice says behind me. "I'll buy it from you."

It's a trio of men stumbling past, drunk, and I brace myself, but they only continue on, laughing. I press my face to the glass again and knock again. Then I remember what Davina said about the pawnbroker having an eye for Catriona.

I call, "Mr. Dover, sir? It's me. I have most urgent business."

I don't give my name—I doubt Catriona would have used her real one. I'm hoping my girlish voice catches his attention. I drum out a light rat-a-tat-tat on the window, which hopefully also sounds feminine.

When the lantern flickers to life, I shade my face to the window and waggle my fingers. A moment later, a key turns in the lock.

Be Catriona, I remind myself as I hurry to the door. As tempting as it is to play the desperate housemaid, wide-eyed and near tears, I cannot screw up again. Slow down. Assess.

I know how to do that, damn it. I'm a cop. It just feels somehow as if I've left that part of me back in the modern world. Another life, another Mallory.

Be Catriona. Be Mallory, too. Evaluate and take control.

It's a moment before the door opens, as if the pawnbroker is peering out to be sure I don't have a thug at my side. When it does open, the man there is younger than I expect. Stereotyping again. I saw this shop, which would fit in any period drama, a pawnbroker down a dark alley. I expect to walk in and find a dusty and grimy wonderland, shelves and cabinets overflowing with an antique dealer's dream. The owner will be a wizened old man with a monocle for peering down at Great-Aunt Gertrude's ruby ring, which I must sell to buy food for my sick baby.

Nope. The guy's maybe thirty-five. Portly and red-cheeked with sideburns that put McCreadie's to shame. His gaze doesn't rise above my neckline, and seeing that, I helpfully undo my coat, tugging out my hair as if it's suddenly grown warm. His gaze gratefully settles on my cleavage. Is "décolletage" the period-appropriate word? Whatever it is, the Victorians were fond of it. Catriona doesn't have a single dress that shows off her ankles, but both her nonuniform ones display her generous assets.

"Miss Catherine," the pawnbroker says. "What ever brings you to my door at this hour?"

I sigh dramatically, which also makes Catriona's boobs bounce. "I have made a dreadful mistake, Mr. Dover. Sold something I ought to have kept. It is most vexing." I raise my eyes to meet his. "I do hope you have not sold it yet."

"I hope I haven't either."

He bustles me in and holds out his hands. It takes me a moment to realize he wants my coat. It's not nearly warm enough in here to take it off. But it isn't my comfort he's looking after; it's his view. I hand over the coat.

As he hangs it up, I glance around the shop. It matches my mental image better than he does. I don't see any jewelry—with the glass windows, he probably locks it up. Mostly it's the vintage equivalent of a modern pawnshop. Instead of used electronics and jewelry, there are everyday items like clothing and tools. Whatever people had of value that they needed to sell, whether it was to get through to the next paycheck or to fund a bad habit. I'd smelled a distinctive sweet smoke outside, as if one of the surrounding buildings housed yet another Victorian melodrama staple: the opium den.

As I move inside, I see what looks like a bank-teller counter, complete with dividers. To give a modicum of privacy for those embarrassed by their need. There are three sections, as if for three clerks, each with a pen and a pad of pawn tickets.

"Now what did you sell me that you need back?" he asks.

"A locket. It's rather unique."

"Ah, the one with the rod of Asclepius. You're lucky, Catherine. I had a student from the medical school in here eyeing it. Said he'd return when he had the money. Offered me a pound for it."

I presume Victorian pawnshops operate like modern ones. You can either sell them something or you can leave it as security on a loan, which you have a certain amount of time to redeem with interest, and after that, the broker can sell it. Catriona would go for option one—the straight-up sale. This guy's telling me I need to pay more than "purchase plus interest." He has a buyer lined up. Or so he claims, but both Catriona and I have seen this stunt before.

"Oh . . ." I say. "That is far more than I can afford." I sigh, letting my breasts sigh with me. "Such a shame. I was prepared to pay nearly twice what you gave me." I glance toward my coat. "But I understand that you must see to your business interests, and I do not fault you for it." I slide a look his way. "Unless you are still willing to sell it to me for less than he offered. It is a firm sale, payable this very night, not reliant upon a poor student's return, a student who, might I guess, was here because he lacked money?"

Dover smiles and dips his chin. "You have a point, Miss Catherine. A very fine point. So rare to see a pretty girl with such a sharp mind."

"Not as rare as you might think, sir. It simply behooves some of us to play to the fool. I would rather not."

Another dip of his chin. "I admire you for it. I believe we can come to some arrangement. Let us open negotiations at one pound."

TWENTY

I get my necklace, and I have money left in my pocket afterward. Dover flirts, but he makes no indecent offers in exchange for the locket.

Outside the shop, I resist the urge to take out the locket for a better look. I'd examined it briefly inside, just enough to be sure it matched Isla's description. It'd be hard to fob off a fake with that snake symbol. Not exactly a common design for women's jewelry.

As I walk, I can't help thinking about the story Isla told. I am a sucker for a good family legend. She said her grandfather gave it to her grandmother because she could not become a doctor in more than theory. Was it a sop? *Oh, sorry you can't be a doctor, dear—here, have a pretty locket with a medical symbol.* Or was it recognition of her loss? A shared understanding?

It's easy to look into the past and presume few women wanted a job or an education. Just those "special" ones, who "aren't like other girls." That's bullshit. Isla—and her grandmother—might not be the norm, but only because someone had encouraged them to dream bigger. Someone said they deserved to use their keen minds however they saw fit.

I can be grateful that Gray isn't a lecher or a raving chauvinist, but that's obviously his upbringing, and I don't think it's as unique as it might seem. For as long as women have had dreams, there would have been men who supported them, and it may be sentimental of me, but I can't help hoping Isla's grandfather was one of them, this locket representing—

A sound cuts me short. I stop in the middle of the road and turn. It's quieter out here than I realized. I don't know how long I'd been in the pawnshop, and when I came out, I'd been too wrapped up in my thoughts to be properly aware of my surroundings.

When I look around, I see that the pubs are all closed. Did they shut down at eleven? That would explain the flurry of activity just before I'd gone into the pawnshop.

I vaguely recall a few drunken revelers on the other street, but then I turned the corner and now I am alone on this narrow, cobbled lane. All the shops are closed, and the apartments above are dark.

The sound comes again. It's a snuffle, like someone crying. I squint up at the apartments. The windows are all shuttered, as if security is more important than fresh air. The cry is clear and unmuffled and comes from the even narrower lane ahead to my left.

Another whimper, one that sounds like a child, and when I hear it, dread creeps down my spine.

I have been here before.

Out at night in narrow and empty streets, discovering I'm more alone than I realized. Hearing trouble in a shadowed lane. The difference is that I recognize this as a potential trap. I'd been so damned confident that night. I was a police officer. I had my cell phone. I would be fine.

I was not fine. If I hadn't tumbled through time, I might have been found dead on the cobblestones the next morning. Strangled to death by a serial killer.

My fingers rise involuntarily to my throat. A woman's cry in an alley. A child's cry in a dark lane. It swirls together, enveloping me in a fog of unreality.

What if this is the way home?

It can't be pure coincidence that I'm back in the Grassmarket at night hearing cries of distress. The rip might have opened again, showing me the way back.

Or it might have opened into a new time that will trap me someplace else.

Do I want to go someplace else?

No. I have Isla's locket, and the reason I worked so hard to get it was that I don't want to go anyplace else. If I can't be home, I want to be where I am, in a household where I am both safe and intrigued by the possibility of more.

Even as I hesitate, the snuffling continues, punctuated by whimpers and soft cries.

It could be an actual child in danger. It could be a rip into another time, maybe even my own. It could also be a trap. Hell, in Victorian Scotland, it could be an actual child *faking* danger to trap me.

I pull out the knife and hold it low against my coat. A flick and the blade extends. Then I affect the most vacant-eyed expression I can manage and step into that alley.

My gait falters as soon as I round the corner. The streetlights don't reach here. Neither does the moon. I can make out a child-shaped form on the ground. A whimper ricochets between the narrow, high walls.

Am I doing this?

Am I giving up a shot, however long, to get home again? Nope, I am not.

I let out a girlish cry as if just seeing the form on the ground. Then I run toward it, saying, "Child? Are you injured?"

I don't even get the last word out before I stop short. That shape could be a pile of rags or could be an actual child. That's not what stops me. It's the paper pinned to the fabric, the word on it, in block letters.

CATRIONA

I stop, and I blink, that sense of unreality seeping back. When a shape swoops from the shadows, I spin to see a black-cloaked figure holding a rope. I see the rope more than anything. A raised length of rope, and in that moment, the last week evaporates, and I'm back in that alley, a killer lifting a length of old rope in exactly this same way.

That is my undoing. First the paper with Catriona's name. Then the rope. There's a shock of "this can't be real" that makes me react a split second too late.

Just like the last time.

This isn't possible. Is not possible.

Unreal. Impossible. Therefore, not happening. Cannot be happening, and so it is a dream, and if it is, then it is the door back. Let that rope fall over my neck. Let that rope tighten around my throat. Let it steal my breath. Let me sink into unconsciousness, and I will rise in twenty-first-century Edinburgh, alive and well.

This is the way home. That is what part of my brain screams. The terrified part that I've tamped down since I awoke four days ago. The little girl who just wants to go home, to her nan and her parents, whatever the cost. Each time she rises, sobbing in despair, I shove her back into silence, and now she roars at the top of her lungs.

This is the way. Just let him do it.

My heart bleeds for that little girl, the most scared and powerless part of me. But she is the voice of fear and cowardice and desperation, and to listen is to surrender. To say I would risk death rather than live this life.

The rope comes down and my hand slams up. It's not the hand holding the knife. It should be, but my moment of shock is enough that when I do respond, it's pure instinct.

My free hand flies up and accomplishes what it could not the last time. It gets under the rope. I grab it, and I twist, and I slam my knife into the bulk of black behind me. The blade sinks into his side, and a man's voice lets out a gasp that's half pain, half outrage.

He falls back, hand going to his side. It's hardly a fatal wound. I've never had reason to stab anyone before, and apparently, I'm not very good at it. I slash at him, but he blocks easily. Then I fight, almost relieved that I no longer need to use the knife. I punch, fist slamming into his face. I kick and, yep, that's a mistake with the skirts, but I manage to hike them up fast enough for a roundhouse kick that slams him into the wall.

As he flies back, something falls from his coat and flutters to the cobblestones. A bright blue feather with a distinctive eye pattern.

A peacock feather.

"You are shitting me," I whisper. I look at him. "Seriously? You're the bastard who killed Archie Evans?" My gaze flits over his outfit. All black, including a mask and what I now realize is a cape.

"Raven, my ass. You're just a damn turkey vulture."

The man stares. I see his eyes, that's all. They could be brown. They could be dark blue or hazel or green. It's too dark to tell, but that hardly matters. I have the killer we've been looking for. That's why my name is on a piece of paper atop that pile of rags. That's why I felt as if I was being followed all night. Because I was. I'm his next victim, not because I'm a threat, but because I'm a message to the men stalking him.

He stands there, blinking at me. Then he says, *"You."*

One word, uttered on a whisper.

A cry in an alley. A rope around my neck. A hundred and fifty years earlier, Catriona is in the same place, hands around her neck. I leapt into her body.

But I wasn't the only one in that alley.

What if my killer leapt into *her* killer's body?

That's why the child's cry led me down this alley. Not a coincidence, not at all. My attacker must have heard the cries that led me to that twenty-first-century alley. He'd replicated that using a child to lure in a hapless housemaid.

Yet as soon as I spoke, with my modern words, my modern attitude, combined with my modern fighting, he came to the same realization I just have.

I'm not Catriona. I'm the woman who'd followed that voice into an alley.

We're both here.

We both jumped through time.

Is that possible? What if I'm leaping to conclusions?

Does it matter? Nope, not when this guy—whoever he is—is currently trying to kill me.

He lunges at me. I slash with the knife, hitting him in the arm, blood spraying. Before I can strike again, his other arm smacks mine hard enough for me to drop the knife. It clatters over the cobblestones, and I hit him, a one-two punch.

My knee rises for a blow, but of course it goes nowhere, trapped by my skirts. That mistake gives him time to slam a fist into my jaw. I reel back. He goes to hit me again, but I punch him in the gut hard enough for my dress to rip. He doubles over, retching.

"What's the matter?" I say. "Not the helpless victim you expected?"

He hits me. My fault for getting cocky. He hits me in the stomach, enough to wind me, but I'm lunging at him when boots thunder down the lane.

"What's that?" someone says. "You there!"

"Oh, thank the lord," I begin, in a girlish voice. "I have been—"

My attacker drowns me out, backing into the shadows, hands raised as he bellows, "She tried to rob me. Promised a bit o' fun and then stabbed me."

Two men stride down the alley, their gazes fixed on me.

I try again to speak, only to have my attacker drown me out once more, ranting about how he'd been attacked by this "wench," how I tricked him, stabbed him, look, see his arm?

One of the men grabs for me. I backpedal, and hit the wall. He snatches my bodice and pins me, leaning in, breath reeking of beer. He's big and brawny, built like a damn blacksmith.

My attacker babbles some more. Then he scoops something from the ground.

"Knife!" I shout. "He's got a knife!"

"*I've* got your knife, girl," the blacksmith's friend says, waving the switchblade. "A wicked little piece, covered in that poor man's blood."

I open my mouth. The blacksmith slams me against the wall, my head snapping back into stone. I black out for what only seems like a moment, but the next thing I know, there's a constable there and my attacker is long gone.

"Wh-what's happening?" I manage, my head throbbing. "Where is he? He's the killer. The raven killer."

"Raven killer?"

Peals of laughter.

"There's a feather," I say. "A peacock feather. There on the ground. Look."

The constable does look. So do I. There's no feather. That's what the killer had been grabbing—not the knife but the feather. He also scooped up the paper with Catriona's name on it.

The blacksmith lifts me off the ground, forearm at my throat, making me choke and sputter.

"You stabbed a man," he says. "Lured him into this lane and stabbed him. Do you know what happens to girls who think they can bat their lashes and then murder a man for a few bob? It's the gallows for you." He leers down at me. "Unless you'd like to give us a reason to let you go."

"Now, now," the constable says. He's around forty, broad-shouldered and whiskered. "There'll be none of that. She will pay for her crime in the proper way." He strides to the blacksmith. "Help me escort her to the police office."

The man hesitates as his gaze drops to my neckline. The constable pulls out a wooden baton, keeping it at his side, a subtle threat.

"Let her go, Bill," says the blacksmith's friend. "We don't want trouble."

Bill turns his head and spits. Then he backs up, letting me crumple to the ground.

"You want her, take her," Bill says, strolling away, waving for his friend to follow. "But you'll need to get the little she-devil to the police office yourself."

The constable watches them go. Then he turns to me. He doesn't say a word, just lifts the billy club in warning. I resist the urge to argue my case. I don't consider fleeing. I wouldn't get far, and it would only make this worse.

I rise and lift my hands. "Just tell me where you want me to go."

He points his club down the lane, and I start walking.

TWENTY-ONE

I'm soon glad I didn't try to escape. We don't even make it to the end of the alley before a young constable comes running to help. I'm tempted to ask how they manage that without radios, but professional curiosity will have to wait. Once the second constable joins, I plead my case again. I don't stop walking. Don't resist arrest. I just try to explain.

I leave out the part about my attacker being the raven killer. The reaction last time makes me regret saying that. Without the feather, I have no proof. I'll save that part for McCreadie and Gray.

Instead, I say that I heard what sounded like a child's cries, and went into the lane to find a pile of rags. I was attacked by a masked man with a rope. I had a knife to defend myself, and I stabbed him with it. That's when the two men came.

"I saw no mask," says the older constable.

"Did you see his face?" I ask.

The younger constable jabs me hard in the back with his baton. "Watch your tongue. You're in enough trouble already. You admitted to stabbing a man."

"Because he attacked me. He tried to strangle me."

"We don't know that. We only know you admitted to stabbing him."

I close my mouth against argument. Save it for someone with seniority. Failing that, save it for McCreadie.

I have no idea what to expect from cops in this era. Hell, while I'd never admit it aloud, half the time I don't know what to expect from cops in my own era.

Here, I'm a pretty nineteen-year-old girl being led down dark and empty streets by two police officers. I'm lucky the older one didn't take that blacksmith brute up on his suggestion.

"I am Dr. Duncan Gray's housemaid," I say.

"Bully for you," the younger constable says. "Perhaps you should have stayed in the New Town. Your master finds out where you were, I'll wager you'll be out on your arse."

"I'm asking that he be contacted, please, sir. Either Dr. Gray or Detective McCreadie, who is a good friend of his and who knows me."

The younger constable growls and pokes me again. "What's that supposed to mean? It sounded like a threat."

"No, sir. I'm not familiar with the procedure for arrests, and I'm hoping my master can be contacted, so he knows where I am."

"Well, I don't know no Detective McCreadie. No Dr. Gray either."

"She means Hugh McCreadie," the older man says. "He is a criminal officer. Dr. Gray is the ghoul that cuts up the bodies. Says it's for science."

"She works for *him*?" The younger man pokes me harder. "I know your master. If he weren't some educated toff, they'd be hauling him on the gallows for what he does."

I open my mouth to defend Gray, but that won't help, so I murmur, "I do not know what you mean, sir. I am only the housemaid."

"Housemaid to a monster," the older man says. "That's what happens when you go fobbing off that sort of fellow as a proper gentleman. Blood will out."

That sort of fellow?

I stiffen. "If you mean—"

"You know what I mean, and if you don't, then you ought to be more careful who you work for. He's a right bastard, that one, in every sense of the word. Poor Mrs. Gray. I knew her father, I did. He fixed up my broken arm when I was a boy and never charged my mother a ha'penny. A good man, who had himself a good daughter. Then that husband of hers brings home his bastard like it's a babe he found in the streets. A half-caste bastard no less. Who knows what kind of woman the mother was."

The two men grumble together, speculating about Gray's mother.

Gray's mother . . . who was not Isla's mother. I remember the inscription in that book, and I kinda love Mrs. Gray for that. Her husband brought home his child by another woman, and she raised him as her own, recognizing that the baby had nothing to do with the situation. A good woman indeed.

This is what Davina meant about the scandal. She'd tapped her face and said something about that reminding me. She hadn't meant the scandal of Gray's skin color. She meant the scandal that explained why he *has* that skin color.

While I'm sure Gray endures prejudice on account of his skin, it's even more significant for the fact it signals his illegitimate status.

I don't see the police station as we reach it. I'm too caught up in my thoughts. I catch a glimpse of a stonework entrance that looks like every other stonework entrance—just a door in an endless row of attached buildings along a narrow street.

The next thing I know, I'm being shoved through that door into a dimly lit room that stinks of smoke and sweat. Once my eyes adjust, though, it feels more familiar than any place I've been in this world. Squint, and I could imagine it's a small twenty-first-century police station, housed in an old downtown building.

There's a desk with a uniformed officer behind it. Benches and chairs. Two constables chatting as they head out on shift. Shouts and clatters rise from the building's bowels, presumably the holding cells, where the drunk and disorderly protest the end of pub-crawl night.

The constables are leading me through when one of the exiting men stops short.

"You again?" he says. "I thought you were dead."

I glance around, but he's looking straight at me.

"You're Gray's maid, aren't you?" he says. "The one that got herself strangled a week back. Last I heard you'd been given up for dead."

"I was unconscious for nearly two days," I say. "But I have recovered. I came back tonight hoping for clues to my attack." *Since the police don't give a damn.* "I was attacked again. I think it was the same man."

My younger escort rolls his eyes. "Oh, don't tell me she's tried this before. Said she was attacked by a man in an alley?"

The other constable rocks back on his heels. "She was attacked all right. I'm the one who found her. You can still see a bit of bruising around her neck and on her temple."

"Thank you for finding me," I say. "However, as I said, I have been attacked again."

He shakes his head. "Cannot stay out of trouble, can you?"

"I was *attacked*."

"This time she knifed the man," the younger constable with me says. "Stabbed him twice."

"He *attacked* me," I say. "Tried to strangle me. Like before."

The older constable's eyes narrow. "Twice in a week? Teddy here is right. You do get up to trouble."

I bite my tongue. "May I speak to—"

"You'll speak to whoever we let you speak to," the younger constable says.

The others all nod, and with that, I'm led away.

I spend the night trying very hard to convince myself that this is a singular life experience, and I ought to take full advantage. How many people from the twenty-first century get to spend the night in a Victorian jail? Hell, in the modern world, tourists would *pay* for this.

A mere hundred dollars to sleep in a historic Victorian cell, re-created just for you! Once-in-a-lifetime experience! See what it was like to be rousted from the street and tossed in jail, with a bucket to piss in and rats skittering across the floor!

Okay, in the re-creation, there'd be a portable toilet with a screen. Also no rats. I get the full experience, including two cellmates. One is mentally disturbed and keeps shouting at me, spraying me with spittle and calling me Molly. The other is drunk and determined to snuggle up with me, and lice visibly crawl in her hair.

When something bites my leg, I look down to see a flea. I leap up, smacking at it, to the delight of the drunk woman. Within an hour, I stop panicking at every flea bite. Within two, I am huddled in the corner, knees drawn up, shivering with cold and disgust and fear that threatens to crystallize into full-blown terror.

When I decided not to run from the first constable, I'd shrugged off any fear of a night spent in prison. I was tough. I could handle it.

I can't handle it. The twenty-first-century dweller in me is freaking out, like a teenage spring breaker tossed into a foreign prison cell. I've been around dirt. I've been around rats. Even been around lice and fleas. But this is all that tenfold.

There's a men's holding cell right across from ours, and a guy who keeps ranting, and when I make the mistake of looking over, he leers back from a face with a pit for a nose. It takes everything in me not to scream.

Oh, I try to rationalize. This is simply the face of abject poverty. These poor people, encrusted with filth, crawling with pests, their minds and bodies eaten away by alcohol and mental illness and syphilis. It's tragic, and I should remember that and not be freaking out like that damned spring-break brat, huddled in a corner lest she touch something icky.

But all the rationalization in the world doesn't help when fleas and lice are crawling over me and I'm trying hard not to look at the man without a nose. Then there are the rats, creeping ever closer, bold and disease-ridden vermin waiting for me to drift off so they can snatch a bite.

I try to focus on other things. I was attacked by the raven killer, the very man we're searching for. He might also be the twenty-first-century guy who tried to kill me. Focus on that. Fall into the implications of it and spend the night dwelling there instead.

I can't. I try, and I cannot form a single coherent thought, all my aware-ness consumed by the horror of my surroundings. I am in jail. I am alone. I don't even have the damned locket, the very thing I took all these risks for. The officers confiscated the locket along with my knife and leftover coins, and I doubt I will see any of them again. All this, and I still lost my chance to make things right with Isla.

The night is endless. Then morning comes, and I'm thirsty and hun-gry, and I need to pee but there's a puddle under the bucket, and I don't know how to use it without stepping in that. I'm torn between hoping for breakfast—even bread and water—and knowing I won't dare touch anything that arrives.

While we're in the basement and I can't see a window, the activity level tells me it's well into the morning hours. Footsteps overhead double and then triple. Someone comes to collect a prisoner and mentions the "proc-urator fiscal's office" and I mentally pounce on that, remembering it's what they call the crown prosecutor here. I am overly delighted with my-self for recalling that, which proves my grip on reality is slipping.

A constable collects the drunk woman, saying her husband is here. She howls that she doesn't want to go and tries to cling to me as she's dragged out. I try to ask if anyone's notified Dr. Gray, but passing officers don't even glance my way, as if I'm one of the ranting inmates, screaming nonsense.

Soon I'm envisioning another night in this hellhole. No one is going to contact Gray or McCreadie. Or they have, and Gray has washed his hands of me, like a stray dog abandoned to the shelter.

Then I hear Gray's footsteps, as preposterous as that sounds. Recognizing footsteps? Like that dog hearing her master? It is ridiculous and revolting, and yet I am instantly on my feet, smoothing out my dress.

Then I see him, and my guts twist.

I've come to get a better sense of Gray since I woke in his house. At first, he'd been clipped and cool, either bristling with annoyance or grim with determination. That facade had melted as he relaxed around me, passionately discussing his work or cheerfully examining murder wounds or blissfully digging into a cream pastry. Yet even at his stiffest, it was hard for Gray to fully inhabit the role when he had ink speckles on his cheek, one sock forgotten, or his hair tumbling uncombed over his forehead.

The man who strides into the prison today is different. He is spotless in his attire, as impeccably dressed as McCreadie. Wavy dark hair tamed and styled. Clean-shaven and cold-eyed. The last is the worst. Even when he's only half present, there's a glitter in Gray's dark eyes, a sign that his brain is spinning in twenty directions. Now his gaze is shuttered, and he walks purposefully alongside a young constable.

At a noise, I glance down the hall to see two more officers, both in plain clothes, standing outside their offices, watching. Another clomps down the stairs and hovers there. They've come to see the spectacle. Only the spectacle isn't me. It's the doctor who cuts up corpses and calls it science, but we all know what it really is, don't we? Sick bastard.

I see it in their stares, as cold as his own. In the curl of their lips. I want to snarl at them that, someday, men like Gray will change their entire profession. The work of men like him will help the police catch criminals who'd otherwise remain free. It'll let them convict criminals who'd otherwise walk free. And, just as important, it'll let them exonerate those who should be free, the innocent fingered by circumstance and released by evidence.

"This her?" grunts the officer leading Gray to my cell.

"It is," Gray says.

The constable opens the door, and I walk forward with as much dignity as I can. Before I can leave, the constable stops me with a raised hand.

"Are you sure you want to go with him?" he asks. "You don't need to. You might find this cell more to your liking."

His gaze cuts in Gray's direction.

"I would like to leave with Dr. Gray, please," I say.

"Well, then, come on out. I hear some girls fancy that sort of thing. Got a bit of the ghoul about you, too, I'll wager?" His gaze goes to the blood on my dress. "Take care the doctor does not run out of corpses to practice on. You'd make a pretty little cadaver for carving."

I expect Gray to say something. That underestimates how accustomed he is to this treatment and how well he's learned the futility of rising to the bait. His expression remains neutral, as if the constable is bidding me a pleasant farewell.

When I join Gray, he doesn't even look my way. Just turns on his heel to go.

"Uh-uh," the constable says. "We still have some papers to be signed. You'll wait in there." He points to another room.

Gray heads through the open doorway, crosses the room, and stops at the other side of it, ignoring the chairs and standing ramrod straight.

When the constable is gone, I say, "I did ask for Detective McCreadie, sir. I hoped he could resolve this."

"He did." Gray's words are brittle and sharp, his gaze on the door. "He convinced them that, as you had been attacked before, carrying a knife in the area was a reasonable precaution. The fact that the man fled made it a very difficult case, and the procurator fiscal chose not to pursue it."

"I think it was the raven killer, sir. He was dressed in black, from a mask to a cape. He had a piece of rope like the one found with the first victim. When we fought, he dropped a peacock feather. He took it before he left."

I expect this to get his attention. I'll see a ripple of life beneath the ice, his interest snagged. Instead, his look is long and it's careful, and when he pulls back, his mouth sets.

"You think I'm lying," I say. "Because I was there when Detective McCreadie said a witness described a black cape, and I saw the rope in your laboratory."

"At this moment, it doesn't matter what I think. The point is that you are free. The police contacted Detective McCreadie, who convinced them not to lay charges."

"Then he left without having them release me?"

"He tried. They insisted I come and take charge of you myself."

My mouth opens. Then I snap it shut.

I'm sorry. That's what I want to say. *I am so sorry, Duncan.*

In that moment, he's not "Gray" or even "Dr. Gray." That's Catriona's boss. This is the first time I see Gray as a person undefined by his role in my life. It's like the first time you see a teacher outside school, struck by the shock of realizing they exist outside that relationship.

This is a man who has been humiliated because of me. Humiliated in front of the very people he's trying to help, who demanded his presence so they could sneer at him and mock him.

As a cop, I've had the experience of trying to help someone who doesn't want help from "my kind." But this would be so much worse, because in my case, I know they have cause not to trust a police officer. Here, Gray's tormentors just think he's creepy and weird, and anyone who has been bullied in school knows exactly how that feels.

Gray has grown up with this. Because he's illegitimate. Because he's not white. One might think his life has already inured him to humiliation. It hasn't. I saw that in the practiced hardening of his fortifications.

He pursues his life's work in spite of the sneers and mockery. At some point, he said "To hell with public opinion" and decided to do whatever he wants. I can admire the hell out of him for that, but I can never make the mistake of thinking the sneers and mockery don't hurt.

"I'm sorry," I say finally, because I can't *not* say it.

The moment I do, his chin jerks up, mouth tightening more as he says, stiffly, "It is of no matter."

They will change their tune. I want to tell him that. I want to tell him that thousands of future detectives will appreciate the work done by him and others. Thousands of innocent people will walk free because of it. Hundreds of thousands of victims will find justice because of it.

"It'll get better," I murmur under my breath.

He glances over sharply, frowning, but I don't think he heard my words. He's just on edge and heard my voice and expects mockery. I square my shoulders and open my mouth to say I think he's doing amazing work, as little as my opinion will matter.

Before I can speak, the constable reappears, smirking. "That's all done. Now just follow me. I'm going to take you the long way around. Wouldn't want you getting too close to the dead room. Might see something you like."

Gray's mouth tightens. I keep hoping for a clever rejoinder. I know he's capable of them. But he chooses stony silence as his defense, and all I can do is follow him out.

TWENTY-TWO

After being paraded past the basement offices, we come up a back set of stairs and then need to walk past the main-floor offices. Everyone comes to look. Gray walks with his gaze forward, and I hurry along at his side. When he stops short, I follow his gaze to see a familiar figure sitting in the front reception room.

Gray picks up his pace. "Isla. I thought I—"

"—*told* me to stay home?"

"No, I told you I could handle this."

"Of course you can," she says smoothly. "But I have never been in this particular police office, and I wished to take a look, in case there is something I might do on behalf of the royal women's police-offices-beautification society. I believe new chairs would be in order here. Perhaps flowers for the front desk."

She's joking, obviously. I bite my cheek against a smile, and Gray rolls his eyes and relaxes just a little. The desk clerk, though, snaps to attention.

"We could use new chairs, ma'am," he says.

"I am certain there is much you could use," she says. "Including an exterminator. I believe I saw something furry scamper that way." Her gaze shunts to the side. "It is an interesting building, though. The historic value is immeasurable."

"That it is, ma'am."

She turns to me. "I have taken the liberty of retrieving your possessions, Catriona. We are free to leave."

I nod, and she takes my arm and leads me outside, Gray following. The moment the door shuts behind her, she turns to her brother.

"I am going to take Catriona out for a breakfast tea," she says. "I know you have errands to run. We shall meet you at home."

Gray hesitates. "I do not believe you'll find a suitable tearoom in this part of town."

"Then we shall find an unsuitable one."

He still pauses, his gaze going from Isla to me before he says, "While I am certain Catriona spent a very uncomfortable night, I am not entirely convinced she deserves tea."

I stiffen. That should make me laugh. I don't deserve *tea*? Not exactly a stellar insult.

It's not that, though. It's the layers of distrust woven under those words. He's not sure I was actually attacked. If I was, he's not sure I didn't deserve it—at least in the sense that I've been attacked twice, and that can't be simple bad luck. Either way, he's not sure I should continue to be treated like a valued servant, and he's *quite* sure I shouldn't be left alone with his sister.

"I insist, Duncan," Isla says, and then adds a softer "Please."

Here I see again the back-and-forth between them, the unease of their relationship. Isla is the older sibling, yet she's reliant on Gray as the "man of the house"—even when it's also her family home.

Now that I know their deeper personal history—he is her half brother, illegitimate, a social stigma—does it alter my analysis? No. They behave as a bachelor and his older widowed sister, with no "half siblings" or "uncomfortable circumstances" thrown in. It's an enviable relationship.

"If you insist," he says.

She meets his gaze, her voice soft as she says, "I do. Thank you for understanding."

"There's a decent tearoom a few blocks over. You can walk there—the streets are safe here. Then catch a hansom home, please."

He pulls coins from his pocket, and she gives a wry half smile.

"I do not need you to pay for my cab, Duncan." Before he can close his fist, she plucks the lone sovereign from among the smaller coins. "But if you insist . . ."

They share a smile, and he shakes his head, straightening with, "I shall see you at home. And, while the household is your province, I would like to discuss . . ." His gaze cuts to me.

"Understood."

He gives directions to the tearoom and offers to accompany us, but Isla shoos him on his way. He's about to leave when he stops.

"You found your locket," he says, and I look over sharply, to see it around her neck.

She nods. "I did."

"Good. I heard you were looking for it, and I was concerned."

"It was misplaced, that is all."

They say their goodbyes, and Isla and I head in the other direction.

"You got the locket from my things," I say. "I was worried it might have gone missing." I glance back at Gray, his long legs carrying him out of earshot already. "That is why I came here last night."

"I know."

Is it my imagination or has her face gone as hard as her brother's, her blue eyes chilling?

I open my mouth.

"This is the last straw, Catriona," she says, gaze still forward as she walks. "That is what I took you aside to say, beyond the reach of listening ears at home. You will return to pack your things. If you do so without complaint, without bothering my brother or Mrs. Wallace, without upsetting Alice . . ."

She hands back Catriona's switchblade, along with the few coins that'd been in my pockets. Then she lifts the sovereign she took from Gray. "A month's wages. I will double it if you do not attempt to argue your case now. I am finished with you, Catriona. I cannot trust you, and I cannot have you in our house."

"B-but I got your necklace back."

"You got my necklace *back*?" She looks over, brows shooting up. "Do you think me a fool? You were trying to *sell* my necklace. That's how you came to be attacked last night. Either you flashed it in front of the wrong person, or you tried to sell it to the wrong person."

I inwardly wince. I was attacked in Catriona's old haunt, with Isla's necklace on me, as if I'd sat in that library yesterday, listened to her pleas for its return, and heard only that I should sell it before she searched my room.

"I sold it before my accident," I say. "To a pawnshop. After we spoke, I knew I had to get it back. That's what I was doing. I recovered it just before I was attacked."

"A pawnshop?"

"Er, yes, a place where people sell items for money."

"I know what a pawnbroker is, Catriona. I meant that, if this is your story, it is easily proven. Take me to this shop, and I shall speak to the owner. Let us see whether he confirms your story."

"I have never laid eyes on this girl in my life," Dover says as we stand in his shop. "I certainly did not buy that necklace from her. It's obvious that such a piece would have been stolen, probably from her mistress. I am an honest man who loans money to the poor for their belongings in times of need. I do not deal in stolen goods."

"Of course you don't," I say. "But I misrepresented myself to you, sir."

His eyes narrow at "misrepresent" as if he doesn't know the word and presumes I'm casting aspersions on his character.

"I lied," I say flatly. "I told you it was my grandmother's locket, and I had to sell it to feed the baby. Then I said my brother gave me money to buy the necklace back. There is no baby. I have no brother. I lied, and I'm sorry that I duped you, sir. The truth is that I stole it from my mistress and then regretted it. You had no way of knowing it was stolen goods."

He doesn't take my excuse. Either he'd seem like a fence or a fool, and he won't be either, especially in front of a proper lady like Isla.

When we finally leave, I say, "I warned you, ma'am. He won't admit he bought stolen goods even accidentally, for fear of a police investigation. You could tell he was lying, couldn't you?"

"No, Catriona. I could not, which means either he's telling the truth or I have a poor ear for detecting falsehoods. I believe, at most, that you have sold him goods before and hoped he'd go along with your story in expectation of future business from you."

"Then why would I have tried to dissuade you from speaking to him?"

Her brows lift. "Do you honestly think that trying to stop me from proving your claim worked in your favor? You hoped to dissuade me, and when you could not, you hoped he would lie for you."

We keep walking. My mind whirrs, looking for solutions. No one likes being made to play the fool, and that's what I've done to Isla. She thinks I had no fear of losing my position because my employer is a silly, wealthy woman who fancies herself a philanthropist. Shed a few tears and spin a few lies, and no matter what happened, I'd keep my job.

"You will pack your things," she says. "My offer stands. I will even keep it at two pounds, despite this. Come home, pack, and leave quietly. The alternative?" She looks at me, locking gazes. "I trust you did not enjoy your night in a cell. The courts have no sympathy for servants who steal from their employers."

"I didn't—" I bite it off. "I know you don't believe me, ma'am. Forget the two pounds. I'll go quietly if I must. No bribe required. But is there some way I can make this up to you? I'll forgo my salary. Take on extra tasks. Give up my privileges—"

"No. I am sorry, Catriona, but you are leaving today, without references. I cannot lie to future employers. I would advise you to take the two pounds."

"Is there nothing—?"

"There is nothing you can say. Nothing you can do. No story will get you out of this."

There are moments when you know you are about to do something incredibly reckless and breathtakingly dangerous. And you don't care. It's not leaping before you look. It's looking, seeing the pit of boiling lava, and jumping anyway, because an enraged elephant is charging straight at you, and there's a very slight chance you might land on that tiny island amid the lava.

"What about the truth? No story. The truth."

She sighs. "Please take the two pounds and do not insult me with more lies. I am more worldly than you seem to believe."

"Which is why I'm going to tell you the truth, and if you don't believe it, which I'm sure you won't, then I ask only one thing. Keep your money. I'll go quietly. Whatever I say, though, promise you won't have me sent off to Bedlam?"

Her lips twitch, just a little. "Bethlem Hospital is in London, Catriona."

"Whatever the Edinburgh equivalent is. What I'm about to tell you is going to have you seriously questioning my sanity, and I need you to promise you won't have me committed to an asylum. Just tell me you don't believe me, and let me leave."

She rolls her eyes and assures me that Scottish asylums are nothing like English ones, because they are *Scottish* and thus very much advanced. Finally, though, I get her to agree. No matter what I say, she will not summon the guys in the white coats.

"We should stop walking," I say. "So I can explain properly."

I look around. We're on an Old Town street, bustling with carts and carriages and people.

Isla sighs again. "Would you like something to eat, Catriona?"

"Is there a patio?"

"A . . . ?"

"Outdoor seating?"

She continues to stare at me.

I watch as a passing cart sprays filthy water onto a shopfront. Down a side lane, a guy is openly pissing on the wall.

"Er, right," I say. "A quiet tearoom, perhaps?"

She waves for me to walk, and I break into a trot, keeping pace with her long strides.

TWENTY-THREE

We're on the street I know as the Royal Mile. In the twenty-first century, it's the tourist ninth circle of hell. In this era, it's already inching in that direction, with tidy shops lining the road between Edinburgh Castle and Holyrood Palace. On the way, Isla pulls over at a public pump and hands me a handkerchief to "clean up a little." Right, because I just spent the night in a prison cell.

I glance at the pump, water collecting in a stone basin below, a child filling a bucket from it. "Er, so, cholera. How's the research coming on that?"

Isla arches a brow.

"Public water. Cholera. Is there any connection that you know of?"

Now both brows rise. "You have heard of the work of Dr. Snow?" She doesn't wait for an answer, just nods and says, "We understand the link between some diseases, particularly cholera, and the water supply. You can be assured that is safe. This is Scotland."

I dip the handkerchief in the running water, wash my face, and then wipe off my dress. When I try to hand back the cloth, Isla waves it away, and I tuck it into my coat pocket. The day is warming up, and I have the coat over my arm as we make our way to the tea shop.

I asked for quiet. What Isla provides is a private room in a bustling shop, which gives us privacy to speak, while the outside noise ensures our voices won't echo into the main dining area.

The table is big enough for six, and I sit in the shadowiest seat, well aware that even after washing, I'm not presentable enough for this middle-class tea shop. Isla starts to take the seat beside me, and then opts for the next one over. Yep, apparently, I stink, too.

Isla orders tea and a tray bearing a selection of meats, cheeses, and breads. Breakfast-worthy, even if it's closing in on noon. I don't plan to eat before I speak, but the moment I smell the bread, I dive in. I polish off a slice, and my stomach stops growling.

"Okay," I say, and even that unfamiliar word is enough to have her brows knitting. I resist the urge to replace it. Time to be me. Be Mallory.

"I'm going to tell you my story," I say. "And as weird as it will get, just let me tell it, okay? That's all I'm asking. Let me finish."

A brief nod as she pours her tea, her gaze on the cup. Fortifying herself to endure whatever bizarre story her housemaid is about to dream up. *Lady, you have no idea.*

"Roll back the clock to exactly one week ago today," I say. "I've flown to Edinburgh to be with my nan. She's in hospice care. Cancer. Two weeks to live, tops, which means she's probably already . . ." I inhale. "Yep, I'm trying not to think about that."

Isla's mild brow knit tightens into a full-blown knot.

I continue, "I'm about to say a whole lotta words that will make zero sense to you. Just roll with it. So, a week ago. Long day at Nan's bedside, and I need a break. I decide to go for a jog in the Grassmarket, which is mostly pubs and restaurants and whatever. Safe enough. I'm in a quiet part. Quieter than I should be in at that hour, but hey, I'm a cop, I can handle it."

"Cop?"

"Police officer. Detective, actually. Anyway, I got cocky. I've patrolled worse neighborhoods in Vancouver."

"Van . . . ?"

"Canadian port city. West coast. In 1869, it'd be a trading post. Maybe a fort? That's always one of the wildest parts of being in Scotland. Walking around the Old Town, seeing medieval buildings being used as condos, when in Vancouver, if it's over a hundred and fifty years old, we wrap it in cotton to preserve the historic value."

She's staring. I expect that. I could shorten my story, cut out any side rambles or confusing terminology, but if I have any chance of convincing her, this is how I'll do it. Talk like someone from the twenty-first century. Pepper my story with terms and asides too elaborate for me to concoct on the spur of the moment.

"Like I said, I got cocky. I heard a woman, and it sounded like she was in trouble, and I'm a cop, right? I can't just ignore it. I head into the lane, and I see a flash of this blond girl in an old-fashioned blue dress. She's semitransparent. Obviously, it's some kind of projected image, maybe from a tour. The Victorian Edinburgh Experience, complete with murdered pretty girls! I figured that was the source of the woman's cries that brought me running. A malfunctioning tour video. Before I could leave the alley, I was attacked. Fought like hell, but the guy got a rope around my neck. Eventually I passed out. I woke in a strange house, hoping to God it wasn't the killer's lair. I looked in the mirror, and holy shit, it's the blond girl from the alley. *I'm* the blond girl from the alley. In her body. In her house. In her time."

I stop there. Isla has her fingers on her teacup.

I take a sip of mine and lean back.

When thirty seconds of silence pass, I say, "Do I get to gather my belongings before you kick me out?"

Her gaze falls to mine. "What you're saying is that you're from the future."

I make a face. "I was trying not to use those exact words. Seriously clichéd B-movie dialogue."

She doesn't react. It's as if I'm not speaking. Or as if she can't hear me over her own mental dialogue, screaming at her to run while she still can, before the madwoman attacks.

"Look," I say. "I don't expect you to believe me. Obviously. That was just my last-ditch effort. Nothing to lose, right?"

"You're a police detective. From Canada. In the year . . ."

"Two thousand and nineteen. One hundred and fifty years from now, which I figure must have some significance. I was attacked where Catriona was attacked exactly a hundred and fifty years earlier. Two women strangled in the same spot. Do not ask what happened or how or why. I'd love to figure that out, but I don't think I'm going to solve that particular mystery, detective or not."

"Your name is?"

"Mallory Elizabeth Atkinson. Elizabeth after my nan, the one who is—was—will be—dying of cancer."

I take a moment there, finding my voice before I continue, "Mom was born in Scotland and came to Canada after university. She went to the University of Edinburgh for law. Dad's family is originally from Scotland, but they emigrated . . . well, it'd be around now, actually. Mom and Dad met at a Burns Night supper in Vancouver. It's a thing, celebrating Robbie Burns, wearing kilts, eating haggis, drinking scotch to burn away the taste of the haggis."

"Your mother studied law," she says, as if that's where her mind stopped.

"She's a defense attorney. Partner in a law firm. Dad's an English prof at UBC, teaching English classic literature. Dickens, Brontë, Hardy . . ."

"Charles Dickens is *literature*?"

"Hey, he's one of my favorites."

She's quiet. I sip more tea.

"How old are you?" she asks.

"I turned thirty in March."

Her brows rise, and I laugh under my breath. "Yeah, thirty in my world is a little less dignified. Hey, when the average life span is over seventy years, you get extra time before you need to grow up."

"Are you married, then? Children?"

I shake my head. "I can say my career got in the way, which is partly true, but if I'd met the right guy, I'd have made it work. I'm sure I'll get married someday. Kids are another thing altogether. Women can go to college, get advanced degrees, and take on amazing jobs, but that doesn't change biology. The baby clock is ticking and . . ." I shrug. "I try not to think about it too much. There are options if it's what I want later, married or not."

When she goes quiet again, I lean forward. "If you want to test me, feel free, but if you're just seeing how deep my delusion goes, can we skip it? Please? Tell me I'm full of shit, and we go our separate ways. Just do me a favor. When I do find a way home and Catriona comes back, kick her ass to the curb."

"Kick her . . . ?"

"Sorry. Let me try that again. *Please, ma'am, heed my words well and dinnae allow the wee lassie to tarry in your abode.*"

Her lips twitch. "We don't actually speak like that."

"Would you prefer 'kick her ass to the curb'?"

"It *is* much more picturesque."

"Yet, alas, not permitted here, particularly for women. Feels like being at my dad's parents' place, them threatening to wash my mouth out with soap for a 'hell' or a 'damn.' I need to learn Victorian curse words." I channel Gray with "What the devil is going on here?" I shake my head again. "Nope, not the same."

I sober and meet Isla's gaze. "My point is not to let the real Catriona come back. If I show up on your doorstep acting like her, presume it *is* her and send her packing. She *was* stealing from you. I found her stash of money. Also found a box of candies some guy sent you and a letter Lady Something-or-other sent your brother, which by the way, you do not want to read."

"A letter?"

"Of a most scandalous nature," I say, affecting an upper-crust accent.

At her frown, I only say, "The point, again, is that you've done enough for Catriona." I push back my seat. "Speaking of which, you have done enough for me, too. Thank you for breakfast, but I can tell I've outstayed my welcome. May I get my stuff?" I clear my throat. "Sorry. May I collect my things, ma'am?"

She doesn't answer. I swear I hear someone's distant pocket watch ticking off the seconds of silence.

Finally, Isla says, "If you are not Catriona, how did you retrieve my locket?"

I tell her, and her face gives away nothing. Then she says, "And the attack last night? Was that connected to my necklace?"

I go quiet. Then I say, slowly, "I heard a child crying. Obviously, that made me think of how I was attacked in my time, but I still went to investigate, in case it was another rip through time, one that might send me home. It was a trap. A guy tried to strangle me, just like before. I fought, and this time I was better prepared. Catriona had a switchblade, and I'd brought it along. I stabbed my attacker, and I fought, and eventually, two guys showed up and rescued him."

"Rescued *him*?"

"Yeah, they rescued the guy *attacking* me. He fled as fast as he could."

He's the raven killer. The one your brother and Hugh McCreadie are looking for.

I don't say that. I'm not sure I should, because it could go so much deeper than that. I suspect he could be the guy who attacked me in my world. That I didn't just travel through time. That I brought a twenty-first-century serial killer with me. I don't tell her that. I'm not even sure what to *do* with that.

A moment later, Isla pays the bill and walks out. I take a chance on following. She hails a coach. A "hansom" as Gray called it, and as I recall from my Sherlock Holmes reading, though admittedly, teenage Mallory thought it was a British spelling of handsome and meant they were very fine cabs indeed.

I'm standing there on the sidewalk as the hansom pulls over. I hesitate. Then I follow Isla, and she doesn't stop me. Once the coach is moving, she gazes out the window, as if trying to convince herself she is alone.

When we pass the gardens into the New Town, I clear my throat. "I'll gather my things and not say a word to Mrs. Wallace or Alice."

"No."

"All right, would you like me to say goodbye? Or do you mean you'll bring my things outside?"

"You are staying. For now. I . . ." She looks over. "I do not know what to make of your story. I need time to think. You will have a roof over your head until tomorrow at least."

She pauses and her eyes narrow. "But if you truly are a police detective from the twenty-first century, why would you be trying so hard to retain a position as a housemaid? Surely, it is beneath you."

I shrug. "I cleaned houses for a summer job one year. That's normal in the future. Kids—teenagers—take on crappy jobs for a bit of pocket money and work experience. Never thought I'd be doing it again, but what's the alternative? Walk into a police station and offer my professional services? I'm trying to get back home, whether that means figuring out the trick or solving Catriona's attack or just waiting for the damn planets to align. Hopefully, it'll happen soon. Until then, I need a roof over my head, and I'm willing to scrub floors to get it."

"If what you claim is true, this must be very difficult for you," she says, her voice softening. "Being separated from your family, from your world."

"I figure I must be here for a reason, right? So there must be a way back."

"Of course," she says, a little too firmly. This is just as likely to be some kind of cosmic hiccup, and we both know it.

"For now, I'm focusing on the practical. I'd like to stay in my job, and I hope you'll give me another chance. If you do, though, your brother isn't going to be too happy about it. I got the distinct impression he's had enough of Miss Catriona."

"I can deal with my brother."

She seems about to drop into her thoughts again when her head snaps up. "You've been assisting with Duncan's studies. If you are a police detective . . ."

"Yep, that's why I'm honestly interested. He's doing amazing stuff. I saw how the police treat him. That'll change. Most of us couldn't imagine solving murders without forensics. If there's one thing I'm actually enjoying about my Victorian experience, it's the chance to see early police work and early forensic science in action."

She goes quiet, deep in thought, before she inhales sharply.

"Duncan," she murmurs. She turns to me. "Whatever you do, do not breathe a word of this to him. I don't know if your tale is delusion or scheme or the impossible truth, but I will not be able to save your position if you try to convince him of it. He is a man of science."

"And science can't explain body-swapping time travel. Not even in my world."

"Allow me to handle my brother, and whatever happens, tell him nothing of this."

TWENTY-FOUR

When we arrive in the town house, Isla waves for me to follow her. We go all the way up to the attic. She opens the locked door I've presumed is for storage.

I follow her inside to find a laboratory. Shelves of boxes and jars, each meticulously labeled. There's a tiny desk, with papers and journals piled on top. Most of the room, however, is a long table, half of it consumed by a still.

"What do you see?" she asks, waving at the apparatus.

"You're cooking up moonshine. Cool." I catch her eye. "Joking. That's what it looks like to me. A moonshine still from a hillbilly-feud movie set amidst the coal mines of Civil War–era Kentucky."

"You do realize none of that makes sense to me."

"Yep, that's why it's fun to say." I walk over and touch one of the beakers. "It looks like a way of making alcohol. Don't ask me how it works. I got a C in chemistry."

"You studied chemistry?"

"Not by choice. It's part of the high-school curriculum." I pause. "High school is the North American term. I can't remember what they call it over here. It's the teen years, roughly thirteen to eighteen."

"We have the High School on Calton Hill. Duncan attended. I have heard it was used as the model for similar schools in America. You attended such an institution? Your parents must have been quite well off."

184 . KELLEY ARMSTRONG

"They were, but everyone goes to high school. It's mandatory. College and university are optional. Maybe half of us go to that."

"Half of *everyone*?"

I shrug. "More among the middle and upper classes. It's not free, unfortunately. Either your parents need to be able to afford it, or you need to take out loans, or you need to get a scholarship, academic or athletic. My parents paid for mine. I had a chance at a softball scholarship, but it was only partial and not for the school I wanted, so I turned it down."

"What did you study?"

"Criminology major. Sociology minor."

"Criminology? Is that what my brother does? Or is it the study of police techniques?"

"Neither really." I pull out a stool and perch on it. "Criminology is the study of criminal behavior. Everything from identifying predictive patterns to understanding underlying causes."

She's watching me carefully, almost like lip reading, as if she's struggling to process as fast I speak.

"Studying the causes of criminal behavior," she says. "What would you say about your own situation then?"

"I'm presuming you mean Catriona, because I've never so much as swiped a chocolate bar." I lean one elbow on the lab table. "I'm not an expert, and I didn't know the real Catriona—just what I've heard of her."

"Analyze her based on that then."

"Ah, a pop quiz. Testing the parameters of my delusion. All right." I settle better on the stool, getting comfortable. "Apparently, Catriona came from a decent family, meaning she didn't *need* to fall into a life of crime. I could speculate that she chose it, but that'd be presumptive without additional data. What was her home life like? Her early experiences? A middle-class family doesn't mean a perfect life. If she was abused—physically or sexually—she may have fled and fallen into crime as a way to make a living. She didn't give it up when she came to work for you. Is that because she enjoys it? She shows sociopathic tendencies, but you'd need a psychiatrist to diagnose that. She wasn't spending her money. She was saving it. To escape life as a housemaid? Can't say I blame her. Maybe it's ambition combined with a lack of ability to empathize with others. She sees other people as only a means to an end."

Isla stands there, watching me after I've finished.

"All of that is pure speculation," I say. "Like I said, I don't have enough data for more."

When she still doesn't speak, I say, "Tell me what parts of that don't make sense in your world, and I can explain further."

"No need," she says. "The concepts I do not understand I can interpret in context. I still do not understand what has happened to you, but I cannot continue telling myself you are inventing falsehoods."

I say nothing. I just sit and wait. Finally, she says, "I . . . I accept this. I may yet be proven wrong, but I accept it. Now we must determine the next course of action."

We discuss it and, in the end, the "next course of action" is that I'll remain a housemaid. Isla isn't happy with that. I'm her social equal, and to have me scrubbing her floors makes her uncomfortable. More uncomfortable than it makes me.

For me, it's not a class issue. I don't "deserve" better by dint of my background or education. If I balk at scrubbing floors, it's because I've worked my ass off to get where I am in my profession, and this is not a place I ever expected to return to. Yet if I had to, even in the modern world, I *would* clean toilets . . . while busting my ass to get a job I preferred.

Right now, this position is a safety net. It's sheer luck that I ended up in an eccentric household willing to overlook the idiosyncrasies of my speech and behavior. Do I go out into the world and attempt to get something like a shop-clerk position—only nominally better than being a maid—at the risk of being fired the first day because I don't know my ha'pence from my thruppence?

No. With Isla accepting my story, I have more than a safe place to hide. I also have someone I can ask for help navigating this world.

That's the deal we strike. I will continue on in this job, and in return, she will alleviate her conscience by letting me ask questions.

"We will also work together to find the way back for you," she says. "And if you ever need someone to talk to about it—being separated from your world and how difficult that must be—I am here to listen."

"I appreciate that," I say softly.

Which leaves one unresolved issue.

"You ought to be working for my brother," she says. "He needs an assistant, and you are not merely a literate apprentice. You are, in your world, Hugh McCreadie's equal, yes?"

"In theory, yes. But I can't tell Dr. Gray that."

"Yet you can help him in the guise of an apprentice."

I answer carefully. "If you mean with his studies, there's the issue of how much I should tell him at the risk of disrupting history. If he'd even believe me, which he won't while I'm Catriona."

"I am not asking you to advance my brother's work. He can do that himself. You understand it and can aid him more than any apprentice. You can also help Hugh and Duncan with this case."

Right. The case. The fact that the killer they're looking for may be a twenty-first-century serial killer. The fact that I can't tell them that. I can't even tell Isla until I'm certain I'm right.

But if he is a modern killer, then there is no way in hell, as a law-enforcement officer, I can just continue to play at being a housemaid. He won't screw up by leaving evidence behind. Hell, they couldn't *use* most of the evidence he might leave. This guy would have a hundred and fifty years of knowledge in his back pocket. Just flip through Netflix and you can find more information on serial killers than the most dedicated Victorian could dig up. All the ways other killers have gotten away with it. All the ways they've been caught.

"I *would* like to work for Dr. Gray when that's possible," I say. "Something tells me he won't be eager to have me back after last night."

"Leave that to me," she says.

Isla goes to speak to her brother. I'm still not quite sure what their situation is. The fact that Gray is quick to hand her money for cab fare suggests she's not a wealthy widow. On the other hand, the fact she teases him about it says she's not destitute either.

The basic arrangement seems to be what I presumed from the start. I'm guessing Gray isn't exactly on the hunt for an eligible future Mrs. Gray. Isla is widowed and childless, and has returned to the family home to keep house for her brother. Therefore, whatever his own feelings about me right now, if she says she doesn't want to fire me, that's ultimately her call.

When she returns, she motions me into the library.

"He'll come around," Isla says as she closes the door behind me.

I take my bucket and brush to the fireplace, so I can work while we talk.

"Please don't do that," she says.

"The fireplace needs cleaning, and Alice doesn't need any extra chores."

She continues to hover, but I wave her away and say, "So I'm right. Dr. Gray isn't happy with me. Is it because he was dragged down to the police station? That was humiliating."

She sighs and sinks into the chair behind the desk. "Duncan would not blame you for that. The problem is that while my brother can be single-minded, he does raise his head now and then to analyze the world around him. You were attacked twice in a similar manner. The first could be misfortune. A second time, though?"

"It seems like proof that I'm involved in criminal activities that could endanger his household, including you."

"He says you claimed your attacker is the killer they've been seeking."

I stop scrubbing the soot. "He thinks I'm lying."

"Was it the same person?"

"Yes."

She leans forward. "Who randomly attacked the housemaid helping to catch him? I may enjoy a rousing melodrama, where every person and event is linked by pure coincidence, but that is fiction."

"I agree. This is *not* coincidence. I told Dr. Gray about the peacock feather, which disappeared. I didn't tell him about the paper, because it also disappeared. The killer took both."

"Paper?"

"I went into that alley and saw a bundle of rags, meant to look like a fallen child. On top of it was a piece of paper with 'Catriona' written in block letters. That was supposed to startle me. Throw me off balance and let him attack me. I had the feeling I'd been followed that night, and I think that wasn't paranoia. The killer targeted me."

She frowns. "Targeted *you*? Or Catriona?"

"Catriona. Presumably because she's Dr. Gray's housemaid, and Dr. Gray works with Detective McCreadie. Do I love this theory? Nope. But I know my attacker was the raven killer, and he knew who he was attacking—Catriona, maid to Dr. Gray."

I set down my scrub brush and continue, "The only other possibility is that whoever attacked me was impersonating the raven killer. What he wore matched what a possible witness reported seeing, but I'll need to go over the newspaper and broadsides and pamphlets again and see whether that made it into a newspaper, which would explain how a copycat killer would have known what to wear."

"I can send Simon to fetch the latest papers for you."

"I'd appreciate that. As for the peacock feather, it fits. For Evans, it was a messenger pigeon or stool pigeon. For Catriona, the proud and vain peacock."

"Is it possible—?" Isla begins.

Mrs. Wallace taps at the door. When Isla calls a greeting, she opens it and says, "Caller for you, ma'am. A messenger from Mr. Bruce with a chemist request."

Isla tells the housekeeper to bring the messenger into the drawing room. Then she turns to me. "Poor timing, but duty calls. I would like to speak on this more after Simon brings us the papers. Perhaps this is how we might investigate the case, you and I together."

"The women shut out by the men, proceeding on their own?"

"As they often must."

It's early evening when Alice brings a message that Dr. Gray requires my assistance in the funerary parlor, and I nearly drop my broom and race for the stairs. I'm down there in two minutes flat to find the business dark and empty. Apparently, the assistance required is that the place needs cleaning, as I've neglected to do so in the last few days.

Once I realize I'm alone, I become uncomfortably aware of how empty and quiet it is. The raven killer tried to strangle me. That note he left tells me he knows who I am, which means if he wants to finish the job, he'll know exactly where to find me.

I slip upstairs and get my knife before I begin work. When I do hear the knob turn, though, it's clearly the front door. I straighten, hoping for Gray. Instead, Isla walks in bearing an armload of papers.

"It is only me," she says with a smile. "Do not look so terribly disappointed."

"Sorry," I say. "But if those are the newspapers, then I'm just as happy to see you."

Her brows rise. "I'm not certain that's a compliment."

"You know what I mean. Your brother is avoiding me, and until he stops that, I'm stuck with this." I wave my dusting rag. "I said I'm okay with it. Doesn't mean I wouldn't rather be examining stab wounds."

"Duncan will come around. He is being prickly, and you need to get used to waiting it out."

We move into Gray's office, and I take a chair as she sets down the papers.

"I don't blame him for getting prickly," I say. "I heard about his, uh, backstory at the police station."

Her lips tighten. "I'm quite certain you did. Yes, our father showed up one night with a child barely old enough to toddle. I was only three at the time, but it is my earliest memory, that little boy in my father's arms, him telling my mother the child is his, and the mother is dead and so she must raise him now."

"That's . . ." I shake my head. "No words."

"Oh, I have a few. Such a thing is not unheard of, but it's still a scandal and an unforgivable insult to my mother. However, it has nothing to do with Duncan, and so she raised him as her own, which was nearly as scandalous."

"Was she supposed to play the evil stepmother and make him sleep in the servants' quarters?"

"Apparently, that would have been more acceptable. No, to her, Duncan was her child, as much as the rest of us."

"Rest?"

She settles into the seat behind Gray's desk. "Duncan is the youngest. I am next. We have an older sister, who is married and visits as little as possible. We also have an elder brother, who was supposed to inherit the undertaking business but dashed off to the Continent before Father was cold in his grave."

"Leaving Dr. Gray to run the business."

"Not Duncan's first choice of occupation, but it did afford him the opportunity to pursue the science of death, and I daresay he enjoys that far more than he would a standard surgical practice. His interest has always been in the science."

"A researcher rather than a practitioner. Whereas your chemistry is more practical? Or more research oriented as well?"

Her lips twitch. "I do believe you have turned this conversation into something of an interrogation, Detective. Learning what you can about those around you. I will play along. My chemist's trade involves both the sale of medicines and the study of new formulations. That poses problems for me professionally. Women may ply their trade as natural healers, with herbs and a mortar and pestle, but when it comes to proper chemistry, it raises the specter of poison. My products are primarily traded through third parties, like Mr. Bruce, who is a chemist in his own right, but not a very good one."

"So he buys your medicine and passes it off as his own. Hope you charge him extra for that."

She smiles. "I should. A surcharge for improving his professional reputation."

"And you've been doing that since your husband passed? Or have you always done it?"

She shakes her head at me. "You *do* want all the sordid details. All right then. Let us get this out of the way. I married young. I married foolishly. A handsome classmate of Duncan's who swept me off my feet, mostly by insisting that my family scandal did not matter to him."

"Seems like a low bar."

"A low bar," she murmurs. "Yes, it should be the lowest possible bar for a suitor to vault, but he was the first to do it."

I frown. "I'm sure your father wasn't the only guy in this world with an illegitimate child. Is it because he brought your brother into the household?"

She glances at me and then at the door. "It is not . . ." She clears her throat. "It is not the fact of Duncan's existence as much as the fact that we accepted him as an equal, given his . . ." Another throat clearing. "Unique heritage."

"Ah, because he's a person of color."

"Is that what you call it? I might have hoped you'd have needed no special term, but yes. Our mother embraced him, and we followed her lead. Or I did and our eldest brother did. Our sister did, too, until she found that society accepted her far better if she distanced himself from her half brother and our unfathomable attachment to him."

"Damn. Okay. So maybe it wasn't such a low bar to hurdle after all. I didn't realize it would be such a big deal for you."

"It is a bigger deal to Duncan, and whenever I face scrutiny for my acceptance of him, I remind myself how much worse it is for him. So yes, accepting me in spite of that put Lawrence in very good stead. It did not hurt that he was handsome and witty and clever, and if Duncan warned me against him, well, that was my little brother being overly protective and so terribly sweet of him. It became far less sweet when Duncan tried to interfere with the courtship and brought our mother to his side, forcing me to elope."

"Ouch."

"Ouch, indeed. I look back on that girl and cringe. Duncan saw through Lawrence's facade, as did my mother, and I found myself wedded to a medical-school dropout who hoped my wealthy family would underwrite his true calling as an explorer in the wilds of Africa."

"Uh-huh."

"Shockingly, they did not, and it was all my fault for not arguing his case eloquently enough. After all, I owed him for having married me, despite the family scandal."

"Asshole."

"I presume that's an insult, and I can think of far worse. The sum of the matter is that when my father died and our older brother traipsed off to Europe, Duncan gave Lawrence the money he needed to travel to Africa, on the condition he would not expect me to accompany him, which suited us both. I moved back into the family home and began my chemist's work, which made enough to allow Lawrence to remain in Africa."

"Seems like an excellent use of income."

"The *best* use. That continued until I received word of Lawrence's death. He did, however, kindly leave me all his debts, which I am almost done repaying two years later."

That's why Gray is so quick to hand over money for Isla's expenses. It's also why she'll joke but won't turn it down. An unspoken agreement between them that, as uncomfortable as their financial arrangement might be, her priority should be ridding herself of this last trace of her asshole husband.

"May we begin our investigating now?" Isla asks, waving at the papers. "Or do you have more questions?"

"I have so many questions, but yes, there's a killer in need of catching. Let's see what we can find."

TWENTY-FIVE

We find no indication that the witness who described "a man in a black cape and mask" also spoke to a reporter. Isla says that at the height of broadside popularity, a witness could expect to make a small fortune selling their story. But that time has passed and writers have learned that it hardly matters whether they quote a legitimate source or not. Making shit up works as well, if not better.

Over the last few days, multiple writers have reported people seeing the killer. All are anonymous sources who saw things like "a man with bird wings" or "a man covered in feathers," as if a killer would walk down the street wearing a costume.

While I discuss the case with Isla, half of my brain is busy analyzing data from the perspective she doesn't have—my suspicion that the "raven killer" is the guy who attacked me in twenty-first-century Edinburgh.

There *is* one section of those questions Isla might be able to help with. If he did cross into the body of Catriona's attacker, how would he find out who he was?

"What kind of ID do you carry?" I ask.

Isla startles from her reading. "ID?"

"Identification. You won't have a driver's license, predating cars here. Probably not a passport either. You don't hop on planes or zip from country to country. Health card? I think we predate free health care, too."

"You do love doing that."

"Doing what?"

"Teasing me with words and concepts I do not know. You realize that I am going to ask you to explain each, and then you'll demand some personal information in return. It is a very clever game."

"It would be, if I had any intention of explaining myself. Can't, though. Butterfly effect."

She fixes me with a hard look.

"Butterfly effect," I say. "Taken from an old story—old to me, not written yet—that involves time travel and the theory that if one could travel in time, one's actions could have catastrophic effects. Simply killing a butterfly could destroy the world."

"That is preposterous."

I shrug. "I agree, which is why I'm not too worried about accidentally stepping on insects. But I do need to be careful what I bring into the past."

"You are saying that you will not tell me about advances lest I invent something fifty years before its time and become wealthy beyond measure?"

"Or get burned for witchcraft."

"We have not burned a witch in over a hundred years. We simply drown them, and only in small English villages, which are usually in England."

"I thought the witch trials were mostly in Scotland. Pretty sure it was the Scots who—"

"Fie." She waves a hand at me and mock-scowls. "You are distracting me from my purpose."

"And you're distracting me from mine. Identification. What do you carry on you when you're out and about?"

"Why should we carry identification? We have records of birth, but we hardly go about with them in our pockets."

"What happens when the police need to see your ID?"

"Why ever should they do that?" She folds the paper with a snap. "Are you telling me that in your world, police go about demanding people prove who they are? That sounds positively tyrannical."

"Er, possibly, yes. But I was just thinking that it's a good thing someone recognized Catriona after her attack. That made me wonder about identification. What do people carry on their person when they go out here?"

"An umbrella."

I laugh. "Good call."

"I take a handbag with a bit of money, but mostly paper, pencil, handkerchief . . ."

An idea hits. "What about keys?"

"For what?"

"The front door."

"Why should I need keys? It is never locked except at night, and if I were out past dark, Mrs. Wallace would leave it open for me."

I'm about to ask whether that's safe when I answer my own question. This is a prosperous street in the New Town. Being in the city, residents will still lock their doors at night, but they're not worried about anyone breaking in midday.

So if my attacker jumped into Catriona's attacker's body, how would he find out who that guy is in this world? Or would he just not bother—pick up and carry on, stealing what he needed?

My fingers itch to grab my phone and start tapping in notes.

"I'd like a notepad," I say. "Or just paper and a pen. Any extras floating around?"

"Check the top drawer. You'll need to use loose paper until I can get you a proper writing journal. If you find one in here, even empty, I would strongly advise you not to take it. My brother knows every notebook in his possession, and if one's empty, he will claim he left it that way because it is exactly the right size and paper for charts or sketches or whatnot."

"Don't borrow blank notebooks from Dr. Gray. Got it. I just won't borrow anything. Considering Catriona's past, that seems best."

I tug on the top left drawer. It seems to stick, and before Isla can say "Try the other one" I yank enough that a box on the desk skates across the polished top. I lunge to grab it, falling out of my chair but landing on my well-cushioned bottom, holding the box.

Isla claps. "Well done. Quite an astonishing display of athleticism."

"It'd be more impressive if I didn't fall on my ass." I sit up. "Catriona's strong, but she's not exactly a gymnast. I'm guessing sports aren't part of a Victorian girl's life."

"Heavens, no. How would one expect to bear children, jostling around the womb in such a fashion?"

"The . . . womb?"

"Of course. If one otherwise engages in sporting activities, it bounces around in the torso."

"And gets lost?"

Her lips twitch. "Presumably. Or becomes untethered from its moorings. Yes, the field of anatomy has advanced enough that a proper physician no longer worries about wandering wombs, but science and popular opinion rarely progress at the same rate. Women are encouraged to engage in only light athletic activity, such as purposeful perambulations about the garden."

"Sounds strenuous."

"I think it is. But I suspect we have different opinions on that."

I start to stand, only to find that the box landed upside down on me, and when I rise, everything tumbles out into my skirts.

I shake my head and right the box, a gorgeous piece with an inlaid mother-of-pearl conch shell on the top. I return the contents, piece by piece, taking my time because they are obviously valuable and delicate. Nah, I take my time because I'm nosy.

My detective brain wants to get a good look at this odd assortment of items Gray keeps so carefully. And they are indeed odd. A big-cat claw fashioned into a brooch. A handful of ancient Roman coins. An ornate hair comb carved from ivory. An enamel scarab inlaid with gems. A few other items, too, that I can't immediately identify.

"Interesting stuff," I say as I pack the box. "Dr. Gray has the travel bug, I presume."

Isla shakes her head. "Those are my father's. He was briefly an army doctor, which is how he met my mother—her father was a physician. The travel suited him. The profession, less so. Marrying my mother gave him the income he needed to quit his position and speculate instead."

"Dr. Gray mentioned that your father invested in private cemeteries."

"That and burial clubs and the business of undertaking in general. While it is not the most prestigious of work, it is very profitable, particularly if one has the knack for selling people on funerals far grander than they can afford."

"That doesn't sound like your brother."

She smiles fondly. "It is not at all my brother, but the business is prosperous enough—and the investments are profitable enough—that

Duncan doesn't need to model himself after our father, much to his relief and mine."

I put the box back on the desk. "Yet he keeps your father's treasures on his desk."

She waggles a finger at me. "You are prying again."

"Occupational hazard."

"Or a very fine excuse. Our mother gave Duncan that box, comprised of all the items she found amongst our father's things when he passed. Items that could have a connection to his mother."

"His birth mother. Who died."

"Presumably. We have questioned that. Mama feared Father might have taken the child from his mother. He wouldn't speak of the matter. Wouldn't speak of Duncan's mother either. Not a name. Not a single fact about her. We suspect she would have, at least originally, been a native of India, but that is pure speculation. Our father would say nothing."

"He erased her."

Isla looks over, her eyes meeting mine as she nods. "That is it, exactly. Erased. As if, whether by birth or background, she did not matter. That upset Mama most of all. More than the infidelity. More than expecting her to raise his illegitimate child. The *erasure*."

She exhales. "That is far more than I intended to say. You are too easy to speak to. It must serve you well as a detective."

"It probably helps that you aren't in any danger talking to me. Not like I'm going to gossip with the neighbors. I haven't even seen the neighbors."

"They are most unpleasant. I would not recommend it." She rises and walks to a cabinet. "Now, while you find yourself writing paper, may I suggest a drink?"

She lifts what looks like a bottle of scotch. "Yes?"

"Yes, please."

I'm a little tipsy as I climb the stairs to my room. It's a lot of stairs, especially after a few fingers of very fine scotch. I blame the booze for the fact that my hand is on the doorknob before I notice light shining underneath the door.

I freeze. I'm sure I didn't leave the light on. I've had the lecture from

Mrs. Wallace on the cost of gas and how I must use oil lamps and candles when possible. I've also noticed that Gray has no problem leaving lights burning all over the place. I could gripe about this, but I don't think he or Isla is the one expecting the staff to use candles. That'd be Mrs. Wallace, keeping her household running efficiently. I have also heard her grumble, quite loudly, when she needs to turn off lights in Gray's wake.

As I watch the space under my door, the light fades and shifts. Someone inside with a flashlight. Uh, no, someone inside with a *candle*. Possibly a lantern. There are still so many parts of everyday life that I need to rethink here. Which reminds me, instead of prying into Isla and Gray's personal lives tonight, I really should have been asking that most unanswerable of questions: How the hell am I supposed to wake up at 5:00 A.M. without an alarm clock? I can't keep asking for Alice's help.

At this moment, the "alarm" I apparently need is one on my door, which I bet they don't have in this world either. My room does have a lock, and Mrs. Wallace has informed me that I'm incredibly lucky in this. Privacy is a rare gift for servants. Which also means that whoever is in my room has a key.

Mrs. Wallace would, I bet. Gray could get one, and he might if he felt compelled to prove I'm a bad seed sprouting irreparably twisted vines.

I'm about to open the door when my fear from earlier slams back.

If the raven killer is from my time, then he knows I'm not Catriona. And he'll suspect *I* know he isn't from the nineteenth century. That makes me a threat. That puts me in danger. Isla literally just told me the damn front door isn't locked until everyone's in for the night, and Gray is not.

I glance around for a weapon. My gaze falls on the door to Isla's laboratory, but it's locked—for our safety, I presume. Then I remember I grabbed my knife earlier. Yep, I've definitely had too much to drink. I ease the knife out.

A drawer opens in my room. Someone's searching it.

I consider my options. Then I ease open the door, as quietly as I can. A figure stands in front of my narrow chest of drawers. She has her back to me, and she's much smaller than I expected.

Alice.

I watch as she riffles through the drawer. She pulls out a silver brush and lifts it into the firelight, turning it this way and that. Then, with a grunt of satisfaction, she replaces it. That brush might be the most valuable thing in here. She's not looking for anything to steal, then. She was making sure it didn't belong to her master or mistress.

Alice tugs the drawer all the way out and reaches inside. With a crow of discovery, she pulls out a letter. It's not until she starts to tug the paper from the envelope that I remember what it is: the letter from Lady Inglis to Gray.

Oh hell, no. We all need to learn our birds and bees sometime, but that is not the way I want this kid doing it.

"Stop right there," I say as I stride in. I snatch the letter from her hand. "That is not addressed to you."

"It is not addressed to you either," she says tartly. When I shift, she flinches, expecting a smack, but she stands firm and lifts her chin. "It belongs to Dr. Gray."

"It does," I say, "and therefore neither of us should be reading it. Apparently, I stole it, though I have no idea why. It is simply a letter from a friend."

When I reach to put it back, she flinches again. I stop and set the letter down. Time to get this out of the way.

"I hit you, didn't I, Alice? Before my accident."

She says nothing, just tightens her jaw.

"I did," I say. "I must have, though I don't remember." I back up and sit on the end of my bed. "I won't do that ever again. If I do, then . . ."

I sigh. "Well, if I do then I'm back to being the old Catriona, and if that happens, hopefully Mrs. Ballantyne will fire me. Otherwise, you should tell her. No matter what Catri—*I* said, you should always tell a grown-up when someone hurts you. A grown-up you trust, and I presume you trust Mrs. Ballantyne."

She doesn't answer.

"Do I seem like myself, Alice?" I ask.

She shakes her head.

"Because I'm not."

"Or because you're *pretending* you're not. You tricked the master, and now you've tricked the mistress. Mrs. Ballantyne is a good woman, and she wants to help, and you're giving her what she wants. That's what Mrs. Wallace says."

"Mrs. Wallace is smart," I say. "Yes, it makes more sense to give someone what they want and lower their defenses."

"You admit it then?"

"I admit it would be a good strategy. But why not employ it sooner? I have a feeling I was always nice to Mrs. Ballantyne. Am I right?"

"You tricked her. Right from the start. Tricked her and then lorded it over us."

I lean back, arms braced on the bed. "Well, then I'm not sure how to prove I've really changed now. I do seem changed, don't I? I don't remember much of my past, and that makes me a different person. Very different."

"*Too* different," she says. "You seem altogether another person, and Mrs. Wallace doesn't like it, so I don't either. Either you are lying, or you are possessed."

"Possessed?" I stifle a laugh, half at the idea and half at how, in its way, this is far more accurate than Alice could imagine. "Have you ever heard of a possessed person being *better* than they were before?"

"Perhaps you are a changeling then. That is a fairy child put in the bed of a human one."

"Oh, I know all about the fair folk. My nan told me stories. If I were a changeling, I'd be the human returned, wouldn't I? The fairies stole me as a baby and replaced me with a wicked fairy child, but now I have come home and banished her."

She considers this and then looks at me.

"Is that what happened?" she asks, in all seriousness, and I bite back a smile by reminding myself just how deep the belief in fairies runs here, in this land, at this time.

"I have no idea what happened," I say. "Only that I am not the person I was, and this one seems better, so I will keep being her for as long as I am able. And if I turn back into my old self, I have warned Mrs. Ballantyne to send me away."

"Did she agree?"

"She did, and so you've nothing to fear from me. If I do hurt you, then it is the old me, and you should tell Mrs. Ballantyne straightaway. Understood?"

She nods, wary gaze on me.

"Now," I say. "I presume you were looking for proof that my personality change is a trick. I'm not sure what you hoped to find. A journal of my confessions perhaps? You are free to continue your search. So far, I have found a pouch of money, sweets sent to Mrs. Ballantyne by a hopeful suitor, and this letter. You may search away."

She continues eyeing me.

"I mean it," I say as I back onto the bed and pick up a book. "Search to your heart's content. You may find more evidence that the old Catriona was a scoundrel and a thief, but none that I am telling lies now."

She watches me for another moment, and then she begins to search.

TWENTY-SIX

I am pleased to say that Alice finds nothing. Not pleased because I feared she might, but pleased to have my searching skills pass the test. It's obvious that Alice has hidden a thing or two in her life, and she spends well over an hour going through my room. She misses the loose floorboard. While she checks the floor, she fails to see the telltale signs, and I show her afterward. Having no plans to turn thief, I'm not the least bit concerned that she knows about Catriona's best hiding spot. Also, I've been drinking, so my judgment may not be at its best. At least I'm not drunk enough to tell her the truth about myself.

She leaves satisfied that I'm not an imminent threat to her family-in-service, and I head to bed. That doesn't mean I get much sleep. Even if the raven killer hasn't realized I'm not really Catriona, he still targeted me. He knows I'm Gray's housemaid. He could come to finish the job. And if he's from the twenty-first century and thinks I know he is, too? He'll definitely try taking me out.

I can't stop thinking about Isla saying Mrs. Wallace only locks the doors at night. Does she ever forget? No one's likely to know if she did, or if she decided to leave it open for Gray. I last saw Gray at dinner, and I have no idea whether he's still out.

The point is that whoever attacked me may try to finish the job, and I'm not exactly sleeping in a house with double–dead bolts and a security system.

I put the switchblade under my pillow.

That's part of what keeps me awake. The rest is this puzzle.

Is it possible that the raven killer is the serial killer who tried to strangle me in 2019 Edinburgh? I itch to grab my phone and start jotting down notes, working through the case for and against that conclusion. I should have taken extra paper from Gray's office, but I hadn't wanted to push my luck. I think of the library downstairs, where there must be paper and pens, but I barely avoided being sacked today. I can't afford to be caught skulking about at night.

Let's start with potential arguments against my theory. The most obvious is the one I considered earlier. How would he survive in this world? Figure out whose body he inhabits? How would he blend in? It's not impossible. I managed it. I'm still weathering the bumps, but I am managing. Therefore, he could do the same, especially with the twin advantages of being in a male body and being from Edinburgh.

I struggle to find solid arguments against the killer being from the modern world, so I switch to the other side temporarily. Signs he *could* be the twenty-first-century killer.

First, the rope. It'd caught my attention the moment Gray lifted it from Evans's body. Something inside me jumped in recognition. I'd easily explained it away, but it still remains a piece of evidence in favor of my theory. Both that killer and this one like to strangle with rope.

The trap is the next obvious factor in favor of my theory. I'd been lured into a dark alley, following sounds of a woman in danger. Might not Catriona then be pulled in by the even stronger lure of a child in distress?

Then there's the moment during our fight when he seemed to recognize me. Recognize the real me, as the victim who'd fought back in the modern world. I'd been fighting for my life and not caring whether I was talking or acting like a Victorian housemaid. That modern talk caught his ear, as the modern self-defense techniques caught his attention. A moment of déjà vu for both of us.

Is that enough?

My defense-attorney mother would say no. It's not enough to convict him of the "crime" of being my modern-day attacker. However, it would be enough evidence for the crown prosecutor to sign off on questioning him. Enough to charge him while I gathered more for trial? Possibly. But that doesn't matter here. Here, my question is only whether it's enough for me to pursue this theory. It is.

Is there anything in Evans's murder that suggests his killer *wasn't* from my time? Fingerprints or other obvious forensic evidence could hint at a Victorian murderer. It's too late to test that with Evans, but I do recall my attacker last night wore gloves, plus the hood that might keep him from shedding hairs. Still, that was also part of his disguise, so I can't read too much into it.

There's nothing in the staging or the method of murder that indicates either a modern or Victorian killer. I'll have to go through that more carefully once I have paper and pen, but a mental rundown pings nothing.

What about the torture? Nope. The old "splints under fingernails" dates back at least to the thirteenth century, from the book Gray lent me. And I investigated a case six months ago where it'd been used. Nothing there. So—

I bolt up in bed.

The water Gray found in Evans's lungs combined with the lung damage and restraints suggests waterboarding. I've seen that, too, and cops I know say it mostly started after the news of waterboarding at Guantánamo Bay. It's a bloodless and effective torture method. One McCreadie laughed at. Pouring water on someone's face? How was that torture? Anyone who has ever been yanked underwater knows how horrible it is. Even if your brain realizes you aren't going to drown, your body reacts with primal panic.

Gray hadn't rolled his eyes quite as hard as McCreadie, but he'd dismissed it, too. Does that mean waterboarding is a modern method of torture? Almost certainly not. If there's a way to terrify another human being, someone found it millennia ago. Yet Gray and McCreadie's disbelief—combined with everyone who web-searched "waterboarding" after the Guantánamo Bay incident—tells me it's not like forcing splints into nail beds. Not something they'd have read in a book or a news article. But if you're a modern killer looking for bloodless torture? Waterboarding would rank at the top of your list.

If this is the same killer, then there's something else I need to think about. Something I've forgotten, being so caught up in the possibility that I've brought a modern killer into Victorian Scotland.

I jumped into the body of Catriona, as she was being strangled by her would-be killer. So, logically, where would my would-be killer have ended up?

In the body of Catriona's killer.

Find him, whoever he is, and I'll have the raven killer.

The next morning starts as expected. Alice has been charged with taking Gray's breakfast to him, meaning I remain in that particular doghouse. Then he's off to work before I need to clean his quarters. Isla leaves before breakfast for some engagement or other.

I'm cleaning Gray's bedroom, my mind working through the implications of my theory, when his unmistakable footsteps pound up the stairs. He's in a hurry, and I glance around, feeling the odd impulse to hide, as if I'm about to be caught somewhere I'm not supposed to be. I continue dusting, presuming he'll run in, grab what he wants, and run out again. Instead, he stops in the doorway.

"You," he says.

"Yes, I am dusting your room, sir. I was not told I shouldn't—"

"I have been looking everywhere for you. Come."

He waves and strides off. I hesitate barely a heartbeat, but it's enough to have him shouting back, "Catriona!"

"Coming, sir."

He continues down two flights of stairs, and I think we're going to the funeral parlor, but he throws open the back door instead. I rack my brain to think of what I might have forgotten to do outside, but that is the domain of Simon and the part-time gardener, Mr. Tull.

When a coach emerges from the stable, Gray grunts and waves me toward it.

"Sir?" I say. "If I'm going out, I need to change my boots and put on a coat."

His look clearly conveys "Not this again" irritation. As much as I don't want to wear my indoor boots through the muck again, I'm really balking because the chill creeping down my spine has nothing to do with the weather.

Isla is gone, and Gray is suddenly very anxious to bundle me off on a coach ride. Has he realized that, with his sister away, he can fire me and tell her I quit?

"In the carriage, Catriona," he says. "Now. We haven't much time."

Not much time before Isla returns?

I want to insist on getting a coat, in hopes of stalling, but Gray is holding the coach door, and his expression warns that a two-minute delay will only annoy him more.

I climb in. Gray rattles off an address to Simon, and we're gone.

As we move from Princes Street into the narrower lanes of the Old Town, I glance anxiously at Gray.

"May I ask where you are taking me, sir?"

He doesn't answer. Doesn't even seem to hear. He's gazing outside, frowning. Then he calls to Simon, telling him where to let us out.

"Dr. Gray?" I say.

He turns sharply to me. "Describe the man who attacked you, please."

"Wh-what?" I stammer.

His brows knit with impatience. "The attack the other night. Or do you think it could have been the same person who attacked you the first time?"

I hesitate. Yes, it's the same attacker—in a way—but I've already said that I didn't see my attacker the first time. I want to tell him it's the same guy, so they'll know the crimes are connected. But what if he's testing me? Seeing whether I'll change my story about not seeing my initial assailant?

I answer slowly. "If I saw the person the first time, I do not recall it."

He leans forward. "Could it be the same man?"

"I . . . would not rule out the possibility, sir. I was attacked in an alley and strangled. This man attempted to do the same, with a rope. If it was the same killer, he may have realized that was more effective than manual strangulation."

He thumps back in his seat and into his thoughts. At least two minutes pass before he says, as abruptly as if we'd never stopped talking, "Describe the recent attacker."

"He was dressed entirely in black, including a mask of some sort."

"Like a theater mask?"

I shake my head. "It was black fabric with holes for eyes and presumably for his mouth, though the lane was too dark for me to make out that. Also too dark for me to see eye color. He wore a black mask, a coat like a cape, a black shirt and trousers. Male. Between five foot eight and five foot nine. Eleven or twelve stone."

"That is very specific."

Damn. Less cop; more housemaid.

I take a deep breath before plowing on with, "I am certain it is the man you seek. The raven killer."

I expect him to grumble at that, to pull back and even dismiss the rest of my description, clearly influenced by my presumption. I won't retract that, though. I would rather damage my reputation with Gray than damage the investigation.

He does not pull back. Does not dismiss me. Just grunts, and then the carriage stops, and he ushers me out. A few words to Simon, and the coach leaves us on the roadside.

I look around. It's a busy street, with the castle rising over the craggy hill in the background. To my left I see a sign that makes me do a double take, seeing my own surname. It's for a James Atkinson, joiner, advertising his services in both cabinetmaking and undertaking. The rough stone building seems half collapsed, with a newer roof patched on. Advertising flyers cover one wall.

I'm still gazing at my surroundings when I realize I've lost my boss. He's moving fast along the narrow road, and I scamper to catch up. I've just reached him when he speaks as if never noticing I'd disappeared.

"Describe the feather."

"The . . . ?"

"The peacock feather," he says impatiently.

"Right. It looked like—" I stop myself before saying it looked like a peacock feather. "It was cut short. To fit inside his jacket, I presume. Less than a foot of quill. It was mostly the eye, and it was kind of ragged. But the colors were really bright."

"Describe."

"The colors?" I pull up an image from my mind. "Green and blue with an orange eye. It looked unnaturally colorful. Garish."

"Peacock feathers usually are."

"Yes, but this was unusually so. It may have been dyed."

"And what happened to it?"

Gray turns a corner before I can answer, and I kick up my pace to reach him.

"The feather fell out as we fought," I say. "Afterward, he stayed in the shadows. The men never even realized he was wearing a mask. Their attention was on me. He reached down, and I thought he was picking up my knife, so I shouted a warning. But one of my so-called rescuers had my knife, and when my attacker left, the feather was gone."

He grunts.

I take a deep breath. "There was also a piece of paper with my name on it."

He wheels so fast I fall back before steadying myself.

"I decided not to mention it because you obviously did not believe me about the feather."

I tell him how I was lured in and how I found my name on that paper, presumably to startle me while he attacked.

"I believe," I say, "that I was made a target because I am your house-maid, possibly even your temporary assistant. If the killer is following the investigation, he may have known I assisted Detective McCreadie at the rooming house. It seems a departure from the first murder, though, and I am not certain what to make of it." I pause. "Unless he planned to torture me for information on the investigation. Strangle me to uncon-sciousness, take me somewhere, and torture me."

Gray only nods abruptly. Then he continues walking.

We turn another corner. It's a quieter area, residential, with buildings that would have been upper-middle-class town houses at one time con-verted to overflowing tenements when the wealthier residents fled across the old medieval wall to the New Town.

Voices sound ahead. A whistle blows. Someone shouts, and a male voice barks a command. Before I can ask where we're going—again—we round yet another corner of these maze-like streets, and I see the crowd ahead. The narrow road has been blocked off, a constable with a whistle warning carts to turn back. It's a wasted effort. The crowd is so thick that no cart could pass, and the constable is left arguing with cart drivers who have no intention of turning back; they want to see what's going on, only adding to the tumult.

Gray strides forward. He reaches back to take my elbow and seems surprised that I'm right beside him, shouldering men out of my way. He still grasps my elbow, so we don't become separated by the crowd. It's at least twenty men deep. Oh, there are a few women, but most of them have been relegated to the edges, the men forgetting their chivalry when they want to see what's going on themselves.

I'm soon glad of Gray's guiding grip. He's tall enough that his head clears the crowd, and he has no compunction about using his size to barrel through. He carries himself like a man of his class, expecting to be obeyed. It works far better than my pokes and squeezes and elbows, and soon we are through, leaving a trail of muttered epithets in our way. When we reach the edge, a constable tries to stop us.

"He's with me," a voice calls.

I recognize it as McCreadie, though I still can't see him. Even this inner circle is a mob of police officers and witnesses and others who seem to have just broken through to the middle. The class or status of the trespassers means the constables don't dare expel them.

Dear God, don't tell me this is a crime scene.

My left eyelid starts twitching as I watch people tramping about. It takes all my strength not to order them aside myself.

Has no one heard of crime-scene containment? No, Mallory, they have not, because they've barely begun using police to solve crimes. Proper protocol is decades away, after they discover the importance of fingerprints and other evidence.

The constable lets us through. As he does, another leans in to whisper something. I catch the words "that Gray ghoul."

The first officer mutters, "He doesn't look gray to me," and they both chuckle.

"Enough of that," a young voice says.

I glance over to see Constable Findlay glowering at the two older officers. Gray waves for him to ignore the insult, and Findlay nods and then leads us to the center, where I stop short, blinking.

There is a woman lying dead beside the steps of a house, with a gate behind her, presumably leading to a yard beyond. That is not what makes me blink. Nor does the fact that she's just lying there, people milling about, some leaning in for a better look, as if she's a display in a wax museum.

A display in a wax museum.

A chill runs through me, because it is exactly the right description. That is why I stop short. I have seen this tableau before, and it takes only a moment to identify the source. Yet another of those macabre museum exhibits Nan had taken me to. I can't quite recall whether this was a special exhibition in a proper museum or more of a tourist wax museum. I remember this scene, though.

A woman lying at the gate leading to a stable. A row of what looked like once-decent residential town houses now decayed into tenement housing. The museum exhibit said she'd been there all night, with people later admitting they'd passed and presumed she was drunk or sleeping rough. It was that sort of neighborhood, after all.

The street was called Buck's Row, somehow shortened from Ducking Pond Row because there was a nearby pond used for ducking punishments. That is the detail from the exhibit that pops out now, one my young brain had tucked away because I wanted to know what a "ducking punishment" was.

Finally, someone had investigated. They discovered a dead woman, still warm, lying on her back. Her throat had been slashed. Later, a medical examiner would discover more. Bruises on her face, as if she'd been struck. Stab wounds to her groin and abdomen. No organs missing. That would come later with other victims.

This is what I see here, in 1869 Edinburgh. It's one of those memories seemingly long vanished, shooting forth in perfect detail, like a stored snapshot awaiting a trigger.

I have seen this before.

Everything is perfectly reproduced, from the victim—a graying brunette in her early forties—to the petticoats in disarray around her.

There is a split second where I think what I saw in the twenty-first century was a re-creation of this very murder. No. This isn't the same murder. It just looks like it. Rendered in as much detail as the killer could manage. Re-creating a murder that will not occur for another twenty years.

That museum exhibit had been on Jack the Ripper. The woman lying dead in Buck's Row?

The first of the canonical five victims.

TWENTY-SEVEN

Polly Nichols. That's the name that comes to mind, and I wouldn't bet my life savings on it, but I'd shout it out at a trivia night.

I'd gone on a Ripper kick in high school. It was right around the time I was solidifying my plan to become a detective, making sure it was more than a childhood dream. Jack the Ripper is the most famous unsolved case in history, so I threw myself into it as a would-be detective. What I eventually realized is that it was a fun little exercise, but ultimately a futile pursuit. It'd been so early in the history of forensics and detective work that one could only blindly speculate on the killer, based on one's favored theory.

Before me lies an exact replica of Polly Nichols's murder. Twenty years before Polly Nichols will die.

Here is the final proof I need. Proof that the guy who tried to kill me two nights ago is from the twenty-first century. He decided to copycat the most famous serial killer of all time.

You bastard.

The curse rings in my head as Gray leads me to the body.

I don't spend one moment wondering *why* the killer did this. I know why. I remember being in Gray's room, going through those newspapers and pamphlets, expecting so much more coverage. The killer expected it, too.

No one had cared. Not really. A journalist strangled and staged to look like a bird? Next, please.

So he decided to do *next*. The next level. You want more? How about a pretty housemaid, slaughtered in an alley? But I thwarted him, and this is my reward.

Oh, it might have nothing to do with me, but I still *feel* responsible. The killer planned to take a young and pretty victim, in hopes that would give him the attention he wanted. Better yet, I was connected to the detective on his trail, and he does love his connections, as if we deserved our fate by offending him.

I did more than offend him. I survived his attack—*twice*—and so he has rethought his plan and decided to make a full right turn. Because he can. He isn't driven by any compulsion to murder in a specific way. He's flexible. And here he's flexed to something far cleverer than staging his victims as birds.

He's stealing from the future. Stealing the thunder of the most famous serial killer of all time. It is breathtakingly clever, and I do not grant him one iota of credit for it, because seeing this poor woman, all I can do is inwardly rage at the pointlessness of her murder, chosen only because she bears a superficial resemblance to Polly Nichols.

What will happen in Jack the Ripper's time now? Will he still kill Polly Nichols in the same manner? He might, if news of this killing never reaches London, but if he does, it will not take long before someone sees the connection and paints history's most infamous serial killer as a mere copycat. *This* killer will be the original.

As I step toward the body, I stop, feeling eyes on me. I look up to see the shocked faces of those nearby as a woman—a housemaid still in uniform—approaches the body. I ignore those looks and scan the crowd. In public murders, especially serial killings, it's basic protocol to get a look at the crowd. My fingers itch to take cell-phone photos, in case the killer is there, gloating and vibrating in excitement at seeing his handiwork admired. Here, with all these people, it would be easy to get close, and I can do no more than survey faces.

Are you here?

I sliced my attacker's arm and stabbed his side. That would be far more helpful in identifying him if people in this world wore less clothing. Even with the sun promising a warm day, all the men are in long sleeves, most also in jackets. Next time, I'll need to aim for the face.

Even if the killer isn't here, I'm sure my own presence will not go unremarked. Newspapers will mention the fair-haired maid who accompanied the notorious Dr. Gray. If the killer didn't realize I was involved in the case before, he'll know now.

Good.

Yes, that puts me in danger, but I was already there, and if he targets me again, I will be ready. I will catch him if I can, and I will see his face if I cannot.

One last slow look at the crowd. Then I bend beside the body. I forget I'm Catriona Mitchell. I become Detective Mallory Atkinson, attending a crime scene, and I kneel a foot from her head. When someone shouts a horrified warning, I startle, realizing what I'm doing. Before I can scramble back, Gray's hand lands on my shoulder, staying me.

"Don't let the lass see this," a voice says, and I look to see McCreadie bearing down on us. "The poor woman has been savaged."

"And Catriona could see that before she wished a closer examination," Gray says placidly. "She has a keen eye and an iron stomach. If she wishes to look, let her."

McCreadie grumbles, but he doesn't tell me to get back. His concern was entirely for my feminine sensibilities. The thought that a layperson—a housemaid—shouldn't get this close to a murder victim doesn't seem to occur to him. Doesn't seem to occur to anyone, from the looks of things.

"How long do I have?" Gray asks McCreadie.

"A runner went to fetch Addington shortly after I sent for you," McCreadie says, his voice low. "I held off as long as I could. I know you like to see victims on the scene when possible, and in this case"—he spares a glance for the dead woman—"it seemed wise to do so. Also, there is the feather."

His gaze travels to the left, and I follow it to see a feather wedged under her shoulder. A peacock feather.

"The same?" Gray murmurs to me.

I start moving aside for a better look at the feather. His hand falls on mine, the warmth of it startling me. He pulls back quickly with a murmured apology and then says, "We have limited time. The feather can be examined later."

"It appears to be the same," I say.

McCreadie says, "I apologize for doubting you."

"I would have doubted me, too, under the circumstances."

I turn to the body. McCreadie squats beside us to listen in.

"I'm afraid I do not have time to make this a teaching exercise," Gray says as he takes a probe from his pocket. "Nor even a lecture. I will discuss my findings later. However, please draw your own conclusions, both of you, and feel free to voice them aloud."

He holds out the probe. I take it automatically. Then I pause and hold it out to McCreadie.

The detective shakes his head. "I will observe only. My stomach is not as strong as yours."

I wait to see where Gray will start. He is the doctor after all. He begins at the neck and uses forceps to examine it quickly before moving down to her abdomen.

I take over examining the neck injuries. Her throat hasn't just been slashed. It's been cut right to the vertebrae. That's the most obvious thing, and I need to see past the horror of it to examine further.

After a moment, I murmur, "Hesitation marks."

I don't mean to speak aloud, and Gray startles as if I shouted. He twists to look at the victim's neck.

"What was that, Catriona?"

I pause a moment, then plow forward. "These marks here, sir." I point to them. "They seemed to indicate that the killer hesitated. That is to say, he did not make the cuts decisively."

"Took him some nerve to work up to it?" McCreadie says.

"Perhaps," Gray says. "I had noted the marks. I was not certain what they indicated but 'hesitation' seems a good interpretation. Thank you, Catriona." He taps the forceps on a spot below the victim's ear. "Did you note these abrasions?"

"I had not. They would suggest strangulation, I believe? Strangled and then her throat cut?"

I reach to check under her eyelids before stopping myself.

"What were you about to do, Catriona?"

"I, uh, I think that book mentioned something about seeing signs of strangulation in the whites of the eyes."

A hint of a smile as he nods. He uses his forceps to nudge up the victim's lids, and I see the red of hemorrhaging. "Now, I promised I was not going to teach, and here I am teaching. Continue to make observations, Catriona, aloud please, as I examine the abdominal injuries."

"I do not wish to disturb you, sir."

"If you mean that in truth, then let me assure you I am capable of listening while also focusing on my work. However, if you feel I am pressuring you, you may refrain from voicing your observations."

I glance at McCreadie, who offers me a small smile and mouths, "Go on."

"She wasn't killed here," I say, which is a bit of a cheat, because there's no way in hell the killer happened to find just the right victim at just the right spot to stage his reenactment. "There's not enough blood on the ground for that. I've, uh, seen animals slaughtered and so I, uh, know the signs."

"You do not need to explain how your knowledge arises, Catriona. I trust it is not from personal experience with murder."

"Only the personal experience of having nearly been a victim of it twice." I get a brief smile from both men for that. I push on. "You'll want to find the actual site of the murder, won't you? It'll have a lot of blood." I pause. "Unless the blood settled after the strangulation. Can you tell how much time passed between that and the throat being cut?"

"I may be able to attempt it if I am allowed to take possession of the body after the autopsy."

"And if Addington doesn't butcher her more *with* the autopsy," McCreadie mutters.

"Examine the edges of the wound, and you'll see they're quite bloodless," Gray says, still working on the abdomen. "My preliminary assessment would be that she was killed elsewhere, by strangulation, and then brought here, where the knife work was done. The blood, as you noted correctly, would have settled by that time, causing a lack of it here at the scene. Hugh? Can you show Catriona how to check for that?"

McCreadie pulls down the shoulder of the victim's dress, as circumspectly as possible, and points out the lividity, indicating the blood has settled.

"We can even tell *how* she was lying postdeath by the pattern," Gray continues. "For that, we'll need to disrobe her, though, which we obviously will not do here. Now, come look at—"

"Sir?" It's Findlay, hurrying over to McCreadie. "I spotted the doctor's coach around the corner."

"Good lad," McCreadie says. "You have keen eyes."

Findlay glances down and bobs his head. Then he sneaks a look at me as we move away from the body.

"It doesn't bother you, Miss Catriona?" he asks. "Looking at that?"

"It doesn't if I remind myself the examination is necessary to find her killer," I say.

"I suppose so." He glances back at the corpse and swallows. "I have never seen one so brutalized."

"This is an extreme case," McCreadie says. "There is no shame in finding it difficult to look upon her."

"Try not to think of the body as a person," I say. "You'll need to, when you investigate her death, but for now, put that aside if you can."

Findlay peers at me intently, obviously not expecting these words from Catriona, and I'm wondering whether I went too far when Gray says, "Catriona is very astute. The object behind us is a piece of evidence. The person within is gone. You honor that person by solving her murder, and you needn't worry about causing insult by examining her remains."

Gray and McCreadie move away to speak, leaving me with Findlay.

"I heard about your attack Wednesday night," he says. "I know Detective McCreadie doubted you at first, but he said the feather proves it. I wanted to say that I am sorry, and I hope you are all right."

"I am, thank you." I look at the crowd and then back at him. "I am sorry for how I treated you. You're a good police officer."

He goes still, and I realize he might think I'm mocking him.

I grimace. "That sounded patronizing. I apologize. I mean it honestly. You're a good officer, and I endangered that, and I'm sorry. If anything ever comes of what I did, I will take the blame. I'll tell Detective McCreadie I stole your notes and that's how I came by the information."

His gaze moves away as he says, gruffly, "It was my mistake."

"No, I will fix it, if need be. I mean that, and I am not saying so in hopes of renewing our attachment." *Dear God, no.* "I am only trying to make amends."

I scan the crowd again. "If I may pass on a bit of advice, take note of faces in the crowd. The killer could be here."

He considers that, again watching me intently. "You have a gift for this. Perhaps more than I."

Is that jealousy? It doesn't sound like it. Just an observation.

I shrug. "I have traveled in the circles of criminals. I know their minds. It's just another way to do detective work. It seems to me that the killer wishes to call attention to himself, first with a bizarre murder and now a horrific one. If that is the case, might he not be here to see his handiwork admired?"

When he doesn't answer, I say, "It was only a suggestion. After all, I am but a housemaid."

McCreadie walks over with Gray.

"I thought of taking note of the crowd," Findlay says to McCreadie. "Being such a gruesome murder, is it possible the killer might be here, watching our horror?"

McCreadie smiles. "That is a capital idea, Colin. Yes, please do that." Findlay nods his thanks to me and moves into the crowd.

A coach drawn by two horses clatters down the lane, and as we look up, McCreadie grumbles. "Trust Addington to insist on bringing his coach where it obviously cannot fit."

It *does* fit, but only by driving all the foot traffic into side streets and alleyways, the displaced shaking their fists at the passing driver.

"Even if his driver can get in," I say, "how is he going to get out again?"

"Easy," McCreadie says. "Addington will expect us to move the body and clear away the crime scene so that he may continue down the lane."

I try not to blink in horror. A crime scene is about to be destroyed so the coroner can visit in his personal coach.

As I stare, a prickle on the back of my neck has me scanning the crowd. I meet eyes. Male eyes, many angry, as if affronted at my presence here, front and center. That would include most of the other officers, unfortunately.

Get used to it, boys. The women at your crime scenes won't always be lying on the ground with their throats slit.

The driver gets as far as he can, then hops down to open the door, as if for royalty. I'm surprised the poor guy isn't expected to bow.

A man climbs out of the coach. The doctor's assistant or intern. He's in his late twenties, lanky and red-haired. He pulls out his boss's black medical bag. Then he shuts the door and strides toward us.

"McCreadie," he calls in a voice far too deep and hearty for his youth.

"Dr. Addington."

I squint against the sun, thinking I must be wrong about his age, but my first impression doesn't change as he grows closer. He's ruddy-cheeked, with an unlined face that says he probably hasn't passed his thirtieth birthday.

"Gray!" he calls. "What ever are you doing here?"

There's no malice in his tone. No sarcasm either. His voice warms with the genuine affection of a man greeting an esteemed colleague.

"I heard of the death and thought it a rare opportunity to observe a murder victim in situ."

"Excellent idea." He claps Gray on the arm, and here a touch of condescension tinges Addington's voice. "Now my question, McCreadie, is why someone didn't come to tell me Dr. Gray was on the scene, so I didn't need to come."

"As you are the city's police surgeon, sir, I am required to summon you. Also, I thought, like Duncan, you might wish to see the body, as he says, in situ."

"What ever for?" Addington peers over at the woman's body. "If you would like my opinion, Detective, the poor lady is quite dead." He laughs at his own joke. "Dr. Gray may never have practiced medicine, but even he can tell you that."

Gray stiffens. And there it is. The reason for Addington's mild condescension. He is a "proper" doctor, and Gray is not.

"You still ought to have sent someone to tell me Dr. Gray is here," Addington chides McCreadie. "I was in the midst of seeing a patient when your messenger arrived. How much more convenient for me to finish that up and have a cup of tea before strolling down to Dr. Gray's house to conduct the examination."

"Your convenience is my utmost concern, Dr. Addington," McCreadie says.

Addington slaps him on the arm. "There's a good chap. Now let's see if you can clear this mess away so my coach may pass through, and with any luck, I can flee this wretched place before the stench ruins this suit forever."

He turns to Gray. "Would you be a good chap and deliver her to your examination room?"

"Is that where you want her?" McCreadie says. "At Dr. Gray's and not in the police office dead room?"

Addington shivers. "Why ever would I wish to examine her *there*?

Dr. Gray's offices are so much better supplied and so much more convivial. We have this arrangement for a reason, McCreadie."

"I am only making certain," McCreadie murmurs. "So I might convey your decision to my superiors, who are of the opinion that this case may be different."

"How? She's dead. Murdered. Nothing *different* in that. I shall await her at Dr. Gray's offices."

So this is how Gray gets away with examining bodies. They have an arrangement with Addington, who lives in the New Town and wants the prestige of being the police surgeon but not the inconvenience of carrying out autopsies in an actual police station. Cleverly done.

"Dr. Addington," Gray says as the other man begins returning to his coach. "Might I beg your indulgence in allowing me to examine the body at the scene. For my studies."

"Of course, of course. She's not going anywhere, is she? Just move her out of the way so my coach can pass."

Gray opens his mouth to argue, but Addington plows on, "Then I'll nip by your house in, say an hour? Oh, and as I have missed my morning tea, could you please have your housekeeper fix me a tray? And if you could have that delightful little maid of yours bring it by, I would be most obliged." He winks at Gray. "I haven't seen her in a while, and I miss the sight of that delectable girl."

He strides away, whistling, without waiting for a response.

"Please tell me he wasn't talking about Alice," I say.

McCreadie snorts a laugh. "No, thankfully. He meant you."

"He failed to see me standing right here?"

"Dr. Addington fails to see anything he doesn't want to see. Including, half the time, the proper cause of death." McCreadie slants a glance at me. "Before you ask, he has not been in his position long. The former police surgeon was an excellent fellow, very deserving of the office. But he retired, and Dr. Addington has connections that saw him elected despite his incompetence. However, it does allow us to take advantage."

I turn to Gray, but he's already at the body, where she's been moved to let Addington pass.

McCreadie winks. "Time for our not-a-lesson to resume."

TWENTY-EIGHT

And so I am back in Gray's good graces. He doesn't say so. Doesn't join McCreadie in apologizing for questioning my attack story, either. His apology comes in action, and from the moment he heard about the feather, the mistrust began to ebb, and I am once again his assistant.

He examines the body while taking time now to explain what he's doing and also keeping an eye on his pocket watch. At the last possible moment, the victim is loaded onto a cart.

And that's when the victim's sister shows up.

The timing is not accidental. While McCreadie seemed to be completely focused on Gray's examination, he was multitasking, having already gotten a preliminary ID on the body and sent officers to track down next of kin. They found the sister and brought her to the scene, and I . . . I will say little about that except that I truly hope the killer is not in the crowd to feed off her grief.

Obviously, I'm horrified at the thought of bringing next of kin to the actual crime scene, but McCreadie is following procedure, where efficiency is the key—get the body identified as quickly as possible. To his credit, when he realizes the sister has arrived, he hurries to the cart and covers the body himself, exposing only her face. I cringe at possible trace contamination from the blanket, but his heart is in the right place, and trace transfer is hardly a concern in a world that doesn't test for trace yet.

As for me, I help in the only way I can—by staying far from the cart and leaving the poor woman to her grief.

I'm bent examining the peacock feather when Gray strides over to scoop it up, making me wince. Again, I remind myself that without fingerprint or DNA testing, there's no concern with handling evidence, but I still inwardly squirm.

"It is the same, yes?"

"If not the exact one, then its exact match," I say. "There's something on the bottom of the quill, where it's been cut off. Hacked off, it looks like. A black staining, like ink."

"Because it *is* ink," he says.

"Ah, right. Hard to find peacock feathers just lying about, so he made do with a peacock-feather pen. Would the dyeing make it cheap or expensive?"

"Cheap," he says. "A substandard feather, dyed."

"Also ragged," I say. "Probably not a new pen, then. Where would one purchase a used peacock-quill pen?"

His lips twitch. "Now you wish to take poor Findlay's job, too? Shall I lose you to Hugh?"

"I was speculating," I say. "But if you are not interested in theorizing . . ."

An unmistakable glitter lights his eyes. "I am far too interested in theorizing, as Hugh would tell you. Not that he complains about me playing detective. He's happy enough for my deductions, though it doesn't keep him from grumbling about them."

"Tell him you are a consulting detective."

One brow arches.

"Sherlock Holmes?" I say.

His expression tells me that, once again, I am ahead of my time. Or behind it. I've lost track.

"Hugh!" Gray calls, waving the feather as McCreadie returns from the cart. "May we take this for examination?"

I open my mouth to protest, but McCreadie shrugs. "If you like."

Gray pockets the evidence as I suppress a whimper.

"There's also a raven feather," McCreadie says. "It was under her body. Would you like that, too?"

"Please." Gray turns to me. "Shall we wash up before we return home?"

"Yes, sir, if we may."

"Let's do that then, and we'll find ourselves a cab. Hugh? Will you join us for lunch?"

"I will not turn down Mrs. Wallace's cooking."

We're having lunch while Addington conducts the autopsy with his assistant, who turns out to be an old guy looking a lot like I'd expected of Addington himself. I delivered their tray and endured Addington's ogling, and then I hurried back to serve lunch. We are settling in to a midday repast of hot soup and cold roast goose when Isla returns.

"I am in time for lunch," she declares, walking in. "Hugh, how lovely to see you."

McCreadie clambers to his feet to take her coat and pull out her chair. Then just as she's about to slide in front of it, he slams it in again.

"No," he says. "You cannot join us, Isla."

"If this is a game, Hugh, I am much too hungry to play it." She takes hold of the chair, but he grips it in place.

"We are discussing a murder," McCreadie says.

Her gaze slides to me before darting away. "I see. Well, I am glad that Catriona is assisting you again, Duncan, but there is nothing about the murder of Archie Evans that I do not know from the papers, and it was a decidedly bloodless affair."

"There's been a second murder. It is different."

"Different how?"

McCreadie pauses and then blurts, "Bloodier."

"How bloody?" She waves off her own question. "Never mind. I am determined to join this meal and this conversation, whatever happened to the poor man."

"Woman," McCreadie says. "Possibly a prostitute."

She frowns. "Was there an outrage committed against her?"

"No, nothing like that. At least . . ." He glances at Gray, who shakes his head. "No outrage. But a gruesome murder. It was very brutal, and you will not wish to discuss it while eating."

"Is that not for me to determine? I am quite capable of leaving if I feel overwhelmed."

"You may be physically able to leave, but you are too bloody stubborn."

"Her throat was cut," I say. "Deeply. Her abdomen stabbed, and her, uh, nether regions also stabbed."

"Catriona!" McCreadie wheels on me.

I placidly spoon up my cream soup. "I believe Mrs. Ballantyne is a grown woman, who ought not to be treated as a child. If she wishes to endure a conversation that may cause nightmares, that is her choice, is it not? She knows the gist of it now. She can make her own decision."

"Thank you, Catriona," Isla says, and she pulls sharply on her chair, wrenching it from McCreadie.

The detective looks to Gray for help, but Gray only shrugs as he slices into his goose. "The girl has a point. Isla now knows what happened to the woman, and the choice is hers. I would strongly suggest"—he slants a look at his sister—"that she not view the body, but otherwise, I accept her choice."

"Good," Isla says as she sits. "Now tell me about this poor woman."

The victim, as her sister confirmed for McCreadie, is one Rose Wright. Widowed and living with her sister, the one who'd come to identify the body.

"Is she a sex worker?" I ask when McCreadie finishes explaining.

McCreadie chokes on a bite of goose.

Isla clears her throat, obviously trying hard to keep from laughing. "I know your vocabulary has been disturbed, Catriona, but we do not generally use that word in company, polite or otherwise."

"Worker?" I say, catching her eye with a look that makes her lose control of that laugh.

Gray only shakes his head, a smile playing on his lips.

"Fine," I say. "Is she a prostitute?"

There's nothing fundamentally wrong with that word. As a police officer, I'd been trained to use "sex worker" instead to avoid the stigma that is associated with "prostitute." The exact same stigma, I realize, that is attached to "sex" in this time period. Of course, judging by what I read of Lady Inglis's letter, Victorians are having—and enjoying—sex. They just don't talk about it. How terribly Victorian of them.

I press on. "The fact that Rose has taken money for, er, her time doesn't mean that's her primary occupation. When I was on the streets, I knew women who'd, uh, sell their favor, if they really needed the money. They had jobs, but those jobs didn't always pay the bills."

"Catriona is correct," Isla says. "While this woman may have engaged in prostitution, do not presume that makes her a prostitute, and even if it does, please do not treat her any less for it."

"I would not do that, Isla," McCreadie says, and there's a gentleness in his voice. Their eyes meet as she nods in acknowledgment.

"I cannot answer the question either way yet," McCreadie continues. "I was not about to interview her poor sister over the body. That will be my first stop this afternoon. Interviewing the family."

"Might I come along?" I ask.

"To the *interview*?" he says.

I hesitate. I'd asked without thinking. Well, yes, I'd been thinking, but only that I wanted to speak to her family and friends.

I have information McCreadie does not. I now know, beyond a doubt, that this is a killer from my own time. I know he's copying Jack the Ripper. I know there may be a connection between the killer and Rose Wright, if he's following his pattern of needing a personal connection.

The problem, of course, is that there is absolutely no reason for "Catriona" to be at those interviews.

"I, er, thought I might be able to help. Perhaps I could go along as your secretary?"

"A female secretary?"

"It is the nineteenth century, Hugh," Isla says tartly. "Women may be barred from many occupations, but they are perfectly capable of being whatever they want, including secretaries."

"I am not arguing that," McCreadie says. "But I thought Catriona would be needed to help Duncan with his examination of the body."

Gray takes a bite of cheese, his face studiously neutral. "If Catriona would prefer to help you—and you have need of her—then I understand. My work is not as interesting as yours."

Here stands the proverbial crossroads. I can stay behind and work with Gray. Or I can convince McCreadie to take me along to witness—and maybe help with—the interview.

I do want to help examine Rose's body; I just want to postpone it until after the interview. That isn't possible.

Pick one, Mallory.

There's no real question. Long-term, I want to help Gray, and so I murmur, "I was not thinking about the body, sir. I would prefer to stay, if it is all right with you."

Isla gives a slight nod of approval. Then she says, "How about we discuss the interview? While I know Hugh is quite capable of handling it on his own, we may be able to come up with interrogative directions he has not considered."

"Certainly," McCreadie says. "I'm always happy to accept assistance. After all"—he winks at Isla—"I'm the one making the salary and the one who'll reap the benefits. Unpaid help is always welcome."

"Oh, you will pay for it," Isla says. "I have a short list of dangerous chemicals I cannot obtain on my own. A police officer, however, would have no such difficulty requisitioning them from the chemist."

McCreadie smiles. "Consider it done."

After lunch, McCreadie conducts an interview. Not the one with the victim's family. The one with the killer's former victim: me.

One would think this might have taken precedence over lunch. One would also think that—having been nearly murdered by a serial killer and escaping through my wits and fists—I'd get a little more, oh, I don't know. Sympathy?

Hey, Catriona, seems you really were nearly murdered by the guy we've been looking for. Why don't you take the day off dusting? Relax. Put your feet up. Anything we can get you? A cold drink, perhaps? A plate of biscuits?

We settle into the drawing room and McCreadie says, "So it seems Catriona escaped our raven killer after all."

"What?" Isla says, in the midst of lowering herself onto a chair.

Naturally, just because I'm about to be interviewed by the police doesn't mean I need privacy or anything. I don't actually care, but yes, it's a little odd to retire to the drawing room, as if we're about to sip a fine glass of port, maybe play a little charades, and instead . . .

I say to Isla, "There was a peacock feather found with the body, which matches the one my attacker dropped. Dr. Gray asked me to describe it before we arrived on the scene, to be sure my recollection wasn't tainted by seeing it again."

I don't blame Gray for that. Standard practice, even if he wouldn't realize it.

"That was a good idea, Duncan," McCreadie says.

"I'd make a good . . ." Gray glances at me. "Consulting detective?"

McCreadie laughs. "As long as you don't expect a cut of my pay, you can call yourself whatever you like. Yes, it appears to be the same killer. I would say it *is*, but we must always leave room for doubt when any exists." He glances at me. "No insult to Catriona."

"None taken. I am satisfied as long as no one continues to doubt that I was attacked by what *seemed* to be the raven killer."

"There is no doubt of that," McCreadie says. "I apologize again for the earlier confusion. Now, would you take me through the events of that evening?"

I glance at Isla. "I think I should be honest here, as to what I was doing out that evening. If I may?"

Isla hesitates. It won't do me any favors to admit I'd stolen her locket. Any lie, though, taints my testimony.

Isla nods. "You may. I would like to say, first, that the matter has been resolved, and I am fully persuaded of Catriona's commitment to this second chance life has given her. I do not hold this—or any—prior action against her."

"Well, now I really *do* want to know what you were doing out there," McCreadie says.

I explain. As I do, both men's moods shift, sparks of outrage from McCreadie and a descending thundercloud of anger from Gray.

"Your locket?" McCreadie says. "She stole your grandmother's *locket*?"

Isla raises her hands. "The old Catriona stole it. The one sitting with us does not recall that and, on realizing what she had done, she took the necessary steps to retrieve the necklace. Dangerous steps that nearly cost Catriona her life."

McCreadie continues to grumble, but his anger will pass quickly. Quick to temper and quicker to laughter, as my nan would say. It's Gray I watch. It's the weight of *his* anger that I feel. His is deeper. His will linger.

"Is there anything else we should know about, Catriona?" he asks finally, that cool gaze turning on me.

Isla tries to cut in, but I beat her to it. "I honestly do not know, sir. Mrs. Ballantyne mentioned the locket, and knowing I have stolen things in the past, I feared I had taken it. I presumed if I had, it would be at the pawn-broker. Fortunately, it was. There may be other things I took before my acci-dent. There may be things I said or did before my accident. Nothing since."

"So you have been forthright with us on all subjects since the accident?"

"*Duncan*," Isla says. "That is an entirely unfair question. Let me re-phrase that with respect to her right to a private life. Catriona? Have you stolen anything since your accident? From us or from anyone else?"

"Only a cup of coffee." At her look, I say, "It was from Dr. Gray's break-fast tray. He didn't finish his morning pot, and so I had a cup."

Isla struggles to suppress a smile, and says gravely, "We shall see that you are allowed your own coffee."

"Thank you."

"Since your accident, have you lied about anything related to your em-ployment or your position as a member of this household?"

"Not to the best of my knowledge. It is possible that I said something that was not true because I don't remember the truth, but I have not in-tentionally lied."

"Since your accident, have you done anything that could harm any member in this household?"

"No."

Isla glances at her brother as McCreadie jokes about her taking a job as a barrister. His anger has already passed. Gray stays quiet. He's not going to say that he accepts my words at face value—I'm not exactly hooked up to a polygraph. But he isn't challenging me further, and that's the best I can hope for.

I continue with my story. McCreadie is impressed by how I fought back and teases that Isla should have a knife of her own, to which she heartily agrees, and he realizes that was a dangerous joke to make. There's a little back-and-forth there, with him trying to talk her out of it and her mak-ing plans to purchase one "posthaste."

Gray pushes to his feet. "You've put the idea into her head, Hugh, and there will be no getting it out. The best you can do is teach her how to use it."

"Use a *knife*?" he sputters.

"Would you prefer a revolver?" Isla says. "Although, now that you men-tion it—"

"I did not mention it. You did."

"I should like a revolver. One of those tiny ones that American ladies carry in their handbags."

"They do not carry pistols in their handbags, Isla. You have been reading too many of those novels of yours."

"But one would fit in a handbag, would it not? That is an excellent idea, Hugh. Thank you for suggesting it."

"I did *not* suggest it."

Gray clears his throat. "Please do continue this lively discussion without me. I have a body to attend to."

He rises and gets to the door before looking at me. When his brows knit, I almost exhale in relief. Okay, so he might not have forgiven me for the locket yet, but he isn't angry enough to bar me from the examination room.

I nod and hurry after him.

TWENTY-NINE

Addington is gone, and Gray is furious about that. The dark cloud of anger hovering over locket-stealing Catriona shifts over a new target. Addington was supposed to come upstairs and speak to McCreadie before he left. That's apparently the real reason McCreadie was having lunch here. He was waiting for Addington's report. Addington and his assistant finished the autopsy and left notes jotted in a nearly indecipherable scrawl.

"He will file a report, won't he?" I ask as Gray glowers at the brief notes.

"Report?" he says without looking up.

"The, uh . . ." I search for a word. "Coroner" isn't used here. "Pathologist" is too much for Catriona. "The report that police surgeons make after an autopsy. There is one, is there not?"

Please tell me there is one.

"He will sign the death certificate stating cause of death," Gray says. "Otherwise, he will make notes to present at court. Detective McCreadie will receive an oral report, but he's going to need to chase Addington down to get it. That is inexcusable."

"Is it possible . . . ?" I clear my throat. "I know you are not licensed to practice medicine—"

His shoulders tense.

I hurry on. "I do not mean any insult, sir. I was only going to say—"

"Surgery," he says. "Not medicine. I studied jointly in medicine and surgery, but intended to pursue the latter."

"All right. Surgery then. Still, the fact that you have the degrees means you're at least as qualified as Addington, licensed or not. I understand the lawyers need the police surgeon on the witness stand, but would it be possible for you to perform autopsies? With him in attendance?"

Gray snorts and slaps the paper onto his desk as he strides from the office. "Addington would never agree to it."

A hesitation, and then he glances back, his chin dipping. "It is an excellent idea, Catriona. I am not dismissing that. Detective McCreadie and I have discussed it, as we have discussed the possibility of both being present at the autopsy, which is quite routine. Criminal autopsies are sometimes even performed in surgical theaters."

"But more witnesses would mean more people to realize Addington is screw—making mistakes."

Gray grunts and pulls open the door to the examination room. "Addington is too well connected for Detective McCreadie to argue with his process. We must simply be thankful that we may confirm his work after the fact. Now, let us do that."

It doesn't take me long to realize the true root of Gray's anger. Yes, he's annoyed that Addington left without speaking to McCreadie. But what truly infuriated him was that preliminary report. On it, Addington listed the cut throat as the cause of death. It is not. As we guessed earlier—and Gray confirms now—Rose Wright died of strangulation.

The killer strangled her, moved her body in front of that gate, and then slashed her throat and stabbed her in the stomach. That could be pure convenience. A bloodless killing with the mutilations added on the staged scene. I can't tell them about the staging, though. Can't say that the killer moved the body there because it resembles the spot where a woman will be murdered twenty years from now. Gray presumes the killer strangled her in a more private location and then displayed her in a busier one, and I need to go along with that.

"May I speculate, sir?" I ask as he measures the abdominal wounds.

"Certainly. That is the process of learning, Catriona. Ask questions and hazard guesses."

"I think he strangled her because that's how he likes to kill. Come up behind a victim and strangle them with rope. It means they don't see him, but it also means he doesn't see them. Doesn't watch their face as they die."

Gray pauses to look at me. "Interesting. You believe he is affected by their deaths?"

"Mmm, I don't think so. I would imagine that only applies in cases where you regret *needing* to kill someone. He's *choosing* to kill. It isn't about caring—it's about *not* caring. He isn't doing it because he enjoys the act of killing. He enjoys hunting his victims and the victory of success and any notoriety that comes with it, but he doesn't care about the act of killing. He does it quickly and efficiently."

I pause, but Gray says, "Go on."

"Archie Evans was a bloodless death. Literally and figuratively, as you said. No one cared. To make them care, he gave them what he thinks they want." I wave at Rose's body. "This."

His head tilts. "You believe he craves attention, then?"

"The elaborate staging of Archie Evans would indicate as much, would it not?"

"It does. It was a theory of my own, which is why I wanted those newspapers the other day." He looks at Rose. "He failed to attain the desired degree of notoriety, and so he progressed to this."

"Escalation."

His lips purse. "Yes, 'escalation.' An excellent word. You seem to have a knack for this, Catriona."

"If you are implying that I understand the killer's mind too intimately, I was asleep when Rose was murdered. Also, I'm not strong enough to strangle someone Archie Evans's size."

"Ah, but you did fight off a killer. I believe you underestimate your strength. No, I don't suspect you of these murders. The killer must have been sizable enough to carry her to the scene, as a cart would have attracted notice. Therefore, it could not have been you. Unless you have developed superhuman strength as a side effect of your memory loss." He peers at me. "Have you?"

I smile. "Sadly, no, though I do seem quite capable of lugging around buckets of soapy water." I glance at him. "How far could *you* carry a woman of her size?"

His startled look makes me laugh. "I was not insinuating that you might be responsible, sir. I mean that you are larger than the man who attacked me in the alley. You seem quite physically fit. I believe Detective McCreadie mentioned something about a propensity for brawling."

"Lies, lies, and damnable lies. I take your meaning, though. How far could I carry this woman? It is an excellent question." He looks down at her. "One that is best answered through experimentation. Sadly, she is in no condition to be slung over my shoulder."

"Yeah, I'm not running along behind, collecting her entrails."

That gets a full sputtered laugh from him. "Such a lack of appreciation for science. You are nearly as bad as your predecessor, young James." He eyes her. "How much do you think she weighs?"

"One thirty," I say. When his brows shoot up, I say, "Uh, nine stone."

"I am not surprised at the unit of measurement but at the speed of your assessment. You are quite good at that."

"I used to work in a carnival, guessing weights."

His eyes spark with interest. "Did you?"

"That was a joke, sir. Is there such an occupation?"

"Of course. It is extremely popular, primarily as a way of discovering one's weight if one does not possess a scale."

I'm not sure whether *he's* joking, so I make a noncommittal noise.

"How much do you weigh?" he asks.

I raise my brows in mock horror. "A gentleman never asks a lady such a thing."

His look of confusion tells me that's not the invasive question it will be in a hundred and fifty years.

"I'd need a scale to be sure," I say. "Probably about the same."

I catch his look and lift my hands. "Oh, no, if you're suggesting—"

"I must conduct the experiment in some fashion. And you *are* my assistant."

"No."

"But science."

His eyes sparkle with mischief, and my heart does a little flip. Oh, no. There will be none of that, Mallory. That way lies madness. Also, serious disappointment, because when he looks at me, he sees his teenage apprentice, nothing more.

"Fine," I say with a sigh. "After you are done checking Dr. Addington's work, you may test how far you could reasonably carry my dead weight. Preferably when I'm not actually dead."

"But *science*."

I shake my head, and we get back to work.

There is no doubt Rose was killed by strangulation. Gray confirms all the signs that allow him to make that determination. Strangled first, and then methodically stabbed to match the marks left on Polly Nichols, which means I'm not the only one who studied the Ripper's crimes.

I am going to speculate further that the killer didn't leap straight into Ripper-style killings because he considers Jack a hack. A butcher, chopping up victims for maximum carnage and shock value. Oh, I know the theories about the Ripper being a doctor, but with Gray I can see a live nineteenth-century surgeon at work, and I can question him under the guise of the current crime. That's a little harder when this victim—unlike the Ripper's later ones—hasn't had any organs removed, but Gray isn't the kind of guy who suspects the motivations of anyone seeking knowledge.

He says that a surgeon would certainly know where to find organs. A doctor should, but the amount of anatomical and surgical experience a regular physician has depends on where and when he was trained. A butcher would have more, at least in the sense of being able to infer anatomical placement from the similarities between humans and pigs.

By no means, then, did the Ripper need to be a surgeon to remove organs from human bodies. And there's no surgical skill displayed with Rose's death. Two slashes to her throat, one twice the length of the other. One long, savage slice to the abdomen and several smaller stabs, plus two to the groin. It's butchery so basic that I suspect an actual butcher would take offense at the comparison.

I think this killer originally wanted to do better than Jack the Ripper. He wanted to be fancy. Be symbolic. And he failed miserably because, quite frankly, no one gave a damn. At least not the degree of "giving a damn" that would put him into the history books. This could, if he keeps it up. Our job is to make sure he doesn't.

When will he strike again? I should know, right? I studied the crimes. Yet it's like not knowing exactly when forensic breakthroughs occurred.

My interest was in facts, not dates. I do know the Ripper's entire killing spree lasted only a month, which means he could take his next victim any time now. This killer will follow the pattern, and *he* does know it. I'm sure of that.

I make notes as Gray rattles off observations. Right-handed killer, judging by the angle of the cuts. Hesitation cuts, as I noted, which supports my personal view that the guy's heart wasn't in his work. The stab wounds suggest a thin-bladed knife. There's no indication that a separate knife was used for the throat. He does, however, find a rope fiber in the neck wound, which he will use under Isla's microscope to compare to any rope discovered in the investigation.

Gray also examines the clothing for fibers and hairs, explaining as he does that McCreadie is not convinced of the usefulness of this, but Gray has read a French paper postulating potential analysis of fibers, hair, and other particles left at crime scenes. There are no hairs, not even the victim's, which suggests the killer removed them. When I say as much to Gray, he agrees that's an excellent idea, but I can tell he doesn't see why a killer would remove hairs when they can't yet be analyzed as evidence.

That's all Gray can get from the body. Then comes the part where he sees how far he can carry me. He tries a few holds before I suggest the firefighter carry—without using that modern term, of course. He agrees that is the most efficient method.

With me slung over his shoulder, Gray walks around the funeral parlor, counting off an impressive two hundred paces before he begins to tire. Then, after catching his breath, he wants to test out stairs. We're on the second story when Isla throws open the stairwell door. I jump, flailing. Gray only tightens his grip while shooing his sister away with a jerk of his chin.

"You are blocking our path," he says.

She leans around him to look at me. "Do I even want to ask what you're doing?"

"Science," I say.

"I see. And more specifically?"

"The killer moved Rose's body after he strangled her," I say. "Before he inflicted the other wounds. She's roughly my weight, and the killer I saw is smaller than Dr. Gray, so this will provide some idea of how far he could have carried her."

"Up a flight of stairs?"

"I am accounting for the elevation progression within the city," Gray says. "Also whether it would have proved overly difficult to carry her down stairs. First, I must get her up them."

"Uh-huh. Well, do not let Mrs. Wallace see you carrying Catriona over your shoulder. I shudder to imagine what she'd think."

"I shall explain."

"No, *please* don't. Finish your experiment and join me in the library for tea."

"Is that an order?" Gray says.

"It is. I invited Hugh to join us, so we may hear his update and share yours."

"We are very busy, Isla. I am not certain we have time for tea."

"I picked up cream pastries this morning. Also, coffee, for Catriona, so she may no longer need to sip piteously at your dregs."

"He hadn't touched the coffee I drank," I say. "Which isn't to say his dregs aren't tempting."

"Are they now?"

Her eyes glitter, and I'm glad I'm slung over Gray's shoulder, so I can make a face at her and roll my eyes.

She laughs and pats my shoulder. "Coffee and tea, cream pastries and lemon cake. Five o'clock in the library. Do not be late."

THIRTY

When we talk to McCreadie, I'm glad I made the choice to stay with Gray. McCreadie's interview brought him nothing, even with the additional questions we brainstormed.

"I know Duncan has theorized that Evans was tortured," McCreadie says as he sips his tea. "Which implies a connection between the two men, but if there is such a connection with Rose Wright, I have no idea what it might be. Her sister is a respectable lady. A laundress. Rose helped when she . . . Well, when she was able. She liked her drink and was often in no shape to assist her sister in the mornings, if you take my meaning."

He means Rose was an alcoholic whose heavy drinking meant she could rarely rouse herself from bed before noon. It's tempting to look at someone like Rose and compare her with her industrious and "respectable" sister, but it's rarely that easy, and I give McCreadie full credit for digging deeper.

Rose was ten years older than her sister. She'd been married, happily enough it seems, and worked in a factory. Five children. The only two who survived infancy both died in the cholera epidemic of 1856, along with her husband. The doctor prescribed laudanum to help with her "nerves"—shockingly, the death of her entire family within a week had sent her into a depression.

From laudanum, Rose moved to alcohol, eventually losing her job and her home, and then going to live with her younger sister, where she helped with the laundry and the children. She went out in the evenings a few times each week, sweeping floors for local shops and then having a drink with friends.

Rose didn't really clean shops in the evening. McCreadie confirmed that easily enough. She was doing sex work. She'd earn enough for the night's drinking and bring home a shilling or two, always apologizing that it wasn't more. I can imagine her planning for it to be more, to bring all those coins to her sister after just one drink.

One drink to take the edge off, banish the ghosts, and boost her self-esteem. One turned into two, which turned into five, and it is a testament to her willpower—or her love for her sister—that she came home with any money at all.

A sad life with a tragic end.

Was there a connection to the killer? My gut says that he needs that. But in this case, he also needed a woman who'd match Polly Nichols close enough to mimic the Ripper. Maybe that was enough. If there was more, it might have only been a passing encounter, like the one we had in the coffee shop.

I'm digging too deep. I know that. Fixating on a connection with the victim. Fixating on the Jack the Ripper connection. Those are distractions. I need to strip them away and focus on the true connection. The one that matters.

Our killer inhabits the body of whoever tried to strangle Catriona a week ago. Forget who's inside that body. Forget *his* motives. Find Catriona's would-be killer, and I can stop him before another Rose dies.

Our killer is my attempted killer . . . in the body of Catriona's attempted killer. Who would want to murder Catriona? I think "who wouldn't" might be the easier question to answer. She stole from those who tried to help her, like Isla and Gray. Fought with those who trusted her, like Simon. Betrayed those who wooed her, like Findlay. Bullied Alice. Gave Mrs. Wallace endless grief. Double-crossed her allies, like Davina. And those are just the people in her life that I *know*.

Are any of those betrayals motives for murder? As a cop, I learned that's a far less useful question than one might think. I've known people who killed a partner to escape horrible abuse, and some still insisted that wasn't a valid motive for murder. I've also known a guy who killed his neighbor for having loud dinner parties and a woman who tried to kill a job rival. In neither case would I remotely see motive for murder, but they still tried to convince a jury of it.

I need to learn more about Catriona. Talk to Davina. Talk to Isla, too. Get Catriona's background from Isla and find out from Davina what Catriona had been up to recently, even if that takes every coin in my stash.

Still, I feel as if I'm about to wade into shark-infested waters trying to find the one shark who did this. I stare at the ceiling, mentally sorting through data and feeling pulled in twenty directions while working with both hands tied behind my back.

I saw Catriona being strangled, but as hard as I rack my brain, I can recall nothing of her killer except the sense that it was a man. Otherwise, the links only further complicate the crime, and I need to constantly pull apart those threads before they hopelessly tangle.

As for the "tied hands" part, well, I'm not a detective here. Not a criminal officer. Not a constable. Hell, I'm not even a man, and for all the times I felt hampered by that in the modern world, it is the difference between having to swim upstream and being kept out of the river altogether.

I have a crime to investigate. I am the person best qualified to solve it, because the killer comes from my world, which I cannot tell the investigating officer. Yet my days are not my own. I'll get up tomorrow and take Gray his coffee, and if I'm lucky, he'll keep me up to date on McCreadie's investigation, and maybe I can add my two cents, but that's it.

I want to tell Isla I need a few days off, so I can go out and investigate.

Go out where? Investigate how? I'd need McCreadie for that, and there's no logical way for me to insert myself into the active part of his investigation.

I'll talk to Isla. Convince her to help me get more access.

Can I tell her about the link between this killer and my twenty-first-century one? I'm not sure yet. I need to work it through more and tread carefully.

The tangled threads make my head spin as they cinch ever tighter. I need paper and a pen so I can get my thoughts out of my head. When the clock strikes midnight, I'm reasonably certain everyone will be in bed, and so I sneak down the back stairs to the second floor and head for the library. I'm creeping across the cold floors when a board creaks, and I freeze.

What if someone catches me in the library at this hour? I can't keep asking Isla to get me out of scrapes.

I tell myself I'm overreacting. If I'm caught, I'll take a book. I'm allowed to borrow them, and it's understandable that I might get one if I can't sleep.

I cock my head, listening, but the house has gone still. I continue on to the library. I consider lighting a lamp, but instead just open the drapery enough to catch moonlight.

Find a book first. That will make my cover story more plausible.

The problem here is that the minute I begin perusing the bookcases, I lose myself in the possibilities, all whispering to be pulled from the shelves. Victorian fiction that I doubt my father has heard of—contemporary works lost to time. Scientific and historical texts of every variety, each promising a glimpse into past theories and thoughts, their gorgeous vellum pages nestled between leather covers.

I ignore all those temptations and head straight to the shelf of texts that might be of interest to a budding forensic scientist. I pull out a translated French book. *A General System of Toxicology, or, A Treatise on Poisons* by Mathieu Orfila. I resist the urge to open it and instead lay it on the desk, ready to grab if I hear anyone.

I'm easing out the desk chair when a whisper comes, like an opening door, and I'm on my feet, book clutched in my hands.

Silence falls again, but as I stand there, holding the book, some sliver of awareness tickles down my spine, the same one I'd felt earlier today, standing near Rose's body and wondering whether the killer could be in the crowd.

With the book under one arm, I slip to the door. I glance down at the leather-bound tome and weigh its use as a potential weapon against the chance this is just a member of the household. I don't want to be found sneaking around holding a fire poker. Nor do I want to come up against the killer while armed only with a book on forensic toxicology.

Damn it, I should have brought my knife. I back up to the fire and grab the poker. Book in one hand, weapon in the other. That will make sense if I explain that I'd been getting something to read when I heard a noise.

I slide into the hall. As I creep down it, I check each room, but the drawn drapes make it impossible to see more than the shapes of furnishings. I reach the hall and consider and then head for the stairs. As I set my foot on the first one, a creak sounds, one that doesn't come from under my feet. I peer down into darkness below. Nothing.

I wait another moment, ears straining. When it stays quiet, I remind myself that this is an old house, prone to creaks and groans.

Uh, no, Mallory, this town house might be a historic building in your time, but it's fifty or sixty years old in this world. With the solid construction, it's no more given to creaking than my condo at home.

Still, any house can be subject to noises, and that must be what I've heard, because it's gone quiet, and it's staying quiet.

I continue down the stairs, poker in hand, hearing nothing more than a creak or two of the floorboards under my own feet. At the bottom I pause to look both ways, and then I stride to the front door. I check it. Locked. Walk to the back door. Also locked.

Good. If there's anyone about, it's only one of my housemates, getting a glass of water or using the water closet.

I return to the library, and I'm pulling open a desk drawer when I am certain I hear a clack from somewhere in the house. I freeze. Then I rise with my book in hand. Halfway to the door, I realize I left the drawer open.

I hesitate but force myself into the hall, where I listen. Listen and hear nothing.

Okay, now I'm being paranoid. The doors are locked. There's no one here. With these high ceilings, I probably heard the echo of the damn drawer opening.

One last peer down the dark hallway, and I retreat to the desk. I reach into the drawer, where I know Isla keeps paper. Next comes the pen, plucked from a holder on the desktop. It's a gorgeous engraved-silver combination dip pen and mechanical pencil that I can imagine my father salivating over. That's the second time I've thought of him in the last hour, and each nudge brings an affectionate smile followed by a surge of panic.

My dad would love this pen.

When I get home, I should find one in an antiques shop for him.

What if I don't get home?

What if Catriona is in my body?

What if I never see my parents again?

Deep breaths to calm my racing heart. What's the saying about long, dark nights of the soul? The witching hour for all my worst fears to toil and boil forth, from a killer in the house to never seeing my parents again.

I cannot control the last part, except in the sense that solving Catriona's murder might be the key to unlocking the gate. Maybe I was brought through time to stop her killer before he struck again. Except it's no longer the same guy, and I'm doing a really shitty job of stopping him.

I press my fingers to my temples, return to the desk, and sit again.

I lift my pen over the blank page to be frozen exactly as I was upstairs. Where to begin? What's the starting thread? The current murders? Catriona's initial attack? Or her second attack—the one I'd faced, which requires the killer knowing she's helping Gray and McCreadie?

Stop. It doesn't matter where I start. Just write it all down.

Current murders. First victim, Archie Evans, chosen because the killer wanted information from him. He knew something—

Wait.

Wait right there.

We'd been checking out Evans's housemates trying to determine what the killer wanted from him. What he'd been tortured for. It had seemed connected to his housemates' anti-immigrant efforts. Except that wouldn't interest a modern-day killer. Whatever his own beliefs, he's not going after Evans to extract information on a nineteenth-century anti-immigration movement.

What *did* he want?

He killed Evans within two days of arriving in this world. He'd barely arrived. What would he want? What *could* he want?

I let my mind drift back to my first day here. Waking in the bed upstairs. Waking in a world and a body I didn't recognize. What did I want?

Answers.

Who am I? Where am I?

I'd gotten them by asking Gray, under the guise of mental confusion.

The killer isn't going to grab a random guy on the street and torture him for information that he could get by feigning a blow to the head until someone took pity and answered.

Where am I? What year is it? What day is it?

Hell, he could get those answers by finding a newspaper stand.

What couldn't he find as easily?

Who am I?

The man whose body the killer inhabits knew Evans. He was connected to him in a way that meant he had the information the killer needed.

Who am I? Where do I live? What do I do for a living?

He wouldn't need to torture Evans for that. Fake a blow to the head and ask, and if Evans got suspicious, then he could kill him. Torture meant he needed more.

What more did I need when I arrived?

Everything. It was like being dropped into a foreign country where you barely speak the same language.

How do I wake up in the morning? What are my duties? How do I perform those duties—where is the mop, the water, the soap?

I'd had my safe cocoon, a houseful of decent people who made allowances for me. Yet I'd needed more, so much more, all the things I'm still figuring out, including information on this body I'm inhabiting. Luckily, I have Isla now, but those early days had been a constant cloud of fear that I'd be found out because I didn't know the first damn thing about Catriona and "memory problems" only got me so far.

The killer had two choices. Live as the person whose body he inhabited or start over. Living as that person meant having a home and belongings and a job, but it also meant understanding that person's life in a way I'd skipped with Catriona.

This is what he wanted from Evans. Not just "who am I?" but the crux of that question—tell me everything about myself so I can fully inhabit this life.

Where am I from? What do I like? How do I act? Who do I know?

That's why he needed torture. He'd captured Evans with the intention of getting as much as possible from him and then killing him, both to cover his tracks and to renew his pursuit of serial-killer fame.

This means that Catriona's would-be killer knew Evans. Knew him well enough that the killer recognized him as a source of invaluable information.

I need to learn more about Evans. He lived with students. Was he also a student? Part-time, maybe? Wait, McCreadie said he was English. Maybe he came for school in Edinburgh?

He wrote for a newspaper. *The Evening Courant.* Was that something done in an office—with colleagues—or freelance? I'll need to ask Isla.

I'm writing feverishly when I catch the distinct sound of footsteps.

I grab the poker, stride to the door, and peer into darkness. It's quiet again.

Goddamn it. Are my nerves working overtime or is someone actually out there? I walk into the hall.

"Hello?" I say, because by this point, if it's just Alice sneaking around to see what I'm doing, I'd rather deal with that than keep being interrupted.

I walk along the hall and through the drawing room and dining room, seeing no one.

"If anyone's there, I'm reading in the library," I helpfully announce to my would-be killer.

I sigh, adjust my grip on the poker, and return to the library. Back at the desk, I pause and peer around. Nothing. I set the poker on the desktop, within reach, and then I'm pulling out the chair when a floorboard creaks behind me.

THIRTY-ONE

I spin just as a dark-cloaked figure lunges out from behind the drapes. He claps a hand over my mouth. I elbow him in the ribs and then wheel and slam my fist into his stomach.

Before he doubles over, I catch a glimpse of an average-sized man with a black mask. Then I realize the "mask" is dark hair falling over his face as he doubles over in pain. I grab his hair and wrench his head up.

"Simon?"

"Surrender," he croaks, raising his arms. "I acknowledge defeat, fair maiden."

"What the hell?" I say as he rises, still holding his stomach.

"Nicely done, Cat," he grunts as he catches his breath. "I suppose I deserved that, trying to spook you."

"By leaping from behind the curtains? Two days after I was attacked and nearly killed in the streets?"

He hesitates. "Two days? It has been a week."

"I was attacked *again* two days ago and spent the damned night in jail for fighting off my attacker." I back up to the desk and fold the papers.

"I-I heard nothing of that," he says. "I do apologize then, Cat. And I cannot help but be grateful I escaped with my life." He rubs his stomach and makes a face. "Who ever taught you to fight like that?"

"The experience of nearly being killed twice in a less than a week."

"No doubt, and again, I do apologize." He glances behind me. "What are you writing?"

"Nothing."

He tries to snatch the pages, and we do a couple rounds of that before he sees I'm serious and stops. He perches on the edge of the desk as I secret the pages away in my bodice.

"What are you doing in here?" I say.

"Uh, it is the house where I am employed?"

"I mean you're inside. At night. How'd you get in?"

"With my key. Because it is . . . the house where I am employed? I came in search of food. I was up late and grew hungry."

"The kitchen is two floors down."

"Yes, but I heard someone moving about as I was in the stairwell. I came to see who it was and warn that I was in the house so that I did not startle them."

"Instead, you *intentionally* startled me?"

"Because you are special." He grins. "You ought to have seen your face. Now, if you are quite finished with the interrogation, I have a proposition."

"Uh-huh."

He leans over and whispers, "I have a penny stick in my rooms."

Is that the Victorian equivalent of inviting me to his room to see his etchings?

"I don't think I need to see your stick," I say. "Not tonight."

"See my stick?" he sputters. "How hard was that knock on your head? I mean I have a penny stick of opium."

I blink before I manage to say, "No, thank you. I'm having quite enough trouble keeping my mind clear these days. That hit on the head is affecting me more than I expected."

I look over at him. "I know you said you had no idea who might have attacked me, but would you mind if I asked you a few questions? About myself? Filling in the holes?"

"Would I mind? You sound as if you are asking a favor of a stranger, Cat. We are friends, are we not?"

"We are, but it is awkward admitting to memory lapses. It makes me feel quite freakish."

He sobers, his voice lowering. "We ought never to feel that way between ourselves. The world gives us enough of that. You may ask what you will, and I will answer as much as I am able and not judge you for your questions." He meets my gaze. "No judgment. Not between us. Yes?"

"Yes. Thank you."

We head down to the kitchen, where we find day-old bread and butter, and Simon makes a pot of tea. Then I question him. I start by asking him about my past. He can't help there—Catriona didn't share any of that. Nor does he know anything about her criminal confederates. In that case, he didn't want to know details. I'll need to speak to Davina.

If Catriona knew her attacker, that puts one degree of separation between her and Evans. Possibly no degrees if all three shared a connection.

Evans's roommates suggested he sold information on their group. To whom? A link shimmers there, between Evans selling his group's secrets and Catriona selling Findlay's police information. Could they have been selling to the same person? Or connected in the same underground web? Evans is friends with someone in that world, whom he uses to sell his information, and Catriona has pissed off—or betrayed—that same person, who tried to kill her for it.

Is that my link?

"Do you know a young man named Archie Evans?" I ask.

Simon stops midbite to look at me. "Uh, yes. The fellow that raven killer murdered. You helped Dr. Gray with the body, did you not? Alice said so." He peers at me. "Are your new memories affected as well?"

"I meant did you know him before he was murdered?"

His eyes narrow. "What are you implying, Cat?"

"I am wondering whether I had a connection to him. He seemed familiar."

Simon relaxes and shrugs. "He wrote for the *Evening Courant*. I've read the paper to you many a time, and I may have mentioned him as the writer."

"Did I ever mention him?"

"Not that I recall."

"He lived with a group of radicalized students. Anti-immigration, anti–anyone who does not look and act like them."

"Are you suggesting you might have hobnobbed with the likes of *them*?"

"I hope not, but I don't remember."

He shakes his head firmly. "You have many faults, Cat, but if bigotry were one of them, we could hardly be friends. It is not."

Well, score one for Catriona. But I also must wonder how well Simon really knew Catriona. He seems like a sweet kid, and when he mentioned Alice, he seemed fond of her. Did he know Catriona abused her? I doubt it, which makes me wonder whether Evans's group really could be the key, and Catriona just knew enough to keep her bigotry from Simon. She was, after all, a master at showing people what they wanted to see.

With that, I hit a brick wall. Simon has nothing for me, and I chat a little longer—not wanting him to feel interrogated and dismissed—before I yawn and declare it past time for bed.

I see the glimmer of a lead in the cord connecting Archie Evans to his killer and possibly to Catriona. That realization has me up just before the clock downstairs strikes five. I leap from bed with the morning light, dress, tear into the hall, and promptly collide with poor Alice coming to wake me. A quick apology, and then I'm racing down the stairs to begin my day by taking Gray his breakfast tray. He's already up, according to Mrs. Wallace, and I skip my morning bread and tea to take his tray to his room.

"Wouldn't want the master's coffee getting cold," I say when Mrs. Wallace grumbles at me for yanking it from her hands.

I take the stairs as fast as I can without toppling the coffeepot. At Gray's door, I pause and inhale. Then I tap and await the invitation before entering.

Gray is hard at work, and seeing that, I have to smile. It's not just the "hard at work before 6:00 A.M." part, which is normal for him. It's the fact that he appears to have done little more than roll from his bed to his desk chair, with the coverlet still draped around his shoulders.

"Might I hope you are in an appropriate state of dress under that, sir?" I ask.

He only grunts, which means it could go either way. I set down the tray and start the fire. I'm so much better at this now, my inner Girl Guide beaming with pride. It helps to make sure the fire is prepped before he retires to bed. It also helps if he doesn't decide to light it at night and work into the wee hours.

I have it going quickly, and by then, he's let the coverlet fall to show, yes, he's decent, with his shirt mostly buttoned. He shrugged off the coverlet without stopping his writing, and I pick it up and begin folding. He gives a grunt that seems to mean he'll do that, but I keep going, neatly folding it and then picking up his socks and laying them out for him. That morning, I am maid-of-the-month material, for the same reason I came racing up with his breakfast.

When I decide I've been solicitous enough to lower his defenses, I say, "Might we discuss the case, sir?"

He keeps writing, and my mood drops a notch. I'm about to try again, maybe ask if there's a time we can discuss it, when he taps his pen into the holder and swivels in his chair.

"You have thoughts?" he says.

I perk up. "I do, sir. I would like to return to the first victim, Archie Evans."

He frowns. "Evans?"

"We have not yet ascertained the purpose of the torture. What information was the killer trying to extract? It suggests Evans knew his killer."

The frown deepens. "It does?"

"Yes." Here I stumble, because I can't tell Gray what I think the killer wanted and how that proves a personal connection. "I believe we should consider the very strong possibility that they knew one another."

His gaze slips back to his notebook, and I feel the ground under my feet eroding.

"I suppose that is a possibility," he says slowly. "Why don't you think more on it, Catriona, and present your theory to Detective McCreadie at tea this afternoon."

"This afternoon?"

"Yes." Gray is already turning back to his work. "As much as I would like to pursue the case sooner, I have a paper due, and I have fallen behind. I hope to have time for an investigative update at tea. Tell my sister, please, in case she would care to join us."

With that, he turns back to his work, and I am dismissed.

I start my dusting in the library, so I can pen a note to Isla, imploring her to allow me a half day off to pursue a lead. I also request a half hour of her time, so I can get advice on how to proceed. I know what I want to do. I'm less certain how to do it in this era.

I include the note with her breakfast tray, which she prefers to be left outside her door after a knock. I don't make it down the stairs before I hear, "Catriona?"

I hurry back up to find her in the hall. She waves me into her room.

Isla's room is the size of Gray's. Both are large enough, but neither is the sprawling bedchamber I expected from the size of this house. All the town house rooms are very much divided by purpose. You cook in the kitchen, eat in the dining room, sit and meet guests in the drawing room, study and read in the library, sleep in the bedroom. Both Gray and Isla have carved out a corner for more in their bedchambers—he has a desk for working and she has a chaise longue for reading. Gray's desk seems shoehorned in, the space not quite big enough to hold it, as if he stubbornly insists on adding this extra purpose to what should be a mere bedchamber. Isla's chaise longue fits much better. One thing they have in common? Their bedrooms both look as if a small tornado touched down.

I start to pick up a discarded dressing gown, but she shoos me away from it and into a chair. Then she proceeds to undress. I struggle not to laugh at that. Victorians have a reputation for prudery, and in some things, it's well earned, but they have no problem with showing off far more cleavage than I would in the modern day, and they apparently have no problem disrobing, in front of a member of their own sex.

With the complicated clothing—and lack of zippers—this is still a time when people of Gray and Isla's stature could expect a valet or lady's maid to help them bathe and dress. Isla doesn't seem to want that, but she strips down and reclothes herself as one accustomed to doing so in front of other women.

I notice her undergarments differ from mine. Instead of the layers of petticoats that Catriona wears, Isla has a lightweight cage-like contraption to achieve that same belled skirt. Probably lighter, but I think I'll stick with the warmer petticoats myself.

I also notice something else. Her discarded drawers might also be crotchless, but they button between the legs. I stare in wonder at this marvel and decide that pockets are all well and fine, but I have a new Victorian fashion goal. Crotch buttons.

She glances over her shoulder. "I don't suppose you know how to tighten a corset? I presume—dare I say hope—they're gone by your time?"

I get to my feet. "Yep. Except for fun."

"Fun?"

"Costume play and, er, intimate play."

"Why would anyone want . . . ?" She shakes her head. "Do not answer that."

"Hey, they're sexy," I say. "And not actually as uncomfortable as I expected. From some of the books I read, they sounded like torture devices."

"That's because you aren't lacing yours nearly as tight as Catriona did. I used to wonder how she moved in it, though I suspect it was less about decreasing her waist than increasing . . . "

"Her boob shelf?" I say, and that makes Isla laugh.

"Yes," she says, "though I never got the impression she used that to woo the lads."

"Nah," I say. "For Catriona, it would have been pure distraction. You can get away with a lot when the guys are staring at your chest. I never realized how much until I suddenly had this." I motion at my cleavage. "It is both a gift and a curse. I will endeavor to use my new power wisely."

I tighten her corset snugly. "Good?"

"Good enough for me, as I am not in the market for a mate, nor do I have the need—or the assets—for distraction." She picks up her corset cover and tugs it over her head. "Now explain this lead you are pursuing."

She sounds so much like her brother that I have to smile. I stop smiling as I remember his reaction to my lead.

"Catriona?" she says when I don't reply. Then she pauses. "Or ought I to call you Mallory? In private at least?"

"I remember hearing a quote about no sound being sweeter than that of our own name, and damn, it feels weirdly good to hear it. But for safety's sake, we should probably stick to Catriona."

"I am quite capable of not slipping up. Mallory is it, then. This lead. You hesitate to share it. Why?"

"Because your brother dismissed the idea."

"My brother does not realize you are a criminal officer."

True, but *she* doesn't know the whole story either.

I consider telling her that I brought the killer with me, but if I tell her, is she obligated to tell her brother? Would I damage their relationship by sharing investigation details she can't pass on? Is that a good enough reason to keep it from her? I'm not sure yet. I only know that I'd rather wait until *not* sharing it endangers the investigation.

Of course, there's another solution to this problem. One I like a whole lot more than keeping secrets from Isla.

"Maybe we should tell Dr. Gray about me," I say. "Then he'd take my theories more seriously."

"We cannot," she says. "Not yet. Please. I need to figure out a way to convince him of the veracity of your story. I came to understand that absolute proof is impossible. He will struggle with that. Moreover, it will be a distraction he can ill afford. He has this case, which is incredibly important for Hugh, along with a paper that is incredibly important for Duncan himself."

She looks over at me. "If it were only a matter of convincing him you are not Catriona, I would attempt it for the sake of the investigation. It is not. It is convincing him of the possibility of passing through time itself, which opens endless potentialities that his mind will not be able to ignore."

When I don't answer, she says, "When we were growing up, our mother always called Duncan's brain a boisterous puppy. Give it a toy, and it will attack with vigor. Wave a brighter, shinier toy in front of him, and it will abandon the first to pursue the second. It is something he has struggled with all his life. He must force himself to focus on one at a time and not be lured away by the promise of another. He has an incredible mind, but it requires incredible discipline."

I understand what she's saying. In the modern world, it might be labeled a mild form of ADHD. But I'm not sure it's right to manage it for him, not at his age. Gray might struggle to avoid distractions, but from what I've seen, once he's found his focus, he holds tight. Otherwise, he'd be with me today, pursuing this case, instead of locked away with his paper.

Isla's concern smacks of older-sibling syndrome, never quite trusting her younger brother can do things on his own, wanting to fix problems for him. Yet I'm a newcomer, and to even suggest she's babying him is to suggest I know the man better. I don't—I just think I might, as an outsider, see him more clearly, my view unmarred by the gauzy layers of his younger selves.

"Please, Mallory," she says. "Trust that I know my brother's mind. We *will* tell him. Once his paper is done or when there is a lull in the investigation. Until then, I will handle any doubt regarding your abilities. Now, the lead?"

"I think the first victim, Archie Evans, knew the killer."

I give my reasoning, insofar as I can without bringing in the part where his torturer was a guy from the future. Without that, it's a weak argument, and Gray was right to set it aside. If she does the same, I *will* tell her, but she only says, "So what do you propose to do about it?"

"Investigate Evans. I've been to his lodgings. I won't be able to speak to his roommates again. I burned that bridge."

"Dare I ask?" she says as she buttons her blouse.

"The ringleader made me throw him into a table."

"*Made* you?"

"It was unfortunate. However, I did score points with the landlady, who seems sick of the little assholes. That will be my way into the house, maybe into Evans's room. I just need a few hours off and, er, directions. Possibly also a bit of advice, so I don't say something rude or weird and get kicked out on my arse."

"In other words, I ought to go with you."

"No, I just need—"

"A companion. One who understands this world and can guide you through it. One who also has not 'burned a bridge' with the young man's friends, in case more information is needed from them."

"I really don't think—"

"I do." She looks at me and smiles. "You do require a half day off, do you not, Miss Catriona? A half day that only the lady of the house can grant?"

"You're blackmailing me into taking you along?"

"I am, indeed. Now gather what you need, and I shall inform Mrs. Wallace that I require your assistance with my shopping today."

THIRTY-TWO

So I'm off playing Victorian detective with Isla. If pressed, I'd admit I'm happy to have her along. Yes, it's helpful having someone who knows the city and the customs and, better yet, that I might screw up and need rescue. But also I like her, and while I'm in this world, she's someone I'd like to get to know better. She's also the only person in this world I can be myself with. So, yep, happy to have her along, even if I worry it's not entirely safe, which is why I'd have gone alone if I'd had the chance.

We walk to the Old Town. If we need a cab, we'll take one home, but it's a gorgeous day, with rare sunshine. Walking also gives us the chance to first pop into a little shop on Princes Street that caters to the "ladies" of the New Town. It's the Victorian equivalent of The Body Shop or Sephora, with everything from creams to cosmetics. The "cosmetics" aren't mascara and lipstick, though. From what I've seen, there's little of that. Instead, they have tiny vials marketed as beauty aids, like mercury for your eyelashes. Or you can lighten your freckles and sunspots with lead sulfate. Isla points those out and assures me that she also avoids them—the advantage to being a chemist.

I pick up a jar of hand cream that smells of tea roses and vows to keep my hands silky smooth. Somehow, I suspect that promise doesn't extend to the cracked hands of a housemaid, but if I'm going to blow some of the cash in my pocket, hand lotion is at the top of my most-wanted list. As I turn the jar over, looking for an ingredient list, the shop clerk fixes me with the kind of narrow-eyed look I haven't gotten since preteen-Mallory would wander into MAC Cosmetics with her friends.

Even after I set down the jar, she keeps glaring. Isla comes over, and I whisper, "Did I miss the 'no maids allowed' sign?"

"No, but it is also possible this isn't the first time you've been in here."

"Ah, right. Light-fingered Cat strikes again."

"Also, yes, this would not be a shop frequented by servants." She lowers her lips to my ear. "And you do not want that cream. It is overpriced and almost certainly adulterated goods. Let me concoct something for you at home."

"Can I concoct it myself? With supervision?"

"You most certainly may," she says with a smile. "I am as delighted to share my work as my brother is, though I suspect you shall find mine far less interesting. If you like the smell of that cream, though, then our work here is finished. We have a gift for the landlady."

She takes the jar to the clerk, who wraps it in the most exquisite packaging. Isla murmurs something, and the woman smiles and stamps the packaging with the store's intricate logo. Then we are off.

On the way, I ask Isla about Catriona. That's a dead end. She knows nothing about the girl except that she seems to have come from a middle-class family. Catriona would say no more about it, not to Isla and not to McCreadie. I'll need to hope Davina has more.

We arrive at the rooming house and slip around to the back entrance, which Isla believes will lead to the landlady's kitchen and personal quarters.

Before we knock, Isla rummages in her small handbag for a tin and holds it out. "Peppermint?"

I peer in at the tiny lozenges. They're the size of Tic Tacs but look more like painkillers.

"Yes. They are only peppermints," she says. "I make them myself."

I take one. It's an interesting consistency, midway between a hard candy and a quick-dissolving mint. Strong but well flavored.

Isla pops two and then knocks.

She chose her gift wisely. The moment Mrs. Trowbridge sees the store stamp, she can't invite us in fast enough. I explain that I feel terrible about the disturbance the other day and the broken table and wanted to bring her a little something. I don't think she needs the excuse. Hell, I'm not even sure she hears it before she's bustling us in.

Within two minutes, I'm searching Evans's room while Isla keeps the landlady occupied. Isla had noticed Mrs. Trowbridge was growing dill, rosemary, and feverfew, which are apparently all treatments for arthritis, and that gave Isla a conversational "in." She explained that her young friend—me—was hoping to see "the poor dead lad's" room and pay respects, and between getting a gift and finding someone to talk herbalism with, the landlady was too happy to question the odd request. She assured me the boys were in class, and I would not be disturbed.

Evans had a room of his own, though it's even smaller than mine. Within twenty minutes, I've completed a thorough search. There are textbooks, all shoved in a dusty corner, suggesting he was a recent graduate. One pornographic novel, tucked away where the landlady won't find it. One hash pipe, well used and also recently used. The residue inside suggests opium.

That pipe nudges a thought, but I push it aside for now. I rummage through his clothing and toiletries, but find nothing hidden there. In a place of prominence lies a scrapbook of his newspaper articles. I thumb through it and then slip it into the bag I brought for our alleged shopping trip. Yes, I feel a twinge of discomfort taking a memento his family would want, but I don't have time to read it here and I doubt I can hunt through old newspapers at the library . . . if there is a public library. Also, it's been a week since Evans's death, and it doesn't look as if any family has either come to collect his things or asked for them to be packed away.

It's only at the end of my search that I find something truly relevant. I'm checking Evan's jackets when I catch the rustle of paper. I try all the pockets. Empty, save for the lint-shrouded remains of a humbug and one lonely penny.

I pat the jacket again. Definitely a rustle. I spread it out on the bed and check the seams until I find a small tear. I rip it open a little more and wriggle my fingers inside to find a folded piece of paper.

I open the paper. It's a jotted list of five addresses. The top two have been crossed off. Beside the next one is a date—several days ago—with a question mark.

I'm folding the note when I see writing on the back, too. I smooth it out. It's written in an entirely different penmanship, and when I see what's there, I blink and have to reread.

> *Catriona Mitchell.*
> *Born 1850, Edinburgh. Family name probably false. Ignore any criminal record under Mitchell, dating back to 1865. I have that. I want something I can use to repay the wench for her backstabbing.*

I'm rereading the note, processing it, when boots clomp on the stairs. I shove the paper into my bodice. Then I grab a notebook from the bedside, check for handwriting, and shove it into my bag.

I'm out the door when one of Evans's roommates crests the stairs. It's the one who'd been studying the other day, the one who'd tried to rein in the others.

He blinks at me in the dim lighting. "What the bloody hell are you doing—" He stops and jabs at the stairs. "Go. Out the back. Thomas is in the front room."

I nod and squeeze past him. Then I clamber down the stairs and wheel into the kitchen, where Isla is having tea with Mrs. Trowbridge.

Isla starts to smile at me, and then rises with a clatter. "My dear girl. You look a fright." She strides over to pat my back reassuringly. "That must have been so difficult for you. I know you were terribly fond of young Archie."

The note I found has my brain whirling, and combined with nearly getting caught in the room, I probably am a little pale. Isla must think I'm faking grief for Mrs. Trowbridge's sake.

"I-I need some air," I say. I turn to the landlady and curtsy. "Thank you so much for your kindness, ma'am. I hope I was not a bother."

"Not at all, child. I am so pleased to know that Archie had a friend who grieves for him." She glares toward the commotion in the front room as the boys tumble in from school. "He ought to have had more. He was a lovely lad."

Isla says her goodbyes and jots something on a piece of paper, promising Mrs. Trowbridge it will be "exactly the thing" for her arthritis. Then she bustles me out the door, and we are gone.

We're around the corner, near the steps in another close. I've given her the note I found, and she's glaring as she reads it.

"Catriona strikes again," I mutter. "Making friends wherever she goes."

"I am not certain whether I am angrier with her, for getting into such scrapes, or this young man for his vindictiveness. So Archie knew Catriona?"

"It's not his handwriting." I show her the book, with his penmanship. Then I flip over the note. "This side, with the addresses was written by him. This other side was not. It's someone asking him to dig up dirt on Catriona."

"He wrote the addresses after receiving this note."

"Maybe? But the note was hidden. The information on Catriona hardly seems something his housemates would care about. I think he was hiding the addresses, which would suggest he wrote them first. Also, it was folded with the addresses inside, and there's no sign of it ever being folded the other way."

She examines the note. "You are correct. That is terribly clever."

"Nah, just basic detective work. It suggests that he jotted down these addresses and then spoke to someone about them. That person wrote the information about Catriona on the opposite side, which meant Evans had to keep the note."

She nods as we walk, and she keeps nodding, as if thinking it through. I'm deep in thought, too. If I mentally shift past the note's connection between Catriona and Evans, there's useful data there on her backstory. I might be able to use that in figuring out who tried to kill her.

Then, without looking over, she says, casually, "What are you not telling me, Mallory?"

I don't answer.

After a moment she says, "Well, I should be glad you are not outright lying and claiming to be hiding nothing. You should be shocked by a connection between the killer and Catriona. Is that not an incredible coincidence? You have already said you are not fond of coincidences, which means you have an explanation for this."

"I'd like to check out this address," I say, tapping the third one, with the question mark and a date beside it.

"Truly? Or is that a distraction?"

"Truly, though it does have the added attraction of allowing me to duck a question I don't want to answer yet. Yes, I am only mildly surprised by a connection between Evans, Catriona, and a third person."

"The third person being the killer?"

I hold out the paper. "Where is this? And don't try withholding your answer for mine or I'll just walk up to those guys, flash my bosom, and ask very prettily."

She snorts. "Somehow, I cannot envision you 'flashing' your bosom *or* asking prettily."

I lower my lashes. "Please, sir, if you might be of assistance. I am trying to find the home of my elderly aunt, who recently moved, and I believe I have been sent to the entirely wrong area. I am but a poor milkmaid from the country, all alone in the big city and so dreadfully overwhelmed." I clear my throat. "Okay, the last part might oversell it."

"Depends on whether you want directions or a coach and escort."

"And a lap to sit in?"

She chokes on a laugh. "Yes, I believe the coach would be sadly over-crowded, forcing you to settle into a lap." She shakes her head and takes the note. "It is about a half-mile walk. Come along."

We're outside a toy shop, and I'm ogling it as if I'm six again, standing outside FAO Schwarz in New York. As a child, I'd have found this tiny shop a disappointment compared to the bright and colorful ones I was used to, but as an adult, it's a straight sugar shot of nostalgia for a world I've only ever seen on Christmas cards and in holiday movies. A place of Victorian magic, with marionettes dancing in the front window and a train set ready to chug around the base.

"Kaplan," Isla murmurs, eyeing the sign. "Is that not what Evans's companions railed against in their pamphlets?"

"Toy stores?"

"Immigration."

I frown over at her.

"The owners are Russian Jewish immigrants," she says.

I'm about to ask whether she knows them. Then it clicks. The store name. Yes, if pressed, I could probably identify Kaplan as a Jewish surname, but that means nothing to me. You certainly can't presume that anyone with a Jewish surname is an immigrant. Or you can't if you're in twenty-first-century Vancouver.

So I ask a different question: "How do you know they're Russian?"

"I misspoke," she says. "They could be from surrounding Slavic countries. They also may not be recent immigrants. I have a friend whose grandfather fled Russia after the execution of Gregory the Fifth. As she says, he escaped one kind of persecution to discover another, but at least this one seemed fifty percent less likely to get him killed. The point is that this is an established business operating under an openly foreign name, and thus it may have attracted the attention of Archie Evans's friends."

I frown at the shop. "I'm surprised it's open, this being the Sabbath."

Her brows rise. "It is not Sunday, Catriona."

"For Jews, the Sabbath is Saturday."

A look passes over her face, almost a sadness. "Ah. I did not know that. My friend never shared much on her faith. It marked her as different, I fear, even with me. Closing on a Saturday would mark them as different." She nods toward the shop. "So they do not. And Saturdays can be quite busy. Some of the local factories have begun allowing their workers to leave midafternoon, to enjoy an extended week-ending with their families."

"Not in the era of two-day weekends yet, are we."

"Hmm?"

I shake my head. "Nothing. As for the shop being on Evans's list, we know the group is anti-immigration. We know he was selling information on their activities to someone. If this place was a target, that might be what he was selling."

I pass over the list. "Any of these others close by?"

"The last one is a block over."

"Let's take a look."

THIRTY-THREE

We're outside the next address. Like the toy shop, it's in one of the better areas of the Old Town. This address is a private residence in a close. Isla buys two fresh loaves of bread at a nearby shop, and we climb the stairs to the right address and rap on the door. It cracks open. After a pause, a woman with a baby on her hip pulls it the rest of the way, still eyeing us with suspicion.

"Aye?" she says.

"We're looking for a Mrs. Ryan," Isla says. "We were given this address."

"There is no Mrs. Ryan here," the woman says in a thick Irish accent and begins to withdraw.

"Wait!" Isla says. She smiles at the baby. "Since we do not have Mrs. Ryan's proper address, we cannot deliver these loaves. Perhaps you would take them?"

The woman studies Isla, her gaze narrowing. Then she smooths out her expression and shakes her head and murmurs, "No, thank you, ma'am. You should find your Mrs. Ryan."

The door closes, and we climb down the stairs to stand in the courtyard.

"Not immigrants then," I say. "And is it me, or was she acting oddly?"

Isla stares at me a moment. Then she laughs. "They were most certainly immigrants. Did you not hear her accent?"

260 • KELLEY ARMSTRONG

"They're Irish. That's not the same thing, right?"

"It is most certainly the same thing." She tucks the loaves into my shopping bag. "We may have some immigration from Eastern Europe and other parts of the world, but the Great Hunger sent the Irish here in droves, and many Scots were not happy to see them."

"The Great Hunger? Oh, is that the potato famines?"

She nods. "It has been twenty years, yet there is extreme prejudice still in some areas. That is why she was wary, and it is why she did not trust the bread. It is also why the family's residence would be on that list. Show it to me again?"

I do, and she says the first two addresses are in an area we shouldn't visit alone, but the remaining one is on our walk back to the New Town.

When we reach the area, I look around at the towering, teeming slums.

"Um, you said the others were in neighborhoods we shouldn't visit alone. Worse than *this*?"

"Yes, worse than this."

I look around us, trying to imagine it.

Isla continues, "There are neighborhoods with buildings ten stories tall, with no running water or sewage. One collapsed on High Street while Duncan was in school. Seventy-seven residents. Thirty-five dead. A lecturer took his medical students to see it. Not to assist with the wounded. Purely as an intellectual exercise. Bodies were still in the rubble and Duncan—" She inhales sharply. "It affected him greatly."

She glances at me. "I know my brother can seem distant and single-minded, but he still sends money each year to the families of those killed. Anonymously, of course. Even I am not supposed to know."

"Is nothing being done, then?" I say, waving around. "About this?"

"Yes, something is being done. They are clearing the slums. You will see notices here and there. The buildings being knocked down, the people sent on their way. No reparations. No assistance. Driven out as if they were rats. For their own good. To convince them to better themselves, because all they need, obviously, is motivation."

Bitter sarcasm drips from her voice. Nothing has changed there either, then. The poor just need a kick in the ass to punt them into the middle class.

"The need is overwhelming," she says, looking about. "In the truest sense of the word. I see this, and I am like Duncan at the site of that collapse. Overwhelmed. I want to run to every door with one of these loaves of bread, ensure everyone has food in their belly tonight. But then what? Perhaps, rather than a single loaf of bread for all, I could sponsor families and see to their needs. Yet most do not want that. Others are beyond that sort of help, lost in a bottle of spirits or laudanum, whichever dulls the pain of this." She waves at the tenements.

My gaze catches on a girl, no more than five, dressed in a sack of a dress, her arms piled high with clean laundry. Then on a man, half drunk in a doorway, staring listlessly, seeing nothing.

"Is it better in your world?" she says. "Please tell me it is not like this still."

"Parts are better," I say. "But not as much as they should be. Where I live—Vancouver—we have a lot of homelessness. People living on the streets. Even after years of patrol, I couldn't help wanting to help. With some, I could, but it never felt like enough. Most didn't want the name of a shelter or a clinic. Addicted to drugs and alcohol, as you say. Or suffering from mental illness. A lot of mental illness. And then, for some, it's a choice, however hard that is to imagine. Eventually, I had to acknowledge that as much as I want to help them all, they're people, not stray cats."

"Not stray cats," she repeats, and her eyes glisten. "Yes, that is exactly the lesson I have had to learn, and it is a hard one."

She pops a mint from her tin. "Take Alice. When Hugh brought her to me, my impulse was to adopt her. Hire a *child* to labor in my home? Absolutely not. Hugh counseled against an adoption, and that may be the worst fight we have ever had. Duncan stayed out of it, but he asked me to employ Alice for a month before making any decisions, and I saw my mistake soon enough. To me, being a child like that, adopted into a well-to-do family, would be a dream come true. The stuff of novels. Yet Alice would have run away had I suggested it. She wants to earn her keep, and anything else smacks of charity and obligation. I am educating her, which she enjoys very much, and I have hopes of easing her into a life where her dreams rise above her station, but it is a slow process."

"And she is not a stray cat."

A wry smile my way. "She is not."

We climb rickety steps to an apartment half the size of my small Vancouver condo. The apartment is home to two Irish families and their children. One of the women is cleaning as the other tends to the smallest of the children and the older ones help their fathers, doing tailoring work by the window.

The apartment is . . . I hesitate to use the word "squalid." That suggests they're living in their own filth, which they absolutely are not. They've made the best of what they have, but no amount of scrubbing will scour away the wood and coal soot stained into every surface, and no amount of polishing the lone window will lift the gloom.

I keep thinking of that jail cell, and how I'd spent the night in the corner, huddled in horror, waiting to escape. These people can't escape. I've seen rough living in Vancouver, and I'd known that behind the tenement doors in the Old Town, I'd find conditions to make our worst look like luxury living. Yet I'm still not prepared for this, and to my shame, I can't wait to get out onto the street again.

"I am glad they took the bread," Isla murmurs after we leave. "I noticed one of the babies has croup."

She continues to talk about what remedies she might send and whether they'd accept a basket of other goods as well. I'm still in too much shock to process her words. Too much shock to also process what I see next.

We're walking down the street, and at a shout behind me, I turn. It's just a man yelling at a kid running past, jostling a woman. But as I turn, someone steps out from a side road and then retreats fast, backpedaling. That alone wouldn't have caught my eye. The street is congested with people scurrying about. I'm not sure why I notice this one, and that is a testament to my preoccupation, because when recognition hits, I can't believe it took even a split second.

"Wait here," I say to Isla as I stride back to the corner.

I peer down it, looking for a retreating figure with dark hair, of average size. While the street is busy, I should still be able to see him. But I don't.

I stride back to Isla as she heads my way. "Did you call Simon to—?" I stop midsentence with a shake of my head. This isn't the twenty-first century, where she can text Simon to come fetch us.

"Is there any reason Simon would be here?" I ask.

"Simon?"

"Did you ask him to pick us up in the area?" I say.

"Certainly not. If we wish a ride home, we will flag down a hansom cab. Are you saying you saw our Simon?"

We return to the intersection. There's still no sign of him.

"Perhaps it was someone who looked like him?" she says. "He's a well-favored young man, but not unusual in his appearance."

"It was Simon. When he saw me looking, he retreated fast."

Her brows furrow. "That is most odd."

"Does he have any connection to this area? A reason he'd be here?"

"No, and there is a funeral this afternoon. He should be at the stables, polishing the carriages."

I motion for us to walk. Isla doesn't push me to talk, just lets me fall into thoughtful silence as she directs us back to the New Town.

Earlier, Evans's hash pipe had caught my attention. Just last night, Simon had offered me opium. I'd made the connection, but hadn't pursued it, no more than if I'd found they both liked to play golf. Yet a shared hobby means the possibility of intersecting lives.

Two young men, around the same age, who both use opium. Not exactly a rock-solid link. But then there's Catriona. Whoever wrote the note in my bag knew tidbits of her past, the sort you might share with friends.

Catriona and Simon are friends. Probably also romantically involved, however casually, and the person most likely to murder a woman is her partner. Yet I struggle to imagine that from the young man I had tea with last night.

Except, if the killer jumped into Simon's body, then that wasn't Simon. I would have never *met* the real Simon.

If the killer knew Catriona and Simon had been friends—occasionally with benefits—he could play that role. And he *would* know it, if that was one of the tidbits he'd gotten from Archie Evans.

Simon claimed he didn't know where Catriona sold her stolen goods, didn't know anything about her past or her confederates. His excuse—that he kept out of that part of her life—made sense, but it could also be the modern killer covering for his gaps in Simon-knowledge.

Catriona had a knack for betraying her friends. Selling them out, as she had with Constable Findlay and, from what Davina said, many others.

Isla hires staff that have been in trouble with the law. Does that include Simon? I got that impression, and while I also got the impression he was trying to steer Catriona away from that life, I must remember that if Simon is the killer, then the Simon I know is not the one Catriona knew, and I can rely on nothing he said.

Could the killer become Simon? He'd need to know Edinburgh well enough to play coachman, but he's presumably from here in the modern world and could figure it out. If he had any experience with horses, he could pull off caring for them and cleaning the stables as much as I could pull off being a maid. He lives over the stables and rarely comes in the house. Or *this* Simon rarely comes in . . . possibly because he's minimizing interaction with people who know the real Simon.

If Simon is the killer, he'd definitely know I'd been helping with the case. He could easily have targeted me. Hell, he watched me leave the night I was attacked. I'd come out the back door and bumped into him dressed in dark colors.

I'd bumped into him last night, too, when he'd hidden in the library and jumped out at me. Jumped out to spook me? So he claimed, but what if I hadn't fought him off? Had there been a length of rope in his pocket? Had he come into the house to kill me in my sleep? He *does* have a key.

What if Simon knew Evans, possibly through a mutual habit? Could Evans have been selling his information to Simon? Probably not. That's the proverbial red herring. Evans was selling information to someone, for some purpose, and while hanging out with Simon, Simon had jotted down information on Catriona, using the paper Evans was carrying.

Catriona had betrayed Simon, and he wanted dirt on her. As her friend, he knew that dirt exists. Evans was a journalist. He could investigate Catriona. Except the situation intensified. Simon followed Catriona and saw her doing something, further betraying him. In a rage, Simon strangled her.

Then the killer from my world took over Simon's body and made contact with Evans. The killer saw an information treasure trove, tortured Evan's for everything he knew about Simon, and then killed him for his first victim.

THIRTY-FOUR

I think this through as we walk. Isla obviously has experience with people being lost in thought—both her brother and herself, I expect—and she recognizes the signs and leaves me to it.

"May I ask about Simon?" I say as we cut through Parliament Square. "Since you've been back from holidays, has he seemed any different to you?"

"Different?"

"Is he acting oddly? I've spoken to him a few times. He seems to be friends with Catriona."

"He is."

"More than friends, I think, which is awkward."

Her brows crease. "More than friends, how?"

"Romantically involved, maybe? Or just fooling around together now and then. Friends with benefits, Victorian-style."

I expect her to laugh at the term, but she frowns at me. "*Simon?*"

"Yes. That isn't the impression you got? They must have hidden it. I guess they would. Premarital sex is verboten here, right?"

"Supposedly, but liaisons between grooms and maids are common. They would hardly flaunt it, but I very sincerely doubt there was any entanglement. Not with Simon."

I thought she'd been going to say Catriona had other romantic interests, which I know she did. When she says Simon instead, that pulls me up short.

"Is he gay?" I ask.

Her brow furrows more. "He is quite a cheerful lad."

"Wrong word. Queer?"

"Odd? No, not really."

"Third time's the charm. Homosexual?"

That has her flushing in a way "premarital sex" didn't. She casts a quick glance around and lowers her voice as she steers me away from others. "I presume that is more acceptable in your world, and I am glad to hear it."

I consider. "Has Oscar Wilde gone to trial yet?"

"Oscar who?"

"That answers my question. He's one of the most famous writers of the Victorian era and another of my faves. When he starts writing, you should read his books and check out his plays. He'll be tried and convicted of indecency, though. For homosexuality."

She sighs. "And that is still in our future. Lovely. As for Simon . . ." She glances over. "Is this important?"

"Anything you can tell me about him is important."

She says nothing, and we've gone clear across to High Street before she speaks again. "I am refraining from the obvious reaction, which is to exclaim that you cannot possibly suspect Simon of these murders based on something as mildly concerning as thinking you saw him following us."

"I *did* see him following us."

"Still, I presume there's more, and it's connected to the things you are avoiding telling me. I hope you are not doing so out of any consideration for my sensibilities. I get quite enough of that from Hugh. A few childhood incidents, and I am forever branded faint of heart."

She walks a few more steps before continuing, "Perhaps the last was well past childhood, but it was entirely Duncan's fault. One does not expect to step into one's place of family business and see one's brother playing with a decapitated head."

"Playing?"

She huffs. "Examining it. But he seemed to be talking to it, and I did not realize Hugh was also in the room, and so it gave me a start."

I sputter a laugh. "Alas, poor Yorick?"

"Yes, only this skull still had a face, which made it so much worse. I fainted, which was primarily due to the heat and the tightness of my cor-set, as I was off to a garden party. The concussion was quite mild, and the nightmares stopped after a few weeks, but you would think I was scarred for life to hear Hugh tell the tale."

"Hey, if you're okay with nightmares and fainting spells, I won't stand in your way. No, I'm not holding back out of concern for your sensibili-ties. Your brother and Detective McCreadie are the reason I'd rather not explain my theory. In order to tell it to them, we'd need to explain the time traveling. So to tell *you* would put you into an awkward position."

"The same awkward position that you are already in."

"Yes, but it's not my brother or my friend."

"I would like to take that responsibility, Mallory."

I open my mouth to protest. Then I shut it. Isla lives in a world of end-less insurmountable walls and locked gates. *Thy name is woman, and so thou shalt not pass.* By protecting her, I'm doing the same thing she's do-ing to Gray, but it feels different to her, and I need to put myself in her place and understand that.

If she chooses to take this risk, do I have the right to refuse her? Es-pecially if not telling her could damage the investigation—rob me of a person to bounce my ideas off? I told myself that when this secret endan-gered the investigation, I'd share it. We've reached that point.

"All right," I say finally, as we approach the gardens leading to the New Town. "May I ask that we finish discussing Simon first? Trust that I have a good reason for suspecting him, answer my questions, and then I'll tell you."

When she hesitates, I say, "You have my word on that, Isla. It's not a trick. I would rather ask these questions without you being influenced by my theory."

"All right. I trust you, and I will prove that by sharing information I would never give to anyone in our household, including my brother. When it comes to the pasts of my employees, I share them with Duncan only as they affect him."

"Need-to-know basis."

"Quite. He must know that Catriona is a thief or Alice a pickpocket. He does not need to know that Simon was a . . ." She clears his throat. "He found himself in trouble because he consorted with men. Older ho-mosexual men."

"He was a sex worker?" I guess.

"Actually, no. That is, I do not think so, in the strictest sense, and if he did accept money, it is no different from a shopgirl accepting rent from a wealthy admirer. Simon . . ." She coughs into her gloved hand. "I apologize if I stumble here, which must seem terribly quaint to you. I consider myself a woman of the world, yet I know the world extends beyond my experience with it. Simon had a friend, a young man who was not quite as handsome but was very charming and garrulous. I believe they were merely friends, but it is none of my business either way. The two of them played a sport of dressing as girls, a very pretty and charming pair of girls who frequented theaters and such establishments and flirted with men who knew exactly what they were and enjoyed participating in the performance. Liaisons were formed, to the financial benefit of Simon and his friend. It is not a world I inhabit, but I see no harm in it."

"All parties were consenting."

"Yes." She turns onto Princes Street and lowers her voice more. "The problem came when Simon's friend extricated himself from an attachment that had proven increasingly worrisome. He found a new benefactor, and his old one killed both him and his new lover."

I should express shock, and I make a noise that approximates it, but I've seen this before. Simon's friend fled a toxic relationship, and he was murdered for it. Too common a tale, whatever the time period.

Isla continues, "It threatened to be quite a scandal, especially given that the murderer was a man of high standing in the city. The police were bribed to look the other way. I fear they were only too happy to wash their hands of the matter. They did, however, need a scapegoat, and their eye fell on Simon."

"Shit."

"He was eighteen, the son of an Irish immigrant, and involved in what they considered 'deviant' behavior. He avoided the gallows only because one of his past lovers had the influence to help him and did not—thankfully—fear getting involved. This man knows Hugh, and through him knew my hiring practices, and so I took on Simon as a groom. I would not presume to say I know him well, but I am quite certain he chose that former life of his own volition, following his own propensities."

"Meaning he likes other men, not pretty housemaids."

"Yes. He was, as you say, friends with Catriona. I saw no hint of anything more."

I ask more questions. Did Catriona and Simon have a recent falling-out? Argue? Not that Isla knows of, but she'd been gone for a month, and Gray rarely notices domestic drama.

Does Simon seem any different? Ilsa describes him as quiet, which is not the guy I've been talking to. To her, he seems like himself, but they've had little contact. He interacts more with Gray, who is not the most observant guy when it comes to his employees.

At that point, I need to tell Isla everything, which means we circle the block around the town house twice. The first time, I'm explaining that I think the killer is the guy who attacked me in the twenty-first century, who was thrown into the body of Catriona's attacker . . . and I think that attacker—and body—is Simon. The second circle is spent in silence as she works that through.

"It makes sense," she says slowly, as we steer to add an extra block onto our walk. "The inciting event is the attack happening in two periods. Two women attacked by two men in a similar manner on the same spot. If you jumped into Catriona, it is logical that your attacker could have jumped into hers."

I don't answer. She's working it through, and we're to the next corner before she says, "Do you know anything of the man who attacked you in your time?"

"I saw his face, but that doesn't help. He was a serial killer who'd murdered two people. Strangled them with a rope, like he'd used on me. I'd seen him earlier that day in a coffee shop. I spilled coffee on him."

Her brows shoot up.

"It *was* my fault. I was distracted, trying to do too many things at once, and I bumped into him. I apologized—I felt terrible—but he brushed me off and then stalked me and tried to murder me."

"That seems excessive."

"In my world, people have been drawn and quartered for less." I glance over at her. "Kidding, obviously. It wasn't an overreaction to the coffee spill as much as an excuse. Some serial killers murder indiscriminately, because it's about the act, not the victim. For others, it's about the victims—picking people who remind them of Mommy or the girl who turned them down or whatever. With this guy, it was a game. He let his victims self-select, so to speak. If someone pisses him off, in a very ordinary way, can he track and kill them?"

"Cerebral," she murmurs. "That's what you and Duncan called the murder of Archie Evans. Methodical and cerebral, lacking passion or bloodlust."

"If I were to speculate, based on the murders in my time and here, I'd say that we're dealing with a guy who thinks he's clever. His driving force is ego. He wants to get away with it, and because he's not compelled to kill in a specific way, he can avoid patterns and connections that would get him caught. Then he arrives here, before the golden age of serial killers."

"The golden . . . ?" She shakes her head. "I don't even want to know what that means. Presumably, they become more common."

"To many people in our time, the first serial killer doesn't strike for another twenty years. He wasn't the first, but he's still the most famous. This guy comes here and thinks he can steal his thunder. Be clever and memorable. Except no one cares. So he goes another route. Replicate those murders. Out-ripper the Ripper."

"The . . . ?" Another head shake. "I definitely don't want to ask about that."

"You do not. The point is that he replicated a future famous murder and will undoubtedly continue on with the rest of the killing spree, meaning we need to stop him before he does."

"Agreed."

"We recognized each other in that attack," I say. "I believe he knows who I am, and I know who he *was*. It's the 'was' part that's a problem. He has the advantage."

"And you think he's now Simon?"

"I'm *theorizing* that he *could* be Simon. What I need from you is either proof that the guy in Simon's body *is* Simon or additional support for the idea that it might not be."

"I honestly can't say either way, Mallory. I haven't had enough contact with him in these last few days."

"Then the next step for me is *finding* proof. I'm not going to approach him directly—that's dangerous if he's the killer, because the killer realizes I'm not Catriona either. Would Mrs. Wallace know Simon better than you?"

"Yes, but she is not . . . fond of Catriona."

"Oh, I know it. I can work around that. I'll talk to her, and maybe talk to Dr. Gray if I can, and then, when I have a better idea either way, I'm going to ask you to send Simon on an errand so I can search his room. Can you do that?"

"Easily."

"Good."

THIRTY-FIVE

I've been in the house for an hour and haven't spoken to Mrs. Wallace yet. First, I told myself I needed to come up with subtle questions. Then, I decided I should do some housework, so she won't grumble about me shirking my duties. The truth is that I want time to think, because I don't like this solution to the puzzle.

It fits. I know my twenty-first-century killer inhabits the body of Catriona's nineteenth-century one. I know he tortured Archie Evans for something, and I could be wrong about *what,* but I am not wrong that Evans was investigating Catriona on behalf of someone who might have been angry enough to kill her.

Is it possible that the note in Evans's pocket isn't from the killer? Catriona certainly had multiple enemies. But that would mean the killer randomly grabbed and tortured the friend of someone *else* Catriona had wronged. Yeah, that'd be one hell of a coincidence and, like Isla, I don't like them.

Simon fits. He's friends with Catriona. She's still up to her criminal ways. She gets him involved in something, and it goes sideways—or Catriona yanks it sideways—and he tries to kill her.

The problem with that scenario? Simon wasn't a thief, wasn't a pickpocket, wasn't any sort of criminal. He was a gay kid who dressed up as a girl to flirt with men and find himself a sugar daddy.

That fits with what I know of Simon, better than I first thought. I'd interpreted flirting, but I can't say it was more than me jumping to stereotypical conclusions about a close relationship between a handsome young man and a pretty young woman. Simon had no problem with her relationship with Constable Findlay. He even gave her shit for playing Findlay wrong. He also gave her shit for not giving up her thieving ways. As for me seeing a different side of him than Isla did, does that mean he's a different guy . . . or just different with a friend versus an employer?

The opium link still bothers me. Seeing him today in the tenements definitely bothers me. I know I saw him. I know he retreated when he spotted me.

I'm almost done dusting the library when a possible explanation thuds into my brain. Dusting rag in hand, I march downstairs to the funeral parlor. I walk in to find Gray deep in paperwork. He looks up as I close the door behind me.

"Didn't you have a funeral this afternoon?" I say.

He blinks, and I realize I've been hanging out with Isla too long today. I need to code-switch before I talk to anyone else in this world.

I half curtsy. "Apologies, sir. I came to clean, expecting to find the offices empty, as Mrs. Ballantyne said there was a funeral today."

"Tomorrow. She has confused her days."

"Then, if I may be so bold, sir, may I ask whether you gave Simon a half day off? Or perhaps dispatched him on an errand into the Old Town?"

He hesitates.

"I saw Simon in the Old Town, sir, and he seemed to be following Mrs. Ballantyne, which is concerning . . . unless you sent him to do so."

He slowly sets down his pen, exhales through his teeth, and then runs a hand through his hair, streaking ink up his forehead.

"May I be blunt, Catriona?"

I plunk into the chair in front of him—as much as one can "plunk" wearing multiple layers of skirts.

He speaks slowly, as if picking through his word choices. "I understand my sister has forgiven you for her locket, and I know you were attacked by this killer we seek. I do not wish to seem mistrusting."

"But Mrs. Ballantyne is your sister, and I have not yet proven myself, and so you were concerned for her safety. You overheard us going out, and you asked Simon to follow us to be certain she was in no danger from me."

"Yes." He straightens. "I am sorry if you are offended—"

"Not offended." I pause. "Also apologizing for cutting you off, sir. You have reason for your mistrust. I spotted Simon and was concerned when he seemed to be following Mrs. Ballantyne."

"You were concerned about *Simon*?"

I shrug. "I am a suspicious person, and it was suspicious behavior. I am glad that we cleared that up." I rise. "Will I see you at tea?"

"Yes, and thank you for understanding my caution, Catriona."

I'm barely in the hall when the back door flies open and Isla zips in, shutting it behind her. She doesn't see me until she turns to find me standing there with my arms crossed.

The one thing about gas lighting? It doesn't exactly illuminate things well, things such as the glower on my face, and she hurries over and whispers, "It is not Simon. I mean, the person who appears to be Simon is actually Simon."

"You searched his room?" My voice rises.

"Of course not. I am hardly a detective. I spoke to him."

"You—?"

Gray leans out the parlor door. "Is everything all right?"

I turn and half curtsy. "Apologies, sir, I was telling Mrs. Ballantyne that she was mistaken about the funeral today and that you invited her to tea with Detective McCreadie. We will retreat upstairs, so as not to disturb your work."

He heads back into the funeral parlor, and I glare at Isla, making sure I'm under the lights so she can see my expression. Then I herd her up three flights of stairs to the attic. Only when her laboratory door closes behind me do I let myself explode.

"You *questioned* Simon? By yourself?"

"You said you could not, and I agreed. So I did it myself." She settles onto a chair. "I was very discreet."

"He could have been a killer."

"He is not."

"You didn't know—" I bite my tongue. This is going to take us right back where we were earlier, with Isla accusing me of patronizing her. We're going to need to talk about this. A long discussion on the danger of what she just did and the fact that she isn't an amateur sleuth in a Victorian novel.

I need to say that without sounding as if I'm treating her like a child, and I'm not in the mental state to navigate that conversation successfully. I'll return to it when I'm calmer.

I take a moment to find my equilibrium and say, "I wish you'd spoken to me, but we can discuss that later. So you talked to him?"

"I was quite clever about it, if I do say so myself."

I bite back the urge to say that "clever" is not the word I'd use for approaching a potential killer without backup. But her face glows with the exhilaration of success, and I can't bring myself to dowse it with a blast of reality. Later, I will. For now, I put myself in her place, her very delineated role, all those walls and barricades that even a progressive family cannot knock down for her.

I have punched a hole through one of those walls, giving her a peek into possibilities beyond. A glimpse of excitement and adventure. Can I blame her for missing the quicksand and the crocodiles and seeing only a glimmering tropical paradise?

She'll *need* to see those crocodiles and that quicksand—the sooner, the better. But I can't treat her like a child. She's a brilliant and capable woman.

"What did you do?" I ask, knowing she's waiting for this.

"I went to the stables and found him within, currying the horses. I asked him to step out. That seemed safer than speaking to him inside."

A sidelong look my way, and I grudgingly acknowledge the precaution with a nod.

She continues, "I pointed out a loose cobblestone as my excuse, so it would not seem suspicious that I summoned him out of doors. Then I commended him for the excellent work he'd done, repairing the path into my garden, how it was quite smooth now, and I no longer caught my heel on the stones."

"Uh-huh."

"He was quite confused, as he did not repair the path at all. He reminded me that it is the gardener's work, and while he will be quite happy to tell Mr. Tull about the loose cobblestone, he did not have the means to do more than temporarily fix it himself."

"Ah."

"I said yes, I only meant for him to tell Mr. Tull about the stone. As for the garden path, I said I was under the impression he'd aided Mr. Tull with that. He said, no, he had not—we'd had two funerals that day—but he was glad the job was to my satisfaction."

"Which proves he really is Simon."

"Quite. An imposter would have agreed to fix the cobblestone and he'd have taken credit for helping with the garden. Therefore, it is Simon, though I am still concerned that you saw him following us."

"That was your brother's doing. The more I considered Simon as a suspect, the less I liked it. I could explain away everything except seeing him today, and so I followed a hunch on that."

"A 'hunch' that Duncan had us followed." Her mouth tightens. "That is not like him. He can be protective, but he knows I venture into the Old Town on my own."

"He wasn't protecting you from unsavory neighborhoods. As long as he thinks I'm Catriona—who stole a locket I knew was very important to you—he's not going to trust me."

"A matter which we shall resolve as soon as his paper is delivered." She rises. "All right then. Have we resolved all questions about Simon? Did anything else connect him to Archie Evans beyond his association?"

"A hash pipe."

"A . . ."

"It's used for smoking opium, and I found residue in it."

Her lips twitch. "I know what a hashish pipe is, Mallory. I am not *that* sheltered. My confusion arises from the nature of the connection. Did Evans have one belonging to Simon?"

"No, but they both use opium."

"And . . ."

I shrug. "I'm not saying they're the only two young men in Edinburgh who do, but it could have brought them into contact. Maybe in an opium den."

"Opium den," she says slowly.

"Wrong time period?"

"No, it's the correct one, but . . . you do realize opium is not illegal."

"What?"

She walks over and squeezes my shoulder. "Poor Mallory, from a time so backwards that it has outlawed sweet opium."

She catches my expression and laughs. "I am teasing you. While opium has its uses, it is highly addictive, whether for personal use or for treating pain."

"But it's legal?"

"As is alcohol, which I might argue has ruined more lives. No, if Simon indulges, it is minor and irregular use. I've seen no indication of impairment. Consider it no different from a young man having a pint or two at the public house, and he would be equally likely to encounter Evans there."

Simon is cleared, which sends me back to square one. Who strangled Catriona in that alley? Who from her long list of enemies finally snapped? That sends me in circles, because I only know that she has enemies. Damn the girl for not keeping a journal.

Dear Diary,
Today the butcher's son threatened to throttle me for stealing from
his weekly deliveries. Tee-hee! What fun!

I really need to talk to Davina. I hate the idea of dealing with her bullshit, and I hate giving her what I know is a small fortune for her information, but I need to stop making excuses, grit my teeth, and get it over with. I'll do that tonight. I'll slip out, making sure I'm well armed and extremely cautious, with plans to be home before the pubs close.

Flip that note from Evans's room then. For the moment, forget the threat against Catriona and return to the list of addresses. If the killer was Simon, I could see no obvious connection to the addresses of immigrants, so I'd brushed off the note as circumstantial. Simon just happened to write on the back of those addresses, which Evans had been sharing with a third party. But if the killer is *not* Simon, is it still coincidental?

Evans was sharing or selling information about his housemates. Why addresses? Were they targets? That makes sense. His asshole roommates are compiling addresses to target the residents with hate crimes or other persecution.

The first two had been crossed off. Removed from the list of possibilities?

Or already "dealt with." There had been a date beside the toy shop. Was that when they intended to act?

Who would Evans share that with? And why? Another group wanting to beat them to the punch? A rival proto-Nazi frat? Like a sick pledge challenge—see who can torch the most immigrant homes and businesses?

Unlikely. It's not as if there are only five immigrant homes and businesses in the city. This might not be Vancouver, but if you include the Irish fleeing the potato famines, I'm going to put immigrants at five percent of the population. That means one in every twenty households fits their definition of outsiders. You can damn well find some yourself without buying a list from some reporter.

So what value *is* the list?

I remember the date beside the toy shop. We're past that date, and there was no sign of damage to the shop. That gives me an idea, and if I'm right, another clue, floating in the ether, seemingly meaningless, will clunk into place.

I need to confirm my suspicion. Can I get to the toy shop and back before tea? I check the clock. I'm cutting it close—very close—but the store will be closed afterward, and every wasted day is another chance for the killer to take his next Jack the Ripper–style victim.

I hurry into the library and pen a quick note for Isla. I don't try to find her—she'd want to join me and then I really would be late for tea. I grab a few coins from Catriona's stash, and I'm off.

THIRTY-SIX

The toy shop truly is a wonderland of a place. From the outside, it looks like a high-end store in the modern world, where the toys are really meant for adults to display as whimsical accents or to place high on nursery shelves where grubby hands can't actually reach them. When I step inside, though, I find actual children milling about under the watchful but kindly eye of a shop clerk.

The clerk is a woman around thirty. Dark-haired and dark-eyed and full-figured. She's smiling at a trio of girls ogling a fully articulated wooden doll.

"You may touch her if you like," she says. "Go on. Pick her up. See how her arms and legs move."

I walk to the counter, and she smiles my way, but it's an absent smile, her attention on the children, enjoying the sight of their wonder. I pause to enjoy it, too, and I feel the weight of the coins in my pocket.

I take out the coins, push them forward, and whisper "Would this be enough?" as I nod toward the girls. The woman glances at the coins and her face lights, only to shutter as she eyes me warily.

"I truly would like to," I say. "If it is enough."

She nods and moves from behind the counter, skirts swishing as she bends beside the girls and whispers to them. They look at me, their eyes widening. She directs their attention to three smaller dolls, not quite as fancy. The girls nod and point. They will take one small doll apiece instead of the one large one to share.

The shopkeeper wraps each doll in blank newsprint as carefully as the New Town shopkeeper wrapped that hand cream in tissue. Then she presents one to each girl. She bends before them and says, "You are to tell your parents that there was a kind woman at the toy shop who bought these for you, and if they have any questions, they may speak to me."

The girls haven't looked at me since first glancing my way, and now all three murmur awkward thanks before running to the door, doll packages cradled in their arms. Before they leave, one blurts back at me, "You are very pretty, miss," and another says, "I like your dress," while the third only giggles and waves. Then they are gone, scampering off down the street.

"That was very kind," the shopkeeper says as she returns behind the counter to count out my change.

When she hands me back coins, I pause. "Was that enough?"

She smiles. "It was. We do not make fancy toys here. Simple and sturdy toys for those who might spare a pence or two for their bairns. Which is not many, even in this neighborhood."

Her dialect and accent are pure Scots, and so I speak carefully when I say, "Are you one of the Kaplan family?"

She tenses, and a sliver of annoyance edges into her voice as she says, "Do I not sound as you expected?"

"No, I am only making sure, because I have a message for the Kaplan family and I did not wish to misdeliver it."

Now her body goes rigid, gaze darting to a door, which I presume leads to a workshop. Through it comes the muffled tap-tapping of a craftsman at work.

"Not that sort of message," I say quickly. "I found this shop on a list of addresses that I fear may indicate danger. Addresses of immigrants, written by those who may mean them harm."

She relaxes. "Ah, all right then. Well, I thank you very much for the warning, but the police have already been informed and thwarted whatever those ruffians had in mind."

"Oh?"

She leans against the counter. "A criminal officer came by last week to warn us that there might be trouble on a certain day. He had the patrols coming past all evening, and my husband and my father slept in the shop here. It would not be the first time we have had trouble. We have been here since before I was born, and still some do not welcome us."

"I am sorry to hear that."

"We are welcome in this neighborhood, because people know us, and they bought toys from us when they were wee bairns themselves. Yet trouble still finds its way from the outside. We have learned to guard ourselves, but this time the police did their jobs. They found young men loitering about, intent on trouble, and they gave them a fright."

"Good."

She smiles. "Very good. We were most pleased."

I double-check, confirming that the date the police were concerned about is the one on Evans's note. It is.

"I do appreciate that you brought us this information." She waves around the shop. "Please, take something with our thanks. Anything you like."

I shake my head. "Thank you, but I am only glad the danger was averted."

"Are there no bairns in your life who would like a toy?" she coaxes.

"No," I say. "No children . . ." I'm idly looking around the shop when my gaze falls on a wooden box.

"Ah." She smiles. "For yourself, perhaps?" She takes the box from the shelf. It's simply constructed but the polished wood shines. When I open the lid, the box plays a tune I don't recognize. On the inside of the lid there's a tin plate showing a girl with a parasol walking over a footbridge.

"Not for me," I say, "but there's a parlormaid in the house where I work."

"You are in service then? What a kind thing to do for a wee working girl." She starts wrapping the box before I can protest. I still try, but she says, "I insist. It is worth less than the dolls."

I'm not so sure about that, but I let her wrap it and hand it to me.

"May I ask one more thing?" I say. "If I were to come into information like this again, I would like to take it to the proper authorities. I hesitated to go to the police because, as you say, they do not always trouble themselves with such concerns. It seems this particular criminal officer is different. Might I have his name?"

She beams. "Certainly. It is Detective McCreadie."

Detective McCreadie, who'd been coming to Gray's town house that night I was attacked, and then turned away, as if he'd forgotten something. Or as if he'd spotted me, followed me into the Old Town, and attacked me.

While there are a few questions I'll want answered by our criminal officer friend, I don't spend more than two seconds seriously considering him for the role of killer.

No matter how much I know about Catriona, I struggle to fully inhabit her. The only reason anyone buys my act is that blow-to-the-head excuse. The imposter-killer might have tortured Evans for background on his new body's life, but there's a limit to how well he'll be able to fool friends. Gray and Isla have known Hugh McCreadie since they were children together. They've been close friends for most of their lives. I cannot imagine the imposter would be able to pull that off.

There's another link, though. The one that sent me to the toy store. The clue I'd seen, floating over the investigation, apparently meaningless until, with a jolt, it'd taken on meaning.

What had McCreadie said about Evans that first night, when Gray was working over his body? That Evans worked the crime beat. The only thing it meant at the time was that it explained how McCreadie knew him. But when I'd considered who Evans might be sharing those addresses with, the answer had been "the police." That would explain why the date had passed and the shop seemed fine.

If Evans worked the crime beat, he would talk to police, and I knew he'd had contact with McCreadie.

From what I know of McCreadie, he's a good cop. If he got hold of that list of targets, he'd do the right thing to warn them. That's why I went to the shop. To see whether I was right that whoever got that list—McCreadie or a colleague of his—had notified the toy-shop owners, who could tell me which police officers were involved.

I have that answer. With it, the obvious suspect is McCreadie himself. Obvious, however, does not mean "only," and I have a much better idea who got the names and passed them on to McCreadie.

I slip in the rear door of the town house. That means circling the block to come in through the mews, but then I can creep up to the second floor, adjust my attire, and ease in with hopes of still being on time—

The clock strikes the quarter hour. Okay, I'm fifteen minutes late. Damn it, I need a pocket watch. Inside, teacups tickle against china saucers. I walk to the drawing room and curtsy in the doorway.

"I apologize for my tardiness," I say. "I had an errand to run, and I had hoped to be back before tea. I will apologize to Alice and Mrs. Wallace for needing to serve in my stead."

"Oh, come and sit down," Isla says. "I explained to Mrs. Wallace that I had sent you on an errand, and Alice seemed quite happy to serve tea in return for a heaping plate from the tray."

I set my package on a nearby table. "I have a gift for her as well, from the toy shop."

Isla cuts me a look, warning me not to say too much, but I ignore her and sit without taking any treats from the tray.

"Detective McCreadie," I say. "I must be honest with you and admit that I conducted a brief investigation into the first victim, Archie Evans."

McCreadie's tea sloshes as his cup clatters onto the saucer. "What?"

"Not alone," Isla says quickly. "I accompanied her."

"That does *not* make this better."

"I had Simon follow them to ensure their safety," Gray says.

"*Et tu Brute?*"

Isla rolls her eyes. "No one stabbed you in the back, Hugh. Catriona had a theory that Duncan found unlikely, and so I accompanied her to young Archie's rooming house. Duncan wondered at our leaving and sent Simon, not knowing we were undertaking an investigation."

"Because you are not *supposed* to be undertaking an investigation. You are a chemist. She is a housemaid."

"They solve crimes," I murmur under my breath. When they hear me, I clear my throat. "It would make for interesting detective fiction."

McCreadie glares at me. "No, it would not. Do you know why? Because you are not detectives."

"All the best detectives are amateurs," Isla says tartly. "Every reader knows that."

When McCreadie's glower deepens, she says, "However, even better would be an amateur team to assist the professional detective. A widowed chemist, a former-thief housemaid, and a medical doctor turned criminal scientist, all helping the clever and handsome criminal officer, who does not need their assistance but humors them most graciously."

"Now you're mocking me," McCreadie growls.

Isla's face softens. "Teasing a little, but never mocking, Hugh. I understand that, in our zeal, we may have overstepped, and I apologize."

"As do I," I say. "All I wanted was proof to either dismiss my theory or support it before bringing it to your attention. However, what we found . . ."

I tell him about the list of addresses. I don't produce the note—I can't with the reverse being about Catriona. I tell him how we visited three of the addresses and realized that, given Evans's roommates' extracurricular activities, it was probably a list of targets for persecution. Then, after we came home, I realized I should have warned the toy shop, as they were singled out for particular attention on the note. In doing so I discovered that they'd already been warned by the police, in the form of McCreadie himself.

"That information came from Archie Evans?" McCreadie says.

"I take it you didn't receive it directly."

"Hardly, or I wouldn't feel as foolish as I do right now, having not realized that the radical group targeting those poor people was the *same* radical group Evans lived with. In my defense, there are, sadly, many such organizations, and while your visit placed this one on my list for closer examination, I did not consider it could be the same group, nor that Evans might be our informant."

"Because Constable Findlay didn't tell you that."

His head jerks my way.

I murmur, "Constable Findlay mentioned something about it."

"Hmm. Well, I would have rather he didn't, but yes, it was young Findlay."

That's why Evans's roommates had known Findlay was a cop. Not because he looked like one—because they actually recognized him.

"Please do not tell Constable Findlay that I said he mentioned it. I would not wish to get him into trouble. I presume he did not tell you which radical group it came from for fear of implicating Evans."

"Who was dead at the time," McCreadie grumbles.

"Dead yes, but his reputation lives on, and I can understand Constable Findlay not wanting to soil that in any way."

McCreadie sighs. "I understand. Yes, Colin has been infiltrating some of these radical groups for me, as he is the correct age to do so. He knew Evans through the young man's reportage. When Evans came sniffing about, I would have Colin speak to him, so I did not have to. Colin must have used that connection to turn Evans into an informant. Clever lad."

"Yes," Gray murmurs. "But it may also have gotten Evans killed."

McCreadie winces. "Someone found out he was selling information to the police, and they tortured and killed him for it. Then the killer realizes he has a taste for murder that mere strangulation did not sate, and so he proceeds to the horrific mutilation of a prostitute."

Isla glances over.

I bite my tongue and keep my expression neutral. I feel terrible nodding and acting like his theory makes sense when I know otherwise. That is not the way to treat a fellow officer. I can only hope that once I've proved my new hypothesis, I can find a way to convince him of the killer's identity so he can make the arrest and claim the closure.

"I am glad to see Constable Findlay doing so well," I say carefully. "He seems a most promising young detective. I have been concerned about him. Does he seem well to you? Normal in his behavior?"

"You mean has he recovered from you breaking his heart?"

"Hugh," Isla admonishes. "First, it is a woman's—or man's—prerogative to change their mind, as I'm sure you know well."

McCreadie's cheeks flush.

Isla continues, "Second, Catriona does not remember what she did to young Findlay. She is only concerned for his well-being. Does he seem well?"

McCreadie shrugs. "Well enough. He's always a quiet lad. He's been a bit absentminded lately, forgetful and distracted, but he has been beside himself with apologies for that. I know he was fond of Catriona, and so I understand his melancholy. Which is not to blame you, Catriona. Isla is right. I might tease, but it is your right to end a relationship, and I am only glad you did it before it became more serious." He sips his tea. "That is far harder on all involved." Another sip. "Now, back to this theory regarding Evans . . ."

Gray and McCreadie continue discussing it. Isla and I add nothing to it—we can't make this worse. They don't notice our silence, though, or they mistake it for agreement. We finish our tea, and the two men leave, still talking about how they should proceed, forgetting all about us.

When they are gone, Isla moves to sit closer to me and whispers, "Constable Findlay?"

I nod. "Does he seem like the same guy to you?"

"I'd hardly know. I haven't seen him since I returned, but even that isn't unusual. As Hugh said, he's such a quiet lad. Hugh handpicked him from the constables shortly after Constable Findlay joined the force. He'd made little impression on the others, being so quiet, but Hugh saw promise in him. He always said the lad only needed a push and a dose of confidence."

"Quiet and shy then."

"Very. I know Hugh encouraged him to join the men for a pint after work and such, but it took effort to make him go. Keeps his own company, he does."

"Yet he was courting Catriona?"

Isla sighs and shakes her head. "I discouraged it. However, Hugh was reluctant to intercede. He thought such a relationship could help them both, Catriona drawing young Findlay from his shell and the boy adding some stability and gravitas to Catriona's life. I feared Catriona was taking advantage of Constable Findlay, but Hugh could not see how she could do so with a young man of very limited means and prospects."

"Well, for a starter, she was selling the trinkets he gave her. Simon told me that. It's also possible she was selling information she gleaned from him. Police information."

She starts another, deeper sigh, and then stiffens. "But if you are suggesting that the killer is in Constable Findlay's body, does that also not suggest the real Constable Findlay tried to murder her?"

"I suspect so."

"Oh my." She falls back in her seat, hand to her chest. "I-I cannot believe—"

She swallows and pulls herself straight again. "Allow me to rephrase that. Can I believe that Catriona would drive a young man to murder? Particularly one inexperienced in matters of the heart, betrayed and cast in the role of fool? Yes. I can. Which does not, obviously, relieve her attacker of blame. Murder is only justified in self-defense, where no lesser course is available. However, that would not keep me from feeling pity and even some responsibility if that is the solution to this mystery."

"Whatever Catriona did to Findlay, it wouldn't justify killing her. It is a motive, though, and it is tragic. We can acknowledge that without blaming Catriona. We can also acknowledge it without blaming you or Detective McCreadie. Neither of you foresaw *that*. If this *is* the solution, which I still need to prove, I'll get the evidence and find a way to present it to him."

"Good. Will you search young Findlay's apartment tomorrow?"

"If I can get his address."

"We'll do that right now. I'll tell Duncan that I wish to send him a basket, in appreciation for all he is doing for the immigrants of Edinburgh." She rises. "Then we will search his apartment on the morrow."

THIRTY-SEVEN

I lied to Isla. Well, half a lie. I do plan to search Findlay's apartment. I'm just not waiting until morning.

Part of that is to avoid taking her. I can't afford to be locked in a battle of wills I might not win. More importantly, I am on a schedule here, and I have no damned idea what that schedule is.

The killer is now copying the murders of Jack the Ripper. He's taken victim one, and he'll take victim two exactly the right number of days later. The bastard is nothing if not precise. I hear the relentless *tick-tick* of that clock, which would be so much more helpful if I could see its damned face.

Was it two days between the first and second Ripper murders? Five days? A week? I have racked my brain for this information and found nothing. I do know that the next murder will be worse. They will all be worse. The clock is ticking, and there's a bomb on the other end of it, and I cannot sleep knowing another innocent woman might die.

I argue with the impulse. Isn't there another way? I stabbed the killer twice. Why not test that with Findlay? Find an excuse to grab his arm and see if he flinches. In a penny dreadful, that would be the solution, but in real life, it's not good enough. I can use those stab wounds as proof—maybe to convince McCreadie—but I need more first.

Would it not be better to search Findlay's apartment tomorrow while he is at work? He isn't known for going out in the evenings. Yes, but that's

Findlay, not the imposter, who will be hunting for his next victim, whether he kills her tonight or not.

But if he is planning to take a victim tonight, I'll already be too late to stop him. True, but what if it's tomorrow night? I have no idea how long it'll take to convince McCreadie that his constable is a murderer.

In the end, there's no reasoning with myself. All that is drowned out by the ticking of the clock. I must try to get answers tonight, so that whether I'm right or wrong, I can plow forward to the next step first thing tomorrow.

I don't wait for late night. I move my coat behind a bush outside the rear door. Then I read in my room until darkness fully falls before I slip downstairs.

I'm on the steps, passing the second level, when a door opens.

"Catriona?"

It's Gray.

"Apologies if I disturbed you, sir. I know it is late. I was peckish and thought I might see if Mrs. Wallace left anything in the kitchen."

"Excellent idea," he says, stepping into the stairwell. "I quite forgot to ask for a biscuit before she went up to bed. We shall raid the pantry together."

I hesitate, but before I can think up an excuse, he's passing me. I follow him down into the kitchen. Once there, he heads straight for a small wooden box. He opens it and deflates.

"Sir?" I say. "There is a bit of leftover cake here."

He turns so sharply you'd think I'd discovered a book on sixteenth-century fingerprinting techniques, and I have to bite back a smile as I hold out the plate. He takes it and then pauses, looks down at it, and opens a drawer.

"We'll divide it," he says.

"That isn't necessary, sir."

He finds a knife and then hesitates again over the slice of cake, as if trapped between the desire to be fair and the desire to eat the whole thing.

I take the knife from him, murmuring, "If I may."

I cut off less than a quarter for myself. "That is all I require. I will leave you to your evening—"

"Not yet. Eat your cake, Catriona. I wish to speak to you."

When I pause, his brows knit. Then a look of horror passes through his dark eyes. "If you think I am attempting anything untoward, I assure you—"

"No, no. You give me no concern on that front, Dr. Gray."

And that's a damn shame.

The thought comes unbidden, and I shove it back with as much horror as he just felt. Still, I can't deny just a prickle of regret that Gray looks at me and sees only his teenage housemaid, while I look at him, leaning against the countertop, nibbling his cake, hair tumbling over his forehead, collar unbuttoned, ink spotting one cheek . . .

I sigh to myself and then I straighten.

Before I can speak, he says, "Good. I know it is awkward to have me seek your company, when you are a young lady in my employ, but you need never worry on that count. What I wish to discuss is the case."

I have to stop myself from blinking at him.

Really, Gray? Really? For the past week, every time I hear your damn foot-steps, my heart skips, hoping you're finally coming to discuss the case. And you want to do it now? When I need to leave—quickly—before I lose my chance to search Findlay's apartment?

"I would like to apologize," he continues. "Not for my mistrust. That you have earned, even if it is a past version of you who earned it, but I am attempting to move past my prejudice."

"Thank you, sir. But—"

"I am apologizing for not properly recognizing your contributions to the case. Earlier, Hugh and I excised you from the conversation, and it is not the first time we have done so. That is inexcusable. You have proven yourself, again and again, and I continue to treat you like a housemaid rather than an assistant. That ends now. I will speak to Hugh about it. You are an integral part of this investigation."

Once again, he's saying exactly the words I've longed to hear . . . right when I can least afford to hear them.

"I apprec—" I begin.

"If we are to work this case as a team," he continues, missing my interjection, "then we must behave as a team. I wish to be more open with you, Catriona. To include you, and not leave you feeling as if you must sneak off and investigate on your own. I understand why you did that.

I want you to know it isn't necessary. If you have theories you wish to pursue, tell me, and I will not brush you off as I did this morning. We shall investigate them together."

I open my mouth. Nothing comes out. He is apologizing for excluding me. For withholding information. For not sharing theories with me.

And what am I doing? Excluding him. Withholding information. Not sharing a theory with him—a vital theory that changes the entire investigation.

I have something to tell you, Dr. Gray.

Isla is wrong. I understand that she doesn't want to distract Gray from his paper. She fears my truth will be too much for him right now. I disagree. He needs to hear it. He needs to hear all of it. He has opened a door for me, and I cannot slam it shut on him.

My mouth opens again. And again, I shut it, because here I face that ugliest of quandaries. Isla trusts me. She has reached out in friendship. I am about to throw over a new female friend for a guy.

It's not like *that.*

No? Am I sure? Didn't I just admit that I find Gray attractive? How much of me wanting to tell him the truth *this very moment* is because it's important for the case . . . and how much is so he won't be angry with me when he finds out?

Am I valuing my relationship with Gray more than my relationship with Isla? I hope to hell not, but I won't take that chance. There is no reason to tell him the truth about myself this very moment. I'll speak to Isla in the morning. I'll be firm, and if I can't convince her, then at least I won't have betrayed her trust. She'll know that I intend to tell him.

"That is what you wish, is it not, Catriona?" Gray says, cake halfway to his lips, brows knit in concern. "Have I mistaken your interest in the case?"

"Not at all. I am glad to hear you intend to include me more. Thank you."

"It is only what you deserve, Catriona. We must be open with one another if we are to work together, in my laboratory or on this case."

I nod and take a bite of my cake, feeling it crumble like ashes in my mouth.

Stop that. You'll resolve this. It'll be fine.

"Now," he says. "Do you have time to discuss the case?"

I feign a yawn. "I wish I did, sir, but . . ."

"It has been a very long day. I understand. Tomorrow then?"

"Yes." I look up at him. "I would very much like to talk to you tomorrow. I have a theory that I think you need to hear."

"Excellent. I shall look forward to hearing it on the morrow."

THIRTY-EIGHT

I leave Gray in the kitchen, where he's puttering about, probably looking for more cake. I slip upstairs and out the back door. The biggest risk here is Simon, in his rooms over the stable, but his light is off, as if he's out for the evening himself. I still take my time and hide in the shadows long enough to be sure he didn't hear me and come out to see what I'm up to. Then I hurry to the mews and zip down the lane.

I feel bad about leaving Gray behind. I feel even more bad about leaving Isla, especially after she's the one who got us the address. I need to deal with that. Discuss options and find a compromise that doesn't endanger her or swaddle her in cotton. Of course, if I'm right about Findlay, we won't need to worry about that. McCreadie will take over, and Catriona's killer will be caught, and—fingers and toes crossed—I will have fulfilled my cosmic assignment and be sent hurtling through the universe to my own time.

I haven't thought much about that lately. There's the case, of course, consuming my thoughts. And I've been finding my footing in this world. Settling in and feeling it settle around me, glittering with possibilities. There are things I'll miss, but this is not where I belong. My family, my job, my friends—and hopefully my nan—wait on the other side, and I will get back to them, with this past week tucked into memory, a grand adventure for the ages.

I yank my thoughts back as I hurry along. The streetlights are still on, people making their way home after social visits, dawdling on a pleasant Saturday evening as the clock ticks toward midnight.

Findlay lives here in the New Town. That shouldn't be so shocking. This case just keeps taking us into the Old Town, as if that's where everyone who isn't wealthy lives. Not true. The New Town isn't like Point Grey in Vancouver, where you can't buy a house for under two million. It's more like a suburb where you can easily spend two million, but you can also get a condo for a quarter of that, or rent someone's nice basement apartment for less than you'd pay in Vancouver proper.

The last is what Findlay is renting. A basement apartment a half mile from Gray and Isla's place. From what I've seen, the Gray family town house lands just above the midway point for New Town home value. The one where Findlay rents the basement would land on the other side of that midway point. It's half the width of the Robert Street town house, with a very subtle ROOM TO LET sign in the front window.

Faint lights glow in the main level, second level, and attic level, with the third dark. If I were to hazard a guess, I'd say the owners live on a couple of floors—maybe the first and second—and rent out the rest. A young man on a constable's salary could afford the basement if he scrimped and really wanted to live in the New Town.

The problem with a basement apartment is that I can't tell whether Findlay is at home. From the front, the lower level is completely black, with no obvious windows. I round the street to the mews, where I count town houses to find the right one.

These being less affluent homes, they don't get individual stables. There seems to be a communal one for horses and then a small garden court-yard behind each house. That makes sneaking up tricky. I'm glad I chose to wear former assistant James's coat, the dark gray color and length blending me into the shadows. I also brought a hat from Catriona's mea-ger wardrobe. In the daylight, it's a jaunty navy blue and quite stylish, which makes me suspect it's a gift she'd tucked away to pawn at the first opportunity. Either way, it does the job, hiding my light hair, with the brim shadowing my face.

There's an exterior basement door, with steps up to the garden. Beside it, a dark square might be a window. A clock inside one of the town houses strikes midnight, and as if on cue, several of the brighter lights go out, including the one on the main level of Findlay's building.

I wait a few minutes, giving whoever is inside time to get to bed. Then I creep forward, sticking to shrubs and a low fence, until I'm close enough to see that, yes, that is definitely a window.

I hunker down and shield the sides of my bonnet, blocking the moonlight. The window stays dark, with no hint of light inside the apartment. I find my knife and clutch it in one hand as I continue on until I'm at the window. Then I bend and peer in. Total darkness. If Findlay is home, he's gone to bed.

Do I dare break in while he's sleeping? Yep. I'm going to take that chance, because I've already accepted that the worst thing that can happen isn't that bad after all.

Worst case, Findlay is home and hears me and confronts me. If he is not the killer, then as Catriona—the former sweetheart who double-crossed him—I can pretend I came to beg forgiveness, slipping in during the night to offer more than a mere apology.

And if Findlay *is* the imposter-killer? Well, that imposter knows I'm also one, and if he catches me in his house, he's going to take full advantage of the opportunity to kill me. While that isn't ideal, I'm not too worried that he'll succeed. I've planned for the possibility of entering the house while he's there, and I have a couple of crude trigger alert systems in my bag. He's never getting the jump on me again. The "not ideal" part comes if we fight and I take him captive for McCreadie. How the hell will I explain that? Pitting Findlay's reputation against Catriona's, I'm sure to lose.

No, if Findlay is the killer and he catches me, I will fight, and then I will flee, and I'll tell Gray the truth. Let Gray and McCreadie take it from there.

All contingencies worked out, my next step is getting into the apartment, which is laughably easy. When my parents bought me all those "junior detective" kits, I'd soon discovered that my lock-picking skills didn't work on anything but the simplest locks, like the bathroom or the old locks at Nan's house. No children's toy is going to teach you how to open a modern dead bolt. But it *had* opened those doors at Nan's.

What does that mean? That ten-year-old Mallory Atkinson, honing her lock-picking skills on her grandmother's doors, had inadvertently been preparing to become a nineteenth-century detective. I open this basement door with no problem.

Once inside, I peer around for the glow of lights. The interior is cold and dark. The next thing is to listen for signs of life. Just the ticking of a clock. Then I bend to check what the floors are made of. I'm wearing my soft-soled indoor boots, but they still make some noise on hard floors. While I could remove them, I'd rather not have to flee in stocking feet. "Time-traveling cop flees killer only to be done in by slippery Victorian stockings" is not the epitaph I care to leave in this world.

From what I can see, the floors are like the basement at the town house—painted wood with lots of throw rugs. I test my tread on the wood. If I'm careless, it'll make a swishing sound, but I don't plan to be careless.

I shut the door without closing it completely, in case I need to make a run for it. Then I take out a box of wooden matches I swiped from the kitchen. It's pitch-black in the hall, and I need that match light. I hold it up to see a corridor with multiple closed doors. Again, not ideal, but if he's sleeping, I'd rather his door is shut.

I make my way down the hall. At each door, I pause, listen, and then crack it open. Room one is a tiny kitchen. Room two is a sitting area. Room three has a sign reading LANDLORD STORAGE. I open it anyway to confirm that, yes, it's storage. The next room is the same. Okay, so this is a really tiny apartment, half the space used by the owners.

There's only one more room, at the front of the house. No water closet, apparently. That's Victorian basement living for you. I take extra time with this last door, which must be the bedroom. When I finally have it open enough to see inside, I send up a whispered "Thank you" into the cosmos. The room is empty. Findlay isn't home.

Back to the external door, which is the only exit. If there'd once been an interior staircase, access has been removed. I close the external door and set up my alert system.

Now that I'm definitely alone, I can light the candle I brought. I even absconded with a tiny candleholder, the sort one might see in an old gothic, the timid maiden making her way through the dark house, candlelight wavering.

My first stop is the kitchen. That's where the window is, so I need to get through this quickly, in case Findlay returns and sees the soft light. This being the kitchen, that's easy. There's nothing here. Almost literally nothing. Findlay might not go out drinking with his mates, but he isn't cooking at home either. There are some basic foodstuffs and nothing more.

I shut the kitchen door as I leave, to be sure no light can be seen through the window. I hesitate at the storage rooms. If I wanted to hide something, would that be a good or lousy place to do it? Depends on how often my landlords took stuff out. If Findlay is the imposter, he won't know that, so I'm going to deduce he wouldn't take a chance.

What exactly *do* I hope to find? I've been wondering that since I first considered searching Simon's apartment over the stables. What could I find to prove the resident is actually a twenty-first-century time traveler? That should be easy. Just turn the spotlight on myself. How would someone searching Catriona's rooms realize she was from the future? Short answer: they wouldn't. I brought nothing with me. Neither did he. And neither of us is going to be comfortable enough in this world to keep a diary.

Based on my room, there is no way anyone could tell that I'm from the future. So flip the question. How would someone know I wasn't Catriona? Again, the short answer is that they wouldn't, because I need to *be* Catriona. I'm not at the stage of storing away her belongings or buying ones better suited to my tastes. There is only one thing in my room to suggest I'm not Catriona: the French book on poisons. Even that is hardly proof. Hell, Catriona *might* read that, if she was looking to kill someone.

Wait. No. There is something else that would betray me, and I only realize it now. My case notes. I've been hiding them under that floorboard. Yes, Alice knows where it is, but if she found the notes, she'd think nothing of them—after all, I *have* been helping Gray and McCreadie with the case. But if the killer came into my room, wanting to prove to himself that I was not Catriona, those notes would do it.

Here I'm looking for a similar telltale sign. What I find is something altogether different.

I've done enough searches as a cop to scan a room and know where to look first. In the living room, it's the settee—an old and ratty thing, the Victorian equivalent of a Goodwill find.

I check the back, looking for holes. I check the cushions. Then I flip it over to find a tear that's been enlarged. Reach in. Root around. Pull out a small notebook.

I open to the first pages and see handwriting that looks like that on the back of Evans's note—the information about Catriona. I take the note from my pocket to check. Yep, same script.

The book is Findlay's case notes. The keen young constable eager to improve his craft, laboriously detailing every aspect of a case, particularly when McCreadie made a connection or uncovered a clue. A personal how-to manual for becoming a detective, and looking at it, I see myself reflected in these pages. I'd been this kind of constable. After helping on a case, I'd write up these notes on my computer and research anything I didn't understand. Teaching myself how to be a detective.

I flip through the pages. Three-quarters of the way through, the handwriting changes. Oh, it's not a marked change. It could pass for the other writing, if the author was in a hurry or writing on an awkward surface. Yet I don't see that. I see someone trying to emulate the original handwriting, with all the stops and starts of practice before the script smooths out.

In these pages, the writer is no longer detailing his job; he's detailing his life. My grandfather—on my dad's side—had Alzheimer's, and he kept a journal just like this. Reminders to himself that became increasingly heartbreaking as the disease sank its claws into him. At first, it was just regular notes like I might jot in my planner. *Dentist appointment—ask about left top molar. Recycling is now the first and third weeks of the month. New parking spot is 18A.* But then it became more. The names of people my grandfather knew. Reminders to do daily tasks, like showering. And finally, reminders of himself, of who he was.

That is what I see here. Those later stages. Copious notes on who Findlay was, everything about him and his job and who he might encounter on a daily basis. There are blank spaces where the imposter can come back and fill things in. There's an entire page on McCreadie, starting with his name and appearance and a few personal details, some of which I know, most I don't—lives alone, never married, engaged once, workaholic, ambitious, estranged from wealthy family. More has been added later, everything from McCreadie's home address to how he takes his tea to his relationships with others.

I stare down at the page and my breathing catches enough that I need to take a moment to calm my racing heart. This is what I was looking for. More than I dared hope for. It's like finding the imposter actually *did* write a diary of his time-travel adventures.

The first part of the book is Constable Colin Findlay's notes for becoming a detective. The second part is the imposter's notes for becoming Constable Colin Findlay.

THIRTY-NINE

With this journal, I am not only certain that the twenty-first-century killer inhabits Findlay, I'm also certain that I was right about why he tortured Evans. In the early notes, I see the sort of specific data plus random facts I might expect Evans to know if he'd been friendly with Findlay. Also the sort of information he couldn't expect Evans to give him over a pint at the local pub.

What do I know about your boss? What kind of question is that, mate?

This data dump required more. It required a poor guy, terrorized and in pain, racking his brain for more to give.

Wait! You mentioned once that your boss didn't get on with his family. That he came from money and something happened. You didn't say what—it was an offhand comment.

That's what I see in these pages. *Tell me everything I've said about Detective McCreadie. About my sergeant. About my coworkers and my friends and my landlords. Every tidbit, no matter how small.*

There's more, too. The same things my grandfather would have noted about his daily life and routines. What was going through Evans's mind when Findlay asked *these* questions? The most banal and obvious aspects of ordinary life, everything from clothing to customs to the value of currency. All the same questions I've been struggling with myself. The questions of a stranger in a strange land. A time traveler in a new time.

If there was any—*any*—possible way I could read these pages and come up with another explanation, like early memory loss, it's erased by the terminology itself, with words like "workaholic." This was written by someone from my world. By the asshole who tried to kill me and then ended up in Findlay's body.

My twenty-first-century attacker is in the body of Constable Colin Findlay. Does that mean Findlay is in his body? Maybe so, but it doesn't mean anything for this case. It's just idle speculation.

Earlier, when I considered Findlay as a possibility, I'd wondered at everything he seemed to know—his comments on McCreadie, his job, Gray, all of which made him seem to be the real Findlay. It's all in here. There's nothing he mentioned, even in passing, that I don't see in these pages.

It's Findlay. I know it is. And I'm in his apartment.

I check the alert on the back door and peer out the kitchen window. Everything is still dark and quiet.

I hurry into the bedroom. I have what I came for, but that won't stop me from looking for more. I find it, too. This guy might fancy himself a clever killer, leaving pristine scenes that would frustrate even a modern forensic team, but he's shit at hiding the more circumstantial evidence.

I'm going to guess that's ego more than carelessness. If McCreadie found Findlay's notebook, he'd never understand the significance of it. Findlay could claim anything from memory issues to investigative practice, learning to detail observations and recollections.

No, the only person who would understand it is the woman who crossed over with the imposter. That makes it safe. It's not as if she's a detective or anything.

I'd bet all of Catriona's ill-gotten gains that the imposter hadn't even *found* what I uncover next. It's an envelope, not only hidden under his mattress but fastened to the mattress itself, so when it's lifted, it won't be seen unless the searcher peers up. In Findlay's list of cases with McCreadie, a perpetrator must have hidden evidence like this, and he remembered it.

I pull out the envelope and find two notes inside. Both are penned in a cramped hand, each letter printed with care, as if by someone of questionable literacy.

Dear Constable Findlay,
Your little kitty-cat is doing you wrong. You think she is so interested in
your job. All those questions she asks! She is interested . . . in selling
every tidbit you give her.
If you want to know more, leave ten bob with the barkeep at the address
below.

A friend

Davina. I'm sure of it. She calls Catriona kitty-cat, and the black-market dive bar is on the street she mentions.

Catriona sold out Findlay, and Davina sold out Catriona.

I check the envelope, but that's the only thing in it. Odd to keep it quite so hidden. A thorough search of the mattress and under the bed confirms nothing fell out.

I'm continuing my search of the bedroom when I find a second note in the same hand, folded and lying right out on the dresser along with some coins and what looks like a shopping list—a few items Findlay must have needed to pick up. In other words, the contents of an emptied pocket, complete with bits of lint.

This is what Findlay had in his pocket the night he tried to kill Catriona. Items the imposter deemed irrelevant but had kept, just in case.

The note is in the same handwriting as the hidden one. From Davina.

Dear Constable Findlay,
Thank you for your generous donation. On Thursday night, come to
the address where you delivered it, wait outside and I will deliver the
proof. You will hear the kitty-cat yowl with your own ears.

A friend

I read the note twice. Then I sink on the bed and read it again. Thursday night. The night Catriona was attacked. Findlay came to the dive bar and waited outside. Catriona was inside, summoned for a meeting with Davina. The two women exit. Davina gets her talking about how she's using the police intelligence she's getting from Findlay. Then he . . .

What did he do next? Follow her? Wait for Davina to leave? Confront Catriona?

I don't know, and it doesn't matter. He overheard, and he tried to kill her. And Davina knew it. If she didn't see the attack herself, she at least knew what happened. She had set Catriona up, and Catriona had been strangled less than fifty feet away. She couldn't help but know why and by whom, and she must have been inwardly laughing her ass off when I came around begging for whatever scraps she might share.

Lost your memory, kitty-cat? What a shame. Pay me, and I'll jog it for you.

It's a good thing I didn't get a chance to meet her tonight and pay for more information. She'd have led me on a wild-goose chase. She sure as hell wouldn't have admitted she sold Catriona out to Findlay, and he'd tried to kill her for it.

I return the note to where I found it. The imposter has no idea what it is, not without also finding that first note, and even then, he wouldn't understand the significance. I do, and together with the note from Evans's pocket, it will put Findlay on McCreadie's radar as Catriona's attacker. I just need an excuse for McCreadie to search this apartment and find it.

Will the note from Evans's room be enough? It's in Findlay's handwriting, which I'm sure McCreadie can—

A noise makes me jump. It isn't my alert, though. This comes from the front of the house. The sound of hooves trotting along the road, which is hardly unusual. What startles me is how loud they are. Far too loud to be coming through a solid wall.

I snuff out my candle, walk to that end of the bedroom, and discover there *is* a window. It's small, just a typical basement window to let in a bit of light or air. It's doing neither because someone—Findlay or his imposter—has covered it with dark fabric as a makeshift blind.

Footsteps sound on the sidewalk right outside the window. Booted footsteps. I can't help lifting the edge of the fabric for a peek. If Findlay returns home from hunting in the Old Town, he'll come this way, passing the town house before circling around to the mews entrance.

It's not him, though. Just a well-dressed couple wandering home, a little unsteadily, as if they were at a neighbor's for drinks. Before I drop the corner of the fabric, a movement catches my eye. Someone across the road. Someone in dark clothing, tucked in beside a shrub.

A figure across the road, watching the house. Watching *this* house. Because I didn't realize there was a damned window. The jury-rigged blind doesn't do a perfect job of blocking all light, and I suspect my candle caught their attention. I'm sure it's Findlay until the figure shifts, and I catch a glimpse of red hair. My gaze shoots lower to see black skirts. A woman dressed all in black, as if in mourning. She's *not* in mourning, though she would likely still have the attire for it.

"Isla," I mutter as I let the drape drop.

Did she follow me? No, that doesn't make sense. If she followed, she'd have come around the back. There's no entrance from the front. She's here for the same reason I am—because she has the damned address. She's staking out the town house, possibly trying to determine whether Findlay is home.

I growl under my breath. Isla's out front, and if Findlay does pass that way, he'll see her, because she's not nearly as well hidden as she seems to think.

Damn it. I should have had that talk with her. I really should have.

I keep telling myself that I'm doing fine in this world, waiting to get home but playing it cool. That is a lie. This investigation has been the only thing keeping me from breaking down in panic and fear at the possibility I might never *get* home. I've been treading water, keeping my head above the surface.

Things aren't so bad here. I met Gray and McCreadie, interesting guys doing interesting things, and maybe I can help. Oh, Gray doesn't trust me after I stole Isla's necklace? Well, that sucks, but until I can mend that fence, I have another to lean on: Isla herself. She's as interesting as her brother, and now that I've been forced to confess my truth to her, she is a true ally. I needed that. Needed it more than I realized, and when she took offense at my warnings, I backed down. I was afraid of losing her trust as I'd lost Gray's. I couldn't afford that. Mentally and emotionally couldn't afford it, and so I screwed up.

Enough of the self-flagellation. At least I saw her, and I can remedy the oversight before she gets hurt.

I relight my candle. One last look around Findlay's bedroom to be sure everything is as I found it. I step toward the hall, only to hear the soft clunk of my alert trigger, telling me someone has opened the back door.

I dart soundlessly to peek out the window. Isla is still there. Which means the person who triggered my alert is the apartment dweller: Findlay's imposter. The killer inhabiting his body.

Two choices. Hide and then flee or confront him. If I were in one of Isla's penny-dreadful detective tales, there would be no question. I'm the detective. The hero of the story. I can't creep out and turn him over to the police. What kind of ending is that? A boring one. Also, in reality, the safe one.

Sneaking out and turning over my evidence would be the obvious answer, if I could turn over *all* my evidence. If I didn't need to tap-dance through an explanation that involves time travel and hope it's enough for McCreadie to arrest his own constable—his *protégé*.

If I fail, the killer will take his next victim. If I fail spectacularly, and the imposter finds out that I fingered him to McCreadie, I will be his next victim. I'm already on his hit list.

I could end this here. I know the man in Findlay's body is a killer. I know Findlay himself tried to kill Catriona. I could live with myself if I had to kill him. Dowse any regret I might have over whether or not the real Findlay deserves it, because in this world, he'd get the death penalty for killing Catriona.

I can hide. Catch him off guard. Kill him. Escape.

I've often wondered—as a purely theoretical exercise—whether I could get away with murder. As a detective with an interest in homicide, I have the advantage. A "crime of passion" where I'm unprepared? No. I'd make a mistake. Everyone does. But premeditated murder? Maybe. In *this* world, absolutely. They are not ready for my level of expertise, no more than they are for that of the serial killer in Findlay's body.

Here is my theoretical question put into practice. I can take what I know, kill Findlay, and escape.

It is a solution . . . and one I don't seriously consider for more than a heartbeat. If I had to kill him to save others—or save myself—I'd do it. But I still have one ace left here. Isla.

If Gray doesn't believe me, I will tell McCreadie the truth, and Isla will back me up. He will listen to Isla, possibly even more than Gray does. I've seen the way McCreadie looks at her. There's history there. Unrequited history? Or just a failure to connect? Doesn't matter. If Isla supports me, McCreadie will come around.

I will hide. I will flee.

Making that choice takes about three seconds. Even during that, I don't stand gaping at the bedroom door. Either way—confront or flee—I need to start by hiding, and I've been doing that as I work it through.

The room contains a bed and a wardrobe. That's it. No closet—wardrobes fill that function in this world. Getting under the bed would trap me. Even hunkering behind it puts me at a disadvantage. So I plaster myself to the wall beside the wardrobe and listen.

I listen for footsteps that don't come.

My alert definitely sounded. That door creaked open, too. I thought I caught a footfall or two. Then nothing.

Did the imposter find the trigger? It was a simple setup. Door opens, hinge gap widens, a nail thumps to the floor. If the person hears and finds it, they'll think it's just a nail that fell out. Nothing unusual there.

Is he trying to figure out where it fell from? Please don't play Mr. Handyman. Be the kind of renter I was, who'd set the nail aside and text the landlord to let them know I found it.

Is a man more likely to try fixing it himself? My dad would, despite the fact that Mom's the one who knows where they keep the hammer and how to use it.

The other possibility? That Findlay realizes it's an alert. Or that he had some junior-detective alert of his own rigged up, to let him know if someone entered his apartment.

I take out my knife. I don't open it. I stand there, holding it, and cursing myself for not having a different weapon. Knives are messy. It'll work if I need to just scare him as I flee, but if I'm forced to do more . . . ?

I won't be forced to do more. I've got this. I just need to get past him.

Damn it, why couldn't he have come home when I was in the kitchen or living room? Someplace where I'd have a *way* to get past him. There's a window here, but I'm not foolish enough to think I can climb up there and squeeze through before he walks in.

One way out. The door. Which is on the other side of Findlay.

I hold my breath to listen. Silence. Then the creak of a floorboard.

Okay, he's not trying to fix the door. He knows someone's here.

I finger my knife. Should I open it up? Or fight my way past without bringing that into play?

What if he has a knife of his own? Then I'll definitely want mine.

I'm about to flip it open when I catch sight of something in the corner. It's nearly hidden in the darkness, but it looks like . . .

Is that a billy club? Oh hell yes. Findlay keeps a police baton in his bedroom, the way I keep a baseball bat.

I strain to listen. The apartment seems silent. Then I catch the softest scuff of a boot. He's halfway down the hall. I take one careful step, lean out, and stretch until my fingers touch the club. They graze wood and start to close, but my aim is off, and the movement starts the baton toppling. I lunge, and it clatters against the wall as I grab it.

I snatch the billy club and jerk back into my spot, clutching it to my chest. There's no cry from the hall. No pound of footsteps. He heard me. He must have, and yet he's continuing his silent approach.

The hunter stalking his prey.

I slide the knife into my pocket and lift the club, gripping the handle. It's wood, smooth with age. There's a ridged section for a handgrip and a worn leather strap to go around my wrist. The weight is different from a modern baton, and I test it out, preparing.

The next noise is so soft I'm not sure I don't imagine it. The slide of a foot. Right at the doorway. Turning in to the room.

I press into the wardrobe, and when I hold my breath, I swear I can hear his. Then another soft-footed step. Another.

He knows I'm in here. And he knows there are only two places for me to hide.

FORTY

I tug a coin from my pocket as quietly as I can. Then I flip it down on the far side of the bed. I want Findlay to dive toward the movement. To react and move without thinking.

He doesn't.

The slide of another step. I wedge as far as I can get into the corner between the wall and the wardrobe. Then I remember my skirts. I'm not wearing a body-hugging cocktail dress. I've got long skirts over layers of underskirts, and they do not "wedge" into that corner with me. I consider pulling them in, but that will cause both noise and movement.

Forget the skirts. Hold my breath. Lift the baton. Be ready.

The edge of a figure appears. Findlay's dark-clad, dark-haired figure. He's moving toward the bed. Then I catch the faintest shift my way, his face turning, checking behind the wardrobe before he focuses on the bed.

I lunge and swing. At the last second, he spins. The club hits him in the shoulder instead of the skull. It should still hit hard enough for him to reel. I feel the solid thwack of it. Yet he barely staggers, and before I can pull back for another blow, he's grabbing at me.

I swing the club. I kick. I even let go of the damn baton with one hand and punch. It shouldn't be that hard. I've fought the imposter before, and he only stood a chance when he had a rope tightening around my neck.

The guy I faced before was a half-assed fighter, all awkward blows and jabs, like someone who's never fended off more than a schoolyard bully.

This is different. This guy grabs the club and ducks my blows and ignores my kicks, and with the damned dress on, I can't do more, and before I know it, I'm up against the wall with a hand over my mouth.

He has one hand on my club and the other over my mouth, but he's not otherwise restraining me. I release the club and pull back for a punch . . . and see him clearly, out of the shadows.

Light brown skin. Dark eyes. And a face at least three inches above where I expect Findlay's to be.

"Duncan?" I say, my voice muffled by his hand. He doesn't seem to notice—or can't hear—the familiarity of the address. He just motions for me to be quiet, brows lifting as if waiting for me to agree.

I nod, and he lowers his hand and steps back.

"What are you doing here?" I whisper.

"Following—" He shakes off the rest and glances toward the hall. "Constable Findlay will be back soon. That's what I came inside to warn. The public houses have closed, and he will be on his way back."

My mouth opens, ten questions leaping into the gap, but I close it and nod. "He's not at a public house, but yes, I was just about to leave. Is— Mrs. Ballantyne is out front."

His brows gather, face darkening. "You brought my *sister*?"

"Uh, no. Didn't you follow her?"

"Certainly not. I followed you. You were obviously in a hurry to leave earlier this evening, and I presumed you were about to follow another clue. Which is why I had that talk with you—vowing to do better, so that you wouldn't feel the need to do such things on your own. But obviously . . ."

He pulls back, and in that movement, I see his hurt.

Damn it, Duncan. I'm sorry. I really am.

"I'm sorry—"

"No need," he says, too quickly to mean it. "You did not trust me yet. I have not earned it." He starts for the hall. "We must get to my sister. She is too reckless by far."

"Not reckless," I say as I hurry after him. "Just restricted. Restricted and restrained and sheltered, and so when she gets an adventure, she isn't prepared to deal with it."

He turns to peer at me, and I realize I'm using my Mallory voice. I wave at the hall. "We'll speak later, sir. I have—I have things I need to tell you, but for now we must get to Is—Mrs. Ballantyne."

We walk two steps. Then I stop so abruptly he bashes into me.

I turn. "There are notes. I can grab them quickly. I just need you to watch me, so you may tell Detective McCreadie that they are where I said they were."

"As I found you here, I am not certain how that proves anything. You may have planted them."

I curse under my breath. Then I stride forward. "Forget the notes. We'll discuss them once we have your sister."

"Are you all right, Catriona? You sound odd."

"I am distracted, sir. Upset at my discoveries and distracted and now concerned about Mrs. Ballantyne."

We reach the door. I wave for him to wait while I peek out. There's nothing to see, though—just the stairwell. We creep out, and I ascend first, scanning the yard.

We jog to the road and then stride along it. Or Gray strides, while I need to stay jogging to keep up.

"You said you knew I was up to something earlier?" I prompt carefully, mostly just to get him talking. He's trying to act normal, but I feel the edge of a chill. I didn't confide in him, and that stings, however much he wants to pretend it doesn't.

For a moment, he seems ready to brush off my question. Then he says, "There was something you were not telling us. Something about Constable Findlay. You discovered something else earlier today, and I had the distinct impression that you did not trust Detective McCreadie with the information."

"That's not it."

"No?" He glances over as we turn the corner. "Yes, perhaps I misspoke. You did not trust Detective McCreadie *or* myself."

"I suspected Constable Findlay, and I know he is very close to Detective McCreadie, so I wanted proof before I took my suspicions to him."

"That is what I presumed," he says. "I followed you, and I saw where you were going, and as it seemed unlikely to be an assignation, I knew you must be investigating Constable Findlay. I am resisting the temptation to lecture you on the dangers of what you did. I know you are not a child, even if you do seem very young to me. However, you are very obviously able to take care of yourself, as you proved when attacked the other day and as you proved again tonight."

"I did not prove it so well tonight," I mutter. "Detective McCreadie wasn't joking when he said you know how to fight."

He shrugs, relaxing a little. "A skill I learned early in life. While my former public school now admits international students, I was an anomaly at the time, and some people do not like anomalies. They mistake difference for weakness. I learned how to teach them otherwise, sometimes with my grades and sometimes with my fists. The problem, as my mother would say, is that I came to enjoy the latter an unseemly amount."

I smile. "Well, you are good at it, which always helps."

"It does, and so I say, as a fellow student of the art, that you have obviously had training yourself. You would do much better without those damnable skirts."

"Tell me about it."

He relaxes more, even offering a faint smile. I'm about to say something else when we turn the corner and I stop short.

Isla is gone.

"Catriona?" Gray says, frowning at me.

I hike my skirts and break into a jog. He follows, and I run as fast as I can to the spot where I last saw her.

"She was right here," I say.

"Are you certain?" He peers across the street and answers his own question. "Yes, that is the town house." He straightens. "Do not panic. She has simply gone home. She saw us round the corner—or heard our voices—and fled, and we shall find her at home, slightly out of breath, acting as if she has been there all along. Yes, no need for panic."

I don't point out that he's said that twice. The reassurance is for himself as he paces, scouring the street and frowning.

"Unless she heard our skirmish in the apartment," he says. "She may have come to your aid. Perhaps she went the other way around." He squints down the street. "Blast it. We shall be running in circles trying to find her, while she will be at home. I know she will be."

I'm only half listening to him. I'm pacing on the sidewalk, thinking. Yes, Isla would have fled if she heard us. We weren't whispering once we came outside. Yes, she could also have heard a crash or a grunt or a cry from in the apartment—it's hard to look back on a fight and know whether you made some involuntary noise.

"I will run home," Gray says. "I am dressed to move faster. Whether she is there or not, I shall return with the coach. You check around the back of the town house. See—"

He cuts himself short. "You have not said whether you found evidence that Constable Findlay is guilty of anything."

"He's the person who attacked me the first time. I am certain of that."

"What?"

"He thinks I double-crossed him." I keep pacing, my gaze on the ground. "A woman I believed to be a friend told him so, and she lured him in that night to the public house where I was seen. I found the evidence in his rooms. Yes, you go home and get the coach. I will check behind the house."

"Not if Findlay is the one who tried to *murder* you. What are you doing?"

I'm standing in the spot where I'd seen Isla as I work this through. It's not as if the imposter could have crept up behind her. That's the thing about town houses—there aren't any side passages to sneak up through. Also no side passages for her to hide in, which is why she'd been so exposed.

Isla found this spot between the front steps and a shrub. It allowed her to see directly across the street, at what she must have realized—while I did not—was the window in Findlay's apartment. I'd missed the window because the blind kept me from seeing it. She didn't see my candlelight after all, and presumed the dark window meant Findlay was not at home.

Had she been tucked in here, deciding her next move? If so, had she circled the block to get in through the basement door?

If she did, for any reason, head around back, then we need to get to her and warn her off. So why am I not asking Gray to do that? Why am I not telling him I'll run to his town house, check for her, and bring Simon with the coach?

Because I am standing where she was, and my gut doesn't like it. Doesn't like it at all.

She can see Findlay's town house perfectly from here. What she *can't* see? Someone approaching on this side of the road.

"Go check the mews lane," I say.

His brows rise at the order. I should reverse course, but I'm so distracted that I shoot him a very Mallory look. The kind I might give a detective partner. Our eyes meet, and there's a moment of connection that jolts through me. He blinks and rocks back on his heels.

"One of us needs to check," I say. "Quickly. Before Findlay returns. I want to look around here a little more. It bothers me."

"Bothers you how?"

"Please check the back door, sir." I meet his gaze again, my Catriona mask in place. "We do not want Mrs. Ballantyne there if he comes home."

"Yes, of course." He glances down the street. "Are you safe here?"

I pull the knife from my pocket.

"All right then," he says. "I suppose I ought to be grateful you attempted to use the truncheon on me instead."

"Knives are messy. Also, they leave distinct wound patterns."

He chokes on a chuckle at that and then jogs off. I bend to examine the ground. No sign of scuff marks where Isla had been standing. If she'd been dragged out, I'd see marks in the dirt, and I don't.

I'm being paranoid. She heard us and took off. It's a quiet night, and Gray isn't exactly soft-spoken.

She's fine. She just—

My gaze catches on something caught on the shrub. As I tug it out, my heart seizes.

"Duncan!" I shout, then quickly amend it to, "Dr. Gray!"

He's less than fifty feet away, and he wheels, running back even faster. I lift what I found. A lady's black glove.

"This was in the shrub," I say. "Is it hers?"

He snatches it from my hand and turns the cuff out. Her initials are sewn there in ivory thread.

"She could have removed her gloves," I say. "And then dropped one as she left in a hurry. But it was wedged in the shrub. As if she put it there."

As if she'd been surprised by the imposter. As if she'd been forcibly removed from her spot. Not dragged but ordered, on threat of violence. She wants to leave a clue. She shoves her glove into the shrub.

I tell myself that's silly. Who would find that glove?

I would, when we realized she was missing, and I guessed where she'd gone. It's a long shot, but a long shot was all she had.

Gray strides in the other direction, and I think I'm being left behind. He gets about ten feet and bends. He lifts what looks like a small white pill. I get closer and see it's one of Isla's peppermints.

"Isla's," I say. "She is fond of peppermints."

"No," Gray says, his voice a growl as he stalks down the sidewalk. "She is not fond of them at all."

I jog to catch up, both of us scouring the dark ground for another spot of white.

"Is it not hers?" I say. "It looks like it. She makes her own, and it's rather distinctive."

"It is hers," he mutters. "A legacy from her damnable husband. He told her once that she suffered from foul breath. It was not her breath. It was her chemicals. But she got it into her head . . ."

Got it into her head that she had halitosis and developed a habit of popping peppermints. A nervous habit.

I spot another and break into a jog. I bend, but it is only a white stone. Then I see another mint, a few feet away.

"A trail of bread crumbs," I say.

Gray doesn't answer. He's processing this, what it means. That his sister has been kidnapped by a killer.

Except he doesn't know that. He knows Findlay throttled Catriona, but that does not necessarily make him a murderer. I've mentioned nothing about Findlay being the raven killer, and I am glad of that now. One look at his face, taut with fear and anger, tells me this is enough. He is afraid for her and yet clearheaded, the panic kept at bay.

"Why would he take her?" he says.

I jump. "Wh-what?"

"If Findlay caught her breaking into his apartment, he would be angry, and we know he is a man of murderous temper. But if he only caught her across the road? My sister is exceptionally clever. She would have an excuse at the ready, should anyone ask why she was loitering about."

I continue on, searching the ground.

"Catriona?"

I bend to what I know is a pebble, picking it up and then discarding it. When I straighten, his hand falls on my shoulder, gripping and turning me to face him.

"What are you not telling me?" he says. Before I can say a word, his face darkens. "Findlay was involved with Evans. You were not investigating him as the man who attacked you. That may be what you found, but it is not what you suspected. We already established that."

"We established nothing, sir, except that your sister is leaving a trail, which indicates she was abducted and in danger."

"You!" he shouts, loud enough to make me jump.

He strides past me, and I spin to see an elderly man talking to someone through a window. The man turns, and even from here, I can see him squinting at this tall, broad-shouldered man marching across the road. He doesn't pull back or flinch. Just squints as if not sure of what he's seeing.

I grab my skirts and race across.

"Good evening, sir," I call before Gray can say more. "I apologize for the abruptness of my master's greeting. We are looking for someone, and he is quite concerned for her safety."

Gray shoots a glare over his shoulder, one that says he doesn't appreciate me running interference. I meet that glare with a hard look. He's worried about Isla and angry with me for—rightly—thinking I'm holding out on him. He's about to unleash that anger on a potential witness, and I'm not letting him do that.

"Ah," the man says, nodding. "I presume you are looking for your wife? A red-haired lady in mourning attire?"

"Yes," I say before Gray can correct him. "That is my mistress."

"Your mistress needs to be kept home," says a voice from the window. It's a woman's voice, though I can't see her through the glazed glass. "She is drunk."

"She is *unwell*," the man says. "I would not speculate on the cause, and as she was dressed for mourning, I would say if it were inebriation, she has reason, poor woman."

"What makes you say she seemed unwell?" I ask.

"She could not walk," the woman inside snaps. "Needed a kind young constable to help her along."

Gray stiffens. "What?"

"My master means to ask whether you might please tell us more?" I say. "She was being aided by a young man in a constable's uniform?"

"He was not in uniform, but I know him," the woman says. "He lives five houses down. Helped me with my door once, when it was sticking. Such a nice young man."

"Would you tell us which way they went?" I ask. Gray has already left, striding across the road.

A hand extends from the window, waving languidly.

"Please," I say to the elderly man. "If it is the young man we think—average height, about my age, with dark hair—our mistress may be in danger."

The woman snorts and mutters under her breath, but the man's brows knit.

"They went around the corner, lass," he says. "To the end and then turned right. I did think it odd that he seemed in such a hurry, but I thought he was being considerate of the poor lady's privacy."

I'm already walking away, calling my thanks as I go.

FORTY-ONE

I hike my skirts and jog to the corner. I don't call to Gray. He'll figure it out, and I'm not going to cause a scene arguing. He catches up as I bend to see another peppermint.

"The gentleman saw Constable Findlay and Mrs. Ballantyne turn this way," I say as Gray walks over.

"Drunk," he mutters. "They see a woman being manhandled, and they presume she is inebriated."

"He may have drugged her with chloroform to make her woozy." I glance over. "Is that a thing? Chloroform as a sedative? Or is that only in fiction?"

He stares at me before muttering, "Yes, it is a 'thing,' as you put it. Every young woman should know that for her own safety."

We're still on the move, scouring the ground for the next mint. How many more before she runs out? And where the hell would he be taking her?

I voice that last question aloud, adding, "Is there someplace private nearby? A park?"

Gray's long strides have already carried him ten paces ahead. "About a half mile away, yes. As for where he is taking her, the answer is obvious, is it not? To his apartment. We have wasted time circling the block. I do not wish to leave you behind, Catriona, but I am going on ahead. Your skirts and your stature hamper you, and my sister is in danger."

I bite back the ridiculous urge to take offense at the comment about my "stature." He's already broken into a run.

"You're wrong, Duncan," I mutter under my breath. "If he was taking her there, he'd have gone the other way around. And he's not going to drag her into a house full of people."

I find another mint at the corner Gray just rounded. When I pick it up, I rise to see him fifty feet away, looking from me to the darkened mew lane. He strides back.

"Blast it," he mutters. "I cannot abandon you."

"Thanks . . ."

He continues as if not hearing me. "You are clearly Findlay's target, and I cannot leave you behind."

"Go ahead," I say. "I can look after myself. But he didn't take her to his apartment."

I jog to the next mint. This one is along the walkway into the gardens behind a town house. I stand over it and peer up at the dark house.

"Why are the shutters all closed?" I ask.

He looks at me as if I'm asking why the moon is out at night. "Because—" He curses and breaks into a run, heading for the back door. I lunge and grab the back of his jacket.

"Careful," I say. "If Findlay is here, you can't let him know *we're* here."

"Maintain the element of surprise. Yes."

"The shutters?"

"They are closed because the owners will have gone away for a lengthy period of time."

"And anyone who sees closed shutters knows that. Bit of an open invitation to burglars, isn't it?"

Or serial killers looking for a place to torture their victims.

"The door is over there," I say, pointing. "Same layout as his place, presumably. He's broken in and been using it. Probably the basement."

Better soundproofing.

I continue, "I can open the door. I'll ask you to stand guard there. Look for light through the shutters. Also listen for noises. Let me know if you hear any."

It's a testament to his state of mind that he no longer questions his housemaid giving him orders. He just nods, his gaze focused on the house, and then moves into position.

I wait, gaze on that window, looking for any change in color. It stays dark, no light escaping through the shutter slats. Has he blacked it out even with the shutters, taking no chances? That would seem to suggest that this is where the imposter took Isla—the mint at the top of the steps confirms it.

Is this where he tortured Evans? Pretended he was taking his friend to his apartment and brought him here instead? It's not as if Evans would know one town house basement from the next. He'd have followed Findlay right inside.

Once Gray is ready, I creep to the stairwell. I was careful before. Now I am ten times more cautious. The worst thing that could happen earlier was that he could have attacked me. Now he has Isla. If I screw up, she'll pay the price.

I check the lock. It's the same as the other one. I take the metal rods from my pocket to pick it. Then I pause at a thought, reach a gloved hand out, and turn the knob. The door opens.

Findlay didn't lock it. Why would he? He managed to get Isla—possibly semiconscious—inside, and that would be a struggle when she's as tall as he is. Bothering to latch the door afterward would be the last thing on his mind. I'm not sure he'd even see the point. Who's going to come creeping around? Surely not his victim's brother and housemaid?

I motion to Gray that the door is unlocked. He comes down the stairs. I don't need to tell him to move quietly. He'd had that down pat when he crept into Findlay's apartment, which makes me think he's done more than help McCreadie with forensics.

I ease open the door so slowly it's painful, and I swear Gray's teeth grind in frustration. I strain to listen. A muffled voice sounds. Findlay's muffled voice, which means it's coming through a door or wall. I nod and open the door the rest of the way, and we slide inside.

As I shut the door behind us, Gray moves past me. I wildly wave for him to hold up, and to my relief, he does. I tiptoe over and, without me needing to say anything, he bends so I can speak into his ear.

"He's talking to her," I whisper. "That means she's all right. We need to proceed with caution. We have time."

Gray's jaw sets. He doesn't like that. This close to him, I feel both his fear and a coiled energy, a taut spring. He wants to charge in there and free his sister. Yet he knows I'm right, and so he only gives a curt nod.

I squint down the hall. The setup is the same as Findlay's place, though since it's a single-family dwelling, the basement seems to be mostly storage. Except his voice comes from our right, from what was the owner's storage room in his apartment. Both doors along that wall are shut. Light emanates from the second one. I point it out for Gray and get another of those curt nods. He's already noticed.

As we move, Findlay's voice comes clearer.

"I'm going to ask you one more time, Isla," he says. "What is your maid up to?"

Isla's voice is weak but firm. "And I will say, one more time, that I have no idea. You know her better than I do. She is always up to something, is she not?"

"Who sent you to my rooms? Detective McCreadie? Your brother?"

"Neither. I found the address in Catriona's room. I was concerned. As you know, she is a former thief, and I feared the address might indicate a future target."

Silence. In that silence, though, I catch a small intake of breath, and my gut clenches. She isn't volunteering these answers. He's torturing her. Each time she doesn't give him what he wants, he does something, and she's stifling her cries.

The imposter continues, "McCreadie went to your house for tea. You discussed the case. He said it was only tea, but I know better. He brings Gray into his confidence. Uses him and takes the credit and keeps me out of it."

"I am certain you could have joined us if you asked."

"I did ask. He made excuses."

To protect Findlay. Yes, McCreadie uses Gray's help, but he's not doing it to take credit. He's doing it to avail himself of whatever resources will help solve a crime.

I remember that first night, when he'd been quick to send Findlay off with a coin for a pint. Giving him plausible deniability, should anyone in the department take issue with McCreadie bringing Gray into his investigation.

Did the real Findlay know he was being sidelined? Did he care? The imposter certainly does, because it meant he was kept out of the center of the investigation . . . into the crimes he was committing.

Findlay continues, "What did he talk about at tea?"

"The investigation."

A sharp intake of breath then. Her sarcasm earned her a stronger punishment, and this time Gray hears it. His chin shoots up, eyes riveted to the door. As Isla catches her breath inside, Gray starts forward.

I grab his jacket, but he jerks free. I lunge and grab it and wrench him back. He wheels on me, face contorting in a snarl.

"Do you want to get your sister killed?" I whisper as I drag him farther from the door.

The look on his face is enough to make me tense for a blow. It's a murderous look, as if I'm the one holding his sister hostage, threatening her life.

"I'm sorry, Duncan," I whisper, abandoning my Catriona voice. "I'm sorry I can't let you go to your sister. Findlay didn't just try to strangle me. He murdered Archie Evans. Murdered Rose Wright. Tortured Evans. Mutilated Wright. If you throw open that door, he will hurt her. I will not let you throw open that door. Understand?"

He stares at me, the fury draining from his face, replaced by . . . Oh, hell, I'm not even sure what replaces it. I only know that in that moment, I am seeing not Catriona's boss but the man within. I see him, and he sees me, and he blinks and then shakes his head, as if throwing it off.

"Please listen to me, Duncan," I whisper. "Whatever you do after this— fire me for insubordination or kick my ass to the curb—I don't care. I care that your sister is in that room, with a guy who will kill her if we startle him."

He holds my gaze. Holds it so fast it's hard to keep from looking away. His chin dips, just a little. Then he glances at the door.

"We need a distraction," I whisper. "Get Findlay away from her without making him think someone's in the apartment. I can do that. When he opens the door, you'll be waiting—"

I stop. My gaze swings to the door. A moment ago, the imposter had been interrogating Isla. But now he's stopped.

I take one cautious step toward the door, holding my breath as I listen, tensed for the muffled sound of pain. Instead, the knob turns.

I backpedal, my arms going out to shield Gray. He's a layperson, and it's like one of those video games where cops have to take out the shooters without killing any bystanders. The principle is hammered into my brain. Protect the bystander.

This works much better if the bystander is willing to be protected. I fall back, arms going up, knife in hand, and suddenly there is no one behind me. For a guy of Gray's size, he moves like a damned ghost. That knob turns and somehow, he's in front of me, and I'm backpedaling into shadow like a helpless maiden.

Findlay steps out. He's heard a noise, right? Our whispering must have been louder than I thought. That's the obvious answer. But no, Findlay strolls out, the door opening to block the big guy lunging toward him, and there's a near-comical moment where I think it's going to smack Gray in the face. It doesn't. Because that's when Findlay hears or senses something. He glances over, almost nonchalantly. And he sees Gray.

FORTY-TWO

This is the moment. This is where the imposter will falter in shock, and Gray will save the day by the sheer virtue of being a big looming shape in the darkness. It seems to happen exactly like that. The imposter falls back, eyes widening. Gray grabs him by the shirtfront and hauls him off his feet . . . and the imposter flinches, head ducking as if to ward off a blow. Then the imposter swings. I see the glint of metal at the last second. A hammer swinging straight for Gray's temple. Before I can open my mouth, it smashes into his forehead.

Gray crumples. And what do I do? Nothing. I stay exactly where I am, and that is one of the hardest things I've ever done.

The attack happened so fast that I didn't have time to burst from the shadows. I'm right where I started, backed up into the darkness, knife in hand, and when Gray goes down, I brace myself to fly out and attack. But I don't get that chance. Gray collapses, and in the next heartbeat, the imposter is behind the open door, shielded from me.

I could still rush forward. That's the hard part—that I choose not to. The imposter hasn't seen me. I'm not invisible. Compared to Gray, though, I am. That's all he saw—Gray lunging at him—and between the shock of that and the relief and delight of outsmarting him, he never thought to look for anyone else.

Now the imposter is behind the door, and he has Gray by the shoulders, and I stay in the shadows as he drags Gray into the room.

"Look who came to your rescue," Findlay calls to Isla. "It's your lucky day. I don't need to torture *you* after all. Let's see if you'll talk when your brother is the one in pain."

The door is closing slowly. So slowly that I have time to dart to the other side and catch it with my boot toe. I wait for Findlay to notice.

Come on, asshole. You already missed a second person in the hall. You can't also miss the fact that this door isn't shutting.

I want him to see it. I have my knife ready. He'll walk over to check the door, and I'll give him an even bigger shock than Gray did.

He doesn't check the door. If he notices it didn't quite shut, he doesn't care. He's riding high on his success and chortling at having leverage over Isla, leverage that may mean he doesn't need to resort to torture, which really isn't his thing. I don't want to know what he'd planned to do with that hammer, but he must have left looking for something to use it for—maybe splints under the fingernails again.

Now he's talking to Isla about how he's going to torture Gray and make her watch, and the glee in his voice could be mistaken for sadism, but I know better. His glee comes from knowing he's going to get what he wants *without* torture. Describing it will be enough for her to cave.

"Where should I start?" he says. "For a doctor, the hands are the obvious choice, but I get the feeling Dr. Gray values his brain more. That was quite a blow to his head. What if . . . ?"

"Stop," Isla says. "Please."

She overdoes her sniffles, but Findlay buys it. After all, she's a poor Victorian widow. It's a wonder she hasn't fainted by now.

I crack the door open. Then I angle myself until I can see inside. The sliver of a view is enough. Gray is unconscious on the floor. Findlay is on one knee beside him, hammer lifted to hit Gray in the head again. I can only see Isla's skirts—she seems to be on a chair just out of sight.

"Tell me what happened at tea today," Findlay says. "What does McCreadie know? What did that little cow tell him?"

Little cow? Is that *me*? Huh.

"Catriona knows nothing," Isla says.

Findlay lifts the hammer. My breath catches, but he only holds it above Gray's head.

"You seem to be doubting whether I'll go through with this," he says. "That's unfortunate. See, the thing about repeated blows to the head is that they're unpredictable. Your brother would tell you that, if he could. If I hit him in the same spot again, it will certainly cause brain damage. It could also kill him. And I don't care. Is that clear, Isla? I don't care if he dies. Just another body to add to my count."

"Detective McCreadie has a lead on Archie Evans," Isla blurts. "On why he may have been tortured."

"Tortured? Who said he was tortured?"

Isla stops. Shit. How little did McCreadie share with his constable?

"I-I do not know," Isla says. "There must have been some evidence—"

"It was her, wasn't it? Catriona?"

"Our *house*maid?" Isla voice rises in convincing incredulity.

"She's been helping him. I know he escorted her as she played detective."

"Perhaps, but as I said, Catriona has nothing to do with any of this."

The hammer swings down. I see it swinging, too fast to be a feigned blow, and I throw open the door and charge at Findlay. He falls back. He might be faking it again. I don't really care. All that matters is that his hammer is no longer on a collision course with Gray's skull.

"You wanted to talk to me?" I say as he scrambles to his feet.

He snarls an oath.

"Is that a no?" I say, brandishing the knife. "I could swear I heard my name. Well, something like it, at least."

He shakes off his anger, finding a sneer instead. "Typical American. I'm surprised you didn't yell yippee-ki-yay, too."

"I'm not American," I say. "Didn't you hear me apologizing for spilling that coffee? I might as well have had a maple leaf tattooed on my forehead."

We're in a standoff. He's five feet away. Gray is on my one side, Isla on my other. Gray is unconscious. Isla's bound to a chair and wisely staying quiet. Either of them makes a target, which is why I ran between the two. The imposter has his hammer, and while it isn't a gun, I'm not about to get in its path.

"You seem eager to talk to me," I say. "Well, to talk about me at least. A little obsessive. Kinda creepy, really. But that's you, I'm guessing. Kinda creepy."

I'm blathering, assessing and distracting, but something there hits an unexpected mark as he blanches. Okay, then.

"Textbook serial-killer behavior patterns," I continue. "I'd hoped for better. More interesting, at least. Please tell me you didn't wet the bed and torture small animals."

That swing goes wide, as his face relaxes, sneer returning.

"So you *are* a police officer?" His laughter rings hyena-like with mockery. "I thought so, from the way you handled that body, all your talk about scanning the crowd for the killer."

Shit. I forgot that. He'd been watching me so intently that day. Not confused by my actions. Studying them. That's why he's been questioning Isla about me. He realized I was a cop. A modern cop. That made me dangerous.

He smirks. "That must have been so embarrassing for you. A police officer murdered by a serial killer. You weren't even chasing me. Just out for a jog. Got yourself jumped like any silly cow."

"You know what's *really* embarrassing? A time-traveling serial killer taken down by a teenage girl in this dress." I wave at myself. "You try fighting crime as a nineteen-year-old Victorian housemaid. Way tougher than killing people as a Victorian constable. You had the inside scoop, and you still screwed up."

He whips the hammer at me.

Isla shouts a warning, but I'm already diving out of the way. The hammer still glances off my shoulder, spinning me around. Then a shot fires. I think I'm mishearing. I must be mishearing. The bullet hole in the wall says I am not.

The imposter curses, and I wheel to see him with a revolver. It's an antique—or it will be, in my day. Right now, it's probably state-of-the-art. He lifts it again, reloaded, and I run, dodging and ducking, not giving him a clear shot.

"Not such a smart-mouthed little cow now, are you?" he calls as his footsteps tromp after me. "Not so brave either."

I run past the exit door as I veer into another room. I need to get him away from Isla and Gray, easy targets for his pistol and his rage.

And then what? I've brought a knife to a gunfight. Damn it, where the hell did he get a gun? Wherever he could, because he's a modern killer. He'll arm himself with the best weapon, which is going to be a gun. I didn't expect it, and that's on me.

I duck around the corner. He's taking his time, each footfall thudding as he walks into the hall.

"You didn't run out the door?" he calls. "You really are pathetic. Let's see. Which room could you be in? How about this one?"

He swings into the room where I'm hiding. "Now, if I were cowering in here, where would I be?"

He stops and chuckles. "I can see your boot."

He strides into the room, heading for an old settee, where my discarded boot peeks out. I crouch behind a chair, knife in hand. One chance. I will get a split second before he realizes the trick. I tense, watching him step into the room. Another step. Just two more—

A shadow looms behind him. A sudden movement. It's Gray, swinging the hammer with all of his might, but he's still dazed, and he puts too much into the swing, and it hits the imposter in the shoulder instead.

The smaller man staggers, but stays on his feet, gun barrel flying up, a point-blank shot that he cannot miss. His finger is on the trigger, Gray at the other end of that barrel.

I fly from my hiding place. I stab the imposter in the back, and I aim for the heart. One chance. That's all I'll get. The knife slides between his ribs. I let go and grab his arm before he can fire the gun. I don't know if he tries, but he doesn't manage it, and the gun falls as Gray slams him backward.

The imposter starts to fall. I dive out of the way, and he goes down, thudding onto the knife handle, the knife driving through his chest. He hits the floor, his face contorted in a snarl. Then his entire body convulses, as if with a seizure. He jerks once and goes still for a moment. When his eyes open, I'm on the floor, pinning him, in case that stab wound isn't as lethal as I expect.

He stares at me. His mouth opens.

"Catriona?"

My own heart stutters. It's the same voice; but it is not the same person.

"Colin," I say.

"You—you have killed me?" he says.

I lean over him. "You tried to do the same to me."

"I-I—" His face spasms in pain, and he shudders. "It was Archie's idea.

All Archie's. He said we had to scare you. Knock you out. Bring you to a basement near my rooms. Frighten you. Punish you."

"You are an officer of the law," I say. "You bring criminals to justice. You don't deliver it yourself."

"Archie hit you, and you did not pass out. You attacked me. I had to defend myself."

"By strangling me?" I swallow my rage and force myself to say, "I am sorry for what I did to you, Colin, but it did not deserve that."

"Do you forgive me?" he says, his voice an almost inaudible rasp. "You must forgive me."

I don't want to. But the terror in his eyes makes me grind out the words. "I understand that you did what you thought you needed to."

His mouth opens, and I don't hear what he says, as I suddenly realize there's an answer here. An answer I desperately need.

"Colin?" I say. "Where were you?"

"Gone," he whispers. "I was gone."

"Gone to another time? Another world? Were you another person? Where did you—?"

Before I can finish, he exhales, and then he is truly gone, taking my answer with him.

FORTY-THREE

We're home now. It's two in the morning. Isla and I are in her quarters sharing a tea tray that Mrs. Wallace dropped off, along with worried glances at Isla and accusing glares at me. She has no idea what has happened, except that her mistress came home with a dirty gown and a shock-slackened face, having endured some ordeal that has me wild-haired and blood-spattered, and Isla insisting that all is fine, that I have saved her life. Maybe so, but Mrs. Wallace is certain Isla's life wouldn't have needed saving if she hadn't been with me.

She isn't wrong about that.

Gray had insisted we go straight home, leaving Findlay dead and the crime scene unguarded. It's a testament to my own shock that I let him do that. There wasn't another option, really. We were bloodied and battered and had to get home before anyone saw us and suspected Gray murdered Findlay. It wasn't as if he could ring McCreadie and summon him to the scene.

Everyone had been quiet on the walk. Isla and I were in shock, and Gray was still muddled from the blow, occasionally stopping on a corner as if uncertain which way to go. He'd rallied by the time we got to the town house and told us he'd let McCreadie know that Findlay was the raven killer but that he seemed to be "not in his right mind." He will suggest that McCreadie have him posthumously accused only of kidnapping Isla and attacking us when we came to her rescue.

That means McCreadie is left with two murders he'll never officially solve. That will be a stain on his career. What would be a worse one? Admitting that his own constable committed the murders he'd been investigating.

There isn't enough evidence to pin the murders of Archie Evans and Rose Wright on Colin Findlay. McCreadie's options are a career stain or career obliteration. He deserves better than either, but the first will have to do.

As for Findlay being "not in his right mind," that's Gray's presumption. Earlier, I'd longed to tell him the truth. Now the case has been solved without that. He was unconscious and heard none of the conversation between myself and the imposter.

Do I still tell him about myself? I want to, but I'm not sure if that's for his benefit or mine. I'll need to discuss it with Isla.

I didn't get one answer I wanted—to know where Findlay went, which would tell me whether Catriona was in my body. Did the killer return to *his* body? Did I kill Findlay only to return the true killer to the other side, where he can continue his work?

I don't know. I may have gotten another answer, though.

How do I get home? I need to die in this world.

If Catriona dies, I can go home. Or that's the theory. Unless the killer didn't return to his body at all. Unless his consciousness is trapped between forms somewhere.

It hurts to think about that. Hurts my head and hurts my soul.

I went to the spot where I crossed into this world, and I am still here.

I found Catriona's attacker, killed him even, and I am still here.

Now the answer seems to be to kill Catriona so I'm free to leap into my own body, my own time? I can't do that. I don't care what she's done—as I told Findlay, it didn't justify killing her. I cannot kill her. Does that mean I'm stuck here, never to see my family again?

Please don't let that be the answer.

Please.

"I must apologize," Isla says as she sips her tea while I sit, lost in my panic and grief. We haven't spoken since we got here. She asked me to her room and accepted Mrs. Wallace's insistence on preparing a tea tray, and then we fell silent.

"You warned me," she says. "I did not listen."

I force my thoughts back on track. "I didn't warn you enough. I was going to, and I chickened out."

"Chickened out?"

"Turned coward. I told myself that I needed to warn you, for your own safety, but then I put it off. Made excuses. Promised I'd get to it later." I look over at her. "I understood that everyone is always telling you that you must not, and I didn't want to be another person putting up walls. I needed to figure out how to explain the danger without alienating you. That's an explanation, but it's not an excuse. I'm sorry."

She shakes her head. "It was an untenable situation. You were pointing out traps on the path, and I was seeing walls. I told myself that I knew it was dangerous and that I was sensible enough to be cautious. After all, I was standing in the open on a respectable street. What could possibly go wrong?"

She shudders, and her voice drops as she says, "It happened so fast. I should have done something, and I am ashamed that I did not."

"Stop. Seriously. You have no reason to be ashamed. I'm the cop who was strangled by a serial killer. Same thing. I knew what I was doing, but it happened so fast."

"You still stopped him."

I make a face. "After he murdered two people, then kidnapped and tortured you."

"My pride was the only thing truly injured."

I meet her gaze. "That's not true. You're going to have nightmares. You're going to have trauma. Even if he didn't do any lasting damage to your body, he did up here." I tap my head.

Her eyes glisten as she drops her gaze. "That was the worst. The pain was minor, but I knew worse was to come, and I was . . ." She shudders again. "Terrified. If you and Duncan hadn't shown up . . ."

"We did. And if we hadn't, you'd have tricked him and escaped. I'm sure of it."

"I will tell myself that. For now, we need to discuss your situation. You cannot remain as a housemaid."

I exhale. "I honestly think it's best if I do. Sure, if you want to hire a part-time maid to fill in when I'm helping your brother, that's fine, but I still need an official job, and 'housemaid' works best."

"You *would* have an official job. As Duncan's assistant. You will help him, and through him, help Hugh."

"Yeah, I'm not so sure Detective McCreadie is going to want my help after this mess. I'm also not convinced anyone would believe that's a real job for a nineteen-year-old girl."

Before she can respond, I blurt, "Findlay came back."

"What?"

"At the end, when his body was dying, he came back to it. That might be my only way home. Killing Catriona. Which I could never do, so . . ." I swallow. "I'm trapped."

"Is that how you feel?" she says carefully. "Trapped in this terrible place?"

I hesitate. Then I say, "It depends on the day. On the hour. I can get caught up in things here, and I'm happy, but then I remember my family, my friends. My fear that Catriona is there, hurting the people I love. I couldn't get that answer from Colin. When I asked where he'd been, he just said 'gone' and then he *was* gone."

She nods. "I apologize if I sounded defensive. I enjoy having you here. I would love to visit your time, but if I could not get back? Yes, I would feel trapped, no matter how wondrous it was, no matter who I might meet there."

"Exactly that. If I could go home any time I wanted, it'd be different."

"We'll figure this out. Find a way for you to get home. I have had some ideas—"

A rap at the door cuts her short. She makes a face at the interruption, and she calls a half-hearted welcome. The door swings open, and Gray stands there, his expression unreadable.

"Duncan." Isla rises. "How did everything go with Hugh?"

"Did you know?" he asks, still in the doorway, half cast in shadow.

"Did I know . . . ?" she says slowly.

"You must have."

"Do you mean about Constable Findlay? Yes, Catriona and I did discuss the possibility—"

"I was unconscious at first," he says, as if she wasn't speaking. "When I came to, I was dazed, and I thought it best to lie there and pretend I was still knocked out. I heard what he said. The man who was not Colin Findlay."

My gut twists, and I push to my feet. "I can explain."

"*Now* you will explain?" His gaze turns on me, the light catching it, and it is ice cold. "Now that you have no choice?" He turns back to Isla. "You knew."

"She—" I begin.

"I am speaking to my sister. Asking a question that does not require an answer, because I could see her face when you were talking to that man. She was neither confused nor surprised. I told myself that I was imagining it. That I was still only partly conscious and hallucinating. That is why I said nothing earlier. I was muddled, still working it through. But when I left to fetch Hugh, my mind cleared, and I could not deny what I had heard. You played me for a fool. Both of you."

"It was me," Isla says. "I forbade—"

"No," I say firmly. "I made a choice."

She glowers at me, but Gray cuts her off with, "I would like to speak to Catriona alone." He turns that cold gaze on his sister. "I insist."

I agree, even as she continues to protest. I give her a look that says I want to do this. He needs to speak to me without his sister coming to my defense.

I follow Gray out the door.

FORTY-FOUR

Gray keeps going down the hall and then descends to the main level. He leads me into the funeral parlor and shuts the door. More silence as we head into the reception room.

Then he turns to me and says, "What year?"

I blink.

"You have traveled through time. From what year?"

I sink onto the settee. "You want to test me. Okay, let's do this."

"No, I am not testing you. My sister will have already done that." He pauses and his eyes narrow. "Is that what Isla said? That I would not believe you? That I am too rigid-minded to accept such a thing?"

"I'd rather not bring Isla into this. Please. Whatever she said or did, I'm an adult." I look down at myself. "Despite appearances." I meet his gaze. "Like I said upstairs, I made choices."

"Including who you were going to share this secret with. Isla. Not me."

I sigh. That's not leaving Isla out of it. But I push through with, "I told her because she was going to kick me out. It was a Hail Mary."

"A . . . ?" He shakes his head. "Fine. Contrary to what Isla may have told you, I believe your story, first because I trust that she tested you on it and second, because I heard that conversation. You were not trying to convince the killer of some far-fetched story. He already knew it because, if I am interpreting correctly, he is from your own time. Now, I asked the year."

"Twenty nineteen. He attacked me in the same spot Catriona was being attacked by Findlay, one hundred and fifty years before. All I know is I was strangled and ended up in Catriona's body, and he ended up in her would-be killer's, which I didn't realize until he attacked me the other night."

"So you knew then it was Constable Findlay?"

"No, I knew my attacker was whoever tried to kill Catriona the first time. He knew I *wasn't* Catriona."

"When?"

"When he attacked me the second time. He expected Catriona. My speech and my fighting techniques told him I was the woman he attacked in our time. That gave him the advantage. I had to figure out who strangled Catriona, and *that* would let me stop the person who killed Archie Evans and Rose Wright."

"You knew all this last night when we spoke. Isla knew your secret as well—she must have, which explains why she let you stay. I tried to talk to you in the kitchen. I stressed my openness to considering any theory you offered. And you . . ." His jaw works. "You decided otherwise."

You rebuffed me.

That's what he means. It's how he feels. I rejected his advances, not romantic but personal and professional, and he is hurt.

Of course he's hurt. I would be, too.

"I made a choice," I say. "I wish I could have made another one but . . ." There's no way to weasel out without throwing Isla under the bus, which I will not do. "This is the one I made. To make sure Findlay was the right guy and *then* tell you everything. My priority was stopping him."

"Because you are a police officer."

"Detective. Vancouver Police Department."

His gaze shutters as his voice chills a few more degrees. "You must have thought it very amusing, all my comments about what a good detective you'd make, praising you as if you were a child showing aptitude."

"No, I only thought that you were very kind to me, and I appreciated it."

"But not enough to trust me with the truth."

"I . . . It wasn't about trust, Dr. Gray. I couldn't risk telling you or Detective McCreadie the truth unless absolutely necessary because I couldn't stop the killer from inside an asylum."

"I would not have done that to you."

"What would you have done?"

His mouth tightens, as if he doesn't like the answer, and he says, "I do not know."

"I agonized over telling you. I did plan to, first thing in the morning. If I made a mistake, then I made a mistake, and I am sorry for that."

He nods curtly, and I know I've lost ground here. So much ground.

Would I make another choice if I could?

Would I have told Gray in the kitchen if I had a second chance?

No. This hurts—hurts more than it should—but I had to choose between losing Gray's trust and losing Isla's, and I wouldn't throw away hers to gain his.

"I'm hoping you'll keep me on," I say. "At least as Catriona the housemaid. Preferably as your assistant, but that's up to you. I'm stuck here until I can get home, which I will do as soon as I can figure out how."

"Yes, I am sure we seem very backwards and provincial to you," he says coolly.

"Not at all. But I have a life there."

"How old are you?"

"Roughly your age, I think. Thirty."

"A year younger. You must have family then. A husband. Children."

"No, and no, and if that seems odd, I'd say to look in a mirror. I've got my career, and it takes up a lot of my time. Too much, maybe. But I still have a life in the twenty-first century. My parents, my grandmother, my friends, my job. This is temporary."

"Of course."

That silence drops again, and I feel the lead weight of it. I want to keep apologizing, but I know it won't help. The damage is done, and it won't be repaired in the next hour. That makes it all the more awkward to have this conversation, where I'm asking to keep living in his house after I've done something that feels, to him, like a betrayal of his trust.

No, it feels like a rejection. Duncan Gray does not make friends easily, I'm sure. He's learned to fortify himself against insult and injury, and he took a chance reaching out and he feels rebuffed. He tentatively opened a door. I didn't shut it. I did something worse—I ignored it. I walked away as if I hadn't even seen it open. That's not what happened, but it's what it feels like to him.

"While I'm here, though, I'd like to help," I say. "If I can. Like I said,

I'll play at being a housemaid for a roof over my head and food on the table. If you really do need an assistant, though . . ."

"And what am I supposed to say to that, Cat—" He stops. "What even is your name?"

"Mallory. Mallory Atkinson."

"What am I supposed to say to that, Detective Atkinson? That I will not allow you to help me when you obviously can? When you're ideally suited to help me advance a science I've dedicated my life to advancing? What sort of man would that make me?"

"I-I'm sorry. I just meant that I understand you feel . . ." I struggle for a word that won't make him close off more, insist he doesn't feel hurt at all.

I start again. "I lied. Misrepresented myself. Withheld evidence from an investigation. I can defend my choices, but I still acknowledge that I did all that, and so you might not be comfortable working alongside me."

"I'm not," he says shortly. "I won't pretend otherwise. I have been seeing you as a child, a girl trying to better herself. I still see that girl, but instead, she's a woman of my own age, a professional officer of the law, and she has been that the whole time and I feel . . ." He inhales, as if steeling himself for an admission. "I feel foolish. I feel I should have stopped long enough to wonder how my housemaid could suddenly read and write and show such aptitude for my studies and detection."

"Because 'She's clearly a time traveler' isn't going to be anyone's first or last guess." I say it lightly, trying to ease the mood, but his expression doesn't change.

"Perhaps not, but I feel very discombobulated, and I will need time to adjust to . . ." He looks at me. Really looks, like he did earlier this evening, when he seemed to see past Catriona to me. This time, he pulls back sharply and shakes his head.

"I will adjust," he says, his voice still frosty. "In the meantime, I can hardly turn down any assistance you might offer."

"I'll be careful," I say. "I won't tell you anything about forensic science that could mess up history."

He shakes his head, relaxing a fraction. "You have an interesting idea of how science works. The other day you mentioned fingerprints. Scientists *have* said that fingerprints can be identifiers. They've studied the phenomenon since before I was born. That does not mean the police are willing to *employ* it. I cannot simply pass along whatever you tell me. I would need to prove it, which would take years, and they still would not use it within my lifetime. It could, however, help in investigating Hugh's cases."

When I don't answer, he continues, "You will need to keep the housemaid position, to explain why you are living in the household of an unmarried man. That would be too unseemly for my assistant, even with my sister here. We will not, of course, require you to fulfill those duties."

"You'll need to have me do some chores to keep up appearances. Except scrubbing out the chamber pots. Please hire someone else for that."

Again, I'm trying to lighten the gloom, but he only nods abruptly. "As you wish."

The ticking of a distant clock fills the silence as it stretches. I want to say more. So much more. But it's not the time. Not yet. When a rap sounds at the back door, I swear we both exhale in relief at the interruption.

Gray strides from the funeral parlor. I hurry after him to see who's come to call at this hour.

When Gray throws open the back door, McCreadie stands there, and for a moment, time circles back, and I'm opening the door to meet the criminal officer for the first time. I half expect to see Findlay behind him, and when I realize I never will again, a pang darts through me. Grief for the loss of a promising young officer, mingled with anger at what he tried to do to Catriona.

"Duncan," McCreadie says. He leans around Gray and nods. "Catriona. You had quite the night, didn't you, lass?"

I murmur something indistinct as I nod.

"I know it is a ridiculous hour," McCreadie continues. "But I need to speak to you, Duncan. It's about the case."

Gray backs up to let him in.

As McCreadie steps inside, he looks at me. "You do not need to tarry with us, lass. You have earned a decent rest."

"No," Gray says. "I believe she'll wish to join this discussion." He glances at me. "As my assistant in such investigations."

"Thank you, sir," I say.

We head back to the funeral parlor sitting room.

"Would you like tea, Detective?" I ask.

"That won't be necessary," Gray says before McCreadie can answer. "If it is needed, we'll get it ourselves. Sit."

There's the distinct air of a command to that last word, and I settle into an armchair.

"What seems to be the problem, Hugh?" Gray says as he leans against the wall, arms crossed.

"Besides the fact that my constable murdered two people and tried to kill Isla?" He pauses. "And Catriona, of course."

Gray uncrosses his arms. "Apologies. I did not intend to be sharp. I am overly tired and out of sorts."

McCreadie's gaze slides between me and Gray, as if he's sensing exactly where that tension comes from. "Understandably so. You have suffered a blow to the head as well, which may explain the rather muddled explanation you gave when you came to my lodgings. I was not quite awake, and I kept telling myself that your story would make more sense once I was. Yet I have taken care of Colin's remains and examined the scene, and I can only say that your recounting of events makes even less sense now. Which is why I am here."

I glance at Gray, whose gaze has turned half toward the window.

"Duncan?" McCreadie says. "Do you have something more to tell me? Something that will better explain what happened tonight? Something that will also tell me who actually killed Colin, because I know it wasn't you. Not unless you stabbed him while on your knees. You must think me a very poor student of your studies if you expected me to believe your story after seeing the wound."

"I killed Colin," I say. "I had no idea Dr. Gray intended to take the blame for that." I pass Gray a hard look, but he's not glancing my way.

I continue, "I stabbed Colin in the back because he was holding a gun on Dr. Gray."

"That does not make this story any more comprehensible."

"It's true, though."

"Which, again, does not make it any more comprehensible." He looks at Gray. "If there is more, I should very much like to hear it."

McCreadie's tone is pleasant, his words a mere request. He doesn't ask whether Gray trusts him. Doesn't remind him of their friendship. Yet Gray flinches as if McCreadie had threatened to storm out the door and never return.

Gray is not a man who makes friends easily. No, strike that. He is not a man others befriend easily. Earlier tonight, he invited me into his circle and, to him, I rejected that overture by deeming him "unworthy" of my secret. Is he now going to do the same to McCreadie?

I can hope, in this moment, that Gray understands I truly did keep quiet out of fear *and* to protect him. That if he keeps my secret from McCreadie, it will be for the same reason. Either way, his gaze shoots to me, and I know keeping my secret is not an option. This is his oldest and most trusted friend. If we are all to work together, I cannot ask Gray to lie to McCreadie for me.

"We have something to tell you," I say.

McCreadie visibly relaxes, as if despite his demeanor, he had feared he might not be worthy of our secret, and seeing that reaction, I understand why Gray felt the same way. We may keep secrets to protect others, but they will only ever feel we didn't trust them enough to share.

McCreadie slaps his thighs. "All right then. I have a feeling this evening is about to get even more interesting."

"You might say that," Gray murmurs.

"Yep," I say. "And while you told me not to fetch tea, I think I'm going to grab that bottle of whisky from your desk, Dr. Gray. I have a feeling Detective McCreadie is going to need it."

"*What* bottle of whisky in my desk?" Gray says, his eyes narrowing. "You have not been cleaning my office, have you?"

"Perish the thought. Isla and I have just been tippling from your bottle."

McCreadie snorts a surprised laugh, and I head out to get the scotch. As I leave the room, I let out a breath, feeling some of the tension seep from my shoulders.

I haven't fixed things with Gray. Not by a long shot. But I will. I'll mend the damage with Gray, and I'll find a way home. Until then, I have found a place here, one I think I'm going to enjoy very much.

ACKNOWLEDGMENTS

So many people to thank for this one. Let's start with my editor at Minotaur, Kelley Ragland, who asked about new series ideas as I began winding down Rockton. This was my dream project but, yes, it's a bit of an oddball, and I hesitated to suggest it, so I came up with a second idea and presented both and, to my incredible relief, she picked this one and shepherded it through the editorial process with her usual enthusiasm and skill.

Thanks to my agent, Lucienne Diver, who encouraged me to pursue—and sell!—this dream project and offered excellent early editorial suggestions.

Thanks to the copyeditor, Terry McGarry, for going above and beyond with her wonderfully keen eye for detail . . . and for helping me straighten out a timeline that *ahem* got a wee bit muddled during my revisions.

And now for the research portion of the acknowledgments. If you're looking for more details on my research, check the author's note. This is just my thank-you section, with the usual caveat that any mistakes in the history or geography are my fault alone.

Thanks to my critique partner, Melissa Marr, for lending me both her editorial eye and Victorian-studies background, both helpful in pointing out overlooked opportunities. Mallory's open-crotch underwear commentary is entirely her fault.

Thanks to Karen Viars. I won a few hours of her research time in a charity auction and used it to have her track down resources on two subjects proving elusive. She found exactly what I wanted and more.

Thanks to Elizabeth Williamson, Allison MacGregor, Heather Campbell-Crayton, and Layla Mathieson, who stepped in when COVID-19 upended my plans for on-site research in Edinburgh. They read the manuscript and flagged a few things I got wrong about their city, along with some always-appreciated typo catches.